Out of Esau

Out *of* Esau

A NOVEL

Michelle Webster Hein

Counterpoint
BERKELEY, CALIFORNIA

Out of Esau

Library of Congress Cataloging-in-Publication Data
Names: Webster-Hein, Michelle, author.
Title: Out of Esau : a novel / Michelle Webster Hein.
Description: First hardcover edition. | Berkeley, California : Counterpoint, 2022.
Identifiers: LCCN 2021060646 | ISBN 9781640094123 (hardcover) | ISBN 9781640094130 (ebook)
Subjects: LCGFT: Pastoral fiction. | Novels.
Classification: LCC PS3623.E39768 O98 2022 | DDC 813/.6—dc23/
eng/20220303
LC record available at https://lccn.loc.gov/2021060646

Jacket design by Dana Li
Book design by Laura Berry

COUNTERPOINT
2560 Ninth Street, Suite 318
Berkeley, CA 94710

www.counterpointpress.com

Printed in the United States of America

1 3 5 7 9 10 8 6 4 2

For Scott, my first reader

and for Alyosha and Silas, who taught me how to see again

Out of Esau

Esau, Michigan

1996

PART I

1

The woman began attending Esau Baptist in late October. An unlikely month, Pastor Robert thought. Spring proved the more common time for people to take up churchgoing—that season of new life when the winter ice had cracked and shrunk to slush and you could smell the snow melting into mud. In January, a family or two usually arrived, freshly resolved to tend their souls, only to drift off a few weeks later. But autumn in Esau, Michigan, struck Pastor Robert as too ominous for new beginnings. That particular October had seen an incessant, stinging rain, which had pin-hammered the abundant heaps of fallen leaves into dense, matted mounds that refused to burn. Night arrived before supper and lingered until after breakfast, framing a series of dim gray days that never quite shook the darkness.

The Sunday that the woman first came, the first snow came, too. It fell not in large, soft flakes but in flurries of white grit that sketched the village in a coat of powder.

That morning, Robert had taken a walk around the town. He left the parsonage and walked down to the end of his street, past the park, such as it was, with its dented slide and three swings, one broken off at the side joint and hanging down like a sad flag.

Beyond this he passed two blocks of small, scattered houses, some boarded-up and forgotten, others stuffed so full that the owner's belongings muffled the front windows and spilled out into the lawn—a box spring here, a rusted rocking horse there, an old stove and several kitchen cabinets shoved beneath the bright blue awning of a carport. A few of the houses were neatly kept, with plastic birdbaths and iridescent gazing balls filling out otherwise stingy gardens.

The next street was Main Street, and it earned this title by boasting the only businesses Esau possessed—a gas station, Esau Market, Larry's Garage, Frank's Hardware, Karla's Kitchen, and Dwight's Bar, along with a slim, one-room library and an unnecessarily large post office. Through conversations with his parishioners, Robert understood the post office to be a relic of another time, much like the half block of empty storefront between the garage and the market, which housed, a lifetime ago, an art gallery and a grange hall, where dances had been held every month and parties thrown every weekend by local persons renting out the space.

Across from the post office stretched a large open lot dubbed "the field," bordered on one side by a chain-link fence that netted all the garbage blowing by—plastic bags and newspapers and shreds of a hundred other materials. The ground there was littered with pop bottles, empty fifths, smashed cigarette boxes, broken lighters, and occasionally a pornographic magazine, though these were stored rather than abandoned, Robert suspected, since they were always discovered beneath the bushes in the lot's corner. Robert knew this because Florence Butts, one of his congregants, made it her personal mission to plunder the ungodly stores kept there and to inform Robert in detail about what she had found, the assumption apparently being that he could do something about it.

Whenever the weather changed, Robert traded his usual walk in the woods for a walk through the town, and he did so with whimsical purpose. He was trying to see the village with fresh eyes and to reap from it the curiosity it had aroused when he'd first moved to Esau a little over a decade before. Back then the town had compelled him like a secret, with its mixture of quaint and eerie, alive and dead, haunted by a livelier past. He had even felt (though he would never have spoken it aloud) a sense of ownership, or perhaps inheritance. This was the place whose souls God had entrusted to him.

That sense, too, had faded. The village of Esau had come to feel like a dead end, which, if not for the eagerness of youth, it might have felt like from the beginning. It was, after all, a town whose best days were behind it, where no major roads led, where one single, narrow country road passed through. And if Robert apprehended some residue of charm that morning in the structures and awnings of the town sketched fastidiously out, in the scents of snow and woodsmoke, then he did so with the bitter knowledge of someone who has fallen prey to false promises and realized it far too late.

Pastor Robert had carried these musings into the church service that morning beneath his suit coat, a slim but heavy weight. He had already begun his sermon when the woman and her two children slipped into the back pew, and several heads turned toward them with expressions of mild disapproval. When she looked up at Robert with her large dark eyes, he felt ice cleave his heart—a fright almost, a rising thrill—and he knew not whether it was God or the devil.

He remained duly circumspect. He did not greet her afterward in her pew, as he usually did with new families, but walked past her to the foyer door, where he stood shaking the men's hands as they exited and acknowledging the women with a nod. The visitor, as she passed, reached out, and he unwittingly reached out in return. He found her grasp soft and warm.

"Susan Shearer." Her voice was quiet but clear. "And Willa and Lukas," she added, patting them each once on the back. The children stood on either side of her. The girl, who looked about nine or ten, gazed soberly up at him, and the boy, a few years younger, stared down and stomped his boots on the carpet.

"Pastor Robert," he replied. "Welcome."

She looked about his age—mid-to-late thirties. Her eyes were unusually large, the dark green of deep water, and her cheeks held what looked to be a permanent flush. Her gaze darted off to one side, then the other, but flashed up again to his face, and he thought of a lantern moving through darkened rooms.

Then, apparently sensing she had lingered too long, she dipped her chin to her chest and made busy ushering her children out the door. As she passed, God help him, he looked for a ring, and, God help him, he found one, a tiny white stone glinting atop a gold band.

And then she was gone, then the Fishers and the Clemenses and the Paisleys and Joe Cummings, who paused, as always, to voice his dire political predictions. Chet Weller delivered his warm handshake, along with his weekly joke. Then the giant brood of Plonskis clambered into their giant white van, and the silence in their wake was loud and barren.

Robert returned to the parsonage next door with the ham and potato casserole that Ethel Grable had left for him on the foyer table. Once again he forgot that 350 degrees in the parsonage oven was actually 450 and once again he forgot to compensate. It made for a desolate afternoon—the memory of Susan's warm hand and inscrutable gaze while the casserole burned in the oven. He ate a helping anyway, the charred chunks of ham grisly between his molars, mouth hard at the work of chewing while his mind drifted again and again to Susan Shearer and her hand and her eyes and what she had seen in him when she looked so close.

2

On the drive home, all of Susan's energy drained out of her. She imagined it leaching out the bottoms of her cramped feet, overflowing the old flats that blistered her pinkie toes and rubbed her heels raw, seeping through the balding insulation of the minivan floor, and dripping into the rickety undercarriage, which shook alarmingly whenever she crested fifty.

Lukas sat in back, dismembering an action hero he'd brought along. Willa was gazing out the passenger-side window, and Susan's gaze followed. Field after field rolled past—cornstalks cracked at the knee and toppled face forward into the dirt. The surrounding squares of naked trees all raised their arms. In horror? In exultation? They always seemed to be gesturing toward some purpose.

Susan used to make such observations to Randy long ago, before they were married. She'd always loved language, and back in school, she'd proved that she was good at it. Much better than Randy, which pained him, though it took Susan way too long to realize that. Once, shortly after they'd married, she had observed how the clouds gathered around the sun when it set—the sun's deathbed, that's what she'd called it—and he'd turned toward her with a look of such contempt that she'd since removed all metaphors from her conversation. That concession was quickly joined by a host of others, among them lipstick, solitary walks, evenings out with a friend or two.

Church was her one disobedience. On everything else she had bent until she broke. But had she been following God when she first met Randy, she would have chosen better. She needed her children to believe, too. Before life came for them and found them unprepared.

For years now she'd been attending the Congregationalist church over in Milton, but the old pastor had retired, and she'd found the new pastor's messages cheerful and undemanding. They served as pleasant reminders rather than exhortations. And so she had finally decided to try Esau Baptist.

Close as the church was, it would have been the obvious choice were it not for Susan's aunt, the only Baptist Susan had ever known. She recalled her great-aunt Bess as a humorless woman who lived alone, brought a small bowl of wet green pudding to all family events, and made it a general practice to question the soundness of any act with which she was unfamiliar.

So to Susan's mind, Baptists were too rigid, too riveted on sin, which was why she had first opted for the church in Milton and why she was only now trying out her aunt Bess's old denomination. Lately, Susan longed for blood and resurrection, for commandments etched in stone. She wanted to remember that her difficult life was difficult precisely because she obeyed, because she kept faithful to the vows she had made and, in so doing, faithful to God, no matter how Randy challenged her.

And lately, Randy had been challenging her more than ever. Lukas had started first grade that fall, and now Randy called three times a day to check up on her—once on each break and once over lunch.

"Who are you with?" he'd ask. "Don't lie to me."

Once he had come home in the middle of the day. He'd burst through the bathroom door and found her bent over the bathtub, scrubbing. He seemed embarrassed, reddening as he offered up a few fake coughs.

"I came home sick," he said. But she knew.

Susan had developed a keen attunement to Randy's anger, to the slightest forewarnings of his rages. Over the past few months, his temper had grown larger, more menacing. It was always slinking along just under his surface. But, too, it was in the air. It went with him to work, and it also stayed behind and hung itself on the watchful silence.

It wasn't his fault. Lately she'd had to remind herself of this, take herself through the litany of explanations. Randy was a broken man. His father, the beatings. His grandfather, the shaming. His mother dead at forty, when Randy was just thirteen, leaving him at that most raw and vulnerable age bereft of the only softness in his life.

With all his excuses, he could have been so much worse. He never hit her, though he did hit other things—tables, walls, doors. He provided for his family, even if he hated his job with a fierce and petulant hatred. Still, he left every morning for the factory and took on all the overtime he could.

Susan's mother had always told her that marriage was a journey, not over land but over water. When the storms came, you lashed yourself to the mast, and you rode it out. And if you couldn't do it for your husband, you did it for your children, and you did it for yourself because you wouldn't be able to make it on your own.

Susan had first turned to faith when Willa was born. Back then, time spent in prayer and scripture fortified her like food. She would come away with a fresh sense of duty, a conviction to persevere throughout the coming day, to meet Randy's sharpness with softness, his unpredictability by pausing rather than flying off the handle like she used to do. And these measures seemed at times to improve things. When Susan noticed Randy's temper softening, she would tell herself, *Look, God is testing you, and you are rising to the challenge.* And despite everything he'd suffered, he loved her, and he loved their children. Granted, his love was stunted and harsh at times, but still it was there. She knew it was there, even if sometimes he was too damaged to show it.

But over the past months her faith had seemed to weaken. In the early mornings, when Susan implored God on her knees, she found little comfort or assurance. Without that strength, she couldn't fathom moving forward.

The van crunched over the loose gravel of their driveway, and the carriage shuddered when Susan turned back the key. Whenever she left, Randy jerked the blinds closed so that they caught over the sofa and hung crooked. It made the small gray ranch look even less inviting. Out front the kids' bicycles lay abandoned on their sides. The skeletons of the plants in the beds looked spiny and brittle beneath the dusting of snow.

Usually the first snowfall made things more picturesque, but this one had made everything more desolate. What had the pastor said that morning—when life looks stark, that's God making clear the narrow path. We often fool ourselves, he'd said. We tell ourselves we don't know what we should do, but most of the time, it's obvious. We just don't want to do it.

He'd offered no advice on that score, on how to make yourself keep on doing whatever it was you knew you should be doing. And anyway, when she'd met him afterward and studied his face, she wasn't so sure he even believed it. Something about the way he'd looked at her struck her as too complicated. He didn't fit the part, either. In a small town like Esau, she'd expected to find a white man with a big family. But his skin was darker, and his hair was thick and so black it was almost blue. He was handsome but out of place. Single, presumably, as he wore no ring. His eyes on her were keen and inquisitive.

"Are we going in?" asked Lukas. "Or are we just going to sit here?"

"We're just going to sit here," she said.

"No!" He must have known she was kidding, but still he stretched the word out into a long, loud whine.

"I'm hungry," said Willa. She was always hungry.

The children needed to eat. Randy needed to eat. His work clothes needed to be washed and dried and folded. Lukas needed a bath, and help with his homework. They were out of sandwich bread, eggs, cheese, coffee.

This is how you keep doing the right thing, she thought. You just do it, and it exhausts you too much to do anything else.

3

Her dad was in one of his moods again. Willa knew this because Willa could read moods. Sometimes she thought she might have ESP, like a boy in a book she'd read who could read people's minds. She couldn't read minds, though, just moods. And this one scared her.

He didn't look over when they walked in. That was the first sign. He wasn't looking at anything else either. That was the second sign. He was just sitting in his chair, staring straight ahead.

The pastor had talked that morning about doing the right thing, about how God shows people, plain as day, what the right thing is. But now Willa didn't know what the right thing would be. She thought maybe the right thing would be to walk over and give her dad a hug. But her mom could read moods, too, and she bent down and pulled Lukas's boots off and said in her warning voice, "You two go play in your room."

Lukas said, "But I wanna watch TV." Lukas could not read moods.

So Willa said, "Lukas, do you wanna play Legos?" Which Lukas loved almost as much as TV.

"Yeah," he said. "Willie, let's play Legos."

Willa remembered then that she didn't very much like to play Legos, but at least it would give her father some peace and quiet.

In their room, Willa first checked her angel. She found the wooden figure exactly where she'd left it, on the night table, its feet perfectly inside

Willa's pencil tracing from months before. The wire wings sprouted from the angel's shoulders at the same angle. The face smiled blankly forward with the same half-circle grin, the same black dots for eyes. Five wire curls stuck up from the angel's head, two on each side and one in the middle. Willa breathed in deep and felt herself settle. Then she walked to the closet and pulled the Legos bin down.

A few months back at bedtime, Willa had noticed with a stab of fear that her angel was facing the wrong direction. So she'd taken a pencil and held the angel still and outlined her feet on the night table. Since then, the angel had comforted Willa, but it had also worried her. It comforted Willa to find the angel standing exactly where she'd left it, but it scared Willa when too much time had passed without checking.

Then, a couple of weeks ago, Willa had dashed to her bedroom after school and found the angel turned halfway around. She could barely breathe until she rushed out and found her mother, who said, yes, she'd dusted the bedroom that day and moved things around and did it really matter so much? Willa had giggled with relief, all giddy and dizzy. Of course it didn't matter, Willa told her. And she'd skipped back to her room and picked up the angel and put her down again exactly where she should be. She'd sat on her mattress and stared at the figure until her breath slowed down and she started to wonder, What was she so afraid of?

Willa and Lukas played Legos for what felt like forever. Down the hallway, she heard nothing except the kitchen sounds of pot lids and drawers, the refrigerator door slapping shut, the tapping of a spoon. Silence was good sometimes, but this one felt like the silence in a scary movie, when everyone's waiting for something bad to happen. Willa could read silences, too.

At dinner, no one talked. Dad chewed with loud smacks and Mom chewed quietly and Lukas poked at his food while he chewed. Willa had given up chewing because she couldn't break the beef apart with her teeth, and its rubbery strings made her gag. She'd eaten the noodles and the sauce, and she'd gulped down the chunks of cauliflower whole. She folded the beef in a corner of her plate and covered it with a napkin. Maybe she could make it to the end of the meal without her dad noticing. Then she could scrape the meat into the garbage when she cleared the table.

Willa shoved her hands under her legs and balled them into fists. She rocked side to side over her knuckles and squeezed her jaws together. She needed to check the angel again. It was like needing to pee.

"May I go to the bathroom?" she asked.

Her dad continued to chew. His cheeks shivered when he chomped. She wanted him to look at her and smile. She wanted him to tease her and call her Willie Bear.

Her mom glanced at her dad, who didn't glance back. Then she turned to Willa and nodded.

Willa stopped in the bathroom first. She paused and flushed the toilet and ran the faucet. Then she tiptoed down the hallway into her bedroom, where she found the angel standing right where Willa had left her.

Back in the dining room, Willa found that her father had moved the napkin off her plate. He nodded at the meat she'd hidden there.

"Eat it," he said. "Now."

Willa studied the strips of beef all wound around each other like a nest of flat worms.

Her mother asked, "Would you like me to cut it up?"

"No," said her father. "She's just trying to get her way. Eat it."

Willa lifted the first strip with her fork, poked it into her mouth, and tried to chew. She was chewing gum, she told herself. Gum that had lost its flavor. Rubber gum. Rubber meat gum.

She couldn't do it.

She closed her eyes and tried to swallow it whole. It stuck in her throat, and she gagged and pitched forward. The meat landed in the middle of her plate, and then a glop of chewed noodles and cauliflower landed on top of it. She looked up and saw her father's face all twisted in anger and disgust.

"Willa!" her mother said. "Are you sick?"

"She's not sick," said her dad. "She's spoiled."

Spoiled? Willa didn't want to be spoiled.

"Randy." Her mother's voice sounded worried.

"Eat it," he said. He said it like they were playing a game and she'd just been sent back to the beginning of the board.

"Randy," her mother repeated.

"Eat it!" he shouted. He slammed his fist down on the table, jumping the plates and wobbling the glasses.

Willa lifted her fork and studied the hill of wet food on her plate. She could do this. She could pretend she was eating eggs maybe, or soup. She turned off some parts of her head. That was something else she could do, when things were too hard at first. It was a little like walking through a house and turning off the light switches one by one. She scooped up a fork-ful and brought it to her mouth.

"No!" her mother cried.

Willa jumped, and the food dropped off her fork. She thought at first that maybe Lukas had cut himself, or a fire had flared up in the kitchen, but she looked up to find her mother leaning over to snatch her plate, then she ran with it to the kitchen, where she dumped it into the trash. The food hit the bottom of the bag with a sloshing sound.

Willa's father shoved the table when he stood. "Goddamnit, Suzy," he said, and he kicked a cupboard, which he did sometimes to show that he was serious.

"Randy," her mom said. "I can't let her do that. I can't just sit there and let my daughter eat her own vomit." She said the last part in a whisper, like she could barely get the words out, like she hoped Willa wouldn't hear.

"So you're just gonna let them walk all over you," her dad said. "You're gonna teach them it doesn't matter what the fuck I say." When he said *fuck*, he kicked the cupboard again.

"I was going to eat it," Willa said.

Willa's mom kept staring at her dad like she had just learned something new about him, something horrible.

"I was going to eat it," Willa said again, louder this time. Let her father be angry with her mother, but don't let him be angry with her.

Willa's dad didn't seem to hear her, though. He walked back to the table and picked up his own plate, which was almost empty. He walked it to the kitchen and dropped it, plate and all, into the garbage. "Tasted like vomit anyway," he said, and he stomped over to the entryway, pulled on his coat and boots, and slammed the door behind him.

"You didn't have to do that," Willa said to her mother, who had come back to the table and dropped back down into her seat. Her mother raised her head and fixed Willa with a look that she couldn't read. It wasn't exactly angry, and it wasn't exactly sad. It was like she'd woken up from a bad dream and still didn't know where she was.

"You didn't have to do that," Willa repeated. "I could have just eaten it."

4

The ladder rattled as Randy leaned it against the gutter. Piece of shit, he thought.

Then it was his arms, he realized. His hands. He couldn't stop shaking. It wasn't even that cold out. The snow didn't give him permission to get all shaky. He could be such a fucking woman sometimes.

He shook out his arms and stomped to the garage, where he grabbed the spade and a pair of work gloves and hitched a garbage bag to his belt loop. Then he stomped back to the ladder and climbed up.

He was a man, he told himself, doing what men do. Laying down the law when it needed to be laid down. Cleaning out the gutters. The first snow had fallen and frozen the leaves still clumped in the eavestroughs. Someone had to clean them out, and it sure as hell wouldn't be Susan, though she had a hell of a lot more time on her hands than he did. But he was taking care of it. He was working all week *and* all weekend. He was working his fucking ass off and *freezing* his fucking ass off, and no one gave a shit.

Well.

He reached the gutter and rested the spade on the ladder's top rung. He opened the bag at his side and pulled on his work gloves and dug with the spade to loosen the leaves, then scooped up a fistful and shoved it into the bag.

Back inside, with the vomit, he hadn't been serious. Not really. And then Susan had jumped in, like some fucking savior, like his children

needed saving. He wouldn't have made Willa do it. He wouldn't have followed through.

But he also knew maybe he wouldn't have stopped her.

It didn't matter. That's the way they'd remember it anyway. They'd remember Randy telling Willa to eat it, and they'd remember Suzy telling her
not to.

Randy had dug out all the leaves within reach, so he climbed down and
moved the ladder along the house. His arms were still shaking. Fucking
ridiculous. More snow was falling, filling up the crevices of his Carhartt,
landing on the skin between his gloves and his sleeves and melting there,
wet and cold. He shook his arms out again, climbed up and started back in
with the spade.

He did everything he was supposed to do, and he was the bad guy. He
was the bad guy, and look at his life. Work, work, and more work, and all of
it for someone else. He slaved away in a shop for nine hours a day, sometimes
more. He did the same fucking thing over and over and over, all day long.
And then he'd come home and eat some low-budget shit that Susan said was
all they could afford, like it was his fault, like he could do anything more
than he was already doing. He was already laying down his motherfucking
life.

He didn't even have friends anymore. He used to. He used to play cards
Friday nights with Shaner and Bert and Dawson until Dawson got so damn
full of himself. Always bitching about the line workers at the plant, where
he'd made manager and landed an office and a salary and three weeks of
paid vacation while Randy just stayed where he was. And staying where you
were in a place like that was really just falling behind.

Fucking Dawson blowing ass about his big degree. Truth was, Dawson
was dumber than a stump. Randy was smart. Randy had potential. Course,
no one knew that. Just Susan, and she probably resented him for not living
up to it.

Willa would grow up, and she'd remember this. She'd tell people what
he almost made her do. They'd be so sorry for her, having an asshole like
that for a dad. She'd ship off to college with the smarts he gave her, and he'd
still be hauling ass for Dawson, cutting his knuckles on mufflers or steering

wheels or whatever the hell else they still couldn't teach a robot to make, and then he'd retire on a shit pension they'd cut in half ten years down the line.

And for all this misery, he'd be to blame.

Put that way, why the fuck go on?

He dropped another fistful of leaves in the bag and shoved them down, but he shoved too far and lost his balance.

A slowed moment. Randy grasped with his left hand but missed the gutter and grabbed the ladder instead. His weight tipped the ladder sideways onto one foot, and it started to fall. He stretched wildly for the gutter again and missed. The white ground with its prickles of grass bent toward him.

He thought, *I could die,* and in the same moment, he thought, *Things could be different. I could be different.*

He landed almost softly. The bushes along the corner of the house had caught the ladder's fall and slowed him just before his body met the ground. He rolled away from the ladder, onto his side, and lay there for a while.

The snow caught his attention, and so he watched it fall—followed flake after flake drifting sideways or blowing briefly upward. He watched for so long he almost thought he could hear the flakes landing, and when he came around to sitting up and checking himself over, he started to wonder if maybe he had jarred something loose. He felt calm, he realized. He couldn't remember the last time he'd felt calm. And almost happy. He thought of Susan and Willa and Lukas, warm inside. He would take a break, he thought, see how everyone was doing. He'd make sure everyone was okay.

But walking inside, the sameness of everything struck him, the hopelessness, the rage that had spent itself into exhaustion. Off in the corner of the living room, Willa was reading a book. Lukas was watching a cartoon on low. Susan was folding laundry and stacking it in piles across the couch.

"I just fell off the roof," he said. It was almost a lie, but if he told them that he only fell off the ladder, Susan wouldn't understand how serious it could have been.

Willa blinked up from her book. "Oh, no," she said. "Are you okay, Daddy?" But her concern sounded fake, like a performance for somebody else, and he didn't answer her.

Lukas kept staring at the TV.

Susan shook out a pair of pants and folded them up before looking over. Her eyes were empty, he thought. Purposely emptied.

"Well," she said. "You look like you're all right." And she turned back around to place the pants on a pile.

"I could've died," he said. His voice came out more high-pitched than he'd intended, almost whiny, like a child's complaint. His surge of goodwill now felt small and weak, a tiny flame in a windstorm.

"Well," said Susan, not even bothering to turn around. "You didn't."

"Yeah," he said. "Too bad for you guys, huh."

Susan said nothing, just went on folding clothes with her back to him. He watched her hips as she bent over and stood back up, followed the shirt seams that traced her waist. He thought briefly, at least she was his. But what if she wasn't. She didn't touch him the way he wanted her to. She went along with sex, but always with the same dutiful movements, looking off at something just over his shoulder. Thinking, probably, about someone else.

"I said," he repeated, louder this time, "too bad for you guys."

This time Susan turned around, a work shirt half folded in her hands. She glared steadily at him for a long moment, then glanced over at Willa, who had buried her nose back in her book. She dropped the shirt into the basket and stalked over.

"How do you expect me to answer that," she hissed, once she'd come close enough not to be overheard. "After what you told our daughter to do?"

She spoke with a fierceness he couldn't remember hearing before.

"I wasn't serious," he said, and he backed up a step. "Wasn't my fault she took me serious." He knew, even as he said it, how stupid he sounded.

"You weren't serious?" she rasped.

"Nope."

"So you were just joking."

Silence.

"After you screamed and slammed the table and scared the hell out of her." Susan's voice broke, and her eyes teared up. She shook her head. "She would have done anything you told her to do. And I just sat there and almost let it happen."

He had done it, Randy thought. He had gone too far.

"No more. You hear me, Randy?"

"What, you want an apology?" He tried to keep his voice light, disbelieving. "For something I didn't even do?"

"An apology?" she asked. "No," she said, and shook her head. "Not unless you're planning to change. Otherwise, I'd rather you just went back outside and left us alone."

She turned and stalked back to the laundry.

Randy stood there for a minute or two, watching his family carry on with their lives the same as if he hadn't been standing there at all. Then he trudged back out into the snow, back to the ladder and the gutters and the steel-gray sky.

The falling snow didn't look beautiful anymore. It looked like work drifting down to bury him, like shoveling and scraping and overtime at the shop to pay for the heat it would take to keep his family warm through the winter ahead. Standing there, he felt dizzy, off-balance, the snow swirling around, like something big was shifting underneath.

He charged back inside.

"I'm sorry!" he shouted. Susan jumped and whirled around. He hadn't meant to shout. "Suzy, I'm sorry," he said, this time in a quieter voice.

He shook his feet out of his boots and crossed to Willa's chair. When she glanced up from her book and caught sight of him standing there, a trace of fear raced across her face and disappeared. He dropped to his knees and rested his hands on her lap. He could feel her narrow bird bones beneath the thin muscles of her upper legs. He had a flash of his daughter as a baby, with that look, even back then, of a sober all-knowingness. He'd been so terrified that he'd drop her or twist her neck, hurt her somehow without meaning to. And here she was, still so small. How could he forget that, how small she still was?

"Willie Bear," he said. "Willie Bear, I'm sorry. I wouldn't have made you do it. I wouldn't have let you." His sorrow felt for a moment like a flood. It poured through him, filled him up. He loved her. How could he do these things?

Willa rested her book on the chair's armrest, facedown, to keep her place. It took some arranging to balance it there without bending any of the pages. He felt a twinge of annoyance at her care in keeping the exact page open, as if her book's world deserved just as much attention as the one in which she was actually living, where her father was making a fool of himself, begging a little girl for forgiveness, begging on his knees.

But then she scooted forward, her hands free, and she hugged his neck. He stretched his arms around her in response, but his hug felt loose with only Willa's slim body to fill it.

"It's okay, Daddy," she said. "I forgive you."

Randy tried not to clench. That's what you're supposed to say, he told himself, when someone says sorry. He forced himself to hold on to his daughter a moment longer before patting her back and pulling away. But she kept talking.

"It's okay, Daddy," she said again. "Everyone makes mistakes."

He could hear, in her words, his own pardon, but he could hear, too, her casting them each in their roles. Herself, the saintly child; her father, the fuckup. Herself, the hero, the one who forgave, even then; her father, the storybook villain, whose path would keep playing out to the same unavoidable end.

5

It was on the bulletin board of the Tulsa Public Library that Leotie saw the flyer for their free "computer beginner" class. Now that she was sitting in it, she understood, one, why it was free, and two, what "beginner" meant. First off, the teacher was late, and then they'd spent fifteen goddamn minutes getting everyone's computer turned on. The class was already half over, and the teacher, a twentysomething who smiled too much, was just now showing them on the overhead screen where to click for the internet. Apparently Leotie was the only one who knew that.

The rest of the class was a bunch of humpbacked, slack-jowled seniors bused in from the center. Leotie had gone there once, just after she got out. Her bossy roommate Peg had suggested it. Anyone over fifty was welcome there, so at fifty-four, Leotie qualified. Free snacks and coffee. Games. It might help her make some friends on the outside—that was the idea. Leotie snorted, remembering.

The girl-teacher told everyone to double left click on the little *e* box with the swirly mark. Then she moved slowly down the rows, pausing at each computer. From the sounds of it, half the class had single clicked and the other half had right clicked and Leotie's neighbor had decided that "double click" meant "just keep on clicking till you break the damn thing." Leotie was the only one who didn't need help, besides a giant homeless man asleep in the back corner. For Leotie, the internet popped right up, with a picture of the library and a list of rules you were supposed to obey. Leotie clicked

I agree , and the square blanked before the word *Yahoo!* blinked across the top of the screen, above an empty bar and, next to that, a button that read *Search*.

This was where Leotie needed help. And at the rate they were going, she was never going to get it.

She clicked on the bar and typed *Robert Glory*. After a moment or two, the screen brought up the same list it always did: Robert Glory the artist. Robert Glory the Canadian. Robert Redford, of all people. Morning glory varieties. Glory handcrafted jewelry. Leotie kept scrolling, past the Richard Glorys and Glory Stoneware and the real estate in Glory, Wyoming, while the librarian led the other students on searches they suggested—RV sales and weather forecasts and hosta varieties. Leotie breathed in, strained to pull the air deep into her lungs, but her chest, as usual, felt tight and too shallow. If she wanted to find him, it had better be soon.

A big cackly broad with a cloud of stiff white curls called out, "You got any healthy recipes for fried chicken?" Like the teacher had the whole internet committed to memory.

Leotie snorted again. The seniors' center, it had turned out, was really just a country club for stingy white people. When Leotie had visited, she hadn't fit in at all, what with her brown skin and her frizzy mane of long gray hair. She'd showed up midmorning on a Wednesday. All the men had been drinking coffee at a table, and all the women—every goddamn one of them—had been stitching away in the corner. Leotie had never seen so many needles. Long needles and short needles and needles with strings and needles with hooks. One of the women had asked her name, and another asked where she was from. "Just down the street," she'd said. And then they'd all gone back to their stitching.

It had dawned on her, as she sat there at the seniors' center watching them all needling away, that no respectable person lived just down the street. There was the apartment block of subsidized housing, where she lived, and a couple blocks down from that was the shelter. From the looks of it, all these biddies lived in cushy condos or in prissy little ranch houses on the outskirts of town.

Leotie had sat there at the seniors' center for at least ten minutes while the other women prattled on about their grandkids and their sciatica and their church commitments. Finally one turned to her—a quieter one with an elegant silver bun, the only one she'd considered liking, though she couldn't have said why—and asked her, "Have you ever done any needlework, Leotie?"

By that point, Leotie was just a boiling pot with a lid on top, and, though part of her wanted to tell the woman, *No, but maybe I'd give it a shot*, the other part of her said, out loud, "Nope. Just heroin." Which wasn't even true. And when she said it, she stood up and knocked over her chair by accident (though of course they'd think she did it on purpose) and stomped out.

No going back there. And now here she was in the library, surrounded. Two women on her left were giggling like schoolgirls. One of them declared that she was "just tickled." Tickled. You couldn't have paid Leotie to use words like that. She'd seen far too much to live out her last months or weeks or days—however long she had left—heehawing over the internet.

Leotie's classmates all filed out at the top of the hour to catch their bus, thank Jesus. That left Leotie and the giant homeless man, still sleeping, and the girl-teacher who kept right on smiling as she moved from station to station, x-ing out all the extra windows and shutting the systems down.

"Hey," said Leotie. "You ever look for anybody?"

The girl startled, laughed, and turned around. "You scared me!" she said, with a face that looked the opposite of scared. "I'm sorry," the girl said when Leotie failed to return her smile. "What did you ask?"

"I asked if you ever look for people," Leotie said. "You know, on the internet."

"Ah! You mean celebrities? Yes!"

"No. I mean ordinary people. People you ain't seen for a while."

"Yes, those, too." The girl walked back to Leotie's computer and seated herself in the neighboring chair. "Did you try typing the person's full name into the search engine?"

"Yeah," said Leotie. "I'm no dummy."

"Of course you're not," the girl said, only she said it like she was talking to a dummy. "Let's see. What's the name?"

Leotie cleared her throat. "Robert Glory."

The girl leaned toward her and typed the name into Leotie's search bar. "Is that how you spell it?"

"Yeah, but I already tried that."

"I hear you, but I'm going to throw in some extra tricks. See if we can rustle up anything new." She typed quotation marks on each end of the name. "This keeps the words together," she said. Then, "Is there any word you could add?"

"What do you mean?"

"You know, maybe a job title or a school or something like that. Some identifying characteristic."

"Baptist Bible college," Leotie said, but the words caught in her throat and came out all garbled.

"I'm sorry?"

Leotie cleared her throat again. "Baptist Bible college," Leotie said. "He went to a Baptist Bible college. I can't remember what one."

"Well. That still might help," said the girl, and she typed *Baptist Bible college* after the name and clicked *Search*.

The screen blanked for a few moments. The girl sat with Leotie and waited. "It's thinking," she said.

Leotie tried to say *I know*, but her throat felt thick and full. Her heart pulsed in her neck. It felt like her whole body was throbbing.

One by one, three search results blinked onto the screen. Leotie's eyes raced over them and her mind stumbled over the words.

The first referred to a deceased Robert Glory in someone's family tree back in 1875. The second result was a singing group from Freedom Baptist Bible College. The last was a link to a pastoral directory. *Robert Glory*, it read. *Current pastor at Esau Baptist in Esau, Michigan.*

"Is that who you were looking for?" the girl asked.

Leotie tried to take in air. It felt like she'd come up from the bottom of a well, like she'd just broken water.

"Yes," said Leotie. "I think so. Thank you. Thank you very much." She had to swallow hard to stop herself from crying.

"Well, aren't you sweet," said the girl, Leotie's gratitude just one more big, happy surprise in a long list of big, happy surprises. She moved off to shut down the remaining computers and left Leotie to herself.

Leotie stayed at the library until it closed, clicking back and forth between the two links. At the top of the first was a grainy photograph of a singing group from some years before and a caption, ABUNDANT LIFE SINGERS, 1981. Leotie could just make out the shape of Robert's features in the back row. The second link provided an address and two phone numbers, one for the church and one for the parsonage.

On her way out, after they'd dimmed the lights for the ten-minute warning, Leotie slipped into the reference section and located the atlases. As quietly as she could, she ripped out Missouri, Illinois, Indiana, and Michigan. She'd already burned the phone numbers into her brain.

6

Susan secured her needle halfway through her fabric, lifted her coffee, and sipped it. Already cool.

What was today—Thursday? No, Tuesday. Tuesday morning, to be precise. The week had only barely begun.

Was that good or bad? Susan thought back to Sunday evening, to Randy slumped sobbing on the edge of their bed. For all his faults, Randy only drank every few months. But Sunday he'd driven to the gas station after cleaning the gutters and bought a fifth of Hot Damn! Cinnamon Schnapps. By the time the kids fell asleep, he had downed it all, moving, as he drank, through his typical stages of drunkenness—from a jubilant happiness, which clashed loudly with whatever had just taken place; to a testy phase, in which he could take offense if his sentiments were not returned; to a surly, bleary-eyed silence; and then, finally, to despair.

"I'm a horrible father," he had blubbered from his side of the mattress.

Susan pulled herself upright from her side of the bed, where she'd been trying to sleep.

"No you're not," she'd said. What else was there to say? "At least you apologized," she'd said. "Your father never apologized. Willa will remember that you apologized." She'd felt so angry at his helplessness, how it made him the one to be pitied, comforted. Still, she tried to mask the anger she felt and leverage the moment.

"Randy, maybe this is a wake-up call." She scooted over and rubbed the back of his neck. "This can be a turning point," she said. "This can be the moment you choose to do better."

He'd nodded as he rocked back and forth, cradling his face. Then he dropped his hands. "I will be better," he said, too loudly. He twisted around and tried to focus on her face. She could see him narrowing his eyes, trying to merge her multiple images into one. "You write this down." She could barely understand him because he could barely get the words out. He would never remember this in the morning. "You write this down, Suzy. From here on out, I'm gonna be a better man."

No, Susan decided as she settled her mug back onto the coaster. Better that it was Tuesday rather than Thursday. Better that the week take a good, long time.

She returned her attention to the shoulder strap of Lukas's snow pants. The seam needed reinforcing to last him one more winter. The pant legs were too short, but his boots, she hoped, would make up for that. She pulled the needle until the thread tugged, and then she pierced it back through the strap.

The thing was, Sunday's dinner had shaken Susan more than Randy's tantrums usually did, more than she cared to admit. Maybe if the kids had been home to distract her, or if she'd had work that actually engaged her mind—maybe then she could have avoided mulling over the *why*. Or maybe if the *why* had been more challenging to answer, she wouldn't have minded it as much.

But she knew why Sunday had shaken her so soundly. Willa's dim stare, her lifting her own vomit to her lips, her lighthearted words like little bells of alarm.

You didn't have to do that. I could have just eaten it.

Susan shook her head. What had she been thinking of before? The day of the week. Weekdays versus weekends. She preferred the weekdays to the weekends if she had to choose. At least the weekdays gave her clear tasks and the time to accomplish them, along with the relative freedom of solitude.

Nevertheless, Susan was unaccustomed to so much silence. Randy left for work around the same time the children left for school. Willa was now in fourth grade, and Lukas had started first grade back in September, which meant that each weekday, from seven thirty to three o'clock, barring sick kids or holidays, Susan was alone. Randy's paranoid phone calls were her only interruption. She felt so lonely sometimes that she almost found them welcome.

There was still too much to be done, of course. Women's work was like a gas, she'd observed, always filling its container, regardless of the size. And now that container was a whole house, mute and empty, with no children to distract her, to make her laugh.

Money was tight, and this always seemed to be her fault, so her chief task was stretching it as far as it would go. She sewed and mended, scoured coupons, purchased old bread and meat that was borderline questionable but fresh enough to freeze anyway. She gardened, she canned, she combined the leftover slivers of soap into larger bars or grated them to make laundry detergent. She salvaged everything she could.

In less desperate times, it might have been rewarding work. But there was never enough. Each task was tinged with its meagerness, how little it did to combat the lack. Pennies into a pit.

She'd tried to talk Randy into letting her go back to work. She could clean offices or wait tables again. Anything, really. Anything would help. Randy had stared at her for too long before answering.

"What are you trying to say?" he said.

His question caught her off guard. "I'm trying to say that I can help bring in money again," she'd said. "You know, now that Lukas is in school full-time. I wouldn't mind it. Who knows. It might even be fun."

He had stood there watching her. "You're saying I can't support this family on my own."

"Randy, that's not—"

He let out a guttural yell as he turned and pulled down the bookcase beside him. Susan's antique figurines shattered against each other as they hit the floor, and all the books thundered down.

Susan had made the mistake of underestimating how traditional Randy could be. The man was supposed to work, and the woman was supposed to stay home. It was an old idea, but it belonged to his father and to his grandfather, too. Of course, Randy's jealousy also had something to do with it. Still, when they'd first married, he hadn't cared. Susan had gotten work waiting tables at a Coney Island in Jefferson. She'd enjoyed the job most of the time, and she'd kept it all the way up until Willa was born.

But those days, she realized then, were over. After Randy's outburst, Susan had thrown away the broken figurines and put back the books and swept the floor and never asked again.

Explosions like that Susan could deal with. You paid a price for being married. Susan's mother had paid those prices, too.

But Willa. Willa, as whip smart as she was, with all that senseless adoration. Why did she care so much for her father's opinion? Why should she long so much for her father's approval?

Again the questions reared up, and again she pushed them down.

Despite the fight she'd accidentally started with Randy, Susan didn't think a job was what she needed or even wanted. It was more that she longed for something to sharpen her, to wake her up. Domestic work took up most of her time, but it occupied only the basement of her brain, while a cold, steady wind whipped through the upper stories. Maybe what she wanted was something to think about—something that was worth thinking about. She wanted to think more, to feel more. She wanted to grow.

One day the previous week, Susan had finished her chores early enough—a rare feat—and so she'd walked the country mile to the Esau library. The inside smelled like dust and the spines of old books, and the librarian, a broad-seated woman with ornate eye makeup, a lined upper lip, and hair as matte black as a woodstove, sat in the dark with only one small banker's lamp lit at her desk unless someone entered. When the bell above the door tinkled, the librarian rolled her chair over and switched on the lights. Susan wished she would leave them off. The darkness made the library seem like a secret, and the lights made Susan feel like an interruption. She left quickly, without having found anything she wanted.

Her problem was, it was hard to tell which books were worth reading and which ones were not. She didn't want any romances, of which there were a staggering number. On an adjoining wall was another section of thick, shiny hardcovers by people like Dean Koontz and John Grisham. But Susan didn't want horror stories, and she didn't want thrillers, either.

A book group, she thought. Didn't people join book groups? She imagined trying to explain that one to Randy. She didn't even tell him about going to the library. She just didn't want to have to explain herself. The last thing she needed was Randy thinking she had too much time on her hands, or worse, that she thought she was smarter than he was.

Susan wound the thread's end three times through a loose stitch, pulled it tight, and clipped the length, then folded the snow pants and set them to the side. Next up—one of Randy's thermal undershirts that had torn under the arm. He'd been reaching up to pull a bag of potato chips off the top of the fridge, and the hole had yawned open. She'd poked her finger in, and he'd jerked his elbow down. "What the fuck, Suzy," he'd said.

"A hole," she'd said, and blushed. "You have a hole in your shirt."

They used to be so much more playful together. Sometimes, if she acted in that vein, she could get him to play along. Not so much anymore. But relationships ebbed and flowed, right? That was the nature of relationships. That was what they did.

She reached for the remote and clicked on the television. Both channels (they only got two) were broadcasting morning talk shows masquerading as news, each hosted by a suited man who never stopped smiling and a blond woman who laughed at everything. Susan clicked the set back off.

She slipped an arm up through the shirt, into the sleeve, and pulled it inside out. Randy's sweat had bleached the gray from the fabric and turned it a watery brown. It was thinner, too, than the rest of the shirt, threadbare and almost transparent. Susan cut another length of thread from her brown spool, sucked it to a point, and poked it through the eye of her needle.

She missed Lukas. She missed Willa. Their weekly trips to the library in Jefferson, their walks to the little playground in Esau's town square. Susan was good at mothering. Not at first, of course, but she'd learned to be. It was an important skill, maybe the only important skill she'd ever acquired, besides keeping everyone fed and clothed. Every day to give them what they needed but not always what they wanted. To help them recognize their challenges and enunciate those challenges and experiment with solutions. To play with them and to let them play. To get out of the way when she could.

But now all the hours of silence opened up too much space for troubled thoughts.

Susan yanked a stitch too tight and ripped the seam she'd sewn, pulling the thread out through the fraying fabric. She jerked free the rest of her thread, pinned the tear deeper, and started again.

Susan wasn't scared of Randy, not really. There were lines she felt sure he wouldn't cross, not with her and not with the children. He even left the spanking to her, though he told her when to do it. But there had been times when Susan had wished Randy would hit her. A broken jaw, a black eye. These would be evidence that something needed to change.

Things hadn't always been so dire, though Randy had always been spiny and moody and caustically opinionated. These traits used to make her laugh, back when he'd liked that she laughed at him. These traits used to excite her. They'd pulled her toward him, a dangerous magnet. Later, she concluded that he'd taken her on as a challenge—standing up to him, laughing at him like she did.

They'd met as janitors at the community college, where they worked in exchange for decreased tuition. They both planned to transfer to universities. She'd wanted to become an English teacher; he'd planned to pursue electrical engineering. She'd quit halfway through her second semester for lack of funds. He'd lasted a year and a half. College, which they'd both seen as a launchpad to their sky-blue future, proved more like a dock in a swamp. They'd both made the dean's list and earned the praise of their teachers. These small accomplishments cast their lives since in a hue of insufficient motivation and regret. Her waitress job, his shop job, the fight to get by. They should have finished, no matter the cost. They should have figured out how.

Susan suspected that Randy, for all his bravado, carried the failure more closely than she did—so closely that he probably couldn't even make out what he'd been lugging around all these years. He'd been so cocksure that his would be a better life than that of his father, who retired from the same factory where Randy labored now. She knew too much of Randy's weakness, after fourteen years of marriage, not to read into his perpetual dissatisfaction all his insecurities, everything he'd wanted to believe about himself butting up against the facts of his life.

Over the years, her initial awe of Randy had faded. Now, at his worst moments, when she groped about for a feeling to help her bear him, the best she could find was pity. Which, she told herself, was a kind of love. How else to explain how much his sadness saddened her sometimes. How she ached for him when he betrayed the briefest glimpse of the turmoil he carried always around, of that young boy still inside, who was beaten every time he grieved his mother and countless other times besides. Wasn't it unfair that, by the virtue of tragic circumstance and God-given personality, some had an easier time at life? What else to level the playing field besides those with resilient dispositions coming alongside those with heavier burdens to bear?

Anyway, Susan had made a vow. Before God and before everyone else. And a vow, as her mother used to say with grim determination, was as good as glue. Susan had learned that to be true. After application, a vow became its own force, it hardened into its own physical reality. There was Susan, and there was glue, and there was Randy, and no matter how she picked them up and turned them this way and that, she could not figure out how to pull them apart.

Susan had finished mending the tear, but her thread felt so frail next to the thinning fabric that she decided to reinforce her seam, just to be sure. She turned the shirt in her lap and squinted as she started to sew back toward herself.

It did give Susan consolation that she was doing "the right thing." Sometimes it felt like her only consolation. She was doing the hard work that her easy words had made, and for this work, there must be some reward, if only the trophy of its being endured.

But now, when she thought of Willa, that consolation vanished. Willa was learning what Susan herself had learned as a child—to bend too far, to shrink too small, to surrender her dignity without questioning the cost. Willa was growing up in a certain shape of a life, a room with jagged edges and invisible walls which, Susan feared, for familiarity's sake alone, Willa would re-create in time.

The tear was finally repaired; this gave her a small satisfaction. She pulled the sleeve right-side out and checked her work. Besides a slight pucker at the base of her seam, it looked as though it had never torn open. Randy wouldn't even notice. Even if she hadn't pointed it out, he would eventually have noticed the tear, but he would not notice the fix, just as he noticed a stain on the rug or a dusty shelf but failed to see that the cabinets had been filled again with clean dishes, his dresser drawers with folded clothes.

Sometimes it felt like life without parole, to go on maintaining this invisible normal, to go on serving Randy forever just because one day, long ago, when she was young and brash and stupid, she had said that she would. Then the image of Willa came back to her, Willa with her resolute stare, lifting her spoon to her mouth.

Susan's stomach surged, and her body flushed with heat. She plunged her hand into her basket of sewing notions, grasped around for the thin, hard body of her seam ripper with its scimitar tip. She turned the shirt back inside out and held it up to the light, dug the ripper under her securing stitch and pulled. The thread broke easily, tiny hairs waving and drowning. She jerked along the seam. Dig, rip, dig, rip. It felt good, this tiny rebellion. But when she'd finished and gathered up all the scraps of thread and folded the shirt and tried to decide whether to put it in his drawer or back in the mending basket, she realized she'd only created more work for herself, and she cut a new length of thread and wet it and poked it again through the needle.

7

That Saturday Robert spent more time than usual revising his sermon, and though he assured himself that such attentions engaged his otherwise idle hands and thoughts, he knew also that he did so for the sheer possibility that Susan might show up again and hear the words he had written.

Robert had found over the course of his career that he could only write well when he wrote to himself, and that others would find truth there, too. This practice had humbled him and engaged him and strengthened him, he felt, along with his flock, which was why his message that week explored the subversiveness of sin—how it crept into one's good intentions, masking itself as virtue. He'd been thinking of Susan and how tempted he'd been to look up the Shearers in the phone book and call with a proper welcome. It would be easily justified; he'd done so on several occasions before, though in those cases a sense of duty had motivated him rather than these twin aches of loneliness and longing.

He had also preached often on thanking God for whatever made him uncomfortable, since discomfort reminded him to find his solace in God alone. He hadn't mentioned that he'd been writing about the parsonage, which was so poorly insulated that, in order to meet the monthly budget, he'd closed off the upstairs, kept the bottom level an even fifty-eight degrees in the winter, and combated the summer heat with a solitary fan he carried from room to room. His living quarters, then, contained what was once the guest bedroom and bathroom, now his own, along with a spacious living room and kitchen, both of which served as a constant reminder that the house was intended for a family of five or six.

His congregation held out hopes that he would fill it, whether from sincerity or politeness he could not tell. They told him that he was still young, that he was becoming the man he needed to be, that God had a plan. He was not bad looking; he had been called handsome and saw the truth of it, though he didn't fit the description of a typical Esau man. He tended to forget this until someone at the market or gas station would ask him where he was from. Sometimes they'd even ask if he was an Indian.

"You an Indian?" They usually said it like they hoped he'd say yes.

He never knew how to answer that. He rarely thought of his Native American identity, but he did look the part. His hair was black and sleek, and his skin was brown. Several girls in college had described it as the color of caramel, each one separately and proudly, as though they had fallen in love with the description, which always made Robert deeply uncomfortable.

Robert's mother had taught him that they were Cherokee, though Robert's father had been white. This he had also learned from his mother, as Robert had never actually met the man.

Robert's early memories had grown fuzzy, especially as there was no one to corroborate them. The state had taken him away from his mother at eight years old, when part of their trailer had collapsed on top of him. He had a vague recollection of a head-splitting pain and a doctor's fleshy face hovering over his own, pulling a needle up and pushing it down again with a sickening pressure.

The car had arrived the following morning before they woke. They'd been sleeping together in their one bedroom, in the end of the trailer that hadn't collapsed. He could still remember waking to his mother's body tightening around him as her head jerked up from the pillow and froze fast, listening. His mother yelling after him as the woman in the red sweater led him away—"I'll get you back, Bobby Glory! God as my witness, I'll get you back!"

In the weeks and months that followed, he returned to this memory each evening, to his mother's promise, his mother's arm draped over his own, her smells of cigarette smoke and peach shampoo. Those days, he was still waiting to go back home. He still believed his mother was just a moment away from ringing the doorbell and whisking him off.

The state had moved him from house to house, of course, but his favorite foster parents had kept him from ages eleven to fourteen, and it was there he decided to become a pastor.

Their whole house rang with order. The gleaming linoleum, the plush carpets, the chore chart affixed to the fridge each month with four matching magnets.

The Baptist church they'd attended gave Robert the same sense of neatness and harmony. One could know exactly what was true and what was false. One could exchange the endless chaos of the world for a tidy system of rules and boundaries so complete and controlled that, within it, each question found an answer and even doubt seemed to disappear.

After high school, he attended a Baptist college, then seminary. He performed well. He was intelligent, he knew, and he possessed an uncommonly high level of self-discipline. He'd dated a handful of girls along the way but never seriously. The girls had invaded his studies, his fortress of peace. They had complicated things, distracted him from his work, and aroused desires that could not rightly be satisfied.

In his last year at the seminary, the offer had come from Esau, and he had taken it as an offer from God—an opportunity to minister to a rural community where, the letter stated, the harvest was great and the workers were few. Other members of his graduating class who hadn't performed nearly as well were interviewing at large churches with big budgets and luxurious parsonages. He told himself that this was because they had wives and children, and families put people at ease. This selection ought not to embitter him. His classmates were not to blame. He would gladly accept a similar position, if one were offered.

After he arrived in Esau, Robert's initial optimism wore through. His seminary training had prepared him for rigorous exegesis, theological debate, and other studious diversions of a life of the mind. His parishioners, however, expected that much of his time be spent at Sunday school picnics and church potlucks and even gatherings that had nothing to do with church—birthday parties and retirement parties, housewarming and graduation parties. It baffled Robert that one small congregation could produce so many parties. It wasn't that Robert disliked people; some people Robert liked very much. But he dreaded the demands of small talk, the requirement to feign interest in dull topics, to laugh at jokes that he didn't find funny, to ask questions he didn't care to know the answers to.

Also, the congregants Robert liked were never the ones to demand his attention. Jim Hibbert, for example, once kept Robert after church for over an hour explaining how "the coloreds" were trying to take over Esau's local government. Apparently, an African American family had moved into a house down on Blue Lake Drive, and the father had attended a village council meeting to "whine" (Jim's word) about comments his daughters had received at school. From this, Jim had deduced the man's desire to run for office and ultimately overthrow the current order. When Robert failed to ascend to the desired level of concern, Jim Hibbert shrugged and said, "I guess you're all in this together."

It was that remark, and others like it, that injected into Robert a steel regarding the parties. Generally Robert wrote those comments off as outliers, or he explained them away—his congregants were well-meaning, and their slips must be interpreted in accordance with that understanding. But after another wasted Saturday spent shuffling between a ninetieth-birthday party for Greta Fern's mother and a farewell party for a church family that Robert had never even met, Robert concluded that if he couldn't attend all parties, he shouldn't attend any.

He feared at first that his congregants might find his decision supercilious, but each polite decline was politely accepted, and slowly the invitations dried up. Mostly he was glad for the time and quiet it afforded, but sometimes the space around him spread out wide and cold, a barren field, and not even Robert's scholarly preoccupations could drive that sense away.

In Esau, Robert's late twenties had faded to early thirties, then mid-, then late. Now, at thirty-eight, his options, he knew, were dwindling, even as his yearnings for a family grew. He could only envision someone too young for him and therefore too immature, or else a widow. Marrying a divorced woman—whatever the reason behind the divorce—would relieve him of his post immediately, and single thirtysomething women did not seem to exist in Esau, Michigan.

Perhaps, he told himself that Saturday as he read through his sermon for the fifth time, perhaps that was why Susan had so captured his attention—she was widowed and simply wore the ring to remember her husband or to discourage untoward men.

Ah, he thought, and he chastised himself, the subversiveness of sin—hoping a man had died so that he might justly partake of the spoils. He prayed a quick prayer for forgiveness and returned his attention to the text.

But then, why had she captured his attention so? She was beautiful, yes, and she was at least somewhat like-minded in thought, attending his church as she had. But there was something else there, too. Her face held a thoughtful intelligence and also a sadness, one so familiar he felt he could understand it without its being explained. And her eyes held a secret he'd thought was his alone. A restlessness, a sleeping wildness, an almost-readiness for something.

Come Sunday morning, trying to soothe the excitement in his stomach, Robert directed himself through his daily routine. He woke early to read his Bible and pray. He took his morning walk—a brisk, thirty-minute clip across the field out back and down the old railroad tracks. He met with the Sunday school teachers prior to class and led them in prayer, led the adult class through the next few verses of their in-depth study of Galatians. Despite his efforts to remain calm and steadfast, he vacillated between a giddy hopefulness and the sober counterweight of reality, which reminded him over and over that a beautiful woman with a wedding ring and two children was almost certainly married and would remain outside the realm of possibility forever.

Yet when she arrived—early this time and willowy beneath her long black coat, her eyes brightened by the cold—it required a good deal of will to mitigate his joy into a standard smile and nod from his post inside the door. She nodded and smiled back (too briefly, he thought, as though she had forgotten him), then ushered her children over to the coatrack.

His eyes lingered on the curve of her neck and the sweep of her dark hair as it crested back into its braid. A few tendrils had come loose and fluttered, as she moved, against the skin beneath her ear, and he found himself flushed and wondering if a similar sight had prompted Paul to decree that all women cover their heads in houses of worship. Then Henry Gillis pulled the door open for Rose, his wife, who staggered in slowly under the weight of her back, and an icy blast of wind jolted Robert from his reverie and filled him with a cold, burning shame that, on the Lord's Day no less, his mind had been thus occupied.

His sermon came off well enough, and from the pulpit his gaze passed over Susan as it swept around the room. Each time he found her staring up at him with such bare directness it seemed she could penetrate all his secret thoughts. When she passed him after the service, she looked up at him and smiled a little, then averted her eyes as if embarrassed. He held himself back from speaking directly to her—she was in the midst of a stream of people shuffling out—and he held himself back, too, from watching her walk to her car. He did speak to Lucy Beamer, who ran the quilting circle, to make sure, with as devout a face as he could muster, that the woman had been properly welcomed. She had, it turned out, and she had also accepted an invitation to the women's quilting circle the following Wednesday, which was held upstairs in the church dining and activity room.

Robert thanked Lucy for her hospitality and then steered the subject toward her husband's gout, which afterward he could not remember as better or worse or the same. He just stood there making sympathetic sounds as his heart exulted that in three days he would see Susan again. On his way to his study on Wednesday mornings, he always paused at the quilting tables to greet the ladies and inquire after their work. It would be strange if he did not stop—if they simply heard the back door open and his solitary footsteps descend the stairs. No, no, he must certainly pause on Wednesday for his usual visit, though he must also take care not to linger longer than was his custom.

8

On the way home from church, Lukas kept singing one of the hymns from the service, but only one phrase over and over in the same singsong voice.

"'Onward Christian soldiers, Onward Christian soldiers, Onward Christian soldiers . . .'"

"Lukas!" she said. "Enough already."

He paused for a moment and then continued, a little more quietly.

"Stop," she said.

He lowered his voice to the quietest tone he could manage, the level right above a whisper. She could barely hear him.

"I said stop it!" she yelled, louder than she'd meant to. Lukas stopped.

"Mom," Willa ventured. "Are you okay?"

"Of course I'm okay," she said. But the truth was she felt prickly and angry, like a teenager. She wanted everyone to go away and leave her alone.

Randy could sense it, too. In the kitchen, she dropped a pan in a rush to get the chicken frying, and she swiped it up in a huff and slammed it down on a burner.

"Jesus," Randy said. "What's the matter with you?" He was sitting in the living room chair in front of the television, watching cars race around a track. She could hear the growl of their engines as they rounded the bends. Ridiculous, that people got paid boatloads of money to drive around in circles. Even more ridiculous that someone would make it a point to sit down and watch them.

"Nothing's the matter with me," she said. "I just dropped a pan." But she could hear the clench in her voice.

That pastor wouldn't slump in front of the TV all afternoon, looking mindlessly on as a bunch of grown men chased each other in circles. How embarrassed she'd be if he were to drop by. Didn't pastors do that sometimes? Stop by and welcome new families to their churches? She'd written their names down that morning on a welcome card, along with their address and phone number, and dropped it into the basket on the foyer table. She imagined, as she filled out the card, that the pastor might call. But why had she put down her address? Now she had to worry that he'd show up when Randy was home, which of course he would do if he were planning to show up at all.

Out in the living room, the engines growled around and around. Randy said to the screen, "Cut him off! Just cut him off!"

Susan held her hand above the oil, judging the heat with her palm. Hot enough. She pushed her sleeves up to her elbows and peeled a wing off the heap of raw chicken parts, dipped it in the egg and turned it over in the breading. It settled into the oil with a hiss.

After last Sunday's horror, she had decided to cook Randy's favorite meals on Sundays as a way of calming him down. He was always the worst after church. So delicate, so defensive. She'd splurge a little if she had to, maybe cut back on other nights. Or she could eat less for lunch. Half sandwiches instead of whole, cut out the yogurt. Or maybe some days she could just skip lunch altogether. She'd heard that fasting was a healthy thing to do. Why not try it? She wouldn't mind losing a couple of pounds.

Susan dropped the final piece, a drumstick, from too high above the pan, and when it landed, sparks of scalding oil jumped up and peppered the underside of her forearm. She squealed and hopped back, rubbing the scalded skin with her apron.

"Jesus," Randy said. "What the hell are you doing in there." He said it like a statement, like he didn't really care to hear the answer. On the television, a buzzer started and kept sounding. An announcer was shouting. Bells began to clang. Soon the race would be over.

Throughout dinner, there were no outbursts. The kids ate ravenously, as did Randy. It seemed to Susan that all she could hear was his chewing. She kept glancing over at him to check whether or not his mouth was open, but most of the time it was closed. It sounded like someone had hooked up a microphone that amplified each tiny sound. The pounding of his molars, the snapping of the chicken tendons, the greasy suck of his lips at the skin. When he swallowed, she could hear the muscles of his throat working the meat down.

Susan looked at her plate. She'd eaten a few small bites. She couldn't bring herself to eat any more. The chicken platter was empty. The kids, in a rare move, had both taken seconds.

"You going to eat that?" Randy asked. He nodded down at her food.

"No," she said. "I'm not feeling well."

He traded their plates. "Too bad for you, but more for me," he said.

Susan stared down at his leftover bones jumbled over a smear of mashed potatoes and a few limp green beans drowned in grease. Might as well start fasting now. Maybe she could fast for the same reasons they did in the Bible, to petition God, to bring his mercy down. Maybe then God would answer the prayers she'd been praying all of these years—to heal Randy and redeem him, or, if not that, at least make Susan more capable of bearing her load.

The pastor that morning had spoken of the subversiveness of sin. How believers must remain always steadfast, ever vigilant. They must remember that the enemy besets them with snares on all sides. At each turn, they must pray to discern their own will from the will of God, for the will of the flesh is sinful and self-serving, and it leads to destruction, even under the guise of leading toward the good.

When he'd said that last part, he'd looked at her, and the warning in his eyes struck straight to the tangle within her of fear and of longing, of the struggle to hold fast. He was a bright man, and an eloquent one, but he seemed to be operating on an extraordinarily harsh view of human nature. Were they all really so awful as that?

"Hey. Suzy." It was Randy. He snapped his fingers. "Suzy-Q." She hated when he called her that.

"Yes?"

"Where'd you go?"

"I'm sorry?"

"Did you hear what I just said?"

"No, what was it?"

"I asked why you don't cook like this all the time."

"Ah."

"Well?"

"Well. We can't afford a lot of meat for each meal. So I usually mix it into other things."

"Why you gotta do that?" His voice had gone short and dry. She felt the warning of his tone bloom through her. Her mind had been elsewhere, and she hadn't measured her words.

She could think of nothing to say, and so she said nothing.

"I work my fucking ass off every fucking day." He sprang up. His chair squealed back, and his belly grazed the edge of the table and set the dishes shaking. The children jumped a little in their chairs, echoes of his movement.

"Look at me," he said. "Look at me!"

She looked up at him. His nostrils flared out, his lips glistened with grease.

"I work as hard as I can," he said. "It's not my fault they don't pay me shit. I still deserve to eat like a man at least, not some animal." And he stalked off to the basement.

Downstairs, Susan heard the toolbox drawers jerking open and slamming shut. He was seeking out something to occupy himself, something that would keep him busy until Sunday ended and Monday whisked him off to work again.

Maybe the pastor would call that week. Maybe she could ask him some of her questions, share some of her thoughts. About how right and wrong didn't seem nearly as neat as he'd pretended they were. About the limits of resistance.

9

Back at the apartment, Mavis was sitting on the porch with her papers and pouch, rolling cigarettes on a TV tray, a blanket wrapped around her shoulders. It couldn't be much past seven, but the sun had already set, and Leotie could barely make out Mavis's face as she hunched beneath the porch light.

"You been gone all day," Mavis said as Leotie pulled herself up the steps, gripping the porch rail. Mavis said this without looking up, like either it was no big deal or else it was such a big deal that Mavis didn't even have to look at her to prove it.

"What's it to you?" Leotie said. She rested at the top of the stairs and tried to take in air. The library was only three blocks away, and she walked slow, but she still couldn't catch her breath. It felt like she'd sprinted all the way home.

"Nothing," said Mavis, and she leaned back and put up her hands, like Leotie was overreacting. "We just know you didn't have to work today is all."

When Leotie didn't bother explaining, Mavis held up a cigarette from her stack. "You wanna smoke?"

"I can't even goddamn breathe," said Leotie, but she took it anyway and sat down on the bench next to Mavis, who had already flicked her lighter and was holding it out. Leotie took one more long breath before tucking the cigarette between her lips and sucking in the flame. It was hard not to cough, but she managed it by breathing shallow and letting the smoke relax her chest.

The two women sat for a minute in silence.

Mavis nodded at Leotie's cigarette. "That's some premium tobacco right there," she said. "Now you going to tell me where you was all day?"

"Mavis," Leotie said. "You are one nosy old bitch."

Mavis laughed, and Leotie laughed and forgot to breathe carefully. She sucked in too much smoke too deep, and it started her coughing. She had to hand her cigarette to Mavis. She jerked her rag out of her pocket, muffled her mouth with it, and leaned over her knees.

It used to be there was satisfaction to coughing. It used to be if she coughed long enough, it relieved something. These days, though, when she started coughing, she could never cough enough. It felt like someone had filled her lungs with glue and no amount of hacking could budge it. Of course, whether it felt good or not didn't matter. It was getting harder to stop once she'd started.

So Leotie sat there barking away until Mavis reached around and thumped her back and Leotie's cigarette burned itself out in the ashtray. Finally, Leotie tasted the bitter phlegm freckling her tongue and felt the rag dampening against her mouth. When the coughs slowed, she cleared her throat, spat, and wiped her lips. Then she drew the rag away.

It looked dirty in the dim porch light. She thought she must have gotten it dirty somehow. But when she leaned back to see the rag full in the light, it shone bright red.

"Well shit," Mavis said, and together they stared at it. "Better go see a doctor about that."

Well, Leotie thought, this is some kind of timing. She'd just been thinking, since finding her Bobby earlier that day, that maybe she had some time. She'd landed at the apartment six months before. Isabel, one of her friends inside, knew a group of ragtags who were looking for a roommate. Besides prison, it was the first steady home she'd had since she left her mom's house at sixteen. One month after her release, Longfellow Care Home had given her a job washing sheets and blankets, and she'd kept it since. No benefits, but still, seven dollars and fifty cents an hour, which was enough to pay rent and bus fare and buy groceries and a lottery ticket, or even papers and tobacco if she'd still smoked regular, which she didn't.

She hadn't ever imagined herself living so comfortably as she did now. She had her own room, her own door that locked. Three squares a day and food to pack on work days. People who noticed when she wasn't around. Friends, kind of. Mavis and Timbo and Quentin and even Peggy, when she wasn't bossing. None of them knew about Bobby because he wasn't for them to know. But still. She had people she liked to come home to, people who seemed to like having her around.

She lowered the rag into her lap. Now the shadow of her body didn't hide the redness. Now the blood kept its color in the dark.

Funny. Had she hacked up blood yesterday, it might not have mattered so much. Now the rag in her hand throbbed out a warning. *Hurry*, it said. *Winter's coming, your body's breaking down. Go now.*

THAT NIGHT, Leotie waited until everyone else had gone to bed. Her only trouble was Timbo, who always stayed up late dicking around on the house computer, playing solitaire and emailing his imaginary girlfriends. She cracked her door and shut off her light. When at last she heard his heavy footsteps shuffle past, she crept out, felt her way back to the kitchen, and switched on the small light over the stove. Leotie had to call because pastors moved around. Bobby might not be in the same place he'd been when someone typed his name into that website. She needed to call and make sure.

Leotie picked up the phone and stared at it. She pressed the talk button, dialed the parsonage number, and hung up. The second time she dialed, she let the phone ring. It was only when she heard the ringing that she realized she was calling in the middle of the night. Before she could think to hang up, the line clicked, and a groggy, startled voice said, "Hello?"

"Hello?" he said again when she didn't answer. "Hello? Who is this?" It was a man's voice, clearer this time. She couldn't tell whether it was Bobby or not.

"This is Mavis Singleton," Leotie said. She'd picked out the name before she called. "Hello."

"Hello." He shaped the end of the word like a question, like he was actually saying, *Why is some loony old bat named Mavis calling me in the middle of the night?*

"Sorry," she said. "I forgot how late it was over there." She realized that he was waiting for her to explain herself. "It's not that late over here," she added.

"Oh," the man said. He sounded confused. "Oh, are you a missionary?" His change in tone suggested that this would make sense of everything.

"Yes," she said. She had planned to ask what time the church service was and maybe what people were supposed to wear. Then she would ask who the pastor was those days. Now she had to pretend to be a missionary.

"Ah," he said. "That makes sense."

Leotie couldn't think of what else to say.

"So you're looking for support?" he asked.

"Yes," said Leotie. She tried to sound businesslike, believable. "I need some support."

"Okay," he said. "Are you serving alone?"

Silence. Was she supposed to be serving alone?

"Yes," she said. She had meant that to sound businesslike, too, but instead it sounded more like a question.

"That's . . . brave," he said. "Where are you serving?"

Shitsticks. "Africa," she said.

"Which country?" he asked.

Leotie remembered the world atlas in the living room.

"Just a minute," she said. "There's someone at the door."

She set the phone on the counter, scrambled around the corner, and swiped her hand over the light switch. She flipped the atlas open to the map of Africa, and her eyes raced for a country she knew she could pronounce correctly. When she found it, she rushed back and paused, bracing herself over the counter. She had moved too fast, and her lungs were pulling for air. She waited a moment for her breathing to calm. Then she held the phone to her ear and put her hand over the receiver.

"I'm on the phone," she said to the cupboards. "I'll be with you shortly."

She took her hand off the mouthpiece and said, "I'm sorry. It's busy here. I'm in Congo."

"Ah," he said. She could hear the doubt in his voice. "And who sent you there?"

Was this a trick question? "God," she said.

He laughed. "That's fair," he said. "But I was asking which sending agency. Or maybe it was a church?"

"Yeah," she said. She didn't feel like trying anymore. "It was a church."

"Okay," he said, but his tone said, *It's time to drop the act.* "What is it that you really need?" His voice was sleepy but kind.

"Help," she croaked, and cleared her throat. "I need help."

"This church is a safe place, if that's what you're asking. Small, but safe. I'm the pastor here. I can help with food and clothing. There's a shelter not too far away that might be able to find you a place to stay if that's what you're looking for."

Leotie was silent.

"Is there anything else you need to know?" he asked.

This time she didn't falter. "Your name," she said. "I should probably know your name."

"Now there's an easy question," he said. "The name is Robert. Robert Glory."

10

Circle Wednesday morning wasn't quite what Susan had hoped. The women were stitching a quilt for a missionary family in Papua New Guinea, which sounded like a good thing, until Bertha proudly informed her that all of their quilts shipped to missionary families and that some families had received not just one but two or three. A woman named Florence chimed in with the countries. India, Kenya, Thailand, Togo, Burma, Brazil. Susan's geography was admittedly rough, but weren't all those countries uncomfortably hot? She couldn't help but see the women's efforts as wayward. It seemed they were doing something to assure themselves they were doing something rather than actually caring for those in need.

All of the quilters were nice enough—especially Lucy, who had invited her—but no real conversation took place, at least not at the depth that Susan longed for. Six women came besides herself, five of them in their sixties or seventies. The sixth, Cecelia, was younger, close to Susan's age, but she gave off a purposeful chill, as if to say that, just because their ages might lump them together, that didn't mean they had to share anything else.

Marjorie, who was in her early sixties, Susan judged, with hair wound around her head in long, gray braids, kicked off the conversation—Had Susan grown up in Esau?

Of course they would know that she hadn't. Susan had lived in Esau for twelve years, and she had known from day one that she would always be an outsider. She and Randy had found an affordable lot just outside of town, far enough away from their parents but close enough to Randy's work, and they'd taken out a loan on a manufactured home. The day the workmen dropped off the two halves of their house and fitted them together, Susan drove to Esau Market to buy something easy for dinner. The market's entire inventory, judging by the faded boxes and dusty cellophane, had lived out its shelf life, even though all the items were either canned or frozen or heavily processed. Eventually Susan selected a frozen pepperoni pizza, furry with frost, and a vintage sack of potato chips, though she could not tell if the packaging was intentionally vintage or if the chips had simply sat on the market shelf for decades.

Behind the cash register, the woman (Darlene Dicky, Susan later learned) did not respond to Susan's energetic "hello." She waited until Susan had selected her purchases and carried them to the counter.

"Pizza and chips," the woman said. "Pizza and chips."

"Yes," said Susan politely, thinking the woman might be challenged in some way.

"Big night, then?" the woman asked.

Susan couldn't decide whether the woman was being sarcastic. "I actually just moved into the neighborhood," Susan said. "About a mile down, right off Willis."

"*You* bought that old lot?" the woman said. Her eyes narrowed to a shrewdness Susan would not have expected of her.

"My husband and I," Susan clarified.

"Ah," the woman said, and she seemed to relax. "You're married then."

"Yes." Susan got the sense that she had just passed a test she hadn't known she'd been taking.

"Any kids?" the woman asked.

"No," Susan said, vaguely wondering if this was the response she was supposed to give. Then she added, "But soon. Hopefully."

The woman gave an approving nod as she handed over Susan's change, but her fingers felt as cold as the coins she placed in Susan's palm. "Well then," the woman said. "Welcome to Esau." Her eerie half smile and the chill of her hands had touched off a small panic in Susan's stomach.

Esau, Michigan, wasn't more than thirty minutes outside Jefferson, where Susan had grown up. She hadn't even considered herself to be changing location, really—just setting. But she had failed to fully consider the closed nature of small towns, particularly ones tucked almost secretively into the countryside, far from major throughways.

No one was likely to arrive in Esau unless they intended to arrive there, or on the off chance that they became hopelessly lost. As a result, the facts of everyone who belonged to the town were thoroughly known—their name and jobs and graduation date; the names and jobs of their parents and also grandparents, who had likely attended school in the old one-room schoolhouse still standing at the edge of the town; and their brothers and sisters, with a special interest in those who had committed the unforgivable act of leaving Esau behind.

On top of these biographical facts, the villagers stacked up stories. Lost jobs, accidents, fistfights, affairs, troubling propensities for the arts or theater. All that had been publicly observed as tragic or cowardly or lustful or beyond the pale of standard behavior—all these fragments had been written down upon the collective conscience of the town. These versions of events must have been tossed back and forth—over the dining tables at Karla's and the raised hoods at Larry's, the bar at Dwight's and the rubber mat at Esau Market. All these stories must have been traded, somehow, handled until they hardened into facts. Yet Susan rarely heard the residents of Esau talk much about anything. She couldn't help but suspect that some uncanny force was at work—that some mysterious cloud, the stuff of science fiction, contained all there was to know about the town and that access to this cloud was the true Esau villager's only birthright. How else to explain the things everyone seemed to know, so effortlessly?

At the quilting circle, the older ladies collected the other pertinent information, though again Susan suspected that they had, somehow or other, already ascertained it all—where in Esau she lived, her children's ages, her husband's job (though Susan suspected that this was more to ensure that she still lived with a real, live husband). When she told them he assembled drills at Mack Tool, the factory just north of Henley, they seemed mollified.

"Does he work Sundays?" Marjorie prompted. In other words, Susan interpreted, was that why he didn't come to church?

"No," Susan answered, and the conversation ended there with the whole circle staring grimly down at the quilting edge, pins gripped in their lips.

Eventually Pastor Robert passed through and asked how everything was coming along. He seemed positively springy, Susan noticed, but there was something off about it, like his mind had chosen an emotion that he couldn't quite locate inside himself. Nervous, that's what it was. He seemed nervous.

After he had left, the older ladies took him up as a subject and batted him around. Marjorie kicked it off.

"So, Miss Susan," she said, "what do you think of our fair pastor?"

Florence snorted. "Don't know that I'd call him fair."

"Fair doesn't just mean white, Florence. It also means good-looking."

"Well, then just say that."

"Fine. Miss Susan, what do you think of our good-looking pastor?" Then, without waiting for Susan to respond, she added in a whisper, "We think he wants to get married."

"Of course he wants to get married." This was Florence again. "Everyone wants to get married."

Ethel spoke sternly, pulling a needle up from the fabric. "He'd better get a move on, then."

"How old is he now?"

"Nearly forty."

"No!"

"Not more than a couple years off. I'm sure of it."

"Still has his looks. That's good."

"You can't rush God's plan."

"You sure can't."

"The Lord works in mysterious ways."

"You can say that again."

The conversation went on and on. Susan stitched resolutely at her edge and said nothing. They were treating him like such an outsider, she realized, speaking of him only in reference to his differences—to what separated his experience from theirs. If he did actually want to get married, as they said, then he must be lonely. And she suddenly felt so lonely, too, sitting there. How long had it been since she'd talked with a trusted friend? Did she even have anyone anymore that she could call? Perhaps Robert's lack of a wife made him lonely, but her own presence of a husband made her just as lonely. Maybe even more so, because it took away the hope of a remedy.

"You own an opinion on any of this, Miss Susan?" Marjorie asked.

Susan raised her head. All six of the women were watching her, waiting for her answer.

"He's very . . . eloquent," she said lamely, and returned her attention to her lap.

After circle, Susan remained in the church bathroom until all the other women had gone. She did not want to commit, out of politeness, to attending circle the following week, and she dreaded the awkward leave-taking of new acquaintances. When the church grew quiet, she moved toward what she thought to be the exit, but she ended up in the sanctuary. She decided to leave out the front, but those doors had been bolted shut. Then, turning around, she glanced through the open door in the corner of the foyer and found Pastor Robert seated behind a desk, staring out at her with a frozen, startled expression.

"Hello," he said, a little too cheerfully. "Did you get turned around?" Then, before she could answer, "Did you enjoy the circle?"

"Yes," she said, and then, "No," and then to her horror she burst into tears.

"Oh!" Robert said, and he jumped up, cracking his leg against his desk. He grabbed a box of Kleenex and hobbled out to her, tissues outstretched.

"Thank you," she said, pulling a sheet from the box and holding it to her eyes. "Are you all right? I'm sorry. I don't know why I'm crying." The tears surged up again, and she covered her face with her hand.

"Oh yes. Just clumsy. Maybe you should sit down." And the pastor gestured toward his office.

11

Susan sank into the seat closest to the office door. Robert settled the box of tissues next to her and lowered himself into his chair. His heart pounded furiously, and his face felt flushed and damp. When the deacons had hired him ten years before, they'd encouraged him not to meet alone with women, and it had always been easy enough to comply. But now, so suddenly, here they were, just the two of them, and absolutely nothing to be done about it. Steady, steady, he thought. Think before you speak. She is hurting. You are a servant of God.

Susan was still crying, pulling Kleenex after Kleenex from the box and sobbing quietly into them. Her breath came in short, hard bursts that shook her shoulders. At last the storm left her, and she sat there for a time breathing into her hands. When she looked up at him, her face was red and glistening, and her eyes shone bright with tears.

"I'm sorry," she said again. "I don't know what's wrong with me. I've interrupted your work."

He replied, "Interruptions are also my work," and she laughed a little.

"I hope the quilting circle didn't upset you?" he ventured.

"No! No," she said, the repetition a little less certain. "It wasn't exactly what I was hoping, but that's not why I'm upset."

"Anything you'd like to talk about?" he asked.

Susan's eyes passed around the room. She waited awhile before speaking. "Have you ever noticed," she said, "how trying to do what's right can lead to so many wrongs?"

"How do you mean?"

She was a wonderer. He could see her wondering. She thought a bit longer and said, "You promise you'll do something. Maybe you shouldn't have promised, but you did. So you keep at it. To stay true to your word. To do what's right in the eyes of God. But it shadows everything that comes after. It takes the color out of your life."

Pastor Robert stared down at his hands gripped together in his lap. Was she talking about her marriage? "God doesn't promise that our obedience will make us happy," he said. "Just obedient."

"But what if it's making everyone miserable?" she asked. "What then? In church you said that we nearly always know what to do, we just don't want to do it. But nothing's ever really that simple, is it? I'm sorry." She shook her head. "I'm just trying to figure it out."

Robert waited for her to continue, and after a few moments, she did.

"Take my parents," she said. "My mother stuck beside my father all her life. They're still together today. He's an angry man. He used to clear the whole dinner table with one arm, send it all to the floor. One time I broke his favorite coffee mug, the one he used every morning. My mother glued it back together. When he found the cracks, she told him she'd dropped it. She lied to him all the time, to protect us. He would tell her to spank us sometimes when he didn't feel like doing it, and she'd take us upstairs and paddle the bed and tell us to cry so that he'd think she followed through. Should she have told the truth then? Should she have obeyed? We hadn't done anything wrong." Her voice had grown urgent, imploring. After a pause she continued more calmly.

"I guess I'm saying that you try to do the right thing, but sometimes the right thing makes more wrongs than just doing the wrong thing in the first place. Then nothing's all right, and nothing's all wrong, and how are you supposed to choose then?"

He said, "The Bible tells us not to do evil that good may come."

She stared into him, her eyes wide and fixed, a questioning crease between her brows. "I'm not talking about evil. I'm talking about living a little more . . . gently. Forgivingly. Of everything."

Occasionally, when people had questioned his preaching, Robert had felt an inward slipping and had scrabbled to hold his footing. Now he felt the same phenomenon, only this time he let himself slip with it. When he finally spoke, his voice rasped.

"I don't know," he said, and he cleared his throat. "You're right," he continued. "It isn't always so easy. Or so clear."

They sat together quietly for a time. The heat ticked along the baseboards. Susan swung her crossed leg and studied the carpet. She seemed in no hurry to fill the silence.

"You pray," he said. "You ask God for guidance. You ask him to make his desires your own."

Susan nodded. Then, after a pause, she said, "I'm starting to wonder if sometimes you don't bend a little, too, when life requires it. When there's nothing else you can possibly do."

She stood and stooped over to drop her tissues into the wastebasket and retrieve her purse from beside the chair.

"Thank you," she said. "Thank you for listening. You have helped me."

"I'm glad to hear it."

"May I—" She paused. "Could you," she asked, gesturing to his shelves, "recommend a book?"

He must have looked confused, because she added, "You know, for these questions? For my life now?"

He walked to the shelf and pulled down his tattered copy of Saint Augustine's *Confessions*.

"It's a favorite of mine," he said. "Take your time."

Susan flushed and slipped the volume into her purse. Robert flushed, too, with embarrassment, though he could not have said why. She was the first to request a book in months, maybe years. Perhaps that was why the act felt so intimate.

They regarded one another for a moment.

"See you Sunday, then," she said.

"See you Sunday."

Robert listened to her footsteps fade across the sanctuary. Then he heard the door to the back close. He opened his Bible to the scripture passage for the week: Hebrews 12, the chapter that spoke of running the race with perseverance, of God disciplining his children for their own good.

Robert's eyes rested on verse 4: *Ye have not yet resisted unto blood.* Suddenly he felt exhausted. All this resisting, all this blood. All this self-denial that paved the impossibly long road to holiness. He wasn't sure he had the strength for it anymore.

Seated at his desk, his eyes moved over and over the passage, but his mind moved over her face and over the soft strength of her voice. She continued to ring in his mind like an alarm or a bell, either warning him of something or waking him up.

12

Susan left the church with a sense of elation that deflated steadily the closer she came to home. It had been some time since she'd had the opportunity of an inquiring conversation. This, she realized, was what she'd been searching for at the quilting circle. Someone with whom she could talk about something that mattered. Someone to listen and consider and respond. Her brief words with Pastor Robert had brought this lack to the fore—a lack of which, flogging away at the hard and humble work of life, she had only been dimly aware. His presence, too, imparted a sense of firmness, of uprightness, of immutable truth. The straightness of his back, the fullness of his shoulders, even the prominent crest of his upper lip. She couldn't tell whether she found herself more attracted to him or to the unencumbered purpose with which he seemed to live his life.

Looking down into herself, she saw a great, empty space—a large room with bare shelves, waiting to be filled. It brought her back to her first semester of college all those years before when her English professor had handed out the syllabus, though back then the sense had been hopeful rather than despairing. He had led them week by week through the class schedule, stocked with names of writers she recognized but hadn't ever read. Homer, Tolstoy, Thoreau. She'd felt such excitement at the prospect of all that knowledge and of the concrete plan for etching it into her mind. In that moment, she had watched her best life roll out before her, had witnessed herself taking those first timorous steps.

It almost hurt to remember that now. How could she have forgotten that she'd been meant for more than this—forgotten not for weeks or months but for years and years?

She had built her home as best she could. She had raised her children to where they went off on their own for hours and hours each day. At last the onslaught of all that work had suspended itself and opened up the opportunity to remember. She used to read. She used to argue. She used to laugh, for God's sake. What had happened?

Susan had driven home without taking any notice of what she was doing, but when she pulled into her driveway and quit the shuddering engine, gathered the collar of her coat against the cold and slipped up the path of smashed snow and into the chilled and shadowy house, she saw her life with fresh eyes—its smallness, its dullness. Everything reflected how unremarkable she'd become. There was the stuffed chair, hideously floral, and the sofa with its threadbare arms and cushions. The giant TV—she had always hated the TV. The dining room table scarred from dropped knives and the burnt circles of pot bottoms. The kitchen behind its partition of counter, its surfaces choked with small appliances and cords and boxes that wouldn't fit into the cupboards and the plastic tufts of bread bags suffocating their leftover heels.

She lived almost all of her life in this one open room. At that moment it looked so ugly as to be almost unreal, the stage of a low-budget play no one would go to see.

It was Wednesday. Laundry day, bathroom-cleaning day. She thought of all the damp socks and pant legs souring in the hamper, the yellow drops dried round the rim of the toilet bowl. After Randy's post-lunch phone call, she pulled Pastor Robert's book from her purse and carried it to her bedroom, burrowed under the bedcovers. She barely made it through the first few lines before the music of the language began to lull her. *Thou madest us for Thyself, and our heart is restless, until it repose in Thee.* She didn't decide to sleep, but sleep took her anyway, quickly and deeply, a wave falling over a castle of sand and pulling it into the sea.

13

On Wednesday, after the bus screeched to a stop in front of their driveway, Willa helped Lukas down the bus steps before dashing ahead of him into the house to check her angel. There it was, its feet perfectly outlined within its tracing. Willa stood for a moment beside her bed and let the relief rush through her. This was the best she felt, checking the angel after a whole day away. The worst she felt was on the bus ride home, when she was afraid it had moved. But the badness and the goodness together felt right, too—kind of like math, when one side equaled the other.

Back at the front door, Lukas was sitting in a puddle of melted snow, trying to work his boots loose. Willa squatted down and gave each sole a good tug, and Lukas yanked them off the rest of the way and tossed them onto the rug.

"Where's Mom?" he asked.

Willa turned around. You could see almost the whole house from the front door, and their mother wasn't in it. Usually she was in the kitchen. Usually she stopped whatever she was doing and met them at the door.

"Mom?" Willa called.

"Maybe she ran away," Lukas said.

Willa felt a giant hand squeeze her stomach. "Don't be stupid, Lukas," she said.

"Don't call me stupid," he said. But she was already running toward their mother's room.

They found her, though it took Willa a moment of pure terror before they did. Willa froze in the doorway, heart banging, and Lukas crossed the room and lifted up the blanket. Their mother was curled in the corner, her head behind a pillow, her body a small bump under the bedspread, like the sheets had bunched up underneath.

"Mom!" he cried, and she gasped and sat up and blinked at them.

"Well hello," she said. "Is it that time already?" The hair on one side of her head was smashed flat. Her cheeks were too red, her eyes too puffy. Maybe she was sick.

"Are you sick?" Willa asked. "You look sick."

"No," she said, and she laughed a little. "Just lazy I guess." The laugh was a fake one. Willa had learned to tell the difference. It was in the eyes, and her mother's eyes weren't smiling. Fake laughs were meant to cover something up, which meant that something needed covering, and Willa felt sick thinking what that something might be.

Mom scooted off the bed, knelt, and wrapped one arm around Lukas. She motioned for Willa, and when Willa walked over, her mother pulled her close.

"I've missed you two," she said. Her breath was sour, and her eyelashes were bent. Her eyelash paint had stuck to her eyelids in tiny black patches. She must have been sleeping a long time.

"You guys up for a snack? How about it?" She stood and shuffled them toward the kitchen. On the counter she set down two bowls, two spoons, and the giant bag of HappyO's. Willa and Lukas looked at the bag. Then they looked at each other.

"Mom," Lukas said. "It's not breakfast."

Their mother turned from the fridge, the jug of milk in her hand. She shook her head like she was shaking off a bug. "Of course it's not," she said. "Ha! What was I thinking." She put the milk and the cereal back, and the bowls and the spoons, and she pulled down two plates instead. She took a block of orange cheese from the fridge and pulled a knife from the drawer and began to slice it.

Something was wrong. Willa was pretty sure it had started back when she'd almost eaten the meat and everything else. Since then, her mom had been acting strange. Willa couldn't say exactly how. She usually thought of her mother as the number three. Soft, bendable, open. No painful poky points. Threes invited you to crawl inside of them and take a nap. Willa's father was a seven—sharp and tall, with no low-hanging branches to grab hold of. Just a slope too steep to climb and a high, flat ceiling that no one could reach. But Willa's mother usually made up for that. The problem was, her mother didn't feel like a three anymore. Lately, she felt like an eight, all curled in on herself, or she felt like a one, tall and alone, with no arms at all, and sometimes Willa thought she even felt like a zero, like a big, empty circle you could see right through.

Willa's mother arranged eight crackers and four squares of cheese on each plate. Willa breathed in and out and tried to relax. The same food, the same numbers. This was good. But in the kitchen, her mother spun around in a circle like she was dancing and sang a little song under her breath as she pulled a tub from the freezer. Willa's mother didn't dance around. She didn't sing little songs under her breath. And she always gave them apple juice, but this time she'd forgotten it.

"Mom," said Lukas with a giggle. "You're being silly."

Their mother sang louder in a deep, funny voice, like old-time romantic music on TV. She tucked her chin and made big silly eyes at Lukas while she danced, twirling into a drawer she'd left open.

"Ouch!" she yelled, too loudly. Lukas laughed louder, and she bent over, holding her hip and hopping around in circles like a cartoon character. "Ow, ow, ow!"

Lukas rocked forward and back, giggling.

"Stop it!" screamed Willa. She clapped her hands over her ears and squeezed her eyes shut. Now her mother wasn't a three or an eight or a one or a zero. She wasn't even a number. She was a squiggle, she was a dot. She was not supposed to act like this. Willa screamed again, stretching both words out as long as she could so they'd have to hear her. "Sto-o-o-o-o-p i-i-i-i-i-t!" When she let go of her ears and opened her eyes, she found her mother staring at her.

"What are you screaming about?" she asked, and she sounded so disappointed it made Willa's heart hurt.

Willa couldn't think of what to say. She looked down at her plate. She'd lined up the crackers in four stacks of two, with one cheese square in the middle of each stack. She ate them like that, like sandwiches, in a line from left to right.

"We're waiting," her mother said, still sadly but not unkindly.

"You're acting funny," Willa said to her crackers. "You're not supposed to act like that."

"And why shouldn't I act funny," their mother said. She spun around to face the stove, where she turned the frozen tub upside down over a pot and the block of its contents hit the bottom with a clang. Her voice almost sounded like she was about to cry. "Why shouldn't I act funny sometimes."

But she stopped twirling and singing, and Willa and Lukas ate their cheese and crackers in silence.

Afterward, in their bedroom, Willa checked the angel's feet. Then she took a pencil and traced the shape of the horse that she kept beside the angel, and just for good measure, she traced the purple box, too, where she kept her bracelets and rings. She seated herself on her bed facing her horse and angel and jewelry box, and she took her homework folder out of her backpack. She would always do her homework right there, she decided, where she could check her objects each time she looked up. This decision relieved her. She took another deep breath and decided to start with math.

14

It had been a good day. Randy usually had to settle for bearable, but today life was almost pleasant.

It might have had something to do with the gossip around the shop. Dumbass Dawson's wife had hooked up with some guitar player in a bar bathroom, and now everyone knew about it. Being a pussy, Dawson didn't know what to do. Supposedly Chrissy was all sorts of sorry. Supposedly he hadn't picked his balls up off the floor and kicked her out.

Dawson must've known that everyone knew. Most days, he strutted back and forth in his upstairs office with its Plexiglas wall that let him look out over the floor, or else he walked up and down the assembly line, asking stupid questions and playing up the part of Mr. Bigshot. But today, he'd kept his sorry ass glued to his desk chair, slouched so low no one was even sure he was up there, though Randy could imagine him staring into his computer screen, blinking back tears like a little girl.

The thing was, it made Randy feel better. Chrissy had done what Randy always feared Susan would do, but now that he knew that Chrissy was the type, he could see how Susan was not. Everything about them was different. When Randy and the guys used to play cards over at Dawson's, Chrissy would always dawdle in the room in a tight T-shirt with her hair all done up. At the time, he'd wished Susan would show off a little more. But Chrissy did what she did because she wanted their eyes on her. She'd been hungry for something, Randy realized, in a way that Susan was not. In other words, Randy was lucky. Suzy was one of the good ones.

At home he found her, as usual, puttering around the kitchen. She'd baked corn bread—he knew that smell—and cooked up some kind of stew. He could trust her, he thought. Of course he could trust her.

In the kitchen, he walked up behind her and wrapped his arms around her waist. He thought he felt her stiffen a little, but then she seemed to relax. She patted his arm and reached for a spatula.

"Good day?" she asked.

"Not bad." Susan's hair was tousled, and she'd pulled a bathrobe over her clothes. Randy thought of Dawson coming home to Chrissy, all done up like the whore she'd proven herself to be. "Not bad at all," he said. "Also, tonight's our TV time." At nine, *ER* came on, followed by *Law & Order*. It was the one night of the week he could get Susan to sit down with him and watch TV. Sometimes she even made popcorn. "I thought we could make popcorn," he said.

"Yeah." She pulled some bowls down from a cupboard. "Yeah, I guess we could do that."

The prospect of the evening ahead warmed him like a drug and made his eyes prickle. "I'm sorry I mess up so much. But I love you, Suzy."

She whirled around to study him for a moment. "Gosh, Ran," she said. She turned back to the pot on the stove, and his heart winced a beat before she added, "I love you, too."

15

$\mathcal{T}$hat evening, Susan and Randy sat together on the couch, the popcorn bowl in Susan's lap. Randy was happy for some reason. He sat closer than he usually did and slung his arm over her shoulder, his hand hanging over her breast. She had always loved his hands, wide and thick-fingered and rough on the fingertips, surprisingly soft on the palms.

Susan watched TV faithfully with Randy on Wednesdays, even though she had never really enjoyed it much. She found the experience of TV vaguely insulting, like a one-sided conversation with someone who insisted on treating her like a child. Still, those two hours of programming were the only interest that she and Randy seemed to share anymore. During commercial breaks, they could talk about things so meaningless that they couldn't possibly spark disagreement—who had it out for who, who had done such-and-such. On these evenings, with half of the week gotten through and the heat pulsing from the woodstove and the promise of sleep close by, Susan could almost grasp the sense she'd had all those years ago, when she'd first moved into Randy's railroad apartment.

Back then, they sat up late ashing their cigarettes into plastic cups and blowing smoke out the kitchen window. Susan, never before an exhibitionist, would wear shorts and a tank top, and she could still remember how bold she felt, how exposed. She'd prop up her long legs (smoother then, with no visible veins) on the sill, as though she gave no mind as to how her display might affect him (she did). She'd squeeze her biceps against her small breasts in the hopes of creating some allusion to cleavage. Sometimes an argument would escalate until Randy, in Susan's opinion, went too far, at which point Susan would stomp upstairs. Eventually Randy would follow, and they'd toss words back and forth until their bodies took over. She'd startle awake to the 3:00 a.m. train rattling past and to condom wrappers glittering like Christmas lights over the carpet. Sometimes she'd sneak back downstairs at that early hour and light another cigarette. She'd breathe in the night air and the smoke and the sound of the howling train, already miles away.

There was such beauty in those moments, such peace and pleasant melancholy and post-sex relief. It was easy to mistake the fullness she felt then for happiness, and even easier to assume that the person with whom she felt these feelings was responsible for them.

On the couch, Susan studied Randy out of the corner of her eye. She tried to see him as she had then, when she woke with the train and watched him sleep, as blissful as a child. She tried to summon that sense of him— Randy the rebel, Randy the misunderstood. She tried to open herself to some freshness, some sexual possibility. He would expect sex after this, he always did. She felt a throb of lust between her legs, but it quickly dissipated. She willed it awake again.

The show switched to a commercial, and Randy reached his giant hand into the popcorn. He worked all of it into his mouth at once and licked the salty butter off his fingers. Then he dug his hand back in for more.

Back in the railroad apartment, Susan would have swatted him. She would have told him to knock it off, that he was gross, and he would have laughed at her, and eventually they would have fallen into bed. Back then, they were so soft, really, so easily satisfied. Susan had been free for the first time of her father. She'd been free, too, to believe that the serendipities of her life would always cooperate in forging a future she wanted.

She hadn't bothered enough to envision that future. She and Randy had the newness of sex and endless years ahead and the naive assumption that they could do with them whatever they wanted. That had been enough, then.

What if it could have been anyone? What if she had not been in love with Randy? What if she had only been in love with freedom and youth and life? Susan reached her hand under the afghan and unzipped Randy's jeans, pulled him gently out. It was an automatic motion, and she didn't realize what she had started until she started it. She woke him with her hand, and he said nothing, just moaned once, deep in his throat, when she took him into her mouth. When he couldn't bear it anymore, he turned her over the couch, yanked up at her nightgown and down at her panties. He grasped her hips with his large hands and thrust himself into her over and over. And for a moment, Susan could still believe they had everything they needed.

16

The trucker dropped Leotie off at a country crossroads three miles outside Esau, if her map reading was right. The page she'd torn from the atlas back in the Tulsa library had already been folded and unfolded so many times that the print along the seams had begun to rub off. Now she was finally in the same square as Bobby, only a map inch away.

The problem was, she couldn't walk a map inch, or even half a map inch, for that matter.

Leotie had left home the morning after she'd called Bobby. She'd taken care to look the same as she always did when leaving for work, but in her backpack she'd stuffed all the money she had on hand (eighty-seven bucks), an extra winter outfit, a box of cheese crackers from the pantry, and a bottle of water she could refill at gas stations. She'd put on two sweaters and two pairs of pants, with the bulkier over top to try to hide the extra layer. At breakfast, she ate two helpings of microwave waffles and five sausage links, and when she packed her lunch, she packed two sandwiches instead of one and two cheese sticks and as many puddings as would fit in her sack.

No one talked much that morning, except for Timbo, who always talked too much because he still hadn't caught on that nobody else liked talking that early. Before, his talking had always annoyed her, but that last morning she realized she'd miss it. All of it, really. She'd miss Timbo blabbering and Peggy burning her big stack of toast and the way Quentin folded back his newspaper occasionally to explain how Timbo was dead wrong about whatever he was saying. She'd miss how, during Quentin's lectures, she and Mavis would glance over at each other and try not to laugh. Even the chores she'd miss, even the meals when it was her turn to wash the dishes afterward.

Standing at the front door, drooped under the weight of food and clothes, she thought about just staying where she was. Why not just tell them she was sick? Live out the rest of her days in comfort with her friends? She was pretty sure they'd let her keep on living there even if she had to quit her job.

But then she thought of Bobby and how kind his voice had been, and she simply called, "Bye, all," like she always did, and took bus 9 instead of bus 13 and then, from the station, she hitched her way out to the interstate.

It was a straight shot, mostly: 44 to 70 to US 12. Hitching as an older lady was easier in some ways than hitching as a young one. It helped that she looked a lot older than she actually was. Years before when she'd bummed rides, she was mostly picked up by hornballs who seemed to expect a little something in return for their efforts. Now men still picked her up— truckers, mainly—but their faces were weary and pitying. She could almost see them thinking about their mothers and feeling sexless and satisfied with themselves, which was just as well.

Now Leotie needed one final hitch. She moved off the road, down into the ditch, and pulled a marker and sheet of paper from her pack. Using a telephone pole as a surface, she wrote GOING TO ESAU in big block letters. Then she zipped the marker back into her pack, shrugged it onto her shoulders, and buckled it around her waist. The truck had been traveling due north, so Leotie climbed up out of the ditch, figured west, and started to walk.

It was hard going. Her chest burned to cough, but she moved slow and pushed the coughs down. Her whole body ached besides. Riding in all of those semis had done a number on her back, shaken her bones all around. The night before she'd spent on a shelter floor in Toledo, with her coat for a blanket, her backpack for a pillow. And now she had to pee.

Think about something else. So she watched the bare white land as she crawled past it. Empty field stretched after empty field as far as she could see, fenced in occasionally by single-file lines of tall, bare trees. A ghost farm stood to her right, with old sheds and barns sinking into the ground. In the snow, a couple looked like rib cages from big animals that had just lay down and died.

From the crossroads behind, an engine growled toward her. It sounded too smooth, too sure of itself to stop, but she turned around anyway and held up her sign. The car, sporty and yellow, roared past, and Leotie turned with it, tucked her sign under her arm, and continued down the road.

Esau. A Bible name. Jacob and Esau. They were twins, weren't they? In prison, she'd gone to Sunday services to boost her behavior points. There she'd heard some of the stories. Jacob was the chosen one, if she was remembering right. Esau was the jealous brother, the son that the father loved less. Leotie wondered what could have drawn her Bobby to such a small, sad-sounding town, especially as, last she'd seen him, he'd looked so fancy it had nearly broken her heart. Her own boy, standing there in a tie and sweater vest with all the other ties and sweater vests, singing some pretty song about Jesus. Bobby was in college and touring churches with a singing group. She'd taken seven buses that day just to sneak into the foyer, peek over the edge of an inside window. She left while she could still see the way out, before her eyes turned everything blurry.

It was something she'd done ever since she lost him, checking in on him like that—more often in the early years, then less and less. The morning that the woman had come to take him away, Leotie had sworn to Bobby and to herself that she'd get him back. But first she had to establish proof of a safe and secure residence. She'd bought the trailer years before, when Bobby was still just a baby, with a sizable chunk of change she'd saved by cleaning hotel rooms. Though money had changed hands, Leotie had never actually signed any documents, so when the truck came to drag her home off the lot, that was that.

The agency assigned Leotie a caseworker who helped her get a room at the YWCA and a job serving food at a Woolworth's restaurant. She saved her earnings inside a sock she kept stuffed under her mattress, and when she'd earned enough for a first month's rent, she moved into the smallest, cheapest apartment her caseworker could find—a studio the size of her trailer's old living room and already populated with colonies of carpenter ants and cockroaches, along with an occasional rat. Leotie dug into her savings for some ant traps and rat poison and made an uneasy peace with the roaches. If she could stay there for six months, she could establish proof of residence.

A month into her lease, Leotie went in for a physical exam, another requirement for custody. It was there Leotie learned that, back when she'd given birth to Bobby at the home for unwed mothers, the doctor had tied her tubes. Bobby had been breech, and to get him out, they'd put her under. She'd woken up with a broken body, and she hadn't even known.

In the office, when the doctor told her, it took her forever to understand. He asked if there was some possibility that she was pregnant, and she told him no because there wasn't. The doctor flipped through her chart and paused on a page.

"My apologies. Of course you wouldn't be pregnant," he said. "Not after your tubal ligation."

At first Leotie had almost let his remark pass by, a bit of medical jargon she didn't need to know. Later, she would wish that she had. But the phrase jingled a distant alarm. "Tubal ligation?" she asked. "What's a tubal ligation?"

"You must have given your consent," the doctor said cheerfully, as though she might be joking. "A tubal ligation is the procedure where they tie the Fallopian tubes to prevent future pregnancies. They wouldn't have done the procedure without your consent," he said. "You don't remember agreeing to that?"

"But what does that mean?" she said. Later she would think herself stupid for persisting. The doctor had told her what it meant. It ought to have been obvious.

"It means you can't get pregnant again."

"Ever?" she pressed. "I can't ever again get pregnant?"

The doctor shook his head. "Never," he said slowly. His cheerful expression had wilted into one of concern.

That afternoon, Leotie was scheduled for a shift at Woolworth's, but she fell into bed and woke up nearly four hours later. She had no phone, and by the time she made it into work, Stanley had already called in Deborah, who was rubbing the counter down when Leotie arrived, the bulge of her apron jingling with tips.

"I been sick," she told Stanley after he led her back to the office. "You gotta understand, I been sick." She was still so stunned it was all she could think of to say.

Stanley was a short, squat man with the whitest bald head Leotie had ever seen and a high voice for a man—nasal and whiny. As a matter of practice, he was a grump, but he could also be forgiving if you caught him in the right mood.

"You know the company's policy for a no-call, no-show, Leotie. It's a case of one and done, simple as that. That's not me, that's the big boss." That afternoon, his voice made Leotie's ears ache. It took everything she had just to sit there and keep listening to him. If she hadn't needed her job so badly, she would have stood up and walked out. Instead, she did something she made it a practice never to do. She begged.

"Please, Stanley. I'm begging you. I won't let you down again, I promise."

Stanley studied her with narrowed eyes, then sighed and slapped his thighs. "One more chance, little missy, you hear me? You caught me on a good day, so I'm going to give you just one more chance."

But the news from the doctor was a wound that wouldn't stop bleeding. At first she thought it must have been a misunderstanding until she mentioned it to her caseworker, who told her it was something doctors did when they didn't think a woman was fit to be a mother. He said it just like that, in one gut-punch of a sentence, then moved on to ask how much Leotie had set aside for legal fees.

Later Leotie would learn that doctors sometimes tied the tubes of unmarried women, especially those with brown skin. It was a law, she learned, it was legal. Often it was even encouraged.

She first saw Bobby again in the yard outside his foster house. On her one day off per week, Leotie would wrap her head in a scarf and pull on her nice dress, an A-line piece she'd found at the Goodwill, and she'd take the bus out to Bobby's new neighborhood and walk around. The foster house was situated near a crossroads, which allowed Leotie to spy out any activity in the yard before turning onto the street. Then, one afternoon, there he was, leaping through a sprinkler with another boy his age.

It had been almost half a year since they'd taken him away, and Leotie saw with a stab of terror how much he had changed in that time. He'd put on weight in a good way—he'd been too skinny, she realized—and someone had sheared his thick flop of black hair into a Princeton, a haircut that matched the other boy's blond one.

Leotie was still wrapping her head around the new shape of his body when the foster mother stepped out onto the front porch with a tray of what appeared to be drinks and food. She called the boys, and they climbed the porch steps with happy voices too distant for Leotie to make out any words. They sat down and began to eat, while the mother picked up towels, one at a time, and wrapped them around each boy's shoulders, rubbing them dry. Bobby said something, and the woman laughed, her voice as light and sweet as a glass of lemonade.

It was like watching a television show about the kind of family Bobby deserved, with a brother and a house and a yard and a sprinkler and a mother who fed him all of the food that he wanted, a mother that no one would ever judge as unfit to bear children.

Back at Leotie's apartment, the question continued to throb: What if Bobby was better off without her? It sat heavy on her back as she bent over the red Formica counter at Woolworth's; it breathed in and out of her lungs with the thick, stale air of the city buses; back home again, it asked itself with the scurry of each cockroach, with every view of the toilet half-hidden behind a badly placed dresser. Day after day, night after night, each piece of her life raised itself up like evidence to ask, What if leaving Bobby alone was the best thing she could do?

It was a question she never answered, it was a question that life answered for her. One night something she ate must have been turned, and she got so sick from both ends that she thought she might die. The next day found her still vomiting every twenty minutes or so and green as death. By the time she hunted down a neighbor whose phone she could use, she was two hours late for her shift.

"You're done here!" Stanley's voice over the phone was loud and high and as strained as a motorcycle engine. "I gave you a second chance, missy, and boy did you blow it!"

Because Leotie lost her job, she also lost her apartment and moved back into the YWCA. By that point, Bobby had turned nine without her. He was doing well in school without her. He had learned to sink a basketball without her. (This she had noted on another of her walks through his neighborhood.) And he had found a family without her. The foster mother, Leotie's caseworker said, had started exploring the possibility of adoption. Not only was it impossible for Leotie to win back custody as a homeless mother with no job, it was also beginning to seem like an act of selfishness. She couldn't give Bobby half the life he'd won when they took him away. How could she ever justify taking him back?

As the years passed, Leotie moved from job to job, apartment to shelter to apartment. Two years after losing Bobby, the police picked her up for sleeping in an alley and charged her, falsely, with prostitution. When they released her and she failed, after six weeks, to report an address, they locked her away again, this time for longer. With a criminal record, she knew she had even less of a chance of winning back her boy, but it was time, ultimately, that made the choice. With every day they spent apart—every week, then month, then year—their reunion became less and less possible until it didn't seem possible at all.

Until now. Somehow, at the end of her life, it had become possible again. More than possible, really. Now she needed him almost as much as she had that first morning, when the woman in the red sweater had driven him away. Now here she was, nearly thirty years later, hiking the last deserted road. Dead on her feet, with a chest full of knives. But just three long miles away.

Behind her, another engine growled, grew louder. She turned around and pulled herself upright, held her sign at chest height so that whoever it was could see her face—see that she meant no trouble and didn't have the energy for trouble besides.

The truck drew nearer, an old Ford with a cracked grille and one side of the hood tipped open. It chugged to a stop, and the driver, an old man in a baseball cap, motioned her toward the car.

"Need a ride to Esau Baptist," she said through the crack above his window. "You going by there?"

He jerked his head toward the passenger seat. "I can drop you off at the front door."

Leotie sank into the warm cab, and she couldn't say whether she felt more grateful or more exhausted. The fields whipped by, and the truck slowed as the sign for Esau came into view. A feeling filled her that she recognized, but from so long ago that it took some thinking to figure out just what it was. Excitement, she finally understood. And just beyond it, happiness.

17

Thursday mornings were usually the happiest of the week for Robert. Wednesday-night prayer service had come and gone, and his sermon, by that point, had found its stride. He faced the prospect of three relatively peaceful days where his work lay mostly in puttering around the parsonage and church, fixing this and attending to that, and honing what he had already written.

Yet this particular Thursday morning, bent over his open Bible and sermon notes and oatmeal, cold and congealing, Robert felt in his gut a gnawing dread. There were too many days until Sunday, and there were also too few. He couldn't figure out what to say about Hebrews 12. He couldn't choose an entirely different text—he'd been preaching through the book of Hebrews for months now—yet he couldn't bring himself to speak about "resisting unto blood," either. In light of his conversation with Susan, it struck him as too, well, preachy. Too harsh and direct a response to her questions.

So Robert moved down again to the following passage, verses 14 to 17, which spoke about Esau, a *profane person . . . who, for one morsel of meat sold his birthright.* The subsequent verse read, *. . . when he would have inherited the blessing, he was rejected: for he found no place of repentance, though he sought it carefully with tears.*

This passage had seemed, at first, a sound one to pursue. It contained a clear, rather prepackaged takeaway, and it allowed him to make carefully worded jokes in reference to the name of their town. (It appealed to him, the thought of making Susan laugh, or at least Susan witnessing his ability to make others do so.) He could also unpack the original passages in Genesis, which would illuminate the New Testament text and take up a much-needed chunk of time.

But when Robert returned to Genesis, he found the Hebrews interpretation of Esau remarkably harsh, even misleading. Robert had read the account before, of course, many times. But never had its unfairness struck him so keenly. In the original passage, Esau, on the occasion when he was said to have sold his birthright, was, by his own account, dying of hunger, and Jacob, with his pot of stew, refused to share unless Esau swore away his inheritance. Would not Jacob, the well-fed brother who took advantage of his famished brother's desperation, be more to blame in this particular case?

And then, later on, when their father, Isaac, called for Esau to receive Isaac's blessing, Esau did not appear to have been "rejected," as the Hebrews account suggested, but to have been robbed outright by his scheming brother Jacob, who fed his blind father soup that his complicit mother had made, and wrapped animal skins around his arms and neck to deceive Isaac so that he, Jacob, might receive the blessing instead.

The real Esau entered much later, having gone out into the fields to hunt down a deer himself, as his father had requested. When he discovered that Jacob had stolen the blessing meant for him, Esau begged his father to bless him, too. But Isaac could not retract the stolen blessing, nor could he give Esau the same. So he told him: *By thy sword shalt thou live, and shalt serve thy brother, and it shall come to pass when thou shalt have the dominion, that thou shalt break his yoke from off thy neck.*

In Robert's notes he had collected other passages on Jacob and Esau sprinkled throughout the Bible. He forced down three giant spoonfuls of oatmeal and shuffled through his passages again, seeking out some new illumination.

From Obadiah, a prophet of the most high, *For thy violence against thy brother Jacob shame shall cover thee . . . the house of Jacob shall be a fire . . . and the house of Esau for stubble.*

What violence? Robert wondered.

In Malachi, *Saith the Lord: yet I loved Jacob, and I hated Esau, and laid his mountains and his heritage waste for the dragons of the wilderness.*

In Romans, *As it is written, Jacob have I loved, but Esau have I hated. What shall we say then? Is there unrighteousness with God? God forbid. For he saith to Moses, I will have mercy on whom I will have mercy, and I will have compassion on whom I will have compassion . . . Who art thou that repliest against God?*

And then back to Genesis, to the image of Esau when he and Jacob met again, years after Jacob's trickery: *And Esau ran to meet him, and embraced him, and fell on his neck, and kissed him: and they wept.*

Esau here the picture of compassion, of forgiveness. What had Esau done that was so very wrong? He had only been hungry, and he'd done something human, desperate. A shoot of indignation sprang up in Robert for all of the centuries of judgment against Esau—the wronged one, the robbed one, the one not chosen.

But who was Robert to reply against God?

He rose and walked his bowl to the sink, filled it with water to soak. As he turned toward the bathroom, he caught the motion of a dark figure out the kitchen window. It was an older woman crossing his yard, he noted before she moved out of view. Not secretively, it didn't seem, but with steady purpose. He tried to trace her circuit and spotted her once more out his bedroom window before her footsteps slowed up the front porch stairs and she knocked, loud and rapid, then rang the bell. He opened the door.

She was a short, shrunken-looking figure in clothes awkwardly padded. Her hat was wearing through at the crown, and the outer shell of her coat flapped open in the wind. Her jeans stopped above the tops of her boots, so that her feet appeared clownishly large in relation to the rest of her body. His eyes took all of this in at a glance and then rested on her small brown face with her mouth pulling heavily for breath. She was a vagrant, he thought, about to ask for money. Then she spoke, and her words struck an eerie chord within him.

"Bobby boy. It's me."

A sharp wind whipped a strand of the woman's hair over her face. She drew it back with her pointer finger and flipped it over her shoulder with the back of her hand. The gesture was reminiscent of a model from a shampoo commercial, but its awkward execution betrayed a familiar fingerprint. She planted her feet too wide, like she was daring someone to mock her affectation; she jutted her chin forward, the angle tense and uncertain, like she was challenging someone to a fight she knew she couldn't win. This woman. He knew this woman. This woman was Leotie Glory. This woman was his mother.

It seemed that they stood there for a long time. He should feel something, he thought, yet he didn't, really. A stunned curiosity, nothing more. Another gust of wind blustered over the yard, raising eddies of snowy dust in its wake. The woman shivered and rubbed her hands together.

"You gonna invite an old woman in out of the cold?"

He hadn't thought of that, the cold. He looked down at his threadbare sweater, his around-the-house Dockers thinning at the knees, and thought vaguely that he should put on a coat if she planned to keep standing there. Only then did he apprehend her meaning. He stepped back into the parsonage and gestured inside.

"Come in. Please, come in," he said, and then resented himself for saying it. It sounded too warm and welcoming. What did she want?

"I mean," he added, "what else is there to do?"

She stepped out of her boots and removed her hat and coat. Then she stood there holding them, her eyes darting back and forth.

"Here," he said, gesturing toward the banister. She spent too long smoothing the neck of her coat over the post, then stretching her hat over the top. It seemed she would keep pointlessly arranging them forever.

"That's fine," he said, but his irritation made his words more biting than he'd intended, which irritated him all the more. She dropped her hands and looked down at the floor. How was he supposed to act? Happy? Grateful? The woman could take what she got.

"Coffee?" he asked.

"Yeah. Please."

They sat across from each other at the kitchen table, which, though he'd removed the leaves, still felt too wide for two people to sit opposite. The coffee maker spat and gurgled. Leotie broke the silence.

"Bet you never thought you'd see me again."

"Nope. No, I didn't."

Robert stood and walked to the cupboard. He set out two mugs—*Pete's*

Tractor Supply and *World's Greatest Dad*. Hand-me-downs. She might think he'd spent his whole life relying on the generosity of others. The coffee maker was still bubbling and hissing, but he lifted the carafe anyway and poured, let the last dregs crash and sizzle on the hotplate.

"Thank you," she said when he placed her cup on the table. Her tone was so meek and grateful that he felt a stab of guilt. Life had not treated her well. He must remember that.

"So why now," he asked, "after all these years?"

Leotie took a long drink of coffee, then studied her thumbs as they outlined the mug's decal.

"Guess 'cause I had to find you first," she finally said.

Bobby could never understand—she could never explain—how the basic act of getting him back had become impossible. *I was so poor,* she wanted to say, but it would sound so weak. *They broke my body*—an explanation, not an excuse. *They broke my body because they knew I never deserved you.* Out loud she said, "Don't you got no family?"

She was looking around the room, and Robert's gaze followed hers. The yawning emptiness of the place struck him. The long L-shaped counter, bare except for the coffee machine and toaster. The kitchen's island, now a landing place for books and mail he had yet to sort. The house was cold, of course—it was only him, after all—and dim. He rarely turned on the lights unless his work required it, relying instead on the daylight, which fell in small squares through the curtainless windows and landed on the floor in weak, watery puddles.

"No," he said. "No family."

"Is that 'cause of me?" She laughed to cover how naked her question had been. "Don't answer that."

Laughing, he thought, *at my loneliness.*

"What do you want?" he asked.

"I'm sorry. I just don't know what to say is all."

"What do you want?"

He was trying to keep his voice even, she could tell, but he wore his anger on his face—jaw muscles chewing, eyebrows knotting together. He'd always been so cautious with his feelings. Once, when he was six, Leotie had found a boy's bicycle at a yard sale for fifty cents and brought it back to the trailer.

"Is it mine?" Bobby had asked over and over. "Is it really mine?" The bike had not made him happy like she'd hoped, just preoccupied with not losing it. One tire was flat, and a pedal had fallen off, leaving a jagged rung of metal in its place. But there was a hill out behind the trailer park, and Bobby had coasted down until he could pedal and pedaled down until he could keep going.

"Do you remember that bike?" she asked Robert, searching out the young Bobby in his face. "The bike I bought you?"

"No," he said, though a vague memory of handlebars and a steep green hill flashed through his mind.

"I bought you a bike," she said. "I had to haggle with them, but they sold it half off. Surprised you don't remember. You loved it, you know." She said in defense, remembering, "I wasn't all bad."

"I never said you were," Robert replied, resting his forehead against his palm. He said it wearily, as though they'd had the same conversation a hundred times before. "I never gave up on you," he said. "It was you who gave up on me."

Leotie closed her eyes and let the pain of his words ricochet through her, a slow bullet. "You're right," she finally said. "I tried, and I tried, believe me, but life—maybe now you know just how much life can get in the way. I failed you, but I never wanted to. It just happened, and it went on happening. And you were doing so well without me anyway."

"Well?" Robert repeated, almost angrily. "How would you have had any idea how I was doing?"

"My caseworker. He told me that the mother wanted to adopt you."

"I told her no." Robert almost spat the words. "I told her she couldn't adopt me because you were going to get me back. Because you promised you'd get me back."

How could such an old pain suddenly become so new? Her lungs crushed beneath it, her vision flashed white with it. "Oh, Bobby," she said, and her chest heaved one strained, solitary sob. "Oh, Bobby, you've got to believe that I'm sorry. You've got to believe how truly, awfully sorry I am."

18

The news of Leotie's arrival spread through Esau with a liquid rapidity. Earl Howard, the local farmer who had dropped Leotie off at the church, put the story together himself. Earl had gotten a good look at the dark-skinned preacher over the years, and though the constructive/assumptive approach to truth so often fails humans everywhere, this time it triumphed.

Earl had been driving back from the Tractor Supply down in Henley when he picked up the woman. Once he'd dropped her off, he sped straight home and relayed the news to Margaret that a poor, sickly woman, likely the pastor's mother, had hitched a ride to the parsonage. In his excitement, he parked crooked in the driveway and left the oat mix and the incubator bulbs and the trough replacement hose in the back of his truck, even though any child wet behind the ears could see that another dump of snow was about to fall. He let the door slam and stomped into the back sitting room, where Margaret was ironing pillowcases with a phone pinned between her cheek and shoulder.

Forty-three years with Earl, and Margaret knew the look. "Hey there, Earl," she said into the phone.

On the other end of the line, Darlene Dickey, sixty years a friend to Margaret, apprehended her meaning.

"Well call me back," she said.

And so Margaret yanked the plug on the iron and shuffled into the kitchen, where she opened the teakettle and held it under the faucet.

"No way he knew," Earl said, once they'd settled into their tea and into Earl's accounting of things. "No way he had any idea she was coming."

When Earl had pulled up in front of the church, the woman had asked him where the parsonage might be, and that, he said, was when he knew.

"I just knew," he said. "That's who she was. I'm telling you, you could read her like a book."

When Earl and Margaret had drunk down their tea and large clumped snowflakes had begun to fall outside, Earl hurried back to his oat mix and replacement parts and Margaret back to her ironing and phone call.

By noon that day, a majority of Esau had come to know the news. From her market post, Darlene Dickey informed each of her customers about the town's visitor and that visitor's likely identity. Darlene's patronage that morning included, among others, Frank of Frank's Hardware, who stopped by for a sack of chips to supplement his lunch, and Jed and Willie from Larry's Garage, who had pooled their change for a two-liter of Mountain Dew. Her patronage also included the librarian Mallory Drake, though Darlene greeted Mallory with only a tight-lipped "Hello then," since Mallory had once told Margaret (who, of course, had told Darlene) that there were three ways to spread news in Esau: telefax, telephone, and tell Darlene.

Darlene left the market only once that day, just after lunch, when she hung the BACK IN 5! sign on the door and jogged up Main to the gas station. There she sipped a Styrofoam cup of old coffee while imparting the news to Bethanne Marshall, who squashed her giant breasts against the counter in a sign of interest and tapped her Marlboro Menthol 100s into the ashtray beside the cash register.

And so it was that the news dispersed. Each of those who had learned of the arrival of the pastor's vagrant mother shared it with each person they ran into afterward. It was a Thursday—nearly the weekend but not quite— and it was snowing again, and the people were hungry for diversion. About 80 percent of the town had been apprised by Thursday evening, and by Friday evening the remaining 20 percent had also been enlightened, and by Saturday evening, the occasional attendees of Esau Baptist had promised their less religious friends and family that they would attend the following morning and report back in detail.

Pastor Robert had, of course, been excluded from these conversations. He had informed no one of his mother's arrival and had only betrayed public irregularity by walking to Esau Market (an establishment he rarely frequented, to Darlene Dickey's chagrin), purchasing a loaf of Wonder Bread and a package of puddings and inquiring as to whether Darlene carried bananas. Of course Darlene didn't carry bananas. How had the man lived in Esau for ten years and never learned whether Darlene carried bananas? But as the details of Pastor Robert's purchases circulated, he began to be forgiven for that particular mistake. Earl Howard had pronounced to Margaret (this detail, in turn, had been pronounced to everyone else) that the woman "had barely a tooth in her head," which explained why the pastor, Lord bless him, had purchased the softest foods the market sold.

General opinion, therefore, had evolved into pity toward Pastor Robert and suspicion toward the visitor. *What did she want, after all these years?* the townspeople asked. *What did she mean, bursting in on him like this?*

ROBERT, EVER THE OUTSIDER, had no idea that he had captured the imagination of Esau. He had even less of a clue as to his position among the women as a kind of sex symbol. But no matter his striving for decency and propriety and godly witness, his person was thrust into enough fantasies, musings, and dirty jokes that, had he known even a small percentage of what was spoken or worse, imagined, he would have detonated, at the moment of apprehension, into a cloud of singular atoms. One of Esau's generosities lay in concealing from Robert their flagrant inappropriateness.

And so Robert knew nothing, either, of the gossip regarding his mother. On Sunday, when everyone who occasionally attended the church came all at once, the influx perplexed him. As he grasped at their names and shifted dimly between their keen attentions toward him and also toward his mother, he almost forgot about Susan until she shuffled, late again, into the back pew with her children.

Standing at the pulpit, Robert felt as though he had woken into some supremely uncomfortable dream. It was hard enough to fathom his mother's presence in his sacred space. She sat in the first pew, beside his usual seat.

Everyone else sat in the back as a matter of habit, and so they all served as a backdrop for his foregrounded mother.

Leotie alone could he see in all her detail. She had not, of course, brought church-appropriate clothes, but she had at least opted that morning for a black shirt and pants. The color of her choices camouflaged somewhat their mottled fabric, the frays at the hems and seams. The holes, however, where a shred of knee peeked through here, a shoulder there, were highlighted by the contrast in color. Nor did his mother's wardrobe choice soften the appearance of her hair, which she had carefully teased (he'd caught sight of her in the bathroom that morning and winced) into a weightless gray cloud.

In addition to her hair and her clothes, the woman's face was so brown before all the white faces behind her that she threw the scene into a study of contrasts. Her presence seemed to ask Robert, *Which world is yours?* He remembered a study where Black children were shown a Black doll and a White doll and asked to pick between them. *Which one is prettier? Which one is smarter? Which one looks like you?* He didn't fit, he realized, in a way he hadn't realized before. He didn't look like anybody else there. He looked like his mother.

And there, in the back of the opposite side, sat Susan, her face pale and shapely as the form of a classical statue, her eyes mournfully large.

As Robert read through his sermon, he found himself suddenly and profoundly exhausted. He and his mother had passed three days in each other's nearly constant company, and he could still only speculate as to why she had come. She was ill, he was certain, maybe deathly so. She had gone through some kind of hell to get there. She seemed determined to play by the rules of his life. She washed dishes after meals, made herself scarce when he sat down to his work. She had asked on Saturday what time they should be at the church, and she'd readied herself all on her own.

With details, however, she had not been forthcoming. She didn't talk about where she'd come from or why she'd left or how long she planned to stay. What if she had committed some horrible crime? What if she was running from the law? But she displayed no behaviors that brought her soundness of mind into question.

Still, as the ideas from Robert's sermon mixed with the other ideas in his mind, Robert felt a certain clarity forming. He had decided that week, after much hemming and hawing, to focus on the hope found in Hebrews 12, on the difference between the old covenant with God and the new one. We are not come to the mount that cannot be touched, he told the congregation. We are come *unto mount Sion, and unto the city of the living God, the heavenly Jerusalem, and to an innumerable company of angels . . . And to Jesus the mediator of the new covenant, and to the blood of sprinkling, that speaketh better things than that of Abel.*

Robert could not bring himself to berate the biblical Esau, that *profane person,* who could find *no place of repentance, though he sought it carefully with tears.*

Was he, Robert, Esau? Was he repenting for something he'd never even done? What had he sold for this church, this pretense of belonging, this morsel of meat?

Afterward, in the parsonage kitchen, Robert slid Ethel Grable's broccoli chicken bake into the oven.

"They feed you, too, eh?" his mother had said as they stepped home in the snow, foiled casserole held aloft. "Not a bad setup."

"It's just something they do on Sundays," he said, and he couldn't help but add, "I've told them it's not necessary, but they keep doing it anyway."

He felt bristly. Usually on Sundays Robert came home in silence, let his mind putter around the memories from the morning, filing away pieces of news, taking mental notes on who might require a visit. His irritation had been further piqued by Susan, who had left without saying anything. He'd spotted her over by the coatrack, and then, when he looked for her again, she'd gone. He couldn't figure out how he'd missed Susan's leaving, except that there had been so many visitors, each of them pausing to ask him how he'd been while scrutinizing the woman at his side.

One visitor, Darlene Dickey, who had attended only once or twice in the past decade, had stretched out her hand toward his mother. "And who is *this?*" she had asked, her eyes practically sparking.

Robert had pretended not to hear the question and had directed his attention instead to those coming up behind Darlene, but he cringed as he heard his mother say, loudly (why did she have to say it so loudly?), "I'm Leotie Glory. I'm Robert's mother."

Now as he and his mother sat together at the kitchen table waiting for the casserole to bake, Leotie picked at her fingernails. Her fidgeting made a *snap snap snap* sound. Was there nowhere that he might escape her, that he might be left alone with his thoughts?

And then she said, as though they were already in the middle of a conversation, "I just wanted a chance to know you. I mean now, as a grown-up. And I wanted you to know me, too. I wanted to try and make up for all the time we lost. Before it's too late."

Robert didn't know what to say to this, and so he said nothing.

"You did good today," she said, and she smiled her half-toothless smile. "I was so proud of you."

Robert nodded, then walked over to the oven and pulled the door open a crack to check on their lunch, even though he knew it was far from done.

He didn't say anything because the only thing he could think of to say was *What gives you the right to be proud?*

19

Susan had decided that she and Randy should go on a date. It had nothing to do with Pastor Robert, she told herself. Nothing to do with the sad beauty of his face, with his eloquent words or his voice as it rolled out over the room, smooth and deep and bright. No, Susan had been meaning to set up a date for a while. A magazine article in the dentist's waiting room had prompted her.

Do something new together, the article encouraged. *Take a class. Visit a pottery studio. Attend a talk at the local library.* Novel experiences, the writer claimed, forged new connections and solidified old ones.

So Susan called up her mother and arranged to drop the kids off on Sunday afternoon.

The article had also talked about sex, but Susan and Randy didn't have a problem with sex. The sex they had wasn't bad, or infrequent. Sometimes Susan even felt ashamed of how much she enjoyed its roughness. Randy was predictable (either missionary in bed or bent over some convenient nearby surface), but something about his need usually sparked and satisfied her. She never denied him, and she never wanted to. But he was so unhappy. She was so unhappy. They were so unhappy together.

Since Susan's parents lived in Henley, the attractions of Henley were their only options. The problem was, there wasn't much there. A Wal-Mart, a Chinese buffet, several pizza restaurants. There was a small college, a coffee shop, and a movie theater playing *Romeo + Juliet* and *The Mighty Ducks*

3, neither of which she wanted to see. Susan called the library to see if there might be any events.

"Events?" the librarian had replied. "What are you talking about?"

"Uh—classes? Or talks?" Susan stammered. "Maybe a small concert?"

"Nothing of that sort here," the librarian responded in a disapproving tone. "We're a library, honey, not an opera house. But you might check out the college."

So Susan had called up Henley College and discovered that the college orchestra would be performing that evening. She asked if she could have two tickets set aside and pay at the door, and the man on the other end of the line laughed at her. "We're not expecting a crowd," he said. "And anyway, it's free. It's always free."

AT HER PARENTS' HOUSE, Susan ushered the kids inside and hung up their coats. Then she kissed them each on the head and called a thanks to her mother, who was already leading them off into the kitchen.

Back in the van, Randy said, "Where are we going? I can tell you've already made your little plans." On the surface, his voice sounded annoyed, but underneath his annoyance, Susan thought she caught a note of fondness and an indulgence in his look.

"I thought we could eat dinner at Route 66," she said. It was a new restaurant a few miles out from Henley. It catered to the college families, and a write-up in the paper had called it *delightfully provincial yet elegant.* "Then there's an orchestra concert at the college," she added.

Randy was still studying her, but judging by his sneer, his annoyance was edging out his indulgence. "So you're going to take me out and get me cultured? Is that it?"

Susan laughed a little, but when Randy didn't smile, she stopped. "It's not that," she said, and she reached over and squeezed his hand. "I just thought we could take some time to remember the way things used to be."

"You mean back when we used to go to orchestra concerts together?"

"Okay, so the orchestra is new, but it's good to go out, right?"

"We go out."

"When do we go out?"

"We go to stores sometimes. On the weekends. Or we go for drives."

They did sometimes go for drives. The four of them would pile into the van and wind their way out to the Amish community twenty miles west, where they'd stop at the Amish general store and load up on dry goods, then the Amish bakery, where they'd buy a box of muffins or sticky buns. They'd eat them in what usually seemed a happy silence as Randy drove the country roads back home.

"Yes," Susan said. "We do go shopping. We do go for drives."

"And that's not enough for you anymore?"

"Of course that's enough for me." It was only after she answered that she realized, with a small ping of fear, that it wasn't true. No, it wasn't enough for her. She wanted it to be enough, and it wasn't.

"Obviously it's not enough, Suzy, or I wouldn't be on my way to an orchestra concert."

"I just thought . . ." And here she paused. She needed to measure her words or her date night would shrivel and die. "I just enjoy spending time with you," she said. "Just the two of us. We don't need to do the same things we've always done, do we? We can do new things, too, right?"

They were still parked in Susan's parents' driveway. In the front window, the curtains parted and her mother's face peered out. Susan glanced quickly away so that she wouldn't catch her mother's eye. She was just about to tell Randy that they didn't have to go to the concert when he pulled the gear shifter down into reverse.

"Okay," he said. "Have it your way."

At Route 66, a crowd of people clustered in the vestibule, waiting for their tables.

"Do you have a reservation?" the hostess asked. Susan hadn't ever made a reservation at a restaurant, so naturally she hadn't thought to do so this time. For a moment, she almost considered lying. She could insist that she'd made a reservation and that someone must have overlooked it. But then she shook her head. The hostess said, "Then there's a forty-five-minute wait."

Randy sent her a sullen stare. "I'm hungry," he said, loud enough for the hostess to hear. The girl sent a worried glance back and forth between them.

"At least it's not an hour," Susan said, trying and failing to inject some optimism into her voice. Even to herself, she sounded tired and annoyed.

"At least now we don't have to attend your orchestra concert."

All the benches just inside the door were full, so they stood outside in the late autumn cold. Randy slumped against the wall with his arms crossed. Susan busied herself blowing into her hands. Then Randy said, "I'm waiting in the van," and Susan spent a full minute standing stupidly in the cold, trying to decide whether to follow him, as he probably wanted her to do, or to wait a bit longer for a seat inside so that they wouldn't miss the call for their table. It was with a twinge of rebellion that she went back in and seated herself on the one square of bench now available. She waited there, her heartbeat fast from her small insurrection.

Randy sat in the van for such a long time that Susan began to plan what she would do if Randy did not come in before they were called (she would follow the hostess to the table and place her scarf there and then go fetch him), and she also began to plan what she would do if he came in before their table was called (she would smile brightly and pat the seat beside her and say, "Not much longer now!").

As it happened, Randy came back into the restaurant right when their forty-five minutes expired. Susan had, of course, been watching the clock—not from impatience, but from fear of how Randy would react were the timeline not met. Susan's bright smile and bench pat went unheeded, and before she could say, *Not much longer now,* Randy stomped toward her and said, in a voice loud enough for everyone to hear, "What do I gotta do to get a seat around here? Go outside and rub my bare ass on the window?" Then he laughed the laugh that meant he was embarrassed of himself in this place and dangerously close to losing it.

Two of the hostesses conferred behind the podium in hushed voices, shooting scared glances at Randy, and then one of them stepped forward and called, "Shearer, party of two." Susan's terror—she hadn't recognized it as terror until that final moment—subsided, and they followed the hostess back to their table.

The eating, however, brought new challenges.

"You've got to be kidding," said Randy, scanning the menu.

"Randy," said Susan, quietly, encouraging him to lower his voice. "Let's treat ourselves. We deserve it. You deserve it." It wasn't like Susan to use such language, but she felt a sense of urgency to head Randy's temper off at the pass.

"I deserve it," he repeated. "So you won't give me shit if I drop twenty-five bucks on a rib eye."

"Of course I won't, if that's what you really want." She said this as confidently as she could, though she, too, found herself staggered by the prices. Somehow she had expected the restaurant to be nice without also being expensive. She had not thought this through. They could not afford this meal, and she could never admit that now.

Her face flushed a hot, throbbing red. They didn't belong here. How could she have assumed they would belong here? The silverware was wrapped in fabric. The menus were single rectangles of thick, creamy cardstock with spare black type. The prices were whole numbers with no dollar signs or decimal points. The entire experience made her want to disappear.

Randy ordered the rib eye, the most expensive item on the menu besides the lobster and the surf and turf. Susan ordered the vegetable plate, which, at fourteen dollars, was the cheapest dinner she could choose without requesting an appetizer in place of a meal. (This would have felt too much like a declaration of defeat.)

When the food arrived, Randy said, "Really?" and the waitress said, "I'm sorry, is something wrong?"

In a disbelieving voice, Randy said, "*This* is twenty-five bucks?" but before the waitress could respond, he added, "Never mind. It's here now. I guess I've gotta eat it."

Randy's portion looked small to Susan, too, though of course she wouldn't have said so. His steak was long but narrow and rather flat, like a wallet. Several asparagus stalks were draped together in a complicated braid, and a stack of small potatoes stood beside the asparagus, with a dark red sauce curving toward the steak in a widening crescent. Susan's own plate was six tiny heaps of different vegetables, and she found herself glumly grateful that her hunger was on the wane.

Randy devoured his meal with surprising speed. Susan didn't know if he did so to underscore how insufficient he found it or because he actually enjoyed the taste. When he finished, she was relieved that he did not belch out loud.

Susan tried to take her time and enjoy her plate, but she found each component unimpressive with the exception of the mushrooms. Rather than attributing her lack of enjoyment to the cooking of the food, she attributed it to her own lack of discernment in determining how the chef had prepared it. This struck her somewhere deep and low, a personal failure.

When at last they climbed back into the van, Susan said, "Well, I have no desire to go there ever again." Something about admitting her defeat felt good, almost reckless.

Randy said, "Fuck that place and its pretentious fucking food." But he reached over and took hold of her hand. "I'm still hungry, Suzy," he said, and the space between them warmed and softened, just like that.

"There's always Arby's," Susan said.

"Now *that's* something we can agree on," Randy said.

She'd meant it as a joke, but once she'd said it, she found herself ravenous for it. Her desire didn't feel like hunger as much as it felt like need—the need to stuff herself until she was so full that it hurt.

At the drive-thru, Randy ordered the same thing they always ordered—the five roast beef sandwiches for five dollars and an extra-large order of curly fries. Down the road, they pulled into the driveway of a propane lot, and they ate in silence with the van running. The exhaust smell seeped inside and mixed with the smell of the meat. The bites were dense and chewy and savory and a little sweet with the Arby's sauce, and for a moment, it was everything that Susan wanted—the food itself, yes, but also the two of them sitting beside each other in silence, doing the same shameful thing.

Whoever wrote that article about the importance of new experiences didn't understand it was the ordinary things that kept you where you were—the places you landed together in relief, after the jags you traveled over to get there. What mattered were the things you couldn't imagine doing with anyone else, the things you no longer had to do alone—like eating to fill a void, like eating in a propane lot in your van with the engine running because it was cold and you were starving for something and there was no one else you could bear to bear witness. The new was too difficult precisely because it was exciting, and how many people wanted exciting, really? Everyone thought they wanted it, but, it occurred to Susan, sitting on the warm seat with her stomach stuffed full, that what they really wanted was for the ordinary to be okay and to revel in the moments when it was.

Randy rolled down the window to belch and blow the air out—a thoughtful, if distasteful, gesture. Then he wadded up his wrappers and stuffed them back into the bag. "You ready to go?" he asked.

Susan glanced at the dashboard clock. Her mother wouldn't be expecting them for another hour at least. "We could drive around for a bit," she said. "If you wanted. We could drive over to Coldwater, see what there is to see."

"Yeah," said Randy. "Why not. That sounds good." When he'd pulled out onto the main road, he took Susan's hand again, and they drove like that the twenty minutes to Coldwater, where they stopped at a bakery drive-thru for a doughnut before turning back toward Henley. They talked a little but mostly sat in silence and let the scenery pass, dimly lit by the dying light—field after field of drying corn and houses here and there with heaps of orange leaves sprawling out over the yards and gardens blighted from frost and carved pumpkins on porches beside scarecrows or skeletons still dangling from Halloween.

Susan wondered why it should soothe her, this driving, this moving reminder that the world just kept on spinning and one could have a look whenever one liked at the silent pageant of people standing in windows or raking leaves or stepping out of cars—people isolated, in her mind, to that singular, undramatic moment.

It reminded her of back before they'd married, when she'd taken a plane to visit her brother in Colorado, and though her favorite part of the trip ought to have been the time spent on the ground, instead it had been watching out the plane window as cars shrank into shiny square stones, whole farms into crooked checkerboards, big towns into clumps of tiny roofs in a sea of empty land. It was the only thing she remembered from that trip—how she couldn't wait to get back up into that perspective where nothing was nearly as important as it sometimes seemed to be.

20

Pastor Robert was bent over his desk Wednesday morning, frowning down at the scattered sheets of loose-leaf and several open books. He'd been willing himself to forget—and had finally, for the briefest moment, forgotten—about Susan's presence at the quilting circle upstairs, when he startled at a light knock on the doorframe and there she stood, in tall, slick boots and an open coat, sliding his copy of Saint Augustine's *Confessions* out of her purse.

Robert laughed an embarrassed laugh that lasted too long. He willed himself to stop and cleared his throat. "Ah," he said, nodding at the book. "Finished already?"

"Actually," she replied, "I was wondering if you might suggest something else."

Robert felt himself wince with an unreasonable disappointment. "Well," he conceded, "old books aren't for everybody."

"It wasn't that," said Susan. "I like old books." Robert hadn't invited her in, but she stepped inside anyway and seated herself in the chair nearest the door.

"May I ask what it was, then?" At the prospect of a provoking conversation, a genuine interest was elbowing out his nervousness.

"It's just that . . ." Susan paused for a moment, her brow furrowing for the words. "It's just that he thinks everything is so evil."

"And you disagree with him?"

"Well, yes."

"With which parts?"

"I mean, he begins with babies."

"Yes."

"Have you spent much time with babies?"

"No," he admitted cheerfully. "As a matter of fact, I have not."

"I'm not intellectual," Susan said. "But I'm pretty sure I've spent more time with babies than Saint Augustine has, and I have never once wondered whether one of them was evil."

"No?"

"No."

"Not even when they scream? Not even when they *flail their limbs,* as Augustine puts it?"

"No. When you spend time with babies, you understand they're just trying to tell you that something is wrong."

"So you wouldn't call it evil. You would call it, what, natural?"

"I guess so."

"So maybe, put another way, Augustine is saying that it's part of our fundamental nature to complain, to be dissatisfied."

Susan cocked her head and squinted off into the corner. He followed her gaze, expecting to find a spider or some other object of interest, but he realized, upon turning back around, that she was simply thinking.

She replied, "We can't blame babies for being dissatisfied, can we? Babies are helpless. They hurt, and they can't help that they hurt. They're not just whining for food, like some grouchy adult at a restaurant. They need it. They're doing what they have no choice but to do."

"Because that's their nature."

"But Augustine doesn't call it nature. He calls it malice. He acts like they're just itching to do the wrong thing. Like from the cradle, we're all just itching to mess up."

Robert took a deep breath and let it out, nodded. "I see your point," he said, and he thought a little longer. "The Bible tells us," he continued, "that *all our righteousnesses are as filthy rags.*" When Susan didn't respond right away, he quoted a little bit more. *"We all do fade as a leaf; and our iniquities, like the wind, have taken us away."*

Susan was thinking again, frowning down at her hands in her lap. He fell silent and waited. Finally she said, "But life is so hard already."

"I'm not sure I'm following you."

For a moment, it seemed that Susan would start crying again, as she had at the last visit. But instead she inhaled deeply and then went on. "I mean, according to Augustine, almost everything is evil. Not just babies. Secular books, rhetoric, anything that gives you pleasure but is not directly related to the glory of God." She paused a moment. "I guess I came to this book feeling like doing the right thing was hard enough. And I read this, and I start thinking how I'm doing even worse than I thought I was. Doesn't this ever exhaust you? Don't you ever get sick of believing you can never get anything right on your own?"

"If truth is truth," he responded, "then emotion doesn't enter into it. It can't."

"But other people read the Bible without coming to these conclusions. Why is Augustine's truth a better truth than anyone else's?"

Robert pressed his lips together and dropped his chin to his chest. It wasn't that he hadn't encountered these questions before. It was that her single question was so much bigger than it purported to be, and he didn't have the heart to defend himself anyway. And then he thought, What if the question was that simple? What if his beliefs could be derailed as easily as that?

"I've upset you," she said. "I'm sorry."

"No," said Robert, putting on a smile. "Not at all."

"It just seems way too arbitrary to be so black-and-white about it. You're bound to get something wrong that way, you know? If you make a hard and fast decision about absolutely everything and carve it into stone?"

Robert wished for a moment that they were writing back and forth as opposed to speaking. He needed to think on this a little longer. He wanted to say something about how he'd always considered Augustine as a scaffolding, a sort of extraneous structure that helped him climb closer to God. But instead of a scaffolding, Susan had experienced Augustine as close-walled and lightless, like a prison.

"Is there another way, then, that you personally go about things?" Robert asked. "A way that makes sense to you, that is not so black-and-white?"

Susan thought for a long time, and he let her think. At the beginning of their conversation, the silence had felt awkward, even uncomfortably intimate. But they had settled into a slow and pleasant speed, one that felt more natural to him and also, apparently, to her.

Finally she spoke. "I don't know," she said. "But I guess I find it helpful to see actions as mixed bags, you know? If you're stealing to feed your family, there's some good in that act. Even if you're stealing fruit for fun as Augustine was, there's an explanation that's not all bad. He was young, he was curious, he was discovering something about himself."

"But you must also agree that stealing is wrong."

"Of course it's wrong. But if you're facing hungry children at home, it's a lot less wrong. What if your family is starving, and stealing is your only choice? In that case, it's practically right."

"Hypothetical situations can do more harm than good when it comes to such arguments. Rarely if ever are cases so extreme."

"True," Susan admitted. "But there's desperation everywhere. So many people are missing things they need. It's not always so obvious, either. Maybe they're missing willpower, or experience, or knowledge. Or maybe good decisions in their situation are harder for them than they would be for us. We look at them from the outside, and we think, 'He shouldn't have done that,' or, 'She should have known better.' But we don't understand because we can't. It sounds like I'm just making up excuses for bad behavior." She thought a little longer. "Maybe I am. Or maybe I'm just trying to explain it." She swung her crossed leg and stared at the bare corner of Robert's desk without seeing it. "It just doesn't help, that's the thing," she said.

"What doesn't help, exactly?"

"It doesn't help to shake your finger and say *bad bad bad*. And it doesn't work just to decide, one day, that you're going to do better."

"Because our sinful nature is so strong. Because we must rely on God for change. On our own, we are hopeless."

"What if we're hopeless *with* God, too? I keep asking God for strength to live my life. I came here searching for it. I wanted someone to tell me to keep going, to keep doing what the Bible says is right, because telling myself the same thing was losing its power. But now I feel weaker than ever."

"I'm sorry," said Robert. He felt suddenly responsible for her weakness, liable. His mind scrambled for a meaningful response. "Maybe God is still breaking down your belief that you can do any of this on your own."

"Maybe," Susan said, but she sounded so weary when she said it that Robert felt a pang of sadness for her. "Maybe," she said again.

"I don't know your story," he said. "But it does sound as though you're trying as hard as you can. It sounds like you're trying to do what's best for everyone."

At this, Susan nodded. "Everyone except for myself," she added. "That's just part of being a woman, I guess."

Robert felt a compulsion to disagree, but he stopped himself. A single pastor encouraging a married woman to put her own needs, veiled though they were, ahead of her family's struck him as too risky. The woman was trying to live according to the role that God had given her. Who was Robert to question that? Still, he raked his mind for some softness to add to her thought, some kindness, when a noise at the door startled them both.

"Didn't want to interrupt," Leotie said, glancing between them. "Made lunch. Figured I'd let you know."

Susan started, and her eyes darted to her wristwatch. She let out a small gasp.

"Leotie," said Robert, rising from his desk. "Meet Susan Shearer. Susan, this is my mother, Leotie Glory."

Susan stood and extended her hand. "Hello," she said.

Leotie nodded in reply. She looked hard into Susan's face, so hard that Robert found himself embarrassed. "Didn't mean to interrupt," Leotie said again, still staring.

"You didn't interrupt," Robert said, not because it was true but because he felt the need to break his mother's uncomfortable gaze.

"No," said Susan, staring right back, but openly, almost kindly. "I hadn't meant to stay so long."

"I'll try and think of another book," Robert said.

Susan turned to him with a curious look, and he could see her rewinding her memory. "Oh, yes," she said. "Good. Thank you."

"It was good to meet you," Susan said to Leotie as she passed. Then she turned back to Robert and said, "Next week then," before slipping out into the sanctuary.

It was only the promise of Susan's final phrase that enabled Robert to accept his mother's interruption and to follow her patiently back to the parsonage. Susan would return. He could hardly believe his good fortune. Susan would come back again, all on her own.

21

There was a lot Leotie hadn't taken into account when she'd loaded herself up and set out for Esau. For example, how much she'd be in the way. Her Bobby would be used to his own habits and routines. He would be used to meeting his own needs however he saw fit to meet them. It didn't matter how quiet Leotie could make herself, or how scarce. When he walked in on her just sitting on the couch or poking through the kitchen cupboards, he would pause and take a big breath, like he had to come to terms, each time, with the inconvenience of her.

Of course, he never said that out loud. He didn't say much else, either. Leotie had imagined that they would catch up on all that they'd missed over the years. But how could she share anything when he so clearly wanted anything else but to talk?

Leotie had taken over the meal preparations, which made her feel only a little better than doing absolutely nothing. Back when Bobby was small she'd developed the knack of making good food from whatever she had on hand. Sometimes she would make everyone dinner at the apartment, and they'd all go off about how good it was. Even Quentin would clean his plate and hand her a priggish compliment.

But it was like wrestling a bear to work Bobby for one kind word. What he really wanted to say, probably, was that he'd gotten by just fine on his own, thank you very much. Well, he didn't have to say that because she already knew. Every waking second of every gray Esau day, she knew what a burden she was.

The fact that she was sick complicated things. She tried her best to hide her failing health, but that was getting harder. She slept a lot, which Bobby probably appreciated. She kept her coughing fits to the bathroom, where she could flush the blood down the toilet or rinse it down the sink. In any activity she had to break every ten minutes or so and rest her heart, catch her breath. If Bobby knew (and how could he not know, with her heavy breathing and her always locking herself in the bathroom to cough), he never asked about it, never let on.

And yet, he was a good son. She tried to play the part of a good mom, and he tried to play the part of a good son, and if it was a competition (it felt like that, like a competition), Bobby would've won every round. He bought extra clothes for her—sweatshirts and sweatpants, thick and soft with loose elastic waistbands—and he washed and folded her laundry, what little there was of it. When she asked about a TV, he lugged one up out of the basement and spent the rest of the afternoon constructing a set of rabbit ears from a cardboard box and a roll of aluminum foil. She'd had her doubts, but he'd made it work well enough.

It seemed to Leotie that she had thought about Bobby constantly since she'd lost him, but she'd forgotten so many things. For example, characteristics. Like how he'd shake his hair back and pat it down at the same time. How he'd touch things after he put them in order. His papers on the dining room table, squaring them unnecessarily with his hands. His place setting at supper, smoothing his napkin and straightening his silverware and rotating his plate a little this way and that, even though the plates were white and would have been fine any old way. Fussiness, that's what it was. His fussiness had followed him all these years.

And his aloneness, the way he'd move steady toward whatever he'd chosen, true to his mind as an old dog. She'd forgotten how he used to wander off all the time. She'd forgotten how once, before he'd even turned three, she'd lost him for an hour and had finally found him three trailers down, staring sullenly at a game of checkers as two old geezers moved their pieces back and forth. She shouted his name in relief, and he held his arms out toward her without turning his head from the game board. It was like he knew she'd show up sooner or later and when she did, he'd have to humor her. But from the very beginning, he'd made it clear that he never needed her nearly as much as she needed him.

Funny how much it hurt still but how it also filled her with pride. Her boy cared for himself far better than she'd ever learned to do. He took daily walks and exercised with a weight machine down in the basement. He flossed, for god's sake. Bobby was one of those new men—they hadn't made them like that when Leotie was young. He wasn't afraid of grocery shopping or cleaning the house. He wrote down smart things that sounded like poetry sometimes. At church, it had surprised her how closely people seemed to listen. She could see them nodding and thinking hard and connecting things in their heads. Her son was bright, a leader. He was handsome and self-disciplined and nice, even when he probably didn't feel like being nice.

Leotie took a little credit for all of these things, though of course she kept that to herself. Still, it wasn't a bad legacy, as legacies go. He wouldn't be there on the earth if she hadn't brought him into it and kept him alive for as long as she had, and that was the truth.

When Leotie and Bobby did talk, they talked about small things, everyday things. The weather, the news on the radio. Clinton, Bosnia, O. J. Simpson, the Atlantis space shuttle. Whenever they talked, they walked around the past. That is, she walked into it and he stood on the outside waiting for her to finish. At meals, he'd make small talk about the day ahead or the day behind, and she'd just jump back thirty-odd years. She couldn't help herself. Memories kept leaping up and surprising her. Like one time, she asked Bobby if he remembered the toothless old rottweiler Jim Sandusky kept on a chain in his backyard. "Jim Sandusky?" Bobby had asked.

So Leotie had to explain how the man lived three trailers down and how Bobby used to stay there sometimes when Leotie had to work late, and how one time she came back and Jim had gotten drunk and lost track of Bobby, who'd wandered out to the dog pen and gotten himself tangled up in the chain.

"It's a good thing that dog didn't have a tooth in his head, else you might not be here today." But it was only after she said it that she realized how irre-sponsible it sounded. What had she been thinking, leaving her little Bobby with a drunk like Jim Sandusky? At the time, it had seemed her only choice. Now it seemed inexcusable. Bobby must have thought so, too, because when she trailed off, he failed to comment, and the past dropped down between them like a curtain. They finished their sandwiches in silence.

On Wednesday, when Leotie had come to Bobby's office to tell him that lunch was ready, she'd thought that she'd been doing him a favor. If it weren't for her, she told herself as she hobbled, gasping, over to the church, the man might skip meals altogether. But she interrupted his conversation with that Susan woman, and she could read on his face, when the woman left, how deeply disappointed he was.

"Sorry to interrupt," she said again as the woman's footsteps faded away.

Bobby shook his coat out with a loud slap, then jerked his arms into its sleeves. "Nothing to do about it now," he said.

Leotie had made soup, and she had been proud of her soup, but Bobby ate his without looking up. He barely even seemed to register that she was there.

Finally, Leotie said, "That woman. Susan."

"Yes?" Bobby asked. He was trying to sound bored, but she could sense his interest crouched underneath.

"Who is she?"

"A new parishioner. She's been attending for three weeks. Or so."

"She married?"

Bobby waited awhile to answer. "I'm guessing she is. She has children." She must've made a face because he glared at her. "What?"

"She likes you."

Bobby laughed a short, high laugh. "What is that supposed to mean?"

"You can just tell," she said. "Trust me. Women know these things. You can tell by her body language, by the way she looks at you."

"Stop," he said.

"And women ain't the only ones I can read."

"Mom." He wasn't laughing anymore.

"I'm just saying," she said.

"Just saying what?"

She shrugged. "That woman might not be as married as you think."

Bobby rolled his eyes, an exaggerated motion. This, Leotie thought with a thrill, was how he might've acted as a teenager.

"Mom," he said again, and she detected disappointment in his tone rather than annoyance. "Maybe things work like that where you're from, but that's not the way things work around here." He thanked her for the soup and carried his bowl to the sink, returned to the door. There was a scuffle of coat and shoes, and then the door closed, and she heard his footsteps heavy on the porch, going away.

"Susan," Leotie said out loud to herself. "Susan Shearer." And she jotted down the name on a piece of paper, folded it up, and tucked it into her pocket.

22

Something was off with her mother again. Willa noticed it the second she stepped inside the house, after the bus had dropped her and her brother off. Music was playing, with horns and violins, strange music that was trying to be pretty and sad at the same time. The music was coming from the small radio that Willa remembered seeing in the basement. Willa's mother had never played music before, not that Willa could remember.

Their mother came out from the hallway in big yellow gloves with a red handkerchief tied over her hair. She sang the words *snack time* along with the melody of the music, and she turned the radio down, but she didn't turn it off. It buzzed through their cheese and crackers, beneath the questions their mother always asked and the answers they always gave, answers their mother seemed almost not to hear.

As much as it pained Willa not to sit with her objects while she finished her homework, she decided to stay at the kitchen counter instead. From there, she could keep an eye on her mother, try to get a better sense of what was going on, what felt so different.

Her mother seemed happy enough. If anything, she seemed too happy. Willa could think of nothing that would make her mother happier than usual. She wondered all through her fractions worksheet and her trait inheritance worksheet and her reading journal. Finally she summoned her courage and asked, "Mom?"

But her mother didn't hear her, even though she was standing close by, chopping carrots and dropping them into a pot. Willa tried again, louder than she meant to. "Mom!"

Her mother jumped, and the knife jumped, too, and she let out something between a squeak and a squeal. She turned and jerked her hand to her mouth, sucked at the blood oozing from her palm, and frowned at Willa, then pulled her hand out to study it.

"Willa, it's dangerous to startle someone when they're cutting something. We've talked about this."

"I'm sorry," Willa said. "I was just trying to get your attention."

"Willa." Her mother's voice had changed from her teaching voice to her worn-out voice. "I don't think I could give you any more attention if we were joined at the nose."

"Mom, I just wanted"—Willa floundered for the words—"I just— you're just . . . different lately."

"Different how?" The way her mother said it, it was like she already knew the answer but she wanted someone else to tell her.

"Happier, maybe? But also like you're far away sometimes."

"Willa, honey, we've been through this. Things change. People change. You can't lock the world into the way it is and expect it to stay that way forever."

Her mother's words worried Willa, but the tone of her words took some of the worry away. She was soft, softening. She crossed to the counter and hugged Willa with her good arm, holding the other arm against her chest. Willa let herself sink into her mother's shoulder as she watched the blood from the wound seep into her mother's shirt.

"The more things change," her mother said, "the more you'll get used to them changing." She pulled back and smiled at Willa. "Even if one of the things is me," she added.

But no matter how warm her mother's smile, Willa couldn't believe it.

That night, her father arrived home madder than usual and Willa and Lukas were sent to their bedroom, where Willa tried and failed to make out the growled conversation coming from the kitchen. At the dinner table, her mother's palm was lined with Band-Aids, but the red spot on her chest seemed to have kept opening, like a flower.

Willa did not taste the food. She swallowed it silently, her eyes darting back and forth between her father's angry face, with its heavy forehead and frowning mouth, and her mother's serene one, her eyes on her plate, her mind off somewhere else.

23

Randy had called Susan twice over lunch before she picked up. The first time he'd let it ring and ring. The second time she'd answered and told him she'd missed his first call because she'd been downstairs with the washer running. But the only reason she'd be downstairs would be to put the dirty clothes in the washer or to take the clean clothes out of the dryer and carry them upstairs, which would mean she would have heard the phone. So that meant either she'd been cleaning the basement, which pretty much never happened, or she was lying.

Work that morning had been rough, which made the missed phone call worse. Dawson must've made up with Chrissy because she'd come slinking into the shop in a tube top and skin-tight pants under her open coat, all tits and hair and eyelids. Everyone on the line looked up to watch her strut past the office windows and shimmy her coat off in front of Dawson's desk. They were treated to a slutty half dance before Dawson sauntered over, a giggly Chrissy draped over him, and jerked the blinds shut. A half hour later, Dawson paraded Chrissy up and down the line, spouting off about the new machinery as though his repentant whore gave a shit. But Dawson wasn't talking to Chrissy. He was talking to them. He was saying, *Look what I still got and don't you wish you had this, too.*

And then Randy had called Susan, and she hadn't picked up.

After their date last Sunday, it seemed to Randy that they'd fixed something he hadn't even realized was broken. But then, as the week went on,

Susan kept checking out more and more. She'd never been a big talker, but since Monday morning, when he asked her a question, she'd said as little as possible. At first he tried to be patient. But it pissed him off was what it did. She'd been the one to waste all that money at the restaurant, and he hadn't even given her any grief about it. She'd been the one flapping on about making more of an effort, about trying new things. And now she wouldn't even pick up the phone.

When Randy arrived home, he checked the basement to see if anything looked different, but it all looked exactly the same as far as he could see. The inside of the washer was dry, but he had no way of knowing whether or not it would already have dried. Upstairs, dinner was roasting in the oven. Susan was on her knees digging through a cupboard. He decided he wouldn't ask, and then he asked anyway.

"So you were downstairs before, huh? When I called the first time?"

"I was doing some work downstairs today, yes," she said. She was acting nonchalant, but Randy thought he detected, in her brief glance upward, a hint of fear.

He thought, *Let it go,* but he couldn't.

"And the washer was running."

"Randy, please." Her voice was pleading.

"I'm asking a simple question. Did you run the washing machine today?"

He sounded very calm, he thought, very in control of himself. But Susan stood and called toward the living room, "Willa, Lukas, please go play in your room."

"Hey," he said, and he threw up his hands. "I'm not the one amping this up."

"Shut the door," she called down the hallway. "All the way, please." The door clicked closed and she turned to him.

"We've talked about this, Randy. If you're not going to believe me, then you're not going to believe me. There's nothing I can do to change your mind."

"Well it's your problem if you're lying to me. The only thing you have to do is answer the fucking question."

Susan shook her head.

"No?" he asked.

She closed her eyes as if she couldn't even bear to look at him anymore.

"No what? No you won't answer the question or no you didn't run the washing machine?"

But Susan had already knelt back down. She took a plastic container out of the cupboard and set it on the floor beside the other containers. Then she rummaged through the cupboard for a matching lid, rested it on top.

He said, "So our marriage is falling apart, and you're organizing Tupperware." His voice sounded calm—bored, even—and he congratulated himself. He was the sane one here. He was the one trying to make things right.

Susan kept digging through the cupboard. When she found a matching lid, she set the fitted container off to the side. When she didn't find a lid, she reached up and tossed the lidless container into the trash. He watched her hips bend and twist, watched the pink skin on the soles of her feet shift beneath the holes in her socks.

Randy walked over, and Susan flinched when he kicked halfheartedly at the pile. The lids all slid off the containers. He hadn't even thought to do it in the first place, but then he did it again, harder, and Susan shielded herself with both arms as the tubs shot off his boot at various angles. Then he kicked again, as hard as he could, and his foot met with something heavy—a glass bowl—that ricocheted off another cupboard door and broke. He hadn't thought about that, that one of them could break. He kept on kicking anyway, because he had not meant to do that, but he had to pretend he had, because he was not losing control, he was claiming it, and this was the only way.

24

It was the November deacons meeting, Thursday morning. Robert and the three men gathered about his desk had crawled interminably through the customary sharing and prayer, the allotment of missionary support, the concern about the leaking urinal, and the concern Florence Butts had raised about Robert's carpet selection for the sanctuary, which was supposed to give the impression of stained glass and which, according to Florence, did not. (Florence was always correcting Robert's choices in the visuals of worship; this was a sore subject, as she explained her interference by referencing his lack of a wife whose womanly eye, it was assumed, would have assisted in such matters.)

Robert and the deacons had also finalized the budget for the coming year, in which Robert's salary was to remain the same. It had never been increased, nor had an increase ever been discussed. The first couple of years, no one else mentioned a raise, and Robert, being young and new, hadn't wanted to rock the boat. Then, after three years, he felt he'd waited too long. His needs were met, he told himself each consecutive year. The Lord would provide. Now the sight of the same small sum suddenly angered him. He breathed in deep and allowed himself one disappointed sigh. That particular grievance would have to wait a little longer. The time had come at last for new business.

Robert had practiced variations of what he felt he should say. He'd even gone so far as to write it down. He cleared his throat and started in.

"My mother, as I'm sure you know, has recently arrived. I've come to believe she is sick and in desperate need of health care, which unfortunately I do not have the money to pay for. I was wondering about the possibility of some funds to help me cover it. She has no savings or insurance," he added. "She's lived a hard life."

His words were met with a period of silence during which Cliff Grable stared at the desk and Jack Allen resituated his legs, and Clark Fisher drew back in his chair and crossed his arms over his chest.

"I know it sounds like a lot to ask," Robert said.

"Where do you think the money's going to come from?" This question came from Clark Fisher, the firefighter a handful of years older than Robert whose three children attended a private Christian school and who had a pool—aboveground, but still—in his backyard. His family hosted all of the youth events, since there weren't many kids, and his were evenly spaced over the age groups. He was thick-chested and round-bellied, with a giant brown mustache for which Robert suddenly felt a resentment.

"There is the family fund," Robert said. It should be relatively sizable, he thought, by now. When he began pastoring Esau Baptist twelve years before, the deacons had encouraged him to contribute to the family fund, and so he had, with 20 percent of his income automatically deducted. He'd considered it an act of faith that God would bless him accordingly.

Jack Allen spoke up. "I don't know, strictly speaking, if that fits the purpose of the fund." Jack was a fifty-some-year-old Robert had graciously permitted into deaconhood even though he'd married a divorced, doe-eyed, much-younger woman who had been still married—with two young children, no less—when their romance began. When Jack expressed interest in the vacant seat, the other deacons had objected, but Robert had gone to bat for him. Jack had strayed from the Lord, but he'd repented, returned to the fold. That was the argument. Now Jack was fiddling with the string tie he always wore. Robert imagined grabbing the dangling ends and crossing them, pulling them tight. He tried to relax.

"It's my understanding that the fund was set aside for pressing needs within the pastor's family," Robert said. "She's the only family I have."

"Dependent family," Cliff Grable put in. "The fund is for dependent family." Of course Cliff Grable would bring up the exact vocabulary. He was the one who always quibbled, after Robert's sermons, about Robert's interpretation of various words within the scripture passage. Sometimes he even knew the original Greek or Hebrew. He was elderly, mid-eighties, and so Robert never saw fit to suggest he broaden his myopic focus on words to the context in which they were spoken.

"But she is dependent. On me," Robert said. "Fully dependent. She has no other family, no other means." They already seemed so unified against him. It struck him that maybe they'd already met and discussed this very possibility, forged a unified front.

"There's something else," Clark Fisher said, and he raised his eyes from his hands and turned to Jack, sent him a look that said *go ahead.*

"What?" Robert asked. No one would look at him. "What is it?"

When Jack spoke, he spoke to his hands. "There's a rumor," he said, "that you've been meeting with that new woman." He cleared his throat and then said, "Alone."

"Susan? Mrs. Shearer?" Robert corrected himself.

Jack nodded gravely. He was still staring down at his hands. His forehead was furrowed so heavily that it almost looked as though he was sleeping.

Robert couldn't deny it. It was against his nature to lie. His mind scrambled instead for how anyone could have known, and then it struck him that Susan's vehicle would still have been parked there when all of the other women left the church. It would only take a drive-by five minutes later to check whether or not she had stayed.

Robert took another deep breath and tried to settle himself. He had done nothing in his past ten years to justify any suspicions on their part. He swallowed down his indignation.

"She came into my office weeping," Robert said. "How was I to turn her away?"

"Twice?" asked Clark Fisher, from beneath his repugnant mustache.

They had been watching, waiting for him to slip, Robert realized. All these years, had they trusted him so little? Was this the nature of the faith he had nurtured in them all? Constant vigilance, zero tolerance, suspicion? Militant accountability, regardless of whether you wanted it or not? Because everyone needed it, especially if they didn't want it—that was the point.

And if they were right, well then how easy, how comfortable it was for them to be right, these men with their wives and their children and their warm homes. These men who sought to deny his request to care for his dying mother—the only request he could remember bringing to them over the course of his ten years in Esau, which were marked, before and behind, with sacrifice and deprivation, with sweat-drenched summers and endless, freezing winters, with living like a pauper while funneling nearly one quarter of his meager salary into a fund that they'd likely been padding for his replacement, a future pastor, with an approvable family. Someone who truly belonged there.

He stood suddenly. "It sounds like you've already made up your minds on the matter." He shrugged his shoulders into his coat and stood before them. They were all looking up at him in surprise. He realized that this was the first time, in all of his years at Esau Baptist, that he'd ever conveyed a strong emotion.

He continued. "I hope you will reconsider my use of the funds. For my mother's sake. But if you will not, then I will find another way to care for her."

"I don't think any of us knew how strongly you felt about this," Clark said. He looked around at the others, then back up at Robert. "I think we all understood that your mother had not been"—here he paused—"much of a mother."

Robert caught his reflection in the pane of glass between his office and the sanctuary, his long black coat and his shock of black hair and the shadowed skin of his face. His back was turned to the outside window, to the weak winter sunshine that fell over the faces of the deacons—their winter-white skin, their pale hair, the shine from Cliff Grable's raw pink scalp. Beside them, Robert looked almost comically different, like a count or a phantom.

He thought about responding. *So?* he could ask. He could shame them with some ethical question. *Does it follow that I should not be much of a son?*

But instead he just nodded at them. "Goodbye," he said. He felt happy suddenly. Eager, free. He left them all seated before his desk and pushed open the church's front door. He needed to shovel. It could wait. Everything could wait.

25

On Thursday morning, Susan had to drop a batch of cupcakes off at the school. She waited until just before Randy would've called for his morning check-in. He would spend the rest of the morning skulking around the line, and then when he called for lunch, she'd tell him where she'd been. She'd tell him that sometimes there were things she had to do, and he would just have to get used to it.

It felt good to be out of the house, even for the short trip back and forth from the school. Susan kept her window cracked open, and the outside air smelled of cold and woodsmoke and the sweet rot of leaves. For what seemed like the first time that month, the clouds had cleared, and the sun fell through the naked trees and melted big patches of snow and warmed the ground beneath, where the once-brilliant leaves had all faded into the same tired brown.

The surprising warmth and beauty of the day reminded Susan of the sense she'd had years back, before she'd grown up, before she'd married and borne her children. It was a private and giddy elation that she was there and the world was there, and the number of things she could do in it was limitless. It reminded Susan of when she'd first gotten her driver's license, and her mother had handed her a list of errands and sent her to Jefferson. Susan had stopped at McDonald's for lunch and sat in a booth with her value meal and an almost irresistible urge to shout, to everyone within sight, *We're here!*

We're here together, and there's food in here and sunshine out there, and isn't this wonderful?

Maybe that was why she hadn't pushed herself harder for a different life. She had thought that her world—her plain, small, ordinary world—would always feel so primed with possibility. Of course, she'd been wrong. But this morning, she could at least remember why she had thought that it might be true.

On the way home, Susan drove past her house and kept on driving. Her road ended and turned off into a narrow gravel drive that curved around and around field after cleared field. They were unexpectedly pretty, these fields, almost picturesque in the sideways slant of the late-morning sun, burnished brown under the blue. She drove for some time without seeing anyone at all, and the solitude of her quest began to thrill her. She wished she had a cigarette, though she had not smoked since well before the kids were born. But somehow, on this strange, sunny day in late fall, with the sun promising its eventual return and the flock of wild turkeys high-stepping over the broken cornstalks on the far side of a field, with the warming ground and the kind blue sky and the rest of the day all to herself, Susan felt freed of something. Maybe she was the same person she used to be after all. Maybe age *was* an illusion, and all the traps she'd built for herself were so weak and self-constructed as to be almost imaginary.

Susan drove until the road ended at a rusty gate that sagged shut across the entrance to yet another field. She parked her car there and climbed out and began to walk along the fence. The path was choked for a short distance with dead branches and thickets of vine, but then it opened up into a small meadow that meandered down a hill into another thicket of wilderness. There Susan thought she could make out a small opening, the head of a trail, and at the base of it, a pattern of posts and rails she recognized as the remains of a railroad track. She skipped down the hill and turned sharply into the opening, where she collided with Pastor Robert.

The pastor jumped in surprise and shouted. Susan screamed and fell back onto the ground. She began to laugh at herself, and then she couldn't seem to stop. She tried to explain.

"I just wasn't expecting—" she said, gasping for breath. "I thought I was alone. I mean, I'm sorry if I scared you." But by then her laughter was edging out her words.

Robert laughed a bit, politely, but then sobered and began to study her with concern. "Are you okay?" he asked. He stepped forward and reached out his arm. Susan took his hand and pulled herself up off the ground, brushing the leaves and dirt from her backside.

"I'm sorry," she said. "Yes, thank you." She was still laughing a little— small, fleeting giggles that wouldn't stop rising up into her throat. "I don't know why I'm laughing. Yes," she repeated, and swallowed hard. "Yes, I'm okay. Are you?"

Robert looked down as if to check himself. "No harm done," he said. "I'm surprised, though. I've never run into anyone out here, and I've been walking these tracks for years."

"Well," she said. "I guess today's your lucky day." Inside Susan cringed. Why was she acting so ridiculous?

Robert smiled, but Susan couldn't tell if his smile was genuine or if he only smiled for the sake of politeness. "You're going this way, I assume?" He gestured down the tracks.

"Yes," Susan said, hoping it wouldn't sound as though she had only just settled on that course of action. "Yes, I am."

They walked together in silence for a time. Susan racked her brain for some intelligent thing to say, but after her giggling outbursts, she didn't much trust herself.

Finally, Robert said, "So, have you read anything interesting since yesterday?"

Susan didn't know why the question felt so intimate, but her face burned in response. She was glad he could only see her out of the corner of his eye. "Not since yesterday, no," she said. "You?"

"Unfortunately not," he replied. They walked on for a little longer. Then he said, "I've been trying to wrap my head around the situation of my mother."

"Ah," she said. "How is that going?"

"Not well," he said. "At least, not well from my perspective."

"Has she moved in with you, then?"

"She has."

"Whose idea was that?"

Robert looked down and watched as his boots kicked up little explosions of leaves. "I guess it was hers," he said. "What really happened was that she just showed up one day out of nowhere."

"So you hadn't seen her for a while?"

"You could say that."

"How long?"

"About"—and Robert squinted up at the sky—"about thirty years."

Susan gasped and halted on the path. Robert kept walking but turned around once he realized that she wasn't beside him anymore.

"It is shocking," he said. "I've gotten over the shock by this point. My question now is how to proceed."

Susan shook her head back and forth as if to clear it and started walking again. "But who raised you, then? Your father?"

She realized it was the wrong question when Robert hesitated before falling into step beside her. An ache throbbed in their footsteps.

"The state took me away," he finally answered. "I was eight. So the foster system raised me. It's not as bad as it sounds. I mean, it can be bad. But I was lucky. The homes they sent me to were stable homes, and most of my foster parents lived the kind of life I wanted to live."

"What kind of life was that?"

"A meaningful one, I guess. An orderly one. Disciplined."

"And now?"

"Now?"

"Now, well, are you happy? I mean, are you glad you took the path you did?"

"Is that the question?" he asked. "Or is the question whether I followed where God led me?"

"No, I think that's a different question," she said. "I'm asking if you're happy. Now. Happy with your life."

Robert stopped walking and squinted up at the sky again. "Sometimes," he said, after a pause, "sometimes I wonder how much I'm here because God led me here and how much I'm here because of my own stubbornness, or worse, my own fear." He started walking again. His feet found a pine cone, and he kicked it along for a while. "No," he said finally. "No, I wouldn't say I'm happy where I am now. No."

"And your mother? Does her coming change that at all?"

Robert frowned down at his pine cone. "No," he said. "It doesn't. But it does make it harder to contemplate changing the situation."

"So you would leave."

Robert stopped walking, so Susan stopped walking, too. He turned to look at her full-on. She forced herself to return the look, though it took some courage to do so. Despite his gentleness, Robert intimidated her. He carried himself with such gravity, such heavy thoughtfulness. And his face was so beautiful that she feared she could not look at him without betraying her admiration for it.

"You know," he said, "I think I would." He stretched his arms straight out to either side and then dropped them down. "Yes, if I got the chance, I think I would leave this place behind."

They were facing each other now across the tracks.

"I didn't know that," he said, "before you asked."

"Oh," Susan said. She didn't know what else to say. She realized that she didn't even mind the awkwardness. She would stand there waiting for a long time, as long as he kept standing there, too.

"And what about you?" he asked. "Are you happy now? Happy with your life?"

Susan looked up and watched a flock of geese cut across the sky. She thought about the wild turkeys from earlier, so secure within their order, about the geese taking turns to break through the air. Why should it be so impossible to find such basic cooperation?

She laughed feebly. "Is anyone?" she asked.

26

That afternoon, Leotie set out toward the gas station for rolling papers and a pouch. She hadn't bought for months. Smoking hurt so much anymore it made buying ridiculous. She bummed instead, or took when someone offered.

But now she needed it. She'd done it. She'd found her son. But she was still old and still sick and now a burden. Nothing was ever near as good as you hoped it'd be. She'd forgotten that.

As she crossed the littered field between the church and the rest of Esau, a gust of wind cut at her neck, and she flipped up the collar of her coat and gripped it shut.

This here was a godforsaken place. All wide open and howling, even in the middle of town. On the other side of the field ran the main street, such as it was. Two storefront strips faced off across the narrow road with empty spaces here and there, raw sockets in an old jaw.

On the way back from the gas station, pouch and papers tucked into the pocket of her coat, Leotie passed a diner. She hadn't thought to stop there until she came to the door. The handful of white men and women sitting at the booths all turned in unison to take her in, and they stared long enough to remind her how she looked. Her leathered skin. Her lips crumpling into the gaps between her teeth. Her long hair, once her pride, not black anymore or thick but gray and straggling out from underneath her threadbare stocking cap.

People kept staring. A herd of cows. She could live here for years and still die a stranger.

She stomped her boots on the mat and walked straight-backed to the counter, trying to look sure of herself.

A waitress approached, her apron clanging with each step.

"What'll it be?" she asked. She was youngish, about Bobby's age, eyelids heavy with makeup and purple lips colored outside the lines. She'd clamped up her hair and sprayed her bangs into a hard clump. It looked like she was hoping someone special would show up. Her eyes slid over Leotie in disappointment.

"Just coffee."

Leotie sat there for a long time, rolling and smoking shallow so she wouldn't cough and letting the day get farther along. She looked at life that way sometimes. She'd learned it back when she lost Bobby. She couldn't take the thought of *never again*, so instead she'd had to think *not now* and just wait for time to pass. Coffee, cigarettes, wandering.

Leotie peeled off another cigarette wrapper and placed it flat on the bar, dipped her fingers into the tobacco and sprinkled the brown flakes over the white. Bobby didn't need her hanging around, and he didn't want her, either. How had she ever thought that he would?

She lifted the wrapper carefully and licked the strip of glue, smoothed it down flat with her thumbs. She brought it to her lips and struck a match.

Sometimes Leotie would get the sense that she'd disappeared. She'd be at a library or a coffee shop, and she'd realize that no one had looked at her for a very long time. The first time it had happened, she'd been sitting in a Starbucks, and it had scared her shitless. She'd finally asked the man at the next table for the time. She had to say *'Scuse me* three times, finally shouting it out, before he folded down his newspaper and eyed her suspiciously. When she asked him what time it was, he nodded toward the clock on the wall and straightened the paper. It had struck her then, and several times since, that she actually was invisible for all intents and purposes. She was of no use to anyone.

Leotie breathed in and out and let the new facts settle.

Truth: Bobby didn't want her.

Truth: She might have the money to make it back to Tulsa, but she didn't have the heart.

Truth: Bobby didn't want her. No one wanted her.

Truth: She needed to move, to walk and walk and walk. She needed to get out past herself and think.

She tossed two dollar bills on the counter, pushed back her chair, and stalked out into the evening, against the burn of her lungs and the reluctance of her legs. Across an open lot, the church loomed, with the parsonage crouched behind it, and Leotie left it behind. She followed Main until it veered off onto a narrow side street, and then she kept on walking, past a handful of dimly lit houses skirted in empty fields, past frozen marshes and thickets of woods. She walked until she couldn't imagine walking any more, and then she turned around and walked all the way back.

It was black out when she returned home, but early enough for Bobby still to be awake. He met her at the door, the inside light bright and smeary. It wasn't the light but her vision, she realized. Her head spun with the dizziness of exhaustion.

"Mom," he said. "I've been worried about you." He opened the door with his free hand, and with his other he pulled her gently inside.

Time swirled and skipped, and then she was lying on the couch under a blanket with her son's face hanging over her.

"I think I wore myself out," she said.

"I think you could say that," Bobby said.

"But you don't want me here. I don't want to be here if you don't want me here." Part of her thought she should stop talking, but she couldn't. She needed to make him understand something while she was too tired to stop herself from saying it. "I wanna be here," she tried again. "I wanna be here till I die, 'cause I think I'm dying. But I don't wanna be here if you don't want it."

"Mom," he said as he pressed his palm to her forehead, and it felt good to let her neck release into the pillow. "I am sorry if I have not been welcoming enough," he said. "Your coming did surprise me. But I do want you here. I do."

The kindness in his voice was enough to start her crying, and the crying made her cough. Soon, before she could stand and struggle to the bathroom, she was hacking blood onto her hands. Bobby fetched her a towel and sat with her until she finally finished.

"This has been going on for some time now, hasn't it," he said.

The understanding between them was such that she didn't even have to say yes.

27

By Thursday afternoon, Randy had stopped work five times just to make it to the toilet before he shit himself. He'd called Susan that morning, and she hadn't answered, and that's when it had started. Then he'd called her twice over lunch. Nothing. She was just out getting groceries, he told himself, even though Tuesday was grocery day, and he knew she'd gone on Tuesday because he'd called on his Tuesday-morning break, just to check, and she hadn't answered, and then when he'd gotten home, he'd dug around in the kitchen for new foods, and he'd found them. A small part of his brain assured him that there was some logical explanation, but a bigger, crazier part of his brain kept imagining Susan naked in their bed in the arms of another man. He could see it all so clearly he felt like he'd been cursed with supernatural sight.

When at last Susan answered his afternoon call, he felt so relieved and angry all at once that he almost started to cry.

"Where have you been?" he asked, trying to sound casual.

Doug and Stevo were off in the corner of the break room with their Styrofoam cups of old coffee. Bert and Shaner were camped out on the bench, sucking down as many Newports as they could before the bell called them back to the line.

Susan's voice on the other end sounded far away. "I had some errands to run, Randy. I can't just sit around waiting for you to call."

"What errands?"

"I'm sorry?" she asked, as if she didn't know what he was talking about. Randy couldn't tell whether she sounded bored or angry.

"What errands?" he growled as low as he could.

"I had to run to the school."

"And that took the whole morning? And the afternoon?"

Susan's sigh came over the line in a burst of static. "Please, Randy. Just trust me."

Randy's guts cramped up, and he clenched over. "Susan," he said. He tried to sound calm. "I'm not asking for an explanation. I just want to know where you were." It was everything Randy could do not to scream at her or shit himself. He was a bomb, and she was a balloon floating just out of his reach. If he blew, she would simply float up and away.

Susan sighed again. "I took cupcakes to Lukas's school, and then I took a walk. A long walk."

Relief swirled through Randy's head. Cupcakes and a walk. Nothing suspicious about that. But then the shadow threw itself down again over his mind. "Were you alone?"

"Randy."

"So the answer's no."

"I'm trying to help you. You need something to suspect, and you're going to find it whether I give it to you or not."

"Who were you with?"

"I've got to go now, Randy."

"Who the fuck were you with?" He was biting down hard to keep the words low. Spittle shot from between his clenched teeth and speckled the mouthpiece. The line on the other end clicked off, and Randy gulped down the bile rising in his throat before he said, "All right then, see you later," to the dead air and settled the phone back onto its cradle. Then he walked straight to the bathroom, where he was still cramped over the toilet shitting out the rest of his guts when the bell rang to call him back to work. On the line, he tried to talk himself down. Susan wasn't that kind of woman, he told himself. She never had been. If he couldn't stop acting the way he was acting, he might even scare her into it. Already he could feel himself driving her away against his will. Already he had the sense that she'd slipped into some other world—a neighboring world where she could go and he could not. He needed to shut the fuck up and trust her, he knew that. He imagined himself going home and laying it all down. *I trust you*, he'd say. *I'm sorry that I make it seem like I don't. I'll stop*, he'd say. *No more.*

But then, when he'd made up his mind, a question would lift its head like a small snake and a hundred other snakes would follow.

For the rest of the afternoon, he kept trying to focus, but he smashed his hand with a drill collar and then Quality Control sent back four of his drill bits because their bearings were too loose for code. By the time he'd tightened them all down, he was three bits under quota, and so Dawson called him upstairs. He told Randy that usually when a worker was that far under, Mick wanted him written up, but Dawson knew that they all had those days and so he was going to be nice this time and let Randy off with a warning. Randy was shit sure that Dawson had blasted quota all the time when he was a piss-on back on the line, but Randy couldn't say anything without looking pathetic, so he had to squeeze his fists in his pockets and take it up the ass.

Then, on the day to beat all motherfucking days, his truck wouldn't start. He knew the battery was dead because the engine wouldn't crank, and when he tested the lights, he realized he'd left them on all goddamn day. He needed a jump, and he'd have to get on it fast, before everyone left. Just as he popped the hood and climbed out with the cables, who should come sailing by in his new blue truck but Dave motherfucking Dawson. The truck slowed, and the driver's-side window slid down. Dawson stuck his mug out.

"Randy, my man," he said. He looked like he was trying not to laugh. "Need a jump?"

Randy had been planning to ask Manny or Marty or maybe Annie from the office. They wouldn't lord it over him. But Dawson had caught him standing outside his truck in the freezing cold with a fistful of jumper cables. He'd look even dumber saying no.

So he said yeah, he did, and Dawson made a big show of backing his truck around and pulling up and hoisting his hood. He kept saying how it was no big deal, like he was doing Randy such a big favor that he needed to downplay it.

All the way home, Randy kept coming back to Dawson's truck with the glittery blue paint and the double racing stripes and everything under the hood the same spotless metal, like the damn thing had never been driven at all. Randy's truck was fourteen years old and riddled with rust and half the size of Dawson's. Randy didn't need any prissy glitter or fake-ass racing stripes. His truck was made for working, not showboating around like some woman. Dawson, though, wouldn't see it that way. Dawson, Randy was sure, saw it as proof of something. That Dawson was killing it. And that Randy was not.

Randy pulled into his driveway and shifted into park, and the whole truck shook for a second, like he was stuck over the tracks and a train was coming. With the dying evening above and the dull snow below, his house looked impossibly flat and small. Why'd he do any of this?

Inside, Lukas was watching a show. When Randy entered, he swiveled his neck toward the door and then turned back to the screen without saying anything. Susan was in the kitchen banging shit around.

"Willa," she called. "It's time to set the table."

So this is how it's going to be, he thought. Susan wasn't even going to say hello. She was trying to punish him for his questions earlier. After their conversation that afternoon, he'd tried to reason himself into civility. He'd imagined himself asking about her day or mentioning, when he walked in the door, how good dinner smelled.

"Willa!" she called, louder this time.

No *hello,* no *how was your day,* no nothing. Well, he was sick of it, damn sick. He wasn't going to grovel anymore. He pulled his legs out of his boots and tossed his coat into the closest chair. "Hello," he said, loud enough for everyone to hear.

No response.

"I said hello!" he yelled, opening the door again and slamming it for emphasis. Lukas jumped, and below the kitchen cabinets, Randy saw Susan freeze, a stack of plates suspended in her hands.

"Hello," she said. She tried to sound aloof, like she wasn't scared, but he could tell he'd rattled her.

"Hi Dad," said Lukas.

Just inside the hallway, Willa froze for a moment before crossing to the dining room. She took the plates from Susan and started setting them down on the table.

No one said anything else. Randy sat down in his chair at the head of the table, and Willa worked around him like he wasn't there, tucking the napkins beneath the plates and lining up the silverware. Lukas kept watching his show. Susan kept knocking things around in the kitchen. It was like he didn't exist. Or like they were saying, in their own separate ways, that they wished he didn't. Their husband and father, who laid down his whole fucking life for them.

His anger was like a fire that needed to eat, and he threw everything into it. Each careless clash of glass or silverware, each blast of noise from the television, each moment of Susan's silence, and Willa's, and Lukas's. His cold house, his chipped plate. His visions of the glittery blue truck pulling into the asphalt drive of Dawson's two-story home.

"I'm hungry," he said. The madness burned his voice. He could feel his only power building.

Susan came and took his bowl, filled it in the kitchen, and brought it back.

"It's time to eat," she said to the kids. She walked over and switched off the television. Lukas shuffled obediently into the dining room. Willa settled herself into her chair.

Randy looked down into his bowl. Shit brown and half empty, with splatters across the top like a fucking toilet.

This. This was what he came home to.

He dug his spoon in and brought a bite to his mouth. The broth was barely warm. His teeth crunched into the frozen core of a carrot. Leftovers from the freezer. She hadn't even bothered to heat them all the way through. He bit into a chunk of beef, still crispy with ice. The madness shot through his arms, and in one swift smack he sent the bowl sailing into the wall. It hit with a satisfying crack and dropped to the floor.

28

Willa watched the stew slide down the wall in thick, slow fingers. She could fix this. She could make this right. She stood slowly, as calmly as she could, and walked to the kitchen. She took the cleaning bucket from under the sink, filled it with hot, soapy water, and dropped in a rag.

Her mother, who had been standing frozen in the kitchen, tipping a box of crackers over a bowl, spoke in a voice as small as a mouse. "Willa," she said, as Willa pulled the bucket, with some difficulty, up out of the sink and started carrying it toward the dining room. "Willa, what are you doing?"

But her mother would see. Willa would make things right. She set the bucket on the floor by the bowl, now broken, that her father had thrown. She lifted the cloth from the bubbles, squeezed out the extra water, and began to wipe the stew from the wall.

"Willa," her mother said, louder this time. "You don't have to do that."

But Willa had already wiped up half the mess and was dunking the cloth up and down in the bubbles, squeezing out the water again, reaching back up with the rag. She felt good—proud—doing this thing that had to be done.

"Randy," her mother said, and Willa willed her mother to let it go, to just let her make things right this time. "Please tell her she doesn't have to do that."

"Why should I tell her that?" Willa's dad said, but he sounded more relaxed. He sounded almost as if he was enjoying this. "She can do what she wants," he said.

"Randy," Susan said. "This is not okay."

"No," Willa's dad said. "It's not okay. It's not okay that you run off and don't answer my calls and don't tell me where you've been. It's not okay that I work my fucking ass off and then come home to this." He jerked his head toward the mess on the wall, where Willa was wiping up the final splatters. "As a matter of fact," he said, "I think I'll treat myself tonight. Eat some real food at a restaurant. Willa? Lukas? What do you think?"

Willa's heart rushed as her mouth rushed to speak, to say the right thing. "That sounds good to me," she finally managed.

"Lukas? How about it? You want some french fries? A hot dog?"

Lukas looked toward Willa as if to double-check his answer before he gave it. Willa nodded and forced Lukas a smile. *Just say yes,* she thought. *Just say yes, and everything will be okay.*

"Okay," said Lukas. His face began to brighten. "I like french fries. I like hot dogs."

Willa's dad turned to her mom. "You want to hide things from me?" he said. "Fine." He stood and stomped to the door, grabbed his coat. "Kids, let's go."

Their mother followed them, twisting a dish towel in her hands, and watched them pull on their coats. When Lukas struggled with his boot, she bent down and helped him on with it. "Well," she said, like she felt she needed to say something, only she didn't know what. "Well. You two mind your manners."

Willa and Lukas crammed into the front seat of their father's truck, a rare treat, and he let them play with the radio while he drove through the snow to a restaurant in Jefferson. Inside, he ordered them hot chocolates and hot dogs and french fries. In the corner by their booth stood game machines with buttons and joysticks, and he let them pull up a chair for Lukas and take turns pretending to play.

When the food arrived, their dad squeezed out their ketchup, and they ate in silence, but it was a happy silence, Willa thought, and she wondered why they didn't do this more often, the three of them. It was safe and warm and perfect for that moment, sitting there together with rice pudding for dessert and fat raisins and cinnamon dust and packets of coffee creamers to pour over the top and men stomping their boots off just inside the door and the lights of the city buildings winking beyond the windows and the Christmas angels lit up on lampposts and the smiling waitress asking did they want anything else? Anything else at all?

29

Susan stood at the front window and watched Randy's truck back out the drive, listened to its motor whine off toward Jefferson. She kept standing there, staring out until the odor of burning stew caught her nose.

She fetched a spatula, turned off the burner, and began scraping at the bottom of the pot, but she could not work the tool underneath the stubborn rubble of root vegetables and meat glued fast to the bottom. It seemed the harder she tried, the harder the mass resisted. Before she knew it, she was bouncing the spatula off the bottom in hard, rhythmic thrusts, and then stabbing it down, her whole arm tight as a knife, the stew broth splashing out of the pot, scalding her stomach through her sweater, sizzling and smoking on the burner coils. She realized then that she was yelling—not words but a roar escalating to a long, drawn-out scream that took all her breath. She flung the spatula into the sink and marched back to the door, where she yanked her coat on over her sweater and grabbed the keys from the hook.

In the van, Susan wrenched up the heat, but the streams of air from the dashboard stayed as cold as snow, so she closed them again. She had to slump to peer out the small, melted semicircle at the base of the windshield. The headlights seemed unusually dim, and snow was falling, thick and steady, a never-ending onslaught of tiny, smooth trajectories. She could hardly see anything at all but the rapid flurry of flakes rising against her.

When at last she spied the stop sign at the first intersection of Esau, she braked to a rolling stop and turned right toward the church.

She hadn't intended to drive to the church, but she found herself turning into the parking lot of Esau Baptist, and, from there, steering onto the parsonage driveway. Once she had entered the driveway, the only way to go was forward, and once she had driven as far forward as she could, she shifted into park. At that point, surely Robert and his mother had heard her, surely they were waiting for whoever had pulled in the driveway to come to the door. So what else was there to do but climb the steps and ring the bell and say, to a startled Robert, "I'm so sorry. I just needed somebody to talk to."

Pastor Robert blinked for a moment, then stood back from the door and gestured her into the house. "No need to apologize," he said. "This is God's house, not mine." But Susan detected a distance in his manner, and he met her eyes only briefly before casting them down.

"I'm sorry," she said again, as she caught sight of his mother asleep on the couch. "I'm afraid I've come at a bad time."

"No time is a bad time," he said. "It would be best to keep our voices down, though. She's had a hard day."

"Yes. Of course."

Susan followed the pastor into the kitchen. Only now, passing the doorway to the pastor's bedroom—his comforter neatly draped over the top and one flat, smooth pillow centered at the head—did she realize how incredibly inappropriate it had been to show up there. On the table sat the remains of a half-eaten sandwich and a shallow layer of soup in a bowl. He gestured to a chair at the table and lifted the dishes.

"I didn't mean to interrupt your dinner."

"I wasn't going to finish it anyway. Tea?"

"Okay. If it's not too much trouble." She took off her coat. Then she feared that the gesture might imply that she planned to stay too long, so she pulled it back over her shoulders.

When he'd lit the burner and filled the kettle and settled it over the circle of flame, he returned to the table and seated himself sideways so that he faced the kitchen instead of Susan. It was wrong to be here. Wrong, wrong, wrong. Why had she come?

"So," he said. "What were you hoping to talk about?"

Susan scrambled for the right words. She wanted to backtrack, to tell him it wasn't very important, but that wouldn't justify her showing up on his doorstep in the middle of a snowstorm. "I'm sorry," she finally said. "I needed somewhere to go, and the church was the only place that came to mind." She stood, and her coat slipped off her shoulders. "I'm sorry," she said again, picking her coat up and sliding her arms back into the sleeves. "I shouldn't have come."

The pastor stood, too, his expression touched with puzzlement. "You might as well stay for your tea," he said. "Now that you're here."

Susan flushed. She sat down, suddenly, her coat bunching up against the back of her chair. She felt ridiculous. "Okay then," she said. "I'll have to get going in ten minutes or so." She had barged into his evening, and now she was acting as though he was the one pressing her to stay. "But tea would be nice, thank you," she said, and then kicked herself because she'd already accepted his offer of tea, and he was already making it.

As though to soften this perceived awkwardness, he said, "Very well," and walked to a cupboard, where he took down two mugs and a box of tea bags. "Black tea okay?" he asked.

"Yes, thank you."

With the pastor's back turned, Susan took the opportunity to straighten her coat. She also discreetly bent her neck and pinched her cheeks, as her nose had the tendency to grow bright red in the cold, and pinching her cheeks usually helped to even that out. Looking down, she caught sight of the stew striping her sweater. She should have changed. Why hadn't she changed? She pulled the sides of her coat closed and crossed her arms over her middle.

The pastor was still turned away from her, pouring some sugar into a bowl. He was tall and straight-backed, thin but strong. His torso stretched up from a slender waist into broad shoulders. She could see them shifting beneath the fabric as he moved.

Susan had considered what these meetings might look like to someone outside of them. She knew for certain what they'd look like to Randy. The pastor was an attractive man, and she was a woman, alone, of a comparable age. But Susan felt too desperate to allow these impersonal facts to dictate her behavior. Her admiration for the pastor was beside the point, she assured herself. She was not seeking him out with secret intentions. She was seeking him out because he was kind, and he listened, and he was the first person with whom she'd carried on an unfettered conversation in months, maybe years. He knew she was married, and she had no doubt that he would honor that fact. However, it was also true, since their conversation earlier that day, that Susan had considered what life with Robert might be like. His past and Randy's past held similar levels of pain, but for Robert, the pain had turned him toward God and others, and for Randy, the pain had shrunk him down and shoved him inside himself. What would that be like, she wondered, to live with someone whose instincts inclined toward thoughtfulness and wisdom, selflessness and humility?

But Susan had to remember that such fantasies were just that—fantasies. She had dated enough men, ridden out enough crushes, to know that any glint of romance was doomed from the beginning. She still thought back on how Randy had thrilled her when they'd first begun to date. He'd felt nothing short of electric to her, cliché as it was. His attention had been a spotlight, shining over her stage. And the stage metaphor was apt because new love wasn't love but performance. First, the actors built up the facades of the people they wanted to be. And then exhaustion and bad judgment and all the potholes in the road of life shook down the compelling figures and left two disappointing humans slumped in the dust, struggling to come to terms with the reality of their partner and the reality of themselves, and to keep loving anyway. The pastor, she had to assume, was not nearly as wonderful as she imagined him to be.

He set down the bowl of sugar. "I'm afraid I don't have any cream," he said.

"Just sugar is fine," Susan replied, though she had never taken sugar with her tea. After the kettle rattled and the pastor poured the steaming water into their mugs and set them down on the table, the bowl of sugar sat between them, untouched and somehow accusatory. Finally, she took a spoonful, tapped it into her cup, and dunked it around with her tea bag. She took a sip and cleared her throat.

"I know it's strange that I've come here," she began, and at these words, a rush of heat rippled over her face. She pictured it like a wildfire, moving across her cheeks in a burning line. "I guess I'm here because you're a pastor, and somehow I've gotten to this point in my life where I don't have anyone else to talk to."

The pastor nodded with a solemn expression. He was not looking at her but down at his tea. This observation made Susan so self-conscious that the only thing she could bear less than going on about herself was to stop talking entirely and have to sit across from him in a humiliating silence.

"It's just that I—well . . ." She should have practiced putting words to this. "It's just that every day is so hard."

The pastor nodded again, still studying his tea.

"I mean, just getting out of bed is hard. Making a grocery list. Opening the mail." She couldn't bring herself to add anything about Randy, undoubtedly the most difficult element, and the ridiculousness of the only things she could say made her eyes sting. She closed them for a moment, squeezed back the tears.

When she opened her eyes again, the pastor was gazing at her with a look tender and pained beyond what she would have expected. He nodded once, encouraging her to go on.

"I know this sounds like a funk, maybe, like a bad mood," she said. "But it feels like my faith. It feels like I'm losing it. When I turn toward God, I can't sense Him there anymore. I can't feel comfort. I can't find strength."

Robert took a sip of his tea. "That sounds like despair," he said.

"So you understand this?" she asked, and she had the sense of asking someone who couldn't answer her, the same sense she had when she sometimes spoke to the picture of her grandmother, now four years gone.

"I do," he said. "I do." And Susan knew that he did.

"Thank you," she said, recognizing it afterward as an odd response, and her embarrassment set her eyes burning again. She tried to explain herself. "It's just good to know," she said, "that someone understands."

"God is always there," the pastor said. "At times this does not feel like the truth. But it is still the truth. It is always the truth."

Susan nodded, but this assurance, she realized, was not what she had needed. The understanding alone was what she had needed. "I'm grateful to you," she said.

"I'm afraid I haven't done anything."

"You have," she replied. "You have." She took a big gulp from her tea. "And now I'm afraid I have to get back." She knew Randy and the kids would be gone for a while yet, but the possibility that they might return early terrified her. She wouldn't be able to tell Randy where she'd been. She wouldn't be able to explain herself. Besides, she needed to get home early enough for the snow to cover the fresh tracks her tires would make.

"I will pray for you," the pastor said. The kindness in his voice fell softly over her raw heart, and she let out a small sob and gasp.

"I'm sorry," she said. "I'm not usually so emotional. It's just that"—she laughed a little—"you feel like a friend. How is it that my new pastor feels like my only confidant in life?"

She had meant this to be a humorous observation, something to lighten her little outburst, but the pastor took a deep breath and furrowed his brow down at his cup.

"Are there others you can also talk to—your husband, for example? Your parents?"

Susan could sense, in the way he tacked on the words *your parents*, that the sole purpose of his sentence had been to bring the fact of her husband into the room. The same burning shame she'd felt before refreshed itself, followed by an urgency to explain.

So she said, pressing back against the wave of embarrassment that threatened to drown her, "My husband's not the talking type, I'm afraid." Then, because that sounded so weak and unsatisfying, "He doesn't understand," and because that sounded so cliché, so predictable, she finally added, "He's a very difficult man to live with." And though Susan knew her explanation did not at all capture the problem of Randy, did not adequately convey that he was the chief reason her life was teetering on the brink of unbearable, she left it at that.

The pastor frowned awhile in thought before finally taking a quick breath, as though he'd been working himself up to something. "My fear in our conversations is that you, in a roundabout way, are asking for permission to end your marriage."

Susan shook her head, hurrying her disagreement. "No."

It took a moment of scrambling for her to apprehend that he'd understood, without her spelling it out, that her marriage was the core, the foundation of all her problems. She had thought she'd been walking so delicately around it. She hadn't been *so* very obvious, had she?

Finally, lamely, she said, "That's not what I'm looking for." Only once she'd said it she realized that she'd been looking exactly for that—a grand permission to do the thing she knew deep down needed to be done. But in that moment, when Susan understood the necessity of her leaving, she also understood that she would not do it.

The pastor responded to Susan's deflection with another solemn nod, though whether he actually believed her, she could not say.

"I apologize for my forthrightness. I just felt I should clarify." Susan took a final gulp of her tea and stood.

"Thank you for your time," she said. "And for the tea."

"You're welcome," he said, and stayed seated at the table as she let herself out.

Outside the parsonage, the snow was still falling in fat white flakes. The van refused to heat on the frozen ride home, and Susan's breath vanished instantly on the air, as though to say that any warmth at all would not be tolerated.

She was home long enough to soak and scrape the pot, put the dishes away, and pack the next day's lunches before Lukas burst in the door, bubbling with frenetic exhaustion and adventure. "We had hot dogs!" he cried. "And ketchup and french fries and hot chocolate, and Daddy let us play video games! And we ate rice pudding for dessert! With creamers!"

Randy and Willa collapsed together on the couch, Randy's arm around Willa's shoulders.

"Hi Mom," Willa said, but her voice lacked its usual warmth.

How easy it was, Susan thought, to win children's affections. One evening, one hot dog, one rice pudding was enough to bring them into the game, where they could be persuaded, traded, shifted around.

"You missed out on a good time," Randy said. "Right, Willa?" He jostled her shoulders with his arm.

"Yeah!" she said, too brightly, and Susan could detect a desire to please her father and beneath that a small but unmistakable urge to reach into Susan and twist the knife.

"Well, in that case, would you like to take over bedtime, too?" Susan asked. It was the closest she could bring herself to calling him out.

Spite flashed over Randy's face. He lifted his arm from Willa's shoulders and clapped his hands. "Pajamas!" he called.

"Are you going to read us stories, Daddy?" Lukas asked, his eyes wet and warm.

"You bet," Randy replied, and after Lukas and Willa had danced down the hall to their room, he fixed Susan with a look both joyful and cruel, the look an opponent might give at the point in a hard-fought game where they have suddenly, miraculously gained the upper hand.

30

Friday morning, Robert rose early and ate his oatmeal in silence so as not to disturb his mother, who was still sleeping on the couch. He accidentally dropped the bowl into the sink, wincing for his mother's sake at the crash. But when he turned back toward the table, there she was, already standing in the entrance to the living room. She wavered over to the table, landed her hands along the edge of it, then rotated her backside to settle herself into a chair.

"Thanks for taking care of me last night," she said. "I hope you know how much I appreciate it."

"I do."

Leotie drew a long, ragged breath and patted her knees. "Well. Enough about this old bird. There's trouble in paradise."

"I'm sorry?"

"I'm talking about the chat last night between you and your lady friend."

"Susan is not my lady friend. She's a married woman."

Robert was hoping that his mother would note the warning in his voice, but she said, "Not for long, from the sounds of it."

Robert plugged the drain, turned on the hot water, and bent to fetch the dish soap from its cupboard. "Breakfast might settle your stomach. Can I make you some oatmeal?"

"Sounded to me like she should walk out on that husband of hers."

Robert turned his face toward his mother but kept his eyes on the floor.

"As a pastor, it is not my job to ensure that everyone in my congregation is happily married. But it *is* my job to guide them down the narrow path, where vows made before God are eternal and binding."

His mother let silence fall for a moment before saying, "Well far be it from me to tell you how to do your job." She waited another beat. "But she'd probably be a lot better off running away with someone like you."

"Do you want some oatmeal? Or not?"

After his mother had returned, breakfast-less, to the couch and Robert had washed the few remaining dishes, he stayed in the kitchen to wash down the cupboards and walls. He had done so only once or twice in all of the years that he'd lived there. He wasn't sure it needed doing now. But he wanted to occupy himself in some sort of movement, something that would allow him to think and also remove the expectation of interacting with his mother. Her words had drawn some danger out into the light. His behavior with Susan was unwise, even perilous.

Robert filled a big bowl with warm, soapy water and started at the top corner of the wall. The residue revealed itself in the tinted rivulets that rolled down, and he found the small contrast satisfying enough. He plunged the rag back down into the water, squeezed it out, and brought it up to the patch of wall underneath the first. It reminded him of the hymn "Wash Me and I Shall Be Whiter Than Snow." He would do this for as long as he had to. He would occupy his hands in blameless work and think on good things. He hummed to himself as he worked, quietly, so as not to disturb his mother. *Lord Jesus, let nothing unholy remain / Apply Thine own blood and extract every stain / To get this blest cleansing, I all things forego— / Now wash me, and I shall be whiter than snow.*

Whiter than snow, yes, whiter than snow. / Now wash me, and I shall be whiter than snow.

He tried to picture it, to meditate on the metaphor. Blood of crimson beside snow so white that it glowed. Why was goodness always associated with whiteness, and evil with darkness? Could such a dichotomous comparison really do no harm to someone like him, to someone like his mother?

But the harder he tried not to think of Susan, the more he did. Her hands, of all things, how he loved her hands. They were lean and long, with smooth skin stretched over large knuckles and broad thumbs. They looked, he thought, like the hands of a mother, like hands that knew how to comfort, how to handle anything. *Break down every idol, cast out every foe.*

He had heard her voice, he thought, in church. There were so few people that it was possible to distinguish many of the individual voices. Florence Butts, whose soprano was ragged and strident and always sharp. Rose Gillis, who castigated her solid sense of pitch with a wildly oscillating vibrato. Clarence Rider, who spoke rather than sang the words and compensated for ascensions in pitch by trading them for ascensions in volume. But in the midst of these, he thought he had detected Susan's voice. Simple and strong, with no unnecessary ornamentation. But it had a husky quality to it, a depth, that set it apart from mere melody.

Break down every idol.

An idol was anything you wanted more than God, anything you found yourself prioritizing above your relationship with your Lord and Savior. His mind longed for Susan, and his flesh, and his soul.

Cast out every foe.

The day before, in the woods, Susan had stopped on the path, and so he had stopped, too, and she had leaned in toward a structure of spotted fungus blooming in shelves from a tree trunk. He had watched her there in her study of it and had come so close to some action, some apostasy, he was certain, that would have damned them both.

Now wash me, and I shall be whiter than snow.

That whiteness again, his otherness.

He was now scrubbing the outsides of the cupboards, stretching his rag over his pointer finger and rubbing it along the grooves that outlined the borders of the doors. The dust there, when wiped, accumulated from the white in small flecks, and he began to write a sermon in his head about how it was almost impossible to see the dust with an untrained eye, about how he would have thought it was clean if he hadn't taken a cloth to it and challenged it to reveal itself. That was what our faith required of us, he would say—that constant uprooting of assumption, that assiduous challenging. And maybe Susan would be there to hear it, and maybe then she would forgive him. And the deacons, too. They would understand that he was only human. He had given sin a foothold. But with God's strength, he could break the footing and watch his lapses in judgment roll away.

He had the urge to call Susan and explain himself, perhaps apologize. It was Friday, her husband would not be home. But as soon as he recognized the potential within this choice for sinful dalliance, he squashed it down. No. He would be strong. He would not call, he would not visit. He would not again be so willingly misled.

Which was how Robert came readily to accept his own redemption that very afternoon, when Cliff Grable rapped on the parsonage door and requested a few private minutes of his time. They ambled over to Robert's office, where Cliff apologized on behalf of all the deacons for the harsh turn that the previous day's meeting had taken and approved the use of the family fund to cover the costs of Leotie's medical treatments. The other deacons had agreed to this while again voicing their concerns over the pastor's meeting alone with Susan. To this final point, Robert thanked Cliff for his wisdom and his accountability and assured him that such meetings would no longer be taking place.

In order to ensure his compliance, Robert remained in his office once Cliff had left it, penned a short and informative letter to Susan, and tucked it into the church's mailbox. Then he pulled it back out, walked it to the post office, and slipped it through the mail slot on the side of the building before he could change his mind. Only after he'd pulled back his hand did he realize that his words, when they arrived, could just as easily be retrieved by Susan's husband as they could by Susan herself, and that there was nothing he could do about it.

31

The morning after Randy had taken the kids out to dinner, Susan packed Randy's lunch and left it on the counter, but she didn't fill his thermos with coffee. After the kids left, she disappeared back into the bedroom and didn't come out. He had to pour the coffee himself and fish his thermos lid and cap out of the dish drainer.

"I'm leaving," he called from the door.

No answer.

"I said I'm leaving!"

Still nothing.

He found her in bed, with the covers pulled up over her head and only her hair sticking out.

"Goodbye," he said.

"Bye," she replied from under the blankets.

"Must be nice to just lay in bed all day." Maybe she was tired. Maybe she was sick. He thought about asking her if she felt okay. "Am I gonna have to feed the kids again tonight? Hey." He pulled back the covers, and she shrank down away from the light.

"Leave me alone."

"What are you, sick or something?"

Susan grabbed the blankets and pulled them over her head again. Randy glanced at the alarm clock on the nightstand. He was going to be late.

"I hope you realize how lucky you are," he finally said. On his way back down the hallway, he tripped on a box of Legos. "Goddamnit," he said, kicking the box. It tipped over, and Legos spilled out in all directions. He grabbed his lunch and thermos from the counter. When he turned around, Susan was standing in the hall.

"Lucky, huh?" She was looking around at the Legos on the floor, and then she looked up at him. Her face shivered, and she pressed her lips into a thin line.

"Yeah, Suzy. I'd say you're pretty fucking lucky."

She held out her arms and dropped them. "How," she said. "You tell me how."

"You've got a roof over your head. You've got a house full of food. You've got two healthy kids. You've got me working my ass off every day to support this family while you get to stay home and play house or take naps or do whatever the hell else you want. So yeah, I'd say you're pretty fucking lucky."

Susan just stood there staring at him.

"Look," he said. "I'd love to stand here and rattle off the rest of the list, but I've gotta go or else I'm gonna be late." His voice was softening. He seemed to have made a point. At least she wasn't arguing back. "Suzy," he said, but it was like she didn't hear him. She looked so small suddenly, standing there, so confused. He felt a burst of warmth toward her, generosity. "You go back to bed," he said. "You'll feel better by the time I get home." He walked over and bent to kiss her, but she turned away and walked back into the bedroom and the door swung shut behind her.

"What the fuck," he said to no one.

On his ten o'clock break, he slipped both quarters into the pay phone before turning the lever and listening to them plunk down into the little hole. He slid them out and tucked them back into his pocket. He would give her some time, he decided, and call at lunch. Small steps.

But when he called at lunch, she didn't answer. He returned his quarters and shoved them back into the slot, dialed the number again. Nothing. He waited for the answering machine to pick up, and he left a message. "Hey, Suzy." He tried to sound nonchalant. "Just checking in. Wondering if you're feeling better."

He winced at the sound of his voice—weak, almost cheerful. Lately he'd felt more afraid than he cared to admit. He'd remember Susan's face after that incident with Willa, how strange she'd suddenly felt, whispering so fiercely that her spit flecked his face. Since then he'd often get the sense that he was watching his whole life move away from him on some giant conveyor belt while he stayed stuck to the floor.

But the night before, sitting with the kids, *his* kids, at the restaurant, watching their simple, quiet happiness, he had thought, *This is enough for them, and maybe it's enough for me, too.* And then he had decided that it *was* enough for him and that it had always been enough and that he just had to start acting like it. And then he decided that maybe the biggest problem was Susan, because it wasn't enough for her, even though it should have been so much more than enough—especially for the mother, especially for her.

As Randy mulled over these thoughts, his timeline started to stretch. From his taking the kids the night before to the following morning when Lukas, unasked, had hugged him goodbye and Willa had pecked him on the cheek—those twelve hours of better behavior stretched themselves out into days, during which Randy had demonstrated improvement while Susan had remained stubbornly the same. The night before, he'd read them three chapters of a book about a fourth-grade kid and his little shit brother (*Three chapters?* Lukas had exclaimed, *Three!? But Mom only ever reads us two!*). The next morning, Susan spent breakfast slamming things around in the kitchen, but Randy poured the kids extra cereal and milk and made jokes about Lukas's turkey homework until they were all three laughing—really laughing.

On Friday morning, while he worked the line, Randy drew up each of these details separately, and the time they'd taken swelled and spread and pardoned any previous mistakes. He even grew convinced that, if Susan would just make up her mind to notice all the good things, then their problems would take care of themselves.

Randy established this optimism over the first half of the morning, and he lugged it, with dogged certainty, through the second half. It grew much heavier when Susan didn't answer his calls, and then he opened his same boring lunch—two sandwiches and chips and an apple and a quart of water—which at the end didn't feel like enough. (It never did. It never, ever felt like enough.) His determination drooped more as he plowed through the first half of the afternoon and through the return of two drill bits from Quality Control and the staff meeting with Dawson on changes to the line and the new quota (twenty each day, instead of seventeen). By the time the meeting had finished—late—Randy had only two minutes to call Susan three times in a row with no answer before dragging himself back to the line to ride out the last two hours of the day and fix his bits and flunk his quota and drive home totally hopeless, totally fucking sick of everything.

32

Friday afternoon Willa sat on her bed, relishing each long division problem and checking her objects and listening for her father's truck in the driveway. She had kissed him goodbye that morning, and he had caught her up in a hug and said, *Thank you, Willie Bear.*

Willa finished her long division homework and tucked it into her math folder. She wished it had taken longer. She had figured each problem through twice, once on scrap paper and once on the worksheet. That way, she'd told herself, she could be sure of the answer (even though she'd gotten them all right the first time), and she could show her work neatly, with no scribbles or eraser marks. She had read her science passage on static electricity and begun writing down her answers to the questions when her father's tires crunched into the driveway.

All day long she'd been picturing herself meeting him at the door, picking up right where they left off. But when she folded her paper into her science book, she felt embarrassed, like someone was watching her, even though Lukas, clueless, was deep in a block-building project on the other side of the room. She stacked her books neatly on her bed and walked down to the end of the hallway to wait.

Her father entered in a dark cloud she could almost see. His face looked heavy, like someone was pulling down at it. "Hi Dad," she said, but he didn't seem to hear her. "Hi Dad," she said again, a little louder.

He dropped his coat on the floor. "Susan," he called. "Hey, Suzy!" He kicked off his boots, splattering the entryway with clumps of muddy snow.

From the kitchen, Willa's mom called, "Yes?"

Willa's dad moved slowly across the living room with extra twitches and yanks. He jerked his chin up as he spoke. "You just not gonna answer the phone anymore?" he said. "Is that it?"

Willa's mom didn't answer.

"You'd better have a good excuse," he said. He slapped the wall and left his hand there. From the hallway, Willa could see her mother's arm jump and freeze before it went on doing whatever it had been doing. "So what is it?" he said.

"I couldn't," her mother said. Willa couldn't tell if she sounded scared or bored.

Her father slapped the wall again, and Willa could make out the shiver in his fingers. "So what the fuck is your excuse?"

"I just couldn't today, Randy," she said, and Willa cringed at the small challenge in her voice. "I just couldn't."

Willa's dad stood there for a while. He didn't seem to know what to say. He just nodded a few times, then jerked his chin up. "So that's it," he said. And Willa could feel the rage that would come next, falling like a wave over the house. She stepped forward. Maybe she could stop this.

"Hey, Dad," she said. "I won the spelling bee today." This was news for her mother, too. Willa had saved it because she'd wanted to tell her father first. She always told her mother news first, but this time she'd saved it for her dad like a present and hoped that her mother would say, in front of her father, *Willa! You didn't even tell me!*

But now she had said it, and her father seemed not to have heard her. Or maybe she hadn't made the spelling bee sound like a big enough deal. Maybe they both assumed that the spelling bee was only between the students in Willa's classroom. It wasn't, though. This one was for the fourth, fifth, and sixth grades together, and Willa was only a fourth grader, and she had beaten everyone else. It had taken all afternoon. The teachers had walked all the students straight from lunch to the high school gym, and across the front of the room, lined them up along the edge of the stage.

Everyone else had dropped off save Willa and Ryan Cooper, a sixth grader with a giant head and big, round glasses who had finally misspelled *unanimous*, and Willa had taken it for the win. Afterward, it seemed like every teacher in the school had congratulated her, and almost all of her classmates had high-fived her or said something like, *Wow, Willa, I heard that a fourth grader has never won before,* or, *How did you know all those words?*, or, *So-and-so said you have to be really smart to spell like that.*

So now Willa swallowed hard and took one more step out from the hallway and said, "It was in the high school gym, and it was for fifth and sixth graders, too, and I still won it."

Her father turned toward her, but he looked through her, like he wasn't seeing anything at all. He turned back to Willa's mother, squeezed a fist, and slammed it into the wall. "Talk to me, goddamnit!"

"I've explained myself as much as I can. I'm sorry, Randy. I just couldn't do it today. That's all." After a moment, she added, "Your daughter is trying to talk to you. She's trying to tell you something."

He laughed a little then, but it was an angry laugh. "You think I'm such a shit father," he said. "But I've got news for you, Suzy. Who fed the kids last night? Who read them stories? Who helped them with breakfast this morning? Me, that's who."

Willa thought, *Just let him have this one, Mom. Just let him take it.*

But her mother was shaking her head. "No," she said, her voice small but sharp. "No. You don't get to rewrite history after one good day. You don't get to erase everything that came before."

"Mom," Willa said. "Stop."

Her mother turned toward Willa, her mouth hanging open in disbelief. "Me?" she said. "You're telling *me* to stop?"

"Willa," her dad said, and he held an arm out toward her. She walked into it, and he wrapped it around her shoulders. She closed her eyes. She could feel looks passing back and forth above her, but she tried to rest where she was, to trust. Finally, her father's arm pulled her into the living room, toward the couch. "So what's this about a spelling bee?" he said.

33

Esau was a town that, like the snow, kept on going no matter what and, like its residents, knew better than to make a show of it. Dirk Newberry the postman was no exception. Before the sun rose late and faint that Saturday morning, the snow had sloped up in chest-high drifts along the west sides of the buildings. It mounted the ledges of first-story windows and stretched upward, with the wind's help, almost to the tops of the panes. But Dirk Newberry arrived at the post office that morning an hour and a half early to compensate for how much longer his route would take. He promptly loaded the bound and ordered stacks of correspondence into the passenger seat of his ailing Chevy Cavalier and, thanks to the equally devoted road-clearing crew, slipped the letter from Pastor Robert into the Shearers' mailbox at twelve noon on the nose (five minutes earlier than usual, he noted a little smugly).

The atmosphere inside the Shearers' house, over the course of that Saturday morning, had been relatively peaceful, which surprised Susan. Randy had spoken calmly to the children (so had she, of course, but she always did), and she and Randy had both refrained from speaking at all to each other. Randy had headed out early to shovel the steps and the driveway, and he'd spent a good hour or so banging around in the garage. He'd go out again soon, Susan knew, and shovel some more. She suspected that he actually enjoyed it. He probably enjoyed his work on the line in the same way. It was something that he could hold over their heads, something that he could resent them for putting him through.

At one point in the morning, Lukas wanted to go outside and play in the snow, and Susan talked Willa into going out, too. She watched them from the window, thought vaguely about pulling on her boots and coat and joining them, letting them draw her into play the way they used to. But they were content without her, building up a wall of snow, and so she finally decided that she would read the book she'd checked out from the library— *Pride and Prejudice*, which she'd never read. At first she didn't want to take her book out because Randy would see that she'd been reading and begrudge her, automatically, the handful of minutes she squeezed out of her days to sit and take in a few pages. Her second thought was that she hoped he would notice, and she hoped he would ask her, rudely, if she'd been reading, and she would say, "Yes, Randy. I like to read. Maybe you forgot that about me. But I still like to think. I still like to better myself."

Susan seated herself in the armchair and pulled her favorite afghan over her lap. She read the first chapter slowly and then reread it, savoring its humor. She remained dimly aware of the snow shovel scraping back and forth from the top steps down to the bottom ones, now on the landing, now over the driveway, the snow budging resentfully in great, muffled *whumps*. And then the creak of the mailbox door and a stretch of silence before heavy footsteps on the stairs and Randy stomping over the carpet in his boots, shoving an unfolded letter into her face, then slapping it down into her lap.

Randy said nothing, and his expression was such a riot of anger and fear that she couldn't imagine what had produced it, so she glanced down at the signature on the letter, and then she knew. And then she had no choice but to read the whole thing, as Randy already had.

Dear Susan, it read, *As a pastor, especially an unmarried one, it has been a rule of mine not to meet alone with women. Because of your emotional state that first Wednesday, I suspended that rule, and I have been reminded, both by the deacons and by my own conscience, that our continuing to meet in such a matter is unwise and perhaps even morally dangerous. I will be happy to meet with you again assuming you arrange it ahead of time so that I can ask one of the deacons or their wives also to be present. It is for your own moral standing that I write this, as well as my own. Sincerely, Pastor Robert*

Had Susan read this letter alone, she might have cried, but Randy's glowering compelled her to clear her face of all emotion and meet his furious wait with a quiet "Yes?"

"Who—the fuck—is Robert?" Randy wrenched out each word.

"A pastor," Susan said, gesturing to the letter.

"A *single* pastor," Randy said. "One that you've been meeting with. Alone."

His face was so swollen and purple and pulsing that Susan wondered if it were possible to give oneself an aneurysm. *He could die,* she thought. *He could die right now, and it would be the best thing that ever happened to me.*

"I knew it," he said. The color dropped out of his eyes and mouth, and the corners of his face melted downward. "I knew something like this was going on." He looked so sad and so utterly defeated that for a moment a crest of pity rose up in Susan and obliterated her sadness for herself.

"Nothing happened," she said. She waited for this to register, and as she did, she reached for his hand.

He shook her away. A sound came from his throat like a small, frightened cat. He gripped his scalp with both hands and pulled at his hair. "I knew it," he said again. He was almost crying.

The kids burst in the door, red-cheeked and happy from the novelty of so much snow and their triumph over the cold.

"Mom!" cried Lukas. "Can you make us some hot chocolate?" But Willa had already sensed the illness in the air.

"Come on, Lukas," she said. "Let's finish our fort, and then maybe Mom will make us some hot chocolate."

"But I'm cold," Lukas whined. "I want to be inside."

Randy had collapsed onto the edge of the sofa and was rubbing his eyes hard with the palms of his hands. Willa squinted, studying her father, and then sent her mother a look that said *What did you do?* Out loud, with false cheerfulness, she said, "Come on, Lukas. I think I know how we could make a roof."

The door closed behind them. Randy continued to stare into the floor. Susan's pity weakened.

"Nothing happened," she said again, though this time she found her tone tinged with irritation rather than understanding. "Randy, you're making a big deal out of nothing."

Randy leaned back onto the couch and looked up at her. "I can't trust you anymore," he said. "I never thought I could, and now I know that I can't." He wasn't angry anymore. He was mournful. "It's almost a relief," he said. "I'm not crazy. I was right. I knew it."

"You knew nothing," she said. "You know nothing at all."

"Well," said Randy, and she could detect in his voice the warm up to a blow, "I know that no matter how much you threw yourself at him, he still didn't want you."

Susan stood. The letter, her book, and the afghan fell to the floor. She clenched her hands into fists. "Threw myself at him?" she asked. *"Threw myself at him?"*

Randy said, "Sure as shit sounds like that." He picked up the letter and scanned it. "'Because of your emotional state,'" he read, then slapped at the letter with the back of his hand. "What the hell is that supposed to mean?"

"It means what it says."

"What, you just went boohooing to him about all your problems?"

Susan opened her mouth to speak and then shut it again. But he must have sensed a weakening, a willingness to share.

"You could have talked to me," he said. "I can listen. I can care." His tone was part belligerent, part genuinely hurt, and the hurt part echoed with the times he had listened, the times he had cared. Back when Susan had gotten a biopsy for a lump in her breast, and she'd had to wait a whole week for the results. He had held her each night and rubbed her back, remained obstinate that nothing was wrong until the results came back benign and he finally admitted that yes, he had been scared but that he hadn't wanted to worry her any more than she already was. Back during Willa's birth, when Susan had pushed for four hours, certain that the baby would never come and that she would die there on the table, and how Randy had stayed calm and steady at her bedside, how he had reminded her to breathe, how he'd wept when Willa finally slid free and the doctor laid her in Susan's arms. She had thought then, and countless times since, that the Randy she'd witnessed in the midst of pain and trial was the real Randy, and that the daily Randy was an impostor built from all the blows his father had inflicted upon him over the years.

Now Randy said, "Are you really that unhappy?" Her sadness had stripped him down to himself, and she detected real sorrow in his voice. "Do you still love me at least?"

Two thoughts. One, it wasn't fair of him to save his kindness only for the falling apart. And two, it wasn't fair of her to forget that this kindness still lived in him, deep down, beneath everything else.

"Yes," Susan said because, at that moment, she felt it. She urged herself to backpedal. "Because love is a choice you make. But it's also a choice you can stop making, Randy. It's a choice you can only make for so long, until your heart just gives out." Her voice cracked. "And I'm giving out, Randy. I'm telling you. I don't know how much longer I can go on like this."

"I'm sorry," Randy said as he moved toward her, and his voice was rough with sadness. He wrapped his arms around her. "I'm so sorry," he said into her hair. "I'll do better. I'll do better if you do." The smell of his sweat warred with the spice of his deodorant and the diesel exhaust from his truck and the men's soap he always insisted she buy in addition to the family bars of Ivory, an insistence she pretended to resent. All of these smells together had somewhere along the way become both a comfort and a long, strong arm that reached up inside her and pulled all of her aspirations down. Randy did love her, and Robert did not. What else was there to do but accept Randy's surprising gift of reconciliation?

34

On Monday morning, Bobby made French toast with bananas sliced over the top. He set down the plates with a clang, then clapped his hands and rubbed his palms together. Leotie could tell he was working up to something well before he said, "Eat up, Mom. I'm taking you to the doctor today."

Leotie's stomach, which had warmed at the smells of cinnamon and syrup, flipped and cooled. "Doctor? What doctor?"

"You know," he said. "For the coughing, the heavy breathing." He yanked his chair to the table and stabbed his French toast with his fork. He was trying to sound careless, she could tell, casual. But he sawed into his breakfast with knife strokes so heavy that they screeched across the plate. His mind was set, and (it touched her) he was scared. He folded a wide strip of toast and stuffed it into his mouth.

"But I don't wanna go see a doctor," she said, and winced at her tone. It sounded like the voice of a child. "I didn't come all this way just so you'd take me to the doctor. Could have gone and seen a doctor just as easy down in Tulsa. Didn't come up here so's you'd have to take care of me." Her mind seized on the possibility that Bobby felt he had to do her a favor, and she could earn her freedom by telling him she didn't want it. "Whatever's wrong with me is just gonna stay wrong with me until what's done is done and that's that." Bobby forked another strip of French toast into his mouth and chewed ferociously. He swallowed hard and said, too loud, "I'm not just gonna let you die, Mom."

"Well ain't no way around that," she said. "We all of us just gonna die anyways."

"Mom," he said, his conviction deflating any hope Leotie had of winning the argument. "That doesn't mean I should just let you suffer. There must be medicine. Treatments."

"Don't want no treatments," she said. "Don't trust no doctors. If you knew what they did to me—"

"You told me what they did to you. That was a long time ago," Bobby said. "Things are different now."

"For who?" Leotie asked, but she knew that she had already lost.

It took all day. At the end of it, they returned home with a stage four chronic obstructive pulmonary disease (COPD) diagnosis, an oxygen tank, a nebulizer mask and compressor, a crate of chocolate Ensure, and an appointment to biopsy the masses on her liver, stomach, and pancreas found by the CT scan. They'd conducted the scan after the chest X-ray, which showcased her lungs riddled with several shadows, likely malignant, and also a few blood clots. Because it wasn't enough to be dying two ways, the good Lord wanted to keep her guessing.

She said this to Bobby, who grimaced like she'd kicked him. They were sitting in a McDonald's. He had ordered a grilled chicken sandwich and a water. She was sucking weakly at a large chocolate shake. The doctor had suggested the shake. She needed to "pack on the pounds." He'd said it like it was good news. "You get to pig out on the stuff everyone else *wishes* they could eat." Leotie couldn't tell if he was trying to make the best of a bad situation or if he simply had no empathy at all.

The doctor was a tall white man, lean and fit like a marathon runner, with impossibly white teeth and eyebrows so dark and striking she wondered if he'd filled them in with a makeup pencil. That was what Leotie kept thinking about as all the words poured out of his mouth, all the *masses* and *blood clots* and *malignants* and *biopsies* and *progressive lung disease* and *stage four*. She couldn't tell if his eyebrows made him more attractive or less. Maybe he looked a little like Susan's husband, she thought, and then she decided that he did. Strong eyebrows like his were probably a sign (*Months,* he said, *or maybe just weeks*) that a man was going to be trouble, and she looked then at Bobby's eyebrows, also dark but soft on his face and turned up in concern. *There,* she thought, watching her son, *is a man who would never hurt anyone.*

He smiled at her—a grim, questioning smile—to feel out how she was taking all this, and she smiled back with a tight-lipped nod, not because the news required it, but because that acknowledgment and acceptance was what he needed from her then, and she could give it. And anyway, she was starting to feel the relief of a heavy secret finally freed. Of course she was dying. She had already known that. And now Bobby knew, too, so there was no need to hide anything anymore. And she had already found him, so what else was there to do but surrender?

In the driveway, Bobby came around to the passenger side, opened her door, and offered his arm.

"Ain't no sicker now than I was this morning," she said.

"I know," he replied, "but it's been a long day."

It had. And the knowledge of all the forces at work in her body to bring her down made independent movement both crucial and impossible. She leaned heavily on Bobby's arm all the way up the stairs and over to her chair. He straightened her new oxygen tube, switched on the television, and brought her an Ensure with a straw sticking out. He sat on the side of the couch nearest her, took her nebulizer and compressor out of its box, and began to piece it together.

On the screen, Tom Brokaw soberly dispersed the news. A young mother had thrown her children off the roof and then jumped to her death. A celebrity had gotten arrested for climbing the Golden Gate Bridge to protect a redwood reserve. Mother Teresa was also having problems breathing. News footage showed her with the telltale canister and hose that now matched Leotie's own. Leotie thought, *What a comparison.*

After the international headlines, the news circled back to the murdering mother. The camera zeroed in on the photograph of a fuzzy dark face turned sideways toward a child. The woman, Chicqua, was still in foster care at age sixteen when she'd given birth to twin boys. At twenty-one, her third child was born. Before the incident, she'd told her neighbors that she'd been fighting with her mother, who'd been in and out of jail all of Chicqua's life. "She raised herself," one of the neighbors reported, "along with her kids." And then she dressed her children in neatly pressed clothing and led them up their housing project's fourteen flights of stairs to the roof, where she threw them off and then jumped. Bobby had finished assembling the nebulizer and turned his attention to the story.

"That was you," Leotie said, and when Bobby shot her a questioning look, she nodded toward the screen. "That woman who killed herself. That was you, but you made different choices."

"Or maybe that was you," he said, "but you kept me alive."

Leotie shrugged. "Some people just go crazy. Ain't their fault." But Bobby's compliment hung in the air and warmed her. "I did," she said, and she closed her eyes and let that meager triumph sink down into her small, sore body.

"You need a treatment tonight," he said. "Don't sleep yet." He plugged the compressor in beside her chair, slipped her oxygen tube beneath her chin, and situated the mask over her nose and mouth. "Try to breathe as deeply as you can," he said, checking his watch.

On the TV, a cartoon turkey was dancing above a set of Thanksgiving poll results: "Only 33 percent of people surveyed plan to roast a turkey this Thursday."

When the treatment was finished and Bobby slid the mask up off her face, Leotie was ready with her question.

"Can we have a real Thanksgiving?" she asked. Her voice, after the treatment, rang louder and clearer. Her lungs, for once, lay calm. She felt heady and comfortable, like she could do anything if she could just stand up. She said, "I'll cook."

35

Before the state took Robert from his mother, a traditional Thanksgiving was something he'd only imagined with the help of TV shows and magazine photographs. Everywhere else, smiling families gathered around large tables in large houses with a large turkey and a lot of other foods. The only Thanksgiving Robert could remember with his mother involved a long line at the soup kitchen, where the odor of unwashed bodies overpowered the aromas of turkey and stuffing and pies. Robert had been following his mother to their table with his food when a drunk man stumbled into him. Robert's plate tipped out of his hands and landed facedown on the floor. He got back into line, but by the time he reached the food again, most of it had already been taken.

In foster care, Thanksgiving came to resemble Robert's ideas about what it was supposed to look like. But all the traditions surrounding it—the menus that had to be followed, the old recipes that could not be altered, the points of gratitude that had to be listed—all this privileged knowledge had repeated itself for years before Robert had shown up and would continue on for years after he had left. He felt the cajoling of those around him to smile more, to enjoy himself, and so he tried, but his trying only revealed how morose he felt. His disagreeableness embarrassed him, and the arrival of each November kicked off a growing sense of dread that only made things worse.

During Robert's first year of college, he confided to the resident assistant of his dormitory that he had nowhere to stay over the holidays. Instead of permitting Robert to remain in the building, as Robert had hoped, the RA spawned the idea that Robert should ride home with him to Ohio for all school breaks, an idea that Robert, after much protesting, had no choice but to accept. The following year, Robert requested the smallest and oldest dorm, off in a forgotten corner of campus. When holidays came, he packed his things and took the bus into town. Once he was sure that everyone else in the dorm had gone, he let himself back inside and subsisted on bulk cereal and cold hot dogs and Ramen noodles from his electric kettle and prayed to God for forgiveness.

In seminary, the food improved while the situation remained more or less the same. Robert let everyone think he had somewhere to go, and he made himself scarce until he would reasonably have returned. It was almost enjoyable to be so secretly alone, to feel as though he had gotten away with something.

Then Robert moved to Esau, and his holiday troubles returned. He arrived in September, and that November Florence Butts refused to take no for an answer. Christmas centered mostly around its morning, which happened in private, in single-family households. Easter centered around a church service.

But Thanksgiving centered entirely around a meal, and those gathered implied by their presence an intimacy with everyone else present. And Robert refused to accept that each November would compel him to imply that intimacy with Florence and Lester and Florence's unmarried sister, Millicent, for whom Florence harbored a secret and obvious hope. Millicent jawed on endlessly about how she shouldn't be eating all the food she was eating and about all the deals she'd found on napkins and footwear and light bulbs while Florence nodded approvingly and Lester interrupted occasionally with a question ("Fishing? Your kind go fishing, right?") entirely unrelated to anything else. And so it was that Robert threw in his lot with the Connor Center, a homeless shelter in Jefferson, and pledged his assistance, at the beginning of each November, in the preparation and distribution of the yearly feast.

When Leotie requested a Thanksgiving—a *real* Thanksgiving—Robert knew that, one, he did not want to do it, and, two, he had no choice. In all the chaos of the past few weeks, he'd forgotten to contact the shelter, so they would not be counting on his participation that year. He comforted himself with the fact that Thanksgiving was only three days off. It would be quick to come and even quicker to pass.

"So what do you mean by a real Thanksgiving?" he asked the next morning, after she'd finished her breathing treatment and he'd brought her a cup of coffee and another chocolate Ensure.

"You know," she said. Her voice was garbled but bright, excited. "All the food. Turkey, stuffing, sweet potatoes, cranberry sauce. We already got the family part. We could invite some friends, if you got 'em."

"I think the two of us will be enough."

"You got no one else you wanna ask?"

"Nope." Robert resented the implications of the question. He thought about the fifty-some people of his congregation. Was there anyone at all he would care to invite? Certainly not the deacons. The only two people he would actually consider were Ethel Grable, the organ player, who unfortunately came attached to her deacon husband, Cliff, and Chet Weller, who might obviously be spending the day with his wife and children. It ruffled Robert to think that everyone else in his entire congregation he would prefer to pass the holiday without.

"What about that Susan woman?" his mother said.

"Mother!" he cried.

She started to laugh, and her laughs turned into coughs. He had to lean her forward and thump her back until she stopped. She sat back up and laughed again, weakly. "That look on your face," she said. "But you never know. Her husband's got to be a workingman. Maybe he's got to work that day. She could say she was going to some event at the church. It's not like it wouldn't be true."

Robert took a deep breath to prevent himself from raising his voice. "The point is not to protect her from getting caught. The point is to fear not her husband but God, and to try and live a blameless life. Besides," he added, calming a little in response to his righteous indignation, "I wrote her a letter asking her not to come and visit me unless she tells me ahead of time so that I can be sure someone else is present."

Silence fell, and he felt assured that the subject was over. He bent down to the compressor and jiggled the hose. His mother said, "Well I'll be here."

Robert stood and fixed her with a withering glare. He found her leaning back expectantly, an impish smile twitching on her lips. "You're kidding," he said. "You *are* kidding." He shook his head and knelt back down. "You know, Mom, just because you're dying doesn't mean you can get anything you want."

"Robert Glory, is that a joke?"

"Well now I've got to keep up with you, apparently."

"I like this. A funny son and a real Thanksgiving. What more could an old woman ask for?"

"Another year?"

"Ah!" she cried. "You're killing me!" She gasped and snorted and then they began to laugh in earnest. This time, when the laughter turned to coughing, Robert grabbed a handful of tissues for Leotie to hold to her mouth as he leaned her forward and thumped away.

"We used to laugh a lot, didn't we?" he asked when her coughing had calmed. "I'd forgotten."

"Most times laughter was all we had." She fell back in her chair and gazed up at him. "Look at you, Bobby. You're the best sort of man, the best sort of son. I don't take credit for any of that. But I am so proud."

This was the gift of dying, Robert thought. As a pastor, he'd seen it many times before—the truth rises up through everything, honesty and gentleness prevail. He had felt guilty for how glad he'd been to have a seat in the room at those moments, when people spoke with the purest kindness he had heard and sat together in the silence of exhausted love and forgiveness, without distraction. He had always thought that if people could see what life came down to most of the time, they would live with much less fear. Even as a Baptist pastor, hell never felt like a possibility at the end. It seemed so plain that everyone was going back to God, repentant and grateful.

"I'm glad you came," he said to his mother, and he meant it.

36

On Tuesday evening at dinner, Susan asked, "So what are we going to do about Thanksgiving this year?"

Randy had been watching Susan closely ever since he'd intercepted the letter from the pastor. If anything, she seemed steadier, calmer, warmer toward him, more resolved. For dinner she had made spaghetti, which she knew he loved, and she'd called "hello" when he'd come in the door. At the beginning of dinner, she told Lukas to tell his daddy about the project he had finished at school that day. And then, Susan's question.

"Why are you asking me?" he said. "I don't even know when it is."

"Randy. It's two days from now."

"So?"

"So, it's a holiday. People have talked about it at work, haven't they?"

Randy hated it when Susan talked to him like this, like he had no idea what was going on, especially because most of the time he didn't. "Yeah, Suzy," he said. "We've been discussing our holiday plans over tea and crumpets."

"You haven't talked about it? At all?" Her voice was unbelieving.

"I'm sure it's the same as any other year. We can take the day off for holiday pay, or we can work it for time and a half."

"So?"

"So what?"

"So what are you going to do?" Susan's tone told Randy what an annoy-ance he was. His arms strained, and his chest tightened.

"Why's it matter?" he said.

She fixed him with a look. "Because I need to tell my mom who's going to be there. And I thought, if you weren't working, maybe we could invite your dad again."

"Great," Randy said.

"What?"

It was Randy's turn to send Susan a look.

"He's getting older, Randy. He's not going to be around forever."

"There's a tragedy."

"Randy, I'm trying to do the right thing. I don't want to spend time with him any more than you do. But he's lonely. He's old and alone, and he's lonely."

"He should be. He's earned it."

"Randy, are you going to work that day or not?"

"If those are my only options, I'll work."

"I didn't say we had to invite your dad."

"Hanging out with your dad's not much better."

"What choice do I have?" Susan pushed back her chair and began slam-ming plates into a stack. Willa jerked her head at Lukas, and they scam-pered off toward their bedroom.

A little flame of fear leaped up inside Randy and began to burn. Ever since he'd read the letter, he'd been afraid of Susan's anger, of going too far. He pushed down his fear and said what he most wanted to say anyway. "Well, I do have a choice. And I'm going to work."

RANDY HADN'T SEEN his dad since Thanksgiving the year before, when Susan's mom had run into him in the Henley Wal-Mart and invited him over. She hadn't told Susan, so Susan hadn't told Randy, and when they'd showed up for dinner, there he was, parked in one of the two living room armchairs with sunglasses on and a can of beer.

"Well hello, Ron," Susan had said. "What a surprise."

But Randy had said, "Why the hell are you here?"

There was a point in Randy's life when he had tried to fix things with his dad, back when Susan was pregnant with Willa and he'd just been hired on at the shop, from temp to full-time with benefits, and life had felt promising. He'd stopped by on a Thursday evening in late summer with a case of beer, and they'd sat out on the screened-in porch and drank a lot and talked a little. The crickets and cicadas and bullfrogs had made up for the lack of conversation, and the lightning bugs against the dimming horizon had given them something to watch. In the long, unspoken stretches, Randy had felt peace like a person sitting between them.

He had returned two or three more times, always on a Thursday and always with a case of beer, and then one night, just before Willa was born, his father asked, out of the blue, "You ever going back to college?"

"Probably not anytime soon," Randy said, taking care not to betray the feeling that rushed through him then. His father, who had always ridiculed his plans, was acknowledging them—asking about them, even. The question flooded his head along with the beer, and his eyes burned. "But someday," he said, believing it then more than he ever had.

"Yeah right," said his dad. "They've got you locked in for good now. You're going nowhere."

"You don't know that," Randy said, a little stunned by the sudden cruelty, though he also realized it shouldn't have been surprising.

"You thought you were such hot shit. A real scholar." His father laughed a little, but any pretense of polite conversation had already fallen away.

"I was smart. I could've done it."

"Maybe, maybe not. But the point is, you didn't."

Randy stood, dimly aware of his anger catching up to his shock. It arrived in his fist as it smashed against the side of his father's face.

"Keep the beer," Randy said, as his father gripped his jaw and staggered to his feet. "You need it. Fucking drunk. You fucking asshole drunk fuck." The words hurt to say them. They were not the words he wanted to say. He left before his anger could melt into the terror of sadness, and he never went back.

He didn't tell Susan about the fight. By the time he arrived home, she was already asleep, her face beaded with sweat, her body propped into comfort with all the pillows in the house and covered with a single sheet. She had fallen asleep with her exposed arm hugging her belly and her forehead creased in concentration. He loved her so much at that moment that he could almost understand the tragedy of his father's loss and the jealousy he must have felt in looking at his son, who still had his wife and a future that included her.

And so he'd kept the fight to himself. He didn't want to burden Susan any more than she already was in her pregnant state, but he also knew that his father was broken beyond repair, and that keeping the fight from Susan would keep the old man from being cut off completely from the only family he had.

Recalling this, Randy began to regret telling Susan he'd work Thanksgiving. Of course he didn't want to work Thanksgiving. He got six paid holidays a year and two weeks of vacation, which he hadn't taken in years because he could work it instead for time and a half, and he'd discovered, during a one-week camping trip back when Lukas was three and Willa was six, that the only thing worse than working was not working. He'd built up fire after fire and split too much wood and then just sat there blistering under the sun and slapping at mosquitoes while Susan cooked and washed up and slathered the kids with sunscreen and took them off swimming or hiking. A few times he tagged along, tried to participate, but it was like he didn't know how. His trying only proved how useless he was, apart from earning enough money to keep them all afloat. Working sucked, but not working sucked even worse.

That night, after the Thanksgiving argument, when he'd sunk into his chair in front of the TV, Willa brought her book into the living room and sat near him on the couch. He craned around to look at her and she sent him a little smile, and he surprised himself by reaching back and squeezing her knee.

What if he started small, he thought. What if he took a couple of extra days off around Christmas and took the kids out sledding, all by himself? What if he started giving Susan some breaks? As the TV blared on, these thoughts became plans, and these plans built themselves up into evidence of how much he had changed already, of how far he was willing to go—so much farther than his own father, who had broken Randy's nose twice with his fist, who had once whipped him with a belt until his back bled.

37

Despite Randy's decision to work that day, Susan had still planned to spend Thanksgiving at her parents' house, as always, until her mother called Wednesday morning and demanded to know, in her wounded way, who all was coming and what Susan planned to bring.

"If I've called you once, I've called you a thousand times," she said, after Susan said hello.

Susan knew that her mother had called exactly twice because both times she had left messages that Susan deleted as soon as she identified the source of nasal consternation coming from the machine's speaker. *Susan. This is your mother.*

Now Susan said, "Yes, Mom?" in a more exhausted voice than she'd intended.

"Well don't let *me* interrupt you. I'm just trying to feed your family a holiday meal tomorrow, which would be a darn sight easier if you returned my phone calls. I don't suppose you received my messages."

"Sorry, Mom, what did you need to know?" Susan reached up and pressed the V of tension between her eyebrows.

"Exactly what I already said. I need to find out how many mouths I'll be feeding tomorrow and whether or not I'm to expect any help." When Susan did not immediately respond, she went on. "I was *going* to ask that you take over the pies as well as the green bean casserole. I figured you could do more now that Lukas is in school. But apparently you've become so busy that you can't even answer the phone, so what do I know?"

Susan's mind grasped feebly for something pacifying to say, but she could not bring herself either to lie or to apologize, and so she came up with nothing.

Maybe she didn't want the holiday enough to fight for it. Maybe she didn't want it at all. She had spent every Thanksgiving of her life—*every one*—with her parents. Had she ever enjoyed it? Even once? She remembered the first time she'd brought Randy to one. He and Susan's father had hit it off. Afterward, Randy had kept jerking his shirt collar straight and thrusting out his chin so that his Adam's apple bulged and bobbed. "Think your old man liked me?" he kept asking, even though he already knew the answer. "I did pretty good, huh?"

Susan had been terrified that Randy and her father would not get along, and then she'd felt the birth of a different unease when they did. As she and her mother sealed the leftover casseroles and stuffings into Tupperware and smothered the still-steaming turkey in Ziplocs, their men sat in the living room in the two matching armchairs, each making a show of enjoying the game, their feet propped up on the ottomans. (She could see their feet if she leaned over the counter, white-socked and somehow touchingly vulnerable.)

She did not enjoy football, she reminded herself, so why should she resent this? It made sense, she told herself, with both of them working as hard as they did, that they should get holidays off.

But Susan worked second shift cleaning the community college buildings after her morning classes, and that week she had lugged ingredients over to Randy's apartment and each night baked a different pie.

But she'd liked it, she argued back. She enjoyed baking.

Randy had sat at the dining room table with his homework spread out in front of him. "Look at you," he'd said. "Little Suzy Homemaker. Aren't you adorable." He'd walked over and pressed his groin into the small of her back, but she swatted him away.

"Do you want a real Thanksgiving or not?" she asked.

"You can buy pies at the store, you know. No need to go through all this trouble. Not when Stan the Man is awake."

Stan the Man was Randy's penis.

"Store-bought is not the same, and you know it," she said. "Stan the Man can wait."

But as it turned out, Stan the Man could not wait, and by the time Susan finished the pie—blueberry with zested lemon, her father's favorite—it was well after midnight, and she overslept the following morning and missed two of her final classes before the break.

After that Thanksgiving, more than half of each of her pies still remained, and her first thought was how pointless her efforts had been—there *were* pies, always, for sale at the store. But her second thought, peeking again at the socked feet sticking up from the ottomans, was that, as much as Randy scorned her efforts, and as much as her father had always rolled his eyes at her mother's insistences, it was women who built the stage where men performed all the days of their lives, just as women built men's lives at the beginnings, before they could walk or talk or feed themselves or contain their bodily fluids at will. Was that why men seemed so often to detest women? Because women had attended them in their helplessness, borne witness to their fundamental weakness, and carried forth within them that unremovable knowledge? Even Susan's mother had one day let slip the secret. "Men," she'd said. "They are the weak ones. If only because they can't stand to let themselves see it."

Susan had understood, even before she and Randy had married, that it was really men who needed the protecting. She knew her corroboration to be not noble but inane, and she also knew that she had slipped unwittingly into the age-old charade and no matter which man she chose, she could not break from her destined role any more than a mouse could marry a bird.

Now, on the other end of the phone, her mother was speaking on and on of Thanksgiving in strident aggravation, her breath coming between phrases in little asthmatic gasps. Susan felt a surge of pity for her. No wonder guilt trips and passive aggression had become her only weapons.

"I guess I'm to do all the talking, too," she said, huffing. "I have half a mind to cancel Thanksgiving altogether. You'd probably appreciate it, what with your busy schedule and all."

Susan sensed her chance and pounced. "You know," she said, trying to sound regretful, "that would actually be a relief to me. Randy has to work anyway, and Thanksgiving's tomorrow, and I don't even have half the ingredients I'd need. The grocery store will be a nightmare today."

"Susan!" her mother cried. "Your father will be devastated."

"Mom. He's always talking about how much he hates holidays."

"To say nothing of how I'll feel."

"It was your idea, Mom."

"*I* was thinking only of *you*," her mother retorted. "Which is one thing we have in common, apparently. Goodbye, Susan. Maybe if we're lucky we'll see you and the kids at Christmas."

"Mom," Susan said, but the phone clicked off, and the line went dead. Susan pressed the phone off, then on. She waited for the dial tone and began to dial her parents' number. She could imagine her mother bustling huffily around the kitchen, glancing every now and again at the phone, softening herself to receive Susan's inevitable apology. She reached the last digit and stopped.

No.

Susan was sick of her mother, and she was sick of her father. Her father's small digs, her mother's constant lassoing of accidental injuries. It was like she was always throwing out her limbs and waiting for someone to step on them. Susan pressed the phone off. She would not call. And if her mother called back, she steeled herself, she would not answer. Tomorrow for lunch she would take the kids to China Garden, and then maybe they'd go home and play in the snow, or watch a movie together, or find a book that they all three wanted to read. The prospect of the day filled itself in like a coloring page. It would be a day like the days the three of them used to have, back when she'd had both of them all to herself. Before Willa had started school. Before she'd lost that era of her life (she could see it now, though she could not see it then) that she'd spend the rest of her years pining for.

When the phone finally did ring, she resolutely did not answer it, but when it rang again, she began to doubt herself. A minute later, when it rang the third time, she decided to answer only to tell her mother, firmly, that she, Susan, was simply in a place where celebration that year felt like a burden rather than a joy and she hoped that her mother would understand.

She answered the phone with, "Sorry, Mom. I just can't do it this year."
But an unfamiliar voice replied, rasping and urgent.

"Susan? Susan Shearer? Leotie Glory here, the pastor's mother. I've got to make this quick, so listen up."

38

By the time Willa woke on Thanksgiving morning, her father had already left for work. Her brother was hanging upside down over the end of the couch with the top of his head on the carpet, singing songs to himself. Her mother was in the kitchen squeezing pieces of dough into a ball. She thumped the dough down and slapped its sides and spun it over and thumped it again. Then she picked up her rolling pin by one handle and began to beat the ball down flat. The way she moved her arms was big and wild and even a little scary.

"What are you making?" Willa asked, squinting up at her mother. Beneath streaks of flour, her mother's face shone bright pink. Her eyes opened so wide that she looked surprised. She was happy. Too happy.

"A pie!" she called above the thumping of the rolling pin.

"For Grandma's?"

"Nope," she said. She stopped thumping the dough, but her voice stayed loud. "We're going somewhere new for Thanksgiving." The hint of a secret signaled to Willa that she wouldn't like the news.

"I'm hungry," Willa said. Her mother wanted her to ask where, and Willa was not going to do it.

"Don't you want to know where we're going?"

"Can I have some cereal?"

"Really, Willa," her mother said. She reached up into the cupboard and pulled down the giant bag of HappyO's. Willa got a bowl and spoon and carried the milk over from the fridge. She climbed up onto a stool. Lukas wandered into the kitchen and climbed up beside her.

"I know where we're going, I know where we're going," he sang in his most annoying voice.

"Shut up."

"Willa!" Her mother was holding a jar of canned peaches over a bowl. They dropped all at once with a loud squelching sound.

"I don't care where we're going," Willa said, a little afraid of her own bravery. "I want to go to Grandma's." The smell of the peaches came across the counter, sweet enough to make you sick. "Why aren't we going to Grandma's?"

Her mother shook some sugar into the bowl and dug in her hands. The peaches made loud sucking sounds as she squeezed them around. Her shoulders softened. "I'm sorry that you're disappointed," she said. Her mother should have scolded her. Why wasn't she scolding her? "Grandma canceled this year. But we did receive an invitation somewhere else." Her mother's eyes went sideways and then down. Now she was paying too much attention to the peaches, to her hands, to everything else.

"Where?" Willa asked, and then kicked herself for asking. "Are we going to surprise Dad at work?"

"No, Willa," her mother said, pretending to be sorry. Then she took a deep breath and pulled her mouth up in a smile. "We're going to a celebration at the church."

"At the church? The new church? With other people from the church?"

"Yes! I'm not sure who else will be there, but the pastor's mother called to say they're trying something new, inviting all the families. So there should be kids there for you and Lukas to play with."

"Are you *sure* there will be kids?"

"No, I'm not *sure*. I don't have their guest list. I only know that other kids were invited."

"What if no one else shows up?"

"Of course other people will show up."

"But what if they don't?"

"Listen." Her mother glanced at Lukas to make sure he wasn't listening too closely and then lowered her voice. "The pastor's mother doesn't have long to live, and she has requested a real Thanksgiving, and she has asked us to be there, along with several other families."

"But she doesn't even know us."

"Willa." Her mother shot her a glare before tipping the snotty peaches into the pie crust. She went on, still whispering: "I'm not going to question the way a dying woman chooses to spend her final Thanksgiving. Her invitation is good enough for me, and it ought to be good enough for you, too."

"It's good enough for me," said Lukas, who, despite their mother's whispering, had apparently been listening. His voice was still singsong and whiny.

Willa kicked at Lukas and missed. Her foot banged against the wall.

"Mom!" he wailed. "Willa tried to kick me!"

"Enough!" their mother called over the noise. "Willa, I suggest a change of attitude. This Thanksgiving can go one of two ways, and the choice is up to you."

"It's the pastor," Willa said, and her mother froze over the pie, the top crust hanging down from her hands like a wet towel. "That's why his mom called and why you said yes. Because you're in love with each other." Willa had overheard enough conversations between her parents to collect the pieces, but she hadn't put them together until she said the words out loud. That explained everything else, too—her father's growing anger, her mother's dreaminess and distance.

Her mom was staring open-mouthed at Willa, one hand pressed to her chest. "What . . . on . . . *earth?*" she said with fake slowness. But her pretending couldn't throw Willa off the truth. Willa had hit the nail on the head, as her teacher liked to say.

"It's true," she said, because her mother's reaction proved it. She slid off her stool, left her breakfast behind. Her mother was speaking loudly now, but Willa didn't bother to listen. She walked to her bed and fell forward onto the mattress. She had a book and a blanket and a cup of water from the night before, and she was going to stay right there reading until her mother forced her to get dressed and go. Her father would be so proud of her for refusing, for defending him.

Willa opened her book, one in a series of mysteries that she enjoyed, but she kept reading the same words over and over while her mind wandered everywhere else. To her father, hard at work on a holiday. To her mother rattling around in the bathroom, curling her hair, Willa imagined, and painting her face—so wrong of her. Wrong, wrong, wrong. To her grandma and grandpa, who, she was certain, had not canceled Thanksgiving but who were sitting disappointed in their quiet house on the couch near the sunporch, where she and Lukas could play for hours, turning the wicker furniture upside down to make forts and tunnels. To her grandmother's food, the stuffing and the cranberries and the toasted sugary nuts.

All of this Willa was missing just so her mother could go spend Thanksgiving with the pastor. Willa's mother probably thought he was handsome. He didn't have her father's messy hair with the bald spot in back or his pillow-shaped stomach that sometimes looked like he had a little baby in there. The pastor's mother she remembered, too, having seen her in church. She looked like a witch from a storybook—old and crooked and up to something.

Willa knew, even as she thought these thoughts, how unfair they were, how mean. But then she thought of her father, working away. She had seen factory workers once on a television show. "On the line" meant that they actually stood in a line, just like in school. Only they stood in the same line all day, in the same exact place, and did the same thing over and over again. That was how Willa imagined her father when she imagined him working. Drilling in the same screw over and over and wishing the line would go somewhere. Once Willa had told him that she wanted to work in a factory, too, when she grew up, and his face twisted. She couldn't tell if he was angry or scared. "No you don't," he said. "Do anything else before you do that." No wonder he was angry sometimes. No wonder he was sad.

Willa stayed in bed with her book until her mother marched into her room hours later (or at least it seemed like hours) and pulled a jumper that Willa hated out of the closet. She threw it on the bed.

"We're leaving in thirty minutes," she said. "I suggest you start getting ready."

Willa lay there until her mother left the room. Then she threw the jumper on the floor and began riffling through her dresser drawers for her favorite sweater, her favorite ripped jeans.

She was sick of being the good girl, the one who always did as she was told. Not today. Today, Willa would make her mother pay for this.

39

By the time Thanksgiving morning rolled around, Leotie had come to an understanding of her fate. Dying was not how she'd expected it to be. In most ways, it was just like living. There was happy, and there was sad. There was pain, and then there were times that weren't so painful. There were rivers of fear, and occasional waves—giant, crashing waves that left her cold and shaking—but there was relief, too, that she didn't have to keep herself going anymore. Old worries would come back to her, and she'd realize she could let them go. Money—no need for it. Her teeth rotting out—so what. She would eat on them for a little longer, and then she wouldn't. There was a deep relief in giving up. She hadn't expected that.

Mostly, Leotie veered back and forth between profound exhaustion and mind-bending highs. And it was in the middle of one of the highs that Leotie turned her whole self toward her son. She would not leave him all alone, not if she could help it. Bobby was her greatest triumph and also her greatest regret. A triumph because he was good—purely and generously good—and smart and handsome and responsible and wise. A regret because he had no one to share his life, and this, she knew, was the direct effect of her absence, her failure to pull herself together. She had taught him that those he loved would fail him, that no one would protect him from the world besides himself. And Leotie only had months, or maybe just weeks, to try and set that right.

It was in this storm of feeling that Leotie called Susan. Bobby had scrambled her eggs and toasted her bread and given her her breathing treatment and her morning medicine. He had settled her in her favorite armchair with her coffee and can of Ensure and then left for the grocery store with the list she'd written down for the following day's feast.

It must have been the prospect of leaving life that made it suddenly so rich. Sometimes the plainest moments became unbearably beautiful, like this one, seated in a soft armchair in a quiet house, listening to the silence and all of its interruptions—the heat hissing in the radiator and the distant clicks and shifts of the old house and the small rushes of water, somewhere, through a pipe. Out the window, snow had eclipsed the field and trees except for the undersides of the pine boughs, and if it weren't for the pines, the white of the snowy field might have blended seamlessly with the cloud white of the sky. Beside her, on a TV tray, her waiting coffee sent up long, wet ribbons of steam, and the prospect of sipping it alongside the cool, chocolate richness of her other waiting drink roused a sleeping excitement in her stomach.

Through the fractured distance of years, she recalled a similar excitement. Her past had shattered long ago, and now she sifted through the shards. Christmas as a child, that's what it felt like. Before she'd learned to hate her mother and their lives together, before she'd begun to plot her escape. Christmas in that old trailer in Oklahoma, with the bent, balding fir tree that her mother had salvaged from somewhere and three clumsily wrapped presents below that her mother had said were for her.

In her memory, it was the only Christmas her mother had given her presents. Leotie forgot what the two smaller ones had been, but the biggest contained a large baby doll, peach-skinned and blue-eyed and golden-haired and entirely new, with eyes that slid shut when you laid her down. Leotie still could not imagine how her mother had gotten ahold of it. For a while, Leotie decided she had stolen it. But maybe her mother had found it somewhere. Maybe it had been a gift from a mysterious stranger. Or maybe, that one time, her mother had scrimped and saved and simply given Leotie an honest-to-goodness Christmas.

Leotie had always given Bobby a real Christmas, but she'd had to rely on charity to make it happen. The year that stuck out most in her mind was the year she'd signed them up for the Christmas program at the shelter where they sometimes ate. Every Friday in December, they'd serve a holiday dessert and provide an activity and then, on the Friday before Christmas, a small sack of presents from Santa.

The desserts were good, and the workers were nice, though they were nice in that syrupy, too-nice way that let you know they were doing you a favor and feeling really good about themselves in the process. The activity lady had put up a tree with decorations and made stockings for each kid with their name scrolled across the top in red glitter. One night she'd set the parents up with paper and stickers and crayons and asked them to help their kids write letters to Santa. Bobby wanted a Lite-Brite and a loom kit that he could use to make pot holders. Girlie gifts. Leotie'd been embarrassed.

"Don't you want some Hot Wheels?" she'd asked. They'd seen the commercials on TV. "Or some action figures?"

The activity lady interrupted. She thought a Lite-Brite and a loom sounded like fine ideas.

That was when Leotie had lost it. She didn't need no goddamn stranger telling her how to raise her kid and she knew her son better than some charity lady and if the woman wanted to interfere so much, why didn't she just drop a brat of her own to boss around and on and on and on. The lady just stood there, insufferably polite, saying things like, "I'm sorry if it sounded—" and "I didn't mean to imply that—" and "No, I don't know your son as well as you do."

Leotie's memories returned so clearly she had to wonder if her mind was making things up. She remembered the woman's exact words—she could hear them. She remembered how the woman twisted her gold curls up into a big banana clip and wore dark purple lipstick that wouldn't have worked on anyone else. Her name was Janis. She was about Leotie's age. She was beautiful, sweetly so, with happy, crinkly eyes and a straight, white smile, the kind that cost a small fortune. Leotie could remember thinking that Janis would have made a better mother. She could also remember the thoughts she couldn't put words to at the time—that it was all well and good for a boy to be a sissy in a softer world, but in their world, Bobby would get eaten alive.

Later that night, back at the trailer, Leotie found Bobby crying in the bathroom. He'd been six or seven, and it had damn near broken her heart wide open to find him hiding in a corner of the shower, the curtain pulled closed, sobbing silently to himself.

"Oh God, I shouldn't have done that," she said. At least she'd said that. "I'm sorry, Bobby. We can go back."

But Bobby was too ashamed to go back. So the following Friday she left him with a neighbor and rode the bus out to say sorry to Janis and to tell her that a loom and a Lite-Brite would do just fine, thanks. And that Christmas Bobby woke to two new presents, each of which he wanted.

Too many sins to confess. And too few virtues to make up for them. But this fresh morning she was alive in her son's warm house, with Thanksgiving still to come and maybe, if she was lucky, Christmas, too. She needed to give Bobby something that could begin to make up, if only a little, for everything. And in Leotie's heightened state of feeling, she seized on Susan.

"Absolutely not," he had said when she pressed him again.

But Bobby was going to go on living, and she was not, and this gave Leotie an extravagance of freedom. She'd always skirted social rules, and now she could ignore them completely. What mattered was leaving her son a better life than the one he had now. The problem of the husband, Leotie figured, would work itself out. If he was going to be around that day, Susan would surely decline. And if he happened to be busy? Well, then, he didn't have to know about it. Which was why it made perfect sense for Leotie to start at the top of the list and dial every Shearer in the phonebook, since each was followed only by the first names of the men. Just as she was beginning to fear that Susan had an unlisted number, or that Bobby would return before she called it, she arrived at *Shearer, Randall J.*

Leotie had to lie a tad—just a little white lie, she told herself—to get Susan to come. Everyone from the church had been invited, Leotie had told her, though she couldn't say yet who all would be coming. She was hoping for a crowd.

Of course, Leotie hadn't invited anyone else. No one else was able to make it at such short notice, that's what she'd say.

Surprisingly, apart from this fib, Susan required little convincing, which told Leotie she'd made the right choice. After Susan had been assured that her and her children's presence was welcome, she replied, "Well then, yes, thank you. I think we will come. When should we be there? What should we bring?"

It wasn't until the following day, Thanksgiving Day, that Leotie began to question herself. Bobby kept asking why they had to cook so much food. When she handed over the bowl of sweet potatoes to peel and chop, he said, "Six sweet potatoes? How many people are you planning to feed, anyway?"

Leotie laughed weakly and then began to worry. She wasn't planning on telling him ahead of time. She was planning to wait until the doorbell rang, and then, after the initial surprise had faded, she was sure that things would work themselves out. Probably he'd be upset with her. Maybe Susan would be, too. But all of that hardly mattered. As of right then, she was only leaving one good thing behind her. If this worked, her legacy doubled. All of those years she'd kept herself alive after Bobby had gone—suddenly, all of those years would count.

In Leotie's state, cooking proved much harder than she'd expected. For long stretches of time, she ended up slumped at the dining room table, feebly directing Bobby through the steps. Finally, the foiled turkey rested on the counter, the canned cranberry sauce lay smashed against the bottom of a bowl, and the stuffing and sweet potatoes were crusting over in the oven. Robert pulled two plates from the cupboard.

"Well, dear mother, shall I set the table for our feast?"

As if on cue, the sound of footsteps drifted down the hall, of shoes shuffling across the front stoop. A boy laughed, a woman's voice answered, and the doorbell, finally, rang.

40

It took less than a minute for Robert to piece together exactly what had happened. At the sound of the doorbell, his mother shot to her feet and staggered toward the door with suspicious speed.

"I'll get it," she huffed over her shoulder. "You stay there."

When she opened the door, her words drifted back to the kitchen with a draft of winter wind. "So glad you could make it. We were just setting the table. Everything's ready. Been cooking up a storm all day. Come in, come in. Oh, just leave those anywhere you like."

She was playing some strange role, Robert thought. The role of a grandmother in the movies, one who had spent her whole life cooking and cleaning and hosting holidays in the same farmhouse. This observation distracted him until his mind sparked at the answering voice, which he placed immediately. He leaned back onto the counter and dropped his face into his hands.

Susan.

His mother had invited Susan.

And Susan had agreed to come.

So Susan must think Robert had approved of these plans.

Which meant that Robert could betray his surprise, or he could let all of his annoyance go and decide to play along.

In the entryway, Leotie was asking the children's names.

"Go on," Susan's voice said.

"Are you a witch?" the boy's voice asked. "You look like a witch." Susan's voice lowered to a hissing whisper, and Leotie laughed.

In the kitchen, Robert rubbed at his temples. It was his mother's fault. She had orchestrated all this, and so she could deal with the consequences. He took a deep breath and let it all out. It was her last Thanksgiving, he reminded himself. Her very last one. He slapped his thighs and nodded once to himself and moved toward the front door.

"Welcome," he called as he stepped down the hall. His mother turned toward him with a guilty wince, which he met with a look he hoped said, *We'll discuss this later.* Then he turned toward their guests with a smile. "Hello Susan," he said with a nod.

She looked fresh and pretty—too pretty. She had left her hair down so that it spilled over her shoulders in a profusion of soft curls. She had also worn makeup, an affect he had not noticed before. Her lips looked pinker than usual, and her eyelids shimmered. He purposely had to move his gaze down to the children. The boy had already thrown off his coat and was swinging a plastic box from side to side. "I brought Legos!" he said. The girl still wore her coat and boots. She kept her arms wrapped tightly around herself and scowled at the floor.

"It's Lukas, right?" he asked. "And Willa?"

Lukas said, "Yep," his eyes big and happy. Willa's demeanor did not change.

"Where is everyone else?" asked the girl.

"Wouldn't you know it," said Leotie, "no one else could make it on such short notice. Looks like it'll just be the five of us."

At that, Robert understood that his mother hadn't invited anyone else but that she'd told Susan she had and that he'd have to pretend all that was his idea, too.

"Is that okay with you, Willa?" he asked, trying to elicit some conciliation from the child, who in response tightened her arms around herself and turned her head pointedly away from him.

"Willa," Susan said, and Robert couldn't tell if her tone betrayed warning or surprise. "I'm sorry." Susan cast Robert and Leotie an apologetic glance. "Today's been a little challenging for some of us."

She reached over and fumbled for the zipper at the neck of Willa's coat, and Willa jerked away. A scarlet flush spread up from Susan's neck and into her cheeks. Robert could not recall a time when he had felt so supremely uncomfortable.

"We'll give you a minute," Robert said, with a pointed look at his mother, who followed him back into the kitchen. When they were hidden from view, he turned to her. *What were you thinking?* he mouthed before opening the cupboard and pulling down three extra plates.

The meal began so awkwardly that its effect on Robert felt almost like physical pain. Willa had at last been prevailed upon to take off her boots and to come and sit down, though she refused to remove her coat or unclench her arms or even to look at anyone. Susan's embarrassment was just as palpable as Willa's anger. She seemed a few times on the brink of speaking, but she would duck her chin before she could get any words out. Lukas chattered away directly to Robert about subjects that Robert somehow could not fathom, and he filled the other stretches with singing and nonsense rhyming words, which only served to underscore the silence that met his babbling.

Once the table had been set and the side dishes had all been placed in the center, Robert carried the turkey to the table, peeled back the foil, and proceeded to carve. The carving knife, which Robert could not remember ever using before, scratched pointlessly across the tough skin of the bird. He finally had to use three different knives to get at the meat. Anyone walking in on the scene would have considered this some typical holiday tableau: the man wielding his knife—or, in Robert's case, knives—over the meat while the gathered family looked on in anticipation. The fact that he had seen this scene before, and that he had fantasized about such scenes himself, only made his current predicament more pitiful. He had a sudden and terrible urge to cry as he hacked away at the carcass, coming up against knot after tendon after bone, stacking up a sad heap of crooked chunks of meat. But he swallowed hard and summoned the preacher within himself, the unflappable public speaker, and he let the noise of his feelings go and brought his focus to the task at hand. Finally he found he had cut enough meat to justify passing the platter once around the table.

At last, all of the dishes had been passed and everyone had taken what they wanted, except for Willa, whose plate had been filled by Susan. Lukas finally fell to eating, and a silence descended in which Robert felt uncomfortable even to chew. He was sure he had never encountered a silence so unforgivingly silent. It amplified each sound that each body made. Susan and Leotie chewed as quietly as possible, their eyes cast down on their plates. Lukas chewed with his mouth open. Willa sat sideways in her chair and tapped the tip of her foot against the floor. She had refrained from touching her food at all, so far as Robert had witnessed, or even looking at it.

Robert turned to Leotie, who was seated beside him and had barely spoken at all since her illicit guests had arrived. He nodded toward her ever so slightly, hoping that this subtle movement might encourage her to say something, or, failing that, might emphasize how utterly her scheming had failed. But she looked so slight and sad sitting there, slurping small bites of soft food. He could not bring himself to guilt her. She had tried, and she had failed. But she had tried. And she had done so for him.

"So," he said, and across the table Susan jumped a little. "I thought we might go around the table and say a few of the things we're thankful for."

Willa sighed loudly. Susan prodded her with her elbow. "I think that sounds like a wonderful idea," she said, but Robert couldn't tell if Susan actually thought the idea was wonderful or if she spoke more as a chastisement to Willa's rude response.

"I'll start!" shouted Lukas. His mouth was full. He continued speaking without swallowing. Tiny flakes of food flew from his lips. "I'm thankful for my mom and my dad and my sister and my dog and my butthole."

"You don't have a dog," Willa said in a withering voice.

"But I do have a butthole!" Lukas sang, and he launched into a fit of giggles.

Robert smiled weakly and braved a glance at Susan, who was resting her forehead on one hand in a gesture of defeat. Lukas continued to giggle wildly.

"Okay, that's enough," Leotie said, and Lukas fell silent. It must have been her appearance, combined with the roughness of her voice, Robert thought, that made Lukas afraid of her. "My turn," she said.

Robert sensed the attention of the table turning toward her. Even Willa shifted a little in her seat.

"I'm thankful for my son here, who's taking care of me even though I done nothing to deserve it." She reached over and squeezed his hand almost bashfully, without looking up at him. "And I'm thankful that ya'll are here, too, even if maybe some of you don't want to be. And I'm thankful that after all these years, I'm finally getting a real Thanksgiving." Silence filled the room again after she finished speaking, but this silence felt less awkward. Robert pulled his hand from his mother's grasp and settled it over top of hers.

"Well," he said, turning toward her, "I'm thankful that you came, Mom. And I'm also thankful that you're all here, reluctant parties included. And I'm thankful that my mother's last Thanksgiving can be a real one, with the turkey and the stuffing and all the awkward family interactions that usually mark this day." He spoke without first thinking through what he was going to say. When he'd accidentally mentioned that this Thanksgiving would be Leotie's last, he halfheartedly tried to follow it up with a joke, which, judging by the looks on everyone's faces, had not come across as such.

"Last Thanksgiving?" asked Lukas. "Why is it going to be her last Thanksgiving?"

The adults exchanged glances.

"Sorry," Robert said.

"I'm sick," said Leotie.

"I get sick sometimes," Lukas said.

Leotie cleared her throat. "Not sick like this."

Robert grimaced at Susan. "Your turn," he said.

"So you're going to die?" Lukas asked. "Before Thanksgiving happens again?" He sounded suddenly mournful. He was looking at Leotie with wet, trembly eyes.

"Yes," she said. "And that's okay. I've lived a long life. And if it isn't as long as I'd like it to be, well . . ."

Even Robert could tell that Lukas's silence signaled confusion rather than satisfaction.

Susan straightened in her chair. "My turn," she said. She seemed to be adopting the same damage-control mentality as Robert's own. "I'm thankful, too, to be here. And I'm thankful for all of this delicious food that I didn't have to prepare. And I'm thankful for my kids, even if they might not feel the same way at the moment—"

"What about Dad?" Willa said.

"Willa," Susan said in a warning voice.

But Willa continued. "Aren't you thankful for him?" she asked. "Because I'm thankful for him. And I'm thankful for how hard he works for our family. And I wish he were here right now."

"I'm sorry," Susan said, more to Leotie than to Robert. "We seem to be processing some big feelings today."

"Ain't nothing wrong with being thankful for a dad that works hard," Leotie said.

"No," Robert said, grasping toward Leotie's optimism. "That's a wonderful thing to be thankful for, Willa."

Willa narrowed her eyes at him. He should not have tried to pacify her, he realized. She did not want to be pacified. She wanted, just as he had wanted at her age, to have a say in the things that directly affected her life.

"My mom's not thankful, though," she said. "My mom's glad he had to work today. I can tell."

"Willa," said Susan again, the warning rising in her voice.

"What?" Willa spun around in her seat and faced her mother head-on. "That's not true? You're not happy that you get to spend Thanksgiving with your new pastor boyfriend instead?"

"Willa!" Susan cried out in disbelief, beet-faced with shock. She appeared unable to say anything more. It was clear in Willa's expression of cruel satisfaction that the girl had been secreting the phrase away like a grenade, waiting for the moment of greatest impact. Robert's mind fumbled for anything he could say to redeem the situation. Denial would give the accusation credence somehow, and he could, of course, accept no fraction of the girl's pronouncement. "It sounds like," he began, a phrase to fill the space, though he had no idea of how he would finish it. "Well, it sounds like—" he began again.

His mother interrupted him. "It's my fault," she said. "Young lady, I called and invited your mother. I'd met her before, and I liked her, and I thought it would be nice to have you kids along. And Bobby here didn't even know what I was up to. This was all a surprise to him."

Susan turned her shocked face to Robert. "Really?" she asked. To Leotie she said, "But you said this was a church celebration." Her look shuttled back and forth between them. "That you'd invited everyone."

Leotie lowered her head contritely down and shook it.

"So you've just been pretending," Susan said to Robert, "that this isn't a surprise."

Robert drew in his lips and nodded.

"You thought he wanted us here," Willa said, and Robert watched her face twist as she turned the knife. "But he didn't."

Susan closed her eyes and rested her face in her hands. Still, Robert couldn't bring himself to fault the child. She was astute enough to spy out the subtleties he'd hoped were hidden, but young enough to lift loyalty above all. It was almost commendable, in a way.

Leotie stood suddenly. "Girl," she said. "Willa girl. Come with me."

Willa shrank back and stared from Leotie to Robert and back to Leotie again. She'd seemed so vindictive a moment before, but that brief demeanor had dropped away, leaving a scared little girl with an active brain who'd been tasked with a life too hard for her to handle at the moment.

"Come on," Leotie said. "I'm not gonna hurt you. We're just going to go and have a little chat." And she hobbled out into the living room. Willa glanced at her mother, still holding her face in her hands, then slid from her seat and followed.

"I'm sorry," Robert said to Susan. "I thought it would be better just to pretend."

"What are you pretending?" Lukas asked.

"That I knew," Robert said.

"Knew what?"

Susan dropped her hands and adopted the grim expression of one resigned to her fate. "He's pretending," she said, "that he wanted us here."

"Can I be done?" Lukas said.

Susan looked at the mounds of food still left on Lukas's plate, then waved her hand. "Go ahead," she said. The boy hopped down from his chair and scurried off.

"I'm sorry," said Robert. "For all of this. I *am* glad you're here."

Susan shot him a skeptical look.

"And I'm sorry about the letter," he said. He waited, but she didn't respond. "The deacons," he went on, "had encouraged me not to meet alone with women, and especially as an unmarried man, I have upheld that practice. Until you came and found me that morning."

"I didn't come to you on purpose."

"No. I know."

Out in the living room, Lukas whispered something, and Leotie laughed.

"I thought we were friends," Susan said. "I don't even know that I have friends anymore. That's what I thought we were. Are you not allowed to be friends with a woman?"

Susan's question filled Robert with a keen sense of shame. He saw himself then as Susan might see him—as a child who'd been given instructions for good behavior, the same child who would have done anything his foster parents had asked of him. And here he was, still operating under a set of edicts arbitrary and unreal, simply in the hopes of being accepted as someone good, someone who belonged.

"I like you," Robert said.

"I like you, too," Susan said with a little laugh. At last her face had opened, and she was smiling. "You're supposed to like your friends."

"Not this much," Robert said. "Not like this."

He watched her gaze drop. She took a deep breath.

"Oh," she said.

He thought he might have detected disappointment in her voice, or perhaps just embarrassment, but his initial trickle of bravery was bursting into a flood, and he let it carry him on. "I think my mother knows how I feel, I think that's why she invited you. I don't know what she was hoping for. She overheard our conversation the other day. She knows you're married." He waited a moment. "I'm sorry for all of this."

"Don't be," Susan said. She was still staring at her plate.

For a time they sat quietly together. In the living room, Leotie was telling a story to the children, an old tale that Robert remembered vaguely from his childhood, now that he heard it, though he'd never recalled it before. It was about an owl and a boy and their friendship. She must have told that to him when he was very young. She must have used it to distract him, to pass the time, as she was doing now.

"I am married," Susan finally said, tentatively, "but I could still use a friend."

Her raised eyes sent a question across the table. Robert caught it and nodded. "So could I," he said. "So could I."

"Maybe your mother knew what she was doing."

Robert laughed a little. "Maybe," he said. "Maybe she did."

Lukas danced back into the dining room, followed by a shuffling Leotie and a slightly-less-sulky Willa. They each returned to their seats. Willa took her first bite. Lukas pushed his plate back from the edge of the table. "Is it time for dessert yet?" he asked.

"Dessert?" Leotie said. "I haven't even eaten my dinner yet." She smiled at Robert, then at Susan—gauging the energy between them, Robert suspected. "Nosirree," she said. "I have every intention of stretching this out for as long as I possibly can."

41

Randy turned out to be one of six sorry saps who had opted to work on Thanksgiving. The day before, Dawson had briefed them on the short line. There'd been an extra order for a set of portable magnetic drills, Dawson told them, rubbing his hands together. That meant he was going to have to shake things up a bit. He took them through the specs slowly, page by page, like they'd never seen a spec sheet before. Randy had to hold himself back from clocking Dawson square in the face.

But when Randy arrived Thursday morning, he found himself fine with the quiet and also fine with the change of pace. The other five men, like Randy, worked on in silence. No hydraulic lifts strained in the background, no welding electrodes sparked on and off. No one turned on the radio. Maybe, Randy thought, they didn't want to be reminded of what day they were missing. Two of them were old shits with half their teeth gone. Two were younger—twenties, probably—with no wedding rings. The last couldn't have been more than a teenager, with his plucked-chicken-skin face and his flabby white arms and soft, fat hands that looked like he'd never worked a day in his life.

All five of the guys worked on other lines, so Randy knew none of them, and he wanted to keep it that way. When they broke at ten for a smoke, Randy stayed where he was, pretending to study the spec sheet. At lunchtime, he realized he'd left his lunch in his truck, so he walked out to get it and ended up eating it there in the cab rather than carry it in and small talk with a bunch of strangers.

By the time break rolled around that afternoon, they had almost finished the order, so Randy suggested they just keep on until they could call it a day. The others agreed—he got the sense that they might be scared of saying no—and they capped off the order just after three o' clock, two hours ahead of schedule.

"Fuckers," Randy muttered to no one as he steered his truck out of the parking lot. But he felt happy to be leaving earlier than he'd expected and hungry, too—hungrier when he realized that Susan and the kids would still be at his in-laws', which was only ten minutes down the road, with the leftovers still sitting out on the countertop and the pies still uneaten, if he was lucky, and coffee brewing maybe. So he drove toward his in-laws' house but found no van parked in the driveway.

Eileen answered the door in her bathrobe. "I thought you had to work today," she said.

"I did," he replied. "Got out early."

"Well Suzy's not here, as you can see. She canceled on me. Surprised she didn't tell you that."

"So she's home?" he asked.

"I don't know where she is, but she sure as shenanigans isn't here. She said you had to work and she didn't want to deal with the grocery store anyway. I almost wondered if she had somewhere else she was planning to go." Eileen kept glaring at Randy after she said this, and it took him a moment to realize that she was waiting for him to respond.

"Not that I know of," he said, and once he said it, a balloon of panic broke in his chest.

"You're still welcome to come in," she called as Randy jogged down the steps.

His truck door screeched open. He didn't even bother to wave. He jerked backward out of the drive and roared off toward home as fast as he could.

He knew the house would be dark when he arrived, he knew the van would be gone, but the empty driveway and the darkened windows still hit him like a slug in the stomach. He parked crooked and sprinted up the steps. He fumbled his shaking key into the lock and threw back the door. "Susan!" he called, even though he knew how pointless it was. "Willa! Lukas!" He crossed to the kitchen and checked the counter, where Susan sometimes left a note. Nothing. He stomped around the dining room and living room, searching for a sign. Finally, he spotted it.

A piece of paper dropped on the entryway floor, with *DADDY* printed across the top in big block letters. He snatched it up. A note. Willa had left him a note. She must have dropped it on the floor as they left. It read only, *We went to the pastor's house.*

Randy's fist closed around the paper as anger rose to his head in a flood of dizzying heat. When he rammed his truck into reverse, he didn't bother to check the road. An oncoming car blasted its horn and swerved around him, heading toward Esau. He yanked into drive, slammed the gas to the floor, caught up to the car in a matter of seconds, and barreled around it. He was not going to stand for this.

42

Over the course of the day, Leotie had gone from thinking her plan to invite Susan and the kids was risky (this was before they arrived) to downright idiotic (this was just after they arrived) to maybe, just maybe (after she'd repented for her stunt and wooed the daughter into eating and managed, in the process, a short stint of private conversation between Susan and Bobby) completely brilliant. Once Leotie and the children had seated themselves at the table for the second time, the strain in the room had relaxed. The Willa girl started eating, and Lukas started talking again, and this time Susan and Bobby talked back to him and also to each other. Leotie could almost trick herself into believing that they were a real family—mother, father, daughter, son. And herself, the grandmother, looking happily on at what she'd be leaving behind.

"I have a superpower," Lukas was saying.

"And what superpower is that?" Bobby asked.

Lukas became suddenly shy. "Maybe I won't tell you," he said. He was on his knees in his chair, picking at a spot on his shirt.

"Do you want me to guess?" Bobby asked.

Lukas nodded.

"Can you fly?"

"Nope."

"Can you turn yourself invisible?"

"No."

"Hmmm," Bobby said, tapping his chin. "Can I ask Willa to help me out?"

"No!" said Lukas. "Don't tell him, Willa!"

Leotie glanced over at Susan, who was listening to the interchange with a small smile.

"Willa," Bobby whispered, and the girl smiled a little, though she kept her gaze down on her plate.

"Don't tell him, Willa!" Lukas cried, but his voice was full of joy.

"I won't," Willa said. She was trying to sound annoyed, Leotie thought, but her attempt now was only halfhearted.

"Okay," said Lukas. "I'll tell you. But I need to whisper it into your ear." He climbed down from his chair and up into Bobby's lap. Surprise passed over Bobby's face, and it pinched Leotie's heart to see the sadness there, too. He had wanted this for too many years. A family around him, the trust of small children. He hesitated before reaching around Lukas and resting his hands against the boy's small back. He leaned forward to catch his whispered words.

"Ah," he said soberly. "That is a very special power. And a very unusual one."

Susan asked, "Do I get to hear about it?"

Lukas looked up at Bobby.

"Should we tell your mother?" Bobby asked, but instead of answering, the boy curled up into a ball and nestled his head into Bobby's chest.

"You're warm," said Lukas, and after another moment's surprise, Bobby let his arms settle back over the boy in a resting hug.

"What do we have here?"

A man stood in the entrance to the dining room. He was tall and bulky under his coat, in a way that said he was out of shape but still strong. His jaw was patchy with stubble, and his wiry hair stuck out from his head, but his face had a sickly handsomeness to it, and his pale blue eyes cut through the air.

"Daddy." Willa stood and went to him, hooked her arms around his waist, and turned her face away from the table.

"Randy," said Susan. She had stood up and taken a step back.

"Nice of you to let me know where you'd be," he said to his wife. His mouth smiled, but his eyes did not. "You know, in case I got out early. Which I did." He waited for her to respond. She did not. "Well then," he said. "Happy Thanksgiving to you, too."

He turned to his son, who was still curled up in Bobby's arms. "Come here, Lukas," he said. He did not look at Bobby. He seemed to be treating Bobby as if he wasn't there. "I said come here, Lukas."

Leotie could make out Bobby's reach around the boy tightening ever so slightly.

"Let him go," the man said, but Bobby didn't move.

"I will let him go when he wants me to," Bobby said.

The man stepped closer. "Lukas," he said through closed teeth. "Come here."

Lukas mumbled something into Bobby's chest, but Leotie couldn't make it out.

"Lukas," the man said again. This time it was almost a shout.

"He said he doesn't want to go," Bobby said, in a voice that surprised Leotie. It was strong—challenging, even—and also calm.

"I'm taking my kids, and I'm leaving. You," he said, turning to Susan, "I don't give a fuck what you do. But I'm taking my kids."

Lukas said something else that Leotie couldn't make out.

"You're scaring him," Bobby explained. "He doesn't want to come with you."

"Give me my son!" Randy spoke these words in a scream as he stepped over, spun around, and put his fist through the nearest wall. He pulled it out in a cloud of dust, and flecks of drywall drifted down like snow.

"Randy," said Susan. "I need to speak to you. Outside." She had been watching the showdown in silence, her face frozen in the shock of fear, but now her voice rang out calm and determined. She was used to this, Leotie remembered. She had been managing this man for some time. She approached her husband and took his hand as if to lead him down the hall. He shook off her grasp with a violent jerk. "Randy," she said. Her eyes teared up, and she started to beg. "Please. We need to talk. Please."

As Susan led her husband back down the hallway, the daughter tried to follow. "No," said Susan to Willa. "You stay here." Then they walked out onto the front stoop and closed the door behind them. A channel of icy wind swept down the hall and into the kitchen.

"A harsh world," Leotie said to no one. The boy was still curled up in Bobby's lap. Leotie leaned over to catch sight of his face and saw that his eyes were squeezed shut and he was shivering slightly. The heat from the overworked stove had leaked out the walls, and the house felt cold again. Leotie pushed herself up and out of her chair and stepped into the living room to fetch an afghan. She brought it back to the table and settled it over Bobby and the boy. The girl was still standing in the hallway, watching her parents through the front windows.

"It's good to love your father," Leotie said.

The girl ignored her.

"I loved my daddy, too," Leotie continued. "Loved him a lot more than I loved my mom. Took me half a lifetime to realize he hadn't done nothing to deserve it."

Still the girl gave no sign that she had heard.

"He didn't do nothing to deserve it because he wasn't ever around. My momma was the one that fed me and clothed me and made sure I didn't drink poison or run out into the road." Leotie knew that their stories weren't the same, but she kept going anyway. "The mommas carry all the work, and then they carry all the blame."

"My mom brought us here," the girl said. "That was wrong."

"Why was that wrong?" asked Leotie.

Now the girl turned toward Leotie with all of her attention, and Leotie felt a shiver that seemed to come not from the girl's pointed look or the chilled air of the house but from the deepest point inside of her, radiating out. All the efforts of her day caught up with her at once, and the understanding of how hugely she had failed, and she felt so tired suddenly, and so deathly cold. She longed to lie down beneath a blanket on the couch and fall asleep, but she resisted this urge and struggled for wakefulness, for clarity. She had to try and mend this giant mistake she had made. She took a shallow breath and pushed her body toward the door.

Susan and her husband halted their conversation when Leotie walked out onto the front landing. Susan wore only her thin socks, and she rubbed her arms through her shirtsleeves. Her cheeks and nose shone a vivid pink, and Leotie could not tell if this color was from crying or the cold or both. The man still wore his boots and coat. He turned his cold wolf's eyes toward Leotie, but they were dull now and glazed over, with only a flicker of awareness.

The cold inside Leotie met with the cold outside of her, and she was overcome, for a moment, by the fear that death would take her right then, and the man would take his wife and kids away and Bobby would be left with the same sad life he'd been living before, only now he would be carrying the extra load of loss. But the fear crested and fell, and she was still standing there, with her empty body and her weak voice.

"You're making life harder for everyone," Leotie said to the man. "You know it, and they know it, too." She hadn't planned to say anything, much less that. "Nobody wants to tell you this," she went on, "but I ain't got nothing to lose, so I can speak the truth, and the truth is you're making life harder for everyone."

"You don't know shit," the man said, but there was no more anger in his voice. "You don't know nothing."

Susan ducked past Leotie. "We can talk more once I get home," she said to her husband and slipped inside. The man did not make to follow her.

"So what are you saying," the man said. "You saying I ought to just go off and kill myself?"

"Of course that ain't what I'm saying. What I'm saying is you got two choices. Either shape up or leave them alone. But don't take this out on them. I asked your wife to come today because I'd met her before, and I liked her. My son didn't have nothing to do with it."

"I don't believe it," the man said, but his voice came out too weak to carry any conviction.

Leotie felt a pang of pity for him. She liked him somehow, against her reason. He was fighting for something noble, even if he didn't deserve it. That was men for you, Leotie thought. Always fighting for things they didn't deserve. Which was maybe why they got those things so often. But the man standing there beside her was losing all the fights he should have been winning. And he looked at her when she spoke, and he listened.

"So you're dying," he said. "Suzy told me."

"I am."

"What's that like, to know?" He handed her his coat. "Here," he said.

She took it without comment and settled it around her shoulders, held it shut. Warmth spread over her back and breasts like water. What was it like, to know?

"It's something that makes so much sense you can't understand it. Like looking at your children and knowing they came from you." A few crows came cawing and landed in the yard, frightening away a lone chickadee. They started pecking through the snow. Inside Lukas shouted something and laughed. "Your daughter loves you," Leotie said.

"But are you scared?" he asked.

The crows, having found nothing, lifted off. After a moment, the chickadee returned.

"I been scared a couple of times," she said. "Real scared. But no one knows what happens, much as they pretend. I been close to death once in my life, so close they had to bring me back." She had caught hypothermia once sleeping in an alley. A passing stranger had called 911. "I didn't see no light, but I did feel something on the other side, and I think it was God. But what it felt like was peace. Pure peace, where nothing you'd done mattered no more." Leotie had never told this to anyone, and now she wondered why not. It had been such a relief to come that close to the end and find waiting an unnatural calm, like a bottomless bath.

"I've been a shit," the man said. "A real grade-A asshole."

"You can change."

"I don't think I can."

"You can. Your daughter loves you."

"I don't even know anymore whether she should," he said. "Did you see the rest of them in there? My wife? My son?" He started walking down the steps toward his truck. "If she does love me, she's the only one."

"Your coat!" Leotie called after him, but he didn't respond. Once he reached his truck he turned to look at her, and he stared a moment before nodding. Then he climbed in and drove slowly off.

She felt she should go inside and tell the others that he had left and that he had seemed strange to her—too sad and too real, though how she could communicate that sense of strangeness, she did not know. But she remained there for a little longer, holding his coat around her shoulders, breathing in the smells of diesel fuel and grease and, beneath those, the sharp scent of sweat.

43

Susan reentered the parsonage dizzy with exhilaration. She had said what she had never expected to say. She had told Randy that she couldn't take it anymore, that she would be moving herself and the kids to her parents' house until she could plan what came next.

Susan had not been planning to tell Randy this, nor had she decided any of this beforehand, but as the words left her mouth, she realized that the decision had been forging itself in the back of her brain for months, perhaps even years. When she looked up from her Thanksgiving dinner and found Randy standing there, she knew it. And when he put his fist through the wall, she knew it then, too.

Out on the porch, she focused on the black hairs that curled above his knuckles, his filthy fingernails, the patches of stain on his teeth. She tried her best to avoid his eyes, the wounds her words were writing across the muscles of his face. She would not think of him as a boy—his mother suddenly gone, his home a prison. She would not think of the days their babies were born and how he had wept, or how on her birthday he always made fettucine alfredo with the jar from the store, which, she'd never had the heart to tell him, tasted nothing like the sauce she'd tried at the Italian restaurant all those years before.

She would refuse to think these thoughts, but they would come to her anyway, after Leotie announced that Randy had left and that he'd seemed "a little off somehow." They would come as she sat before the cold piece of peach pie, not as sweet as it should have been and bitter with too much ginger, the overworked crust heavy on the top and slick wet on the bottom, dense as clay. The thoughts came then, as Robert helped himself to an extra piece of pie and Leotie reached over with her unfamiliar hand and rested it atop Susan's own. Susan thought of her own mother, alone that day with the man she had chosen all those years before, and despite herself, Susan felt a nostalgia swelling for the way things used to be, with her children's needs met and some of her own, and all the world around her predictable enough and somehow comforting if she just stuck to the path she had told everyone she'd keep walking.

Around her, the parsonage loomed large and empty and cold, and Susan found, as she lowered a stack of dirty plates into the sink, that she wanted nothing more than to be home before her own sink with her own family's dishes and the evening moving forward as it always did.

When Susan learned what Randy had done, she knew that he had done it just then. She knew because she felt its reverberation within her as she stood there before the sink, wishing herself away. She felt the tremor of warning, the deep echo from a faraway drum. When she considered it afterward, she could almost watch him move through the steps as if he had filmed himself. He entered their bathroom, the one they had shared, the one whose upper walls she'd stenciled with small blue flowers. He brought with him the knife she used for paring the stems from tomatoes, for carving the core out from apples. He undressed and ran the bathtub full, lay down in the water, drew the knife across the inside of both wrists (crosswise, the way you'd cut if you didn't really want to die, he must have known) and waited, hoping that she might come and find him there, and hoping, too, that no one would.

PART II

44

December. Another month, another deacons meeting. How many must he have attended in his time at Esau Baptist, Robert wondered. Cliff Grable meted out his inexorable arguments in favor of the King James Version (KJV) over the easier-to-read New King James Version (NKJV), an update that Robert had suggested, while Robert privately indulged in the math and arrived at the sum of something like one hundred and fifty meetings. Which roughly translated to three hundred hours. Which was an unfathomable number of hours to have spent in this way and which seemed suddenly to hit him all at once with the force of profound exhaustion.

Always, at the Sunday service prior to the meetings, Robert would hand each deacon a copy of that month's business, and invite them to add items (or, in Cliff's case, prepare arguments) as each saw fit. By this point, Robert was thoroughly regretting having mentioned the NKJV at all, especially as he'd had an inkling it would come down to this, as had any of his attempts to update anything.

The NKJV, according to Cliff, had been translated and published by a host of greedy reprobates who did not confess to the inerrancy of scripture. Furthermore, the *thee*s and *thou*s from the KJV served the purpose of differentiating the plural *you* from the singular *you,* an argument whose importance Cliff supported with a seemingly endless number of verses. Furthermore, the NKJV changed key words, many words, and Cliff read out each one from his sheaf of loose-leaf papers. Furthermore, the NKJV left many words untranslated, especially those that revealed unpleasant truths, such as words that referenced hell, of which there were again a staggering number.

Robert finally interrupted Cliff at the tail end of this fourth argument. "Thank you for your research, Cliff, as always. Your case has been scrupulously made. Any other thoughts?" Robert directed this question toward the other two, but the thoroughness of Cliff's arguments, Robert knew, had already trumped his own halfhearted suggestion, and the matter was dropped without further discussion.

"The other matter of business," Robert said, "is the matter of my mother. As you know, after her hemorrhage two weeks ago, they are keeping her in the hospital owing to the round-the-clock care she now requires. I'd like to use the family fund to hire someone for the night watch until my mother passes so that she can die at home, with me. This position is likely to be short-term, as you know, though it would accrue some cost. Eight hours a night at eight dollars an hour comes to about four hundred fifty dollars per week."

Each of the deacons was shifting uncomfortably in his chair.

"But this cost would, of course, enable her to die a dignified death at home. She is miserable in the hospital, as we all would be." He was finished, but the air of awkwardness in the room prompted him to keep talking. "She would very much like to come home," he added. "Very much."

Silence.

Robert had not expected this reaction. The deacons had already approved, albeit grudgingly, Robert's use of the family fund. For this month's meeting, he had also judiciously chosen the NKJV question, which he assumed, with Cliff's tendencies, would likely be denied. And this denial on one order of business, he hoped, would increase their sense of generosity when it came to the other. But now Jack was straightening his string tie, and Cliff was quietly but continually clearing his throat, and Clark was twitching his hideous mustache and shooting eye daggers at the other two, who were returning his meaningful stares with uneasy glances.

Robert sighed. "What is it?" he said.

Clark nodded at Jack, who tugged at his tie once more before beginning, in a timid voice. "It's just that we'd had an agreement."

Robert wasn't sure which agreement they were referencing. He shot a questioning look at Jack, who nodded to Cliff, who cleared his throat.

"About the woman," Cliff said.

"Yes," said Robert, finally understanding. "Directly after our conversation, I wrote her a letter explaining that I would not be meeting alone with her, and I haven't. I actually haven't seen her or spoken with her in a matter of weeks."

"But it seemed wise to invite her for Thanksgiving. Without her husband." This came from Clark, finally participating in the conversation which, up until that point, he'd been directing only with his eyes.

Thanksgiving? How on earth had any of them heard about Thanksgiving?

"Ah," Robert said, and he tried to laugh a little. "That's actually a funny story. My mother invited them without my knowledge."

"Funny?" Clark repeated. "I fail to see how a situation that compels a man to go home and attempt suicide is very funny."

"I'm sorry?" Robert said.

The three of them exchanged glances.

"You're telling me you didn't know," Clark said, his voice unbelieving.

"Did he die?" Robert asked, unable to keep the desperation out of his voice. "Is he dead?"

"No he's not dead," said Clark. His tone had changed from disbelief to impatience. "They've locked him up in the crazy house. His wife is working at the diner now, at Karla's." He paused. "I can't understand how you haven't heard about it," he said, as though Robert's ignorance were his own fault. "Everybody knows. The whole town's talking about it."

Robert shook his head back and forth, dazed. "The whole town's not talking to me," he said, more to himself than to them.

So that explained Susan's silence, her absence from church. He had called her twice since Thanksgiving—once on the Monday following Thanksgiving, when, God help him, he knew her husband would be working. The phone rang and rang until the machine picked up, and Robert hung up in fright. After she'd missed her second Sunday, he called the following Monday, early enough that she would catch his message before Randy did. What he'd said on the answering machine must have sounded so inane after everything that had apparently happened. He'd muttered something about how he was sorry if he'd accidentally ruined her Thanksgiving and how he hoped she'd forgive him and return to church.

When he didn't hear back or see her again, he'd taken that as a sign that he ought to stop contacting her, and he had done so.

He had wondered, of course. He'd spent the three weeks since Thanksgiving wincing in response to those remembered moments—Willa's accusations; his and Susan's shared time alone at the table, when he had, with such painful awkwardness, confessed his feelings for her; his helplessness in response to Randy's arrival, how Robert had weakly flip-flopped back and forth between playing the part of defender and the part of peacemaker and how he had failed at both; how then he'd just sat there, powerless, as another man—a man he couldn't help but view as more real, in some way, than himself (why was that?)—spoke his mind and made his waves and drove away.

"I don't believe this," Robert said.

"Well, believe it or not, it happened," said Clark. "And some think you're to blame."

"Me?"

"Either you or your mother."

"How could my mother be held accountable for the attempted suicide of an unpredictable stranger?"

"Because with or without your knowledge, she invited a married woman and her children to pass Thanksgiving at the parsonage, of all places, without their husband and father. Who, after suspecting that more was going on, which of course he would, having a brain in his head, went home and tried to kill himself. Robert, this is bad. This is very bad. This is a scandal."

"Now, now," said Cliff Grable, who interrupted his own objection with a vicious hacking noise.

"I don't know as I'd go *that* far," said Jack.

"Oh, it is. It most certainly is. My cousin Donnie keeps calling me up to ask if the pastor has driven anyone else to suicide lately. He thinks he's being funny. No. This is all over, everywhere." He directed his attention back toward Robert. "I just don't believe you haven't heard about it."

Cliff growled a little in his throat. "I'm sure he's not lying," he said.

"Are you?" said Clark. "I'm not."

"Now Clark," said Jack. "Give the man a moment to respond."

"Do you really think I'm lying?" asked Robert. "Is your faith in me that weak? And if it is, what have I possibly done to deserve it?"

"Let's all calm down," said Cliff, speaking clearly for once.

"No," said Robert. He felt almost dizzy with anger. "If I do not have your trust," he said. "If I do not have your trust," he said again, but he found that he could not finish. He wanted to say *Then that is your own fault.* He wanted to say what he was realizing, in that moment—that his whole life in Esau had been a kind of unexamined capitulation. He had an overwhelming urge to go and check on Susan, to apologize. How had everyone known, and for so long, except for him?

The three deacons were still sitting in silence, waiting for him to speak. "Why did no one tell me?" he asked. "Before it came to this?"

His mother's words came to his mind. *There's a reason the whole town talks without talking to you.* She had said some variation of this several times, but her experience, he had told her, did not dictate his own. How could everyone else treat him according to his difference when he himself so often forgot about it?

But that's how it gets you, she'd said. *That's how it sticks around.* Looking over the deacons' faces—Clark's distrustful frown unsuccessfully hidden beneath his mustache, Cliff's buggy eyes perplexed behind his bifocals, Jack's sideways gaze and figure listing uncomfortably away—Robert stood up suddenly from his desk.

"I am late to see my mother," he said. He only realized after he had said it that it was a lie and that the deacons would all know as much. He also realized he didn't care. "Her doctor's coming in before lunch," he went on. "I'll have to talk with him about home treatment plans if I'm to do this on my own."

"Now Robert," cautioned Cliff. "No reason to get angry."

"Ten years," said Robert. "Ten years I've served this congregation, and this is how I'm treated."

Clark harrumphed as Robert passed, and Jack gripped his string tie, and Cliff hemmed and hawed wordlessly as Robert lifted his coat from its hook and stepped out the front doors of the church, into the snow-covered everything and the cold.

45

Susan peeked over the diner's food window to check on her pancake order. If Lenny the line cook caught her looking, he'd assure her two or three times that her food was almost finished, and then he'd spend the rest of their cooking time updating her on its progress. *Just three minutes. Just two minutes and change. Counting down to one.* And so on. And she'd have to say *okay* and *great* and *sounds good* and *no rush* until he finally slid the pancakes onto the window ledge and dinged the bell, which was all he had to do in the first place.

On the grill, her pancakes, unflipped, were beginning to bubble. Just before Lenny moved into view, she stepped to the side of the window and backed deftly into the wait alley, where she pretended to busy herself. But the creamers, she already knew, were full, and the ice bin was full, and the yellow counters, despite their brown cracks and stains, were clean, and so there was nothing at all to do.

Through her apron, she squeezed the wad of dollar bills from breakfast. It was Wednesday, she reminded herself, and Wednesdays were slow. Still, the wad was so thin you could hardly call it a wad. No more than fifteen or sixteen dollars, twenty at the most, if she counted up all the change. The only tip she hadn't collected was Herb's, with his pancakes that had to be hot enough to liquefy the scoop of butter on top and his coffee that had to be microwaved for thirty seconds and then filled up as soon as he'd drunk it halfway down. He'd leave you two fat quarters if his demands were perfectly met, four dimes if they were not. It was all so hopeless. But there was still lunch, and if she kept her head and didn't let the rush unsettle her as it sometimes did, then maybe she could walk with forty-five.

The first bill from the psychiatric hospital had come, and she had opened it and checked the amount and then ripped it up into tiny pieces and dropped every last sliver into the trash. Randy's workman's compensation checks had finally begun to arrive, but they only paid a little over half of his usual earnings, which she'd already had to stretch too far as it was. She'd gotten the job at Karla's right away, and even though the tips were hit or miss, the timing had been fortuitous. Dot, who'd waited all the tables weekdays at Karla's, had fallen and broken her hip, and Jeff the owner had burned through a string of unreliable younger girls and was desperately seeking an older, more dependable replacement. He hired Susan on the spot for the day shift, Mondays through Fridays, which started at seven and ended at two. She'd arranged for the kids to catch the bus a block down from the restaurant, so she still saw them off in the morning and then made it home before the afternoon bus dropped them off. But Christmas break began that Friday, and so Susan would have to start driving the twenty minutes to Henley to drop them off at her mother's. She'd also have to somehow cobble together a Christmas for them, though she had put off thinking about that.

How could they celebrate Christmas after everything that had happened? Christmas would never be the same again, not to mention Thanksgiving. Susan and the kids had left the parsonage not long after Randy and had arrived at twilight to a darkened house. The moment she opened the door, she knew that something was wrong. The lights were all off, the TV silent, the woodstove cold. He was taking a nap, she told herself, but she didn't believe it.

"Stay here," she had told the kids. She stretched her arm behind her as if to stop them from following, but she failed to turn around and make sure. She switched on the nearest lamp. The living area of the house, all one open room, showed no sign of Randy, so she turned down the hall and entered the bathroom and screamed. The patter of footsteps behind her reached her ears too late, and she turned to find her children's faces pale in the glow of the bathroom night-light before she slammed the door and locked it. How much had they seen?

"Willa?" she said to the doorjamb, astounded at the calm in her voice. "Call 911. Tell them there's been an accident. Tell them to come immediately." Then she stepped over to the bathtub.

She knew she should turn on the light, but she couldn't bring herself to do it. Not until she knew.

"Randy?" she whispered.

No answer.

"Randy, please speak to me. Please be okay."

"Suzy-Q."

Susan gasped and started to sob. He was still alive, but in the dim light, she could make out the dark pool that had spread from the wrist slung over the side of the tub. She yanked two towels off the rack and wrapped them around Randy's wrists.

"Mama?" Lukas called through the door. "Mama, Mama, Mama." He began to chant mindlessly, as if that evening were the same as any other.

"It's okay, Lukey," Susan said. "Mama will be right out." She reached down and found Randy's forehead with her palm. Still warm.

"I don't want to die."

"Willa is calling an ambulance. They will do everything they can." Her hand was still resting on his forehead. She began to smooth his hair in soothing strokes, and her tears came back. "Just stay with us," she said. "Can you hear me, Randy?"

"Yes." His voice sounded weak but determined.

"Just stay with us until they come."

"I'm sorry," Randy said, and her sobs echoed in his voice. "I just can't go on anymore. Like this, I mean. You need to believe me, Suzy, I'm going to get better."

She hushed him. "Save your strength," she said. "They'll be here soon."

"Promise, Suzy," he said, and beneath her palm he struggled to raise his head. "Promise you'll give me one more chance. Please. I'll be better. I promise I'll be better."

Outside the moon had moved, and a slice of its beam now cut through the back of the blind and fell across Randy's eye, the pupil contracting in the light, though it struck Susan that it might be contracting in death, and fear seized her. What would the rest of her life matter if she had brought him to this? Could any heights of happiness she might achieve ever justify this loss? She thought she could see, in the small world of his face, all of him that she had ever loved and all that she was still tender for. She could see all that she would miss and all that she would regret. So she said, "Yes, Randy. One more chance. I promise. Just stay alive, and I will give us one more chance."

After the EMTs had carried him out on a stretcher, his eyes still wide open and wild with fear, and the ambulance had whined off into the distance, she tried to explain enough to her children without explaining too much.

"Your father had an accident," she said. "But he's going to be okay. We'll go visit him there in the hospital, and soon he'll come back home."

But Willa had stared her down until she had to look away, and then after Lukas had fallen asleep, Willa had stalked out into the dining room, where Susan sat, trying to wrap her mind around the day, and Willa had said, with a strain in her voice that Susan had never heard before, "If he dies, I will never forgive you."

"This is not my fault, Willa," she said, too severely. "You cannot hold me responsible for this." And then her daughter began to cry, and she pulled the girl down into her lap and rocked her back and forth. "I'm sorry," she whispered. "I'm so, so sorry. Everything's going to be okay." She said this over and over, even though Willa had proven too many times that she knew better than to believe it.

Now break was starting in two days, and Randy had been committed for nearly three weeks. Lukas didn't seem terribly worried, but Willa was so tense, so joyless. Her schoolwork was suffering, which had never happened before, and the other night around two in the morning, Susan had heard a strange noise and found Willa standing, apparently sleepwalking, in front of the open refrigerator.

So Susan had Willa to worry about, and she couldn't forget about Lukas in all of this, or Randy, who they visited once a week and who was doing well, the doctors said, which both encouraged and frightened her. And then she had work on top of it all, and all of the work at home that wasn't getting done, and Christmas coming, and far too little money. And in a strange way, this deluge of busyness, overwhelming as it was, relieved her because there, under each of its endless demands, was Pastor Robert, whom, for the sake of her marriage, she needed to forget, even though she couldn't.

In Karla's Kitchen, the bell dinged. Susan fetched the pancakes, with the butter scoop melting at a promising rate over the top, and when she returned to the dining room, there stood Pastor Robert on the mat just inside the door, rubbing his bare hands together, his eyebrows angled down in concern. She was so surprised she didn't even say hello at first. She just stood there, rooted to the spot for a moment, then walked to Herb and set his plate down and turned back to her visitor.

"Well!" he said, gesturing with his palms up to the dining room, which was empty with the exception of Herb slouched in the corner, staring down at his butter and judging its melting potential with a small frown. "Looks like I've got the run of the place."

"Looks like," she said. A shock of excitement jolted through her, but she tamped it down. She had chosen her path, and the well-being of her family depended on her continuing to choose it. Robert seemed different from the last time she'd seen him—now he seemed frantic, a little wild. His eyes were bright, and his cheeks were tinged pink from the cold. The winter wind had blown his hair around. It stuck up from his head at odd angles and added to the untamed energy of his appearance. He seemed troubled, that's what it was—deeply concerned.

"Is everything okay?" she asked.

"Yes," he said. "I mean, everything's okay with me." He paused to stare at the floor, took a sharp breath, and then continued. "I've only just heard. What happened. I came straight here. I had no idea. I didn't even know you were working here. Until just now, when one of the deacons told me. I guess everyone knows, but somehow no one told me. The deacons are furious about Thanksgiving, about everything that happened. I needed to tell you how sorry I am."

Susan froze. Everyone knew? Everyone was talking about it? She had told only her mother and Jeff, the restaurant owner. She felt suddenly, horrifically exposed. She couldn't think how to respond, so instead she said, "How's your mother?"

"I'm sorry?" he asked. He peered at her closely. Then his gaze traveled to Herb, and he finally seemed to understand her need for discretion. "I'm sorry," he repeated. "My mother. She hemorrhaged—a pulmonary hemorrhage, not deathly but serious enough—so I had to admit her to the hospital. She's dying, which you know. She shouldn't have to just waste away in there. I'm trying to bring her home. But then there's the problem of money."

"I'm sorry," she said.

"Well, thanks," he said. "That makes two of us."

He kept standing there. He seemed to have something else to say. Behind Susan, Herb cleared his throat. That would be the half-empty-coffee warning. "Did you want to order anything?" she asked. "Would you like to sit down?"

"I thought maybe I'd pick up some soup for my mom. You know, hospital food being what it is."

Susan pointed to the whiteboard beside the door, on which she'd written the soup of the day. "Chicken noodle okay?" she asked.

"Perfect," he said. Then, "I guess I also wanted to make sure you're holding together in the midst of all of this."

Behind her, Herb cleared his throat again. She turned her palms up and shrugged. "Getting by, I guess."

"And Randy?"

"He's still in the hospital. He's getting better. He keeps saying they're teaching him how to be good."

Robert laughed weakly. "Well," he said. "I hope he tells me. If he finds out."

Susan laughed a little, too.

Robert straightened his back and swung his hands in his pockets, bolstered, it seemed, by her laughter. Then in a quieter voice he said, "What are you going to do after he gets out? Are you going to take him back?" Robert tried to let this question roll naturally, she could tell, though the attention he gave it betrayed him, and he let his smile drop.

Annoyance flared out of Susan before she was able to check it. "You have an opinion, then, on what I ought to do?" she asked. She'd been managing herself and her family just fine, and now Robert showed up, his veiled suggestions. Behind her, Herb rattled his coffee cup. She thought of Randy, too, shut away, hoping. She suddenly felt beset on all sides by men, each of them waiting for her to acknowledge their rightness and follow along with whatever they thought she should do.

"Ah," Robert said, and he stared down with a look of embarrassed surprise at the square of entryway on which he stood, the yellowed linoleum curling up at the edges. "You're right," he said. "It's not my place to tell you anything."

Susan almost laughed then. She'd forgotten his contriteness, his readiness to admit fault. He glanced up at her, and she must have been smiling a little because a flash of hope skittered across his face. "What?" He was asking to be let in on the joke. "What is it?"

"It's nothing," she said. "Go ahead and take a seat. If you want."

On her way back to the kitchen, she passed Herb, who was still rattling his now-empty mug against the edge of the table.

"I know, I know," she said.

When she returned with the coffeepot, he said, "Looks like a four-dime day for old Suzy."

Susan had to stop herself from pouring hot coffee into his lap. "You can keep your dimes, Herb. See if I care." She had halfheartedly tried to lighten her tone, but it came out as irritated as she felt.

"Well, well, well," Herb said. "I think Jeff might have something to say about that."

"Oh, you've still got to pay Jeff for the pancakes," she said. She recognized the conciliation in her voice, and she hated herself for it. "Today you're just getting my services free of charge."

"Isn't that generous," Herb said, as though he didn't know whether to feel mollified or not.

Susan turned to Robert. "Did you want anything else? Other than the soup?" she asked.

Herb picked up on the curtness in her voice and called to Robert. "Isn't our old Suzy just a bucket of goodness and light?"

"No, thank you," said Robert, responding only to Susan. "Just the soup." His initial wildness had faded. She had startled him back into himself. It was just as well.

She brought him his Styrofoam container with the check settled over top. He folded the check around an already-folded bill and handed it back.

"It was good to see you," he said.

The polite thing, she knew, would be to respond in kind. "Yes, well," she said. "I hope your mother enjoys the soup."

He took this in and smiled, a little sadly, then walked back out into the cold.

Behind the cash register, she unfolded his check. A twenty-dollar bill. For a check that totaled two dollars and ten cents. Susan quickly made the change from the register drawer, shoved it deep down into her apron.

After Robert left, the diner filled up with that day's meager lunch rush—eight or nine tables seating themselves in a matter of minutes. When Lenny caught her scanning the grill for the status of her final table's food and kicked off his countdown, she told him, far more harshly than she'd intended, "Just ding the bell, Lenny."

She finished out her shift in near silence and left work with sixty-two dollars. She started the van and sat there on the side of the road, waiting for the heat to kick in and the rear defrost lines to loosen the snow. She had lost the window scraper and had put on hold any purchases not strictly urgent, so she'd been scraping the snow with a three-ring binder instead, which she tried only to use in their driveway, where no one would see her. But the van was slow to heat, and the rear defrosters—it dawned on her as she waited—must have stopped working. Her mind veered back and forth between how much gas she was wasting and how rude she'd been to Robert. Finally, she pulled the binder out from under the passenger seat and climbed out into the cold. She angled the binder's cover up against the frost and began awkwardly to scrape.

46

Leotie was getting the hell out of the hospital, and that was that. She didn't know if she would actually have to hightail it out while no one was looking, but just in case they tried to stop her, she figured she'd escape. Besides, it was more exciting that way.

She chose morning, since she was freshest in the mornings and strangers were more likely to help at that time of day, should she need it. After she'd hacked up all of the phlegm she could and the nurse aide had come in and given her her breathing treatment and her pills and a shot of something (she could never remember what) in her ass and hung her wheat-colored feedbag high up on a pole so that it would drain out through the slick white tube down her nose—after all that was done, she reached under her bed and pulled out her Patient's Belongings bag.

Leotie was wearing two hospital gowns—one forward and one backward—to hide her ass hanging out, so it took some doing to get them both off, then pull on her T-shirt and sweatpants, then roll up her pant legs so no one could spot them under the gowns, then tie her winter coat around her waist and wedge her boots in there, too, and then pull the gowns back on over top and smooth them down as well as she could. When she'd finished, from what she could tell without a full-length mirror, she looked tentlike and lumpy. But she was betting most all her cards on no one looking too close at her, since no one ever looked much anyway.

She sat down for a minute or two and rested, caught her breath, and went to work on the tube.

Peeling the tape off her cheek was easy. Pulling the tube out wasn't hard, either, but it slithered up from her belly impossibly long, like an unexpected animal. When she'd pulled it free, she gagged silently before tucking the tube's end down between her gowns. She peeled the tape off the tube, pressed it back onto her cheek, and shuffled out the door, rolling the feedbag pole alongside her.

The hallway to the elevators was nearly empty except for two nurses giggling behind a desk. Leotie passed them slowly, as she always did on her morning walks. Each of them glanced at her once and beyond that took no notice.

Getting on the elevator was so easy she almost felt stupid for all her efforts. Just as she approached, the closest elevator opened, and a doctor walked out, fully absorbed in her clipboard. Leotie waited a beat, shuffled in, hit the 1 button and, when the doors closed, she slid the gowns over her head and the dripping tube with them, peeled off the tape, yanked on her coat, smashed her feet into her boots, shoved down her pant legs, and kicked her gowns and feedbag into a corner before the elevator dinged and two women stepped on.

The two women—visitors, she guessed, since they weren't wearing uniforms—looked at the corner mess and then back at Leotie, but Leotie kept her poker face until the doors dinged open at the first floor, where she walked straight out the elevator, straight out the hospital doors, and into the parking lot.

Leotie had to pause then to catch her breath, and she smelled the bite of the morning, cold and clean, and the exhaust from an idling bus parked along the curb and the coffee from two cups a young woman was carrying, one for herself and one, evidently, for someone inside, and Leotie felt a little thrill in having walked out of something she didn't want and into something she did, on her own terms, with her own two stubborn legs carrying her own stubborn body, failing though it was.

The sunrise, a pale gold and blue, had broken through the cloud cover at the edge of the sky, and the cars she passed on her way to the street were patterned with frost that looked like etchings of leaves and flowers, and she couldn't believe that frost just happened on its own like that, without anyone doing anything about it.

On the sidewalk, she caught the smells of breakfast from a diner across the road, and she remembered, with almost unbearable joy, the bills she'd shoved into her pants pocket. She crossed the street between crosswalks, pausing to wait at each lane for cars. One man rolled down his window as he passed and yelled, "You're going to get yourself killed!" It made Leotie laugh as she panted over the concrete and into the diner, so warm inside that the windows had fogged over. She landed breathlessly on a stool at the counter.

Behind the counter, a big girl with a young face lifted a coffeepot. "Coffee?" she said. The girl's other hand rested on her belly, which Leotie realized was big in a pregnant way. Her face was young, but now Leotie could see the weariness already in it, and the worry. Leotie could see what the girl must see—the coming labor and the ocean of trouble beyond and the never enough of it all.

But Leotie could also see the day when it would all be finished, the day when the girl had birthed her baby a long time before and raised the child well or not. It didn't matter nearly as much as the girl probably thought it did because life was so fast anyway, and no one ever took it serious enough, or light enough, either. If Leotie had really known that there would come a time when it would all be over, maybe she would have done things differently, or maybe she would have done the same damn things and just not cared so much. Life really was beautiful—that was the thing, because then it was over. And Leotie decided then that she would live in the world a long time, if she could.

She said, "Yes, thanks" to the coffee, and the waitress let her use the diner phone to call Bobby, who didn't answer. She ordered pancakes and scrambled eggs—soft, pillowy foods—and devoured every last bite. She paid early, mostly to prove she had the money, then sat and sipped slow at her coffee and wondered what to do.

Now that her gut was full, all the energy she'd spent finally caught up with her, and a woozy sleepiness hit. Her eyes kept closing on their own, and her chin kept dipping down and then pulling up. At one point, she opened her eyes to see her waitress a few feet off whispering to a fat man with a vest and a mustache—the manager, probably. She stood and walked to the bathroom and sat for a while on the toilet, then shuffled back and lifted her mug.

"One more for the road?" she asked.

Leotie spent as much time drinking the coffee as she could, and just when she'd nearly finished and was starting to panic a little about what to do next, a breathless Bobby hustled in, red-faced, with an open coat, and asked the waitress standing behind the register just inside the door if she'd seen "an older lady, small, haggard." The woman turned toward Leotie, and so Bobby did, too. When his eyes settled on her, Leotie couldn't quite pin down what passed across his face. Relief, yes, but also something else, something like disappointment or annoyance, a twinge of the burden she'd become. He walked over and sank down onto the stool beside her. "Mom," he said.

She thought at first he might scold her, but instead he rested his elbows on the counter and rubbed the heels of his palms into his eyes. Then he dropped his hands and swiveled around to face her, patted his thighs once, resigned and resolved. "Well," he said, "let's get you home."

47

Willa and Lukas climbed on the school bus outside the restaurant in the frosty morning dark, and when the school day had finally crawled past and the bus had crawled out to their home and dropped them off, the world felt like it was already getting ready for bed. Usually, the sky was a dull gray. If there was any sunlight, it looked weak and sideways, like the sun was too far away and coming at them from the wrong direction.

Inside waited Willa's angel and her mother and silence (if you didn't count Lukas's cartoons) and homework and the dark evening stretching out into what felt like forever until her mother told her, finally, that it was time for bed. After her dad's "accident" (her mother's word), they'd stopped going to church, which was fine by Willa, but then the weekends felt even longer than the week, their Saturday-morning visit to the hospital the only interruption in the two long, dark days.

Willa had had to work up the courage to ask her mother why it was so dark all the time. What if the darkness was all in her head? Or what if the world was ending, and Willa was the only one who'd noticed? But when she asked, her mother assured her that the days always grew shorter in winter and that soon they would get longer and longer until the summer came and Willa would be falling asleep before the sun set.

Willa knew her mother must be telling the truth, but even so, she had a hard time believing it. Her mother would say, *I want to hear about your day*, and so Willa would tell her something—about how Mrs. Maple was letting everyone take the long division test again or how Bradley Parsons threw up right into his lunch box, things like that. Then, when Willa stopped talking, it would take her mother a second to come back from wherever she'd gone in her head and say, *Huh,* like she was thinking it over, and then, *Well that's good,* which half the time fit the conversation okay but half the time proved that she hadn't been listening at all.

When Willa asked about her father, her mother would say, *Everything's going to be okay.* But she'd say it in a way that sounded like she was so exhausted she'd say anything just to stop talking. She'd tell Willa that her dad was *just sick right now,* even though he didn't seem at all sick anytime they visited. Willa had witnessed the dark pool on the bathroom floor. After she had called 911, she had angled her ear against the crack under the door, and she'd heard the sobs and the muffled words. Her dad had hurt himself on purpose, hurt himself so much that he almost died. But he was sorry he did it, and he didn't want to die. That's what he'd said, over and over, as she listened under the door. *I'm sorry, I'm so sorry, I don't want to die.* But her mother kept calling it an accident.

A couple of times, Willa asked the biggest question she had—*Is Daddy going to come back home?*—to which her mother always replied, *Of course, Willa. We just don't know when.* Willa could never bring herself to ask the next question on her mind—*Do you want him to?*

Willa wanted to want her dad to come home because he always said, when they visited him, that he wanted to be there. And she knew any good daughter would want her father to return. And she told her mother this whenever she had the chance. "I miss Daddy," she'd say. Or, "I wish Daddy was here." But deep down, in Willa's secret place, she sometimes wished he'd stay locked away forever.

She tried to do her homework, to read, to look forward to something. Christmas was coming up in only a few days, but her mother had been so wiped out from work that she hadn't decorated. Willa had tried to decorate for her, but she couldn't pull out the panel into the attic, and when she asked for help, her mom said, "I just can't right now, Willa. I'm sorry. I just can't." And so Willa let it go.

Even Lukas seemed to be feeling it. He almost never bothered Willa to play with him anymore. Mom let him watch cartoons all the time, which she'd never done before, but the cartoons didn't make him laugh like they used to. It felt to Willa like a cloud had dropped down out of the sky, and they were all just wandering around in it, waiting for something to change.

And then, things did change, kind of. Only they changed in the wrong direction.

It started on Thursday, during language arts block. Willa was feeling perfectly normal until she wasn't. She'd finished her journal entry and looked up from her desk, and suddenly everything seemed strange. The other kids' pencils scratched too loudly, and Mrs. Maple, standing at the chalkboard, looked faded, like she'd been partly erased. Then she turned and said something to all of them, but her voice sounded far away and echoey, like she was talking underwater, and that's when Willa knew she was dying. Her heart started jumping hard and fast, and her throat squeezed shut. She couldn't breathe, and a squealing sound strained from her mouth. An arm circled her shoulders, but Willa had fallen down into her stomach, and she heard Mrs. Maple's voice coming from somewhere high overhead. "You're okay, Willa. You're okay. Just try to relax."

She didn't know how long it lasted. Slowly, her throat opened. Her breathing slowed down, and her heart slowed down, too, and when she opened her eyes, she was sitting in the principal's office, though she couldn't remember if she'd walked there or if someone had carried her. The school nurse and Mrs. Maple and Mr. Hinckley the principal and a bunch of other grown-ups crowded around her with close, worried faces.

"Feeling better now, dear?" Mrs. Maple asked.

Willa nodded slightly.

"You gave *me* quite a scare," Mr. Hinckley said. He sounded annoyed.

All the grown-ups turned to the nurse. She was standing back, surveying Willa with crossed arms. She shrugged. "Panic attack," she said. "Nothing I can do. Call her mom."

After the panic attack went away, Willa was almost glad it happened. For that afternoon, at least, Willa's mother acted like her old self. She asked her lots of questions and listened to the answers. She helped Willa into the house, even though Willa didn't need help, and her mother laid her down on the couch and brought her a mug of hot water with a bouillon cube crushed up in it.

When Willa asked her what a panic attack was, her mother told her, "Sometimes, when you worry a lot, all your worries get clogged up. Kind of like hair in a drain. And then your body has to work really hard to get them all out." She smoothed the hair back from Willa's forehead. "The good news is, you got the clog out. It's all gone now. All done." But her mother still looked so worried that it made Willa wonder how long it would be before she clogged her worry drain again. Then she realized that her wondering was actually worrying, and then she realized that she was worrying about the worrying, and at this rate her worry drain would clog again in no time.

"Are you feeling better?" her mother asked. She was still pushing Willa's hair back from her forehead and looking down at her with a crinkled-up face, like Willa was a math problem she couldn't solve.

"Yes, Mom," said Willa.

But after that, the worrying wouldn't go away. It was like someone had turned up the knob and she couldn't find it to turn it back down. Occasionally, she would forget about the worry, and she would wonder why she felt so relieved, until she remembered, and then she'd start worrying again. She couldn't even figure out what she was worrying about. She just had the feeling that something really bad was going to happen, only she didn't know what.

48

§Susan had decided to return Robert's tip. She'd been mulling it over for two days, and she'd concluded that she resented him for it. She resented his assumption that she needed it, for one thing. She resented that he referenced his own money problems and then handed it over so easily, as if to say that, though his circumstances were dire, hers were absolutely hopeless. She resented how much she needed it, too, and she resented how obvious her needing it must be. The whole transaction, the longer she considered it, made her feel cheap and pitiable.

She had to remind herself that maybe he'd actually meant to give her a five and had only realized later, upon opening his wallet that, in his rush to leave, he'd handed over the wrong bill, in which case he must also have realized that the awkwardness of any attempt to retrieve it could not possibly be worth the gain. In either case, she had to be the one to act, especially after how rude she'd been.

Since she couldn't be sure of his intent, she couldn't know whether to be irritated or embarrassed or perhaps even apologetic. She finally decided to place the change firmly in his palm and say something like *I think you accidentally overpaid*, thereby giving him the chance to contradict her if he wanted.

When she finally stopped by the parsonage, though, she couldn't remember what she'd decided to do. Susan had just endured yet another angst-ridden shift, during which she'd been called "sweetheart" twice and "babe" once, and one man, angry about his undercooked omelet, had grabbed her elbow as she passed and squeezed it so hard she could still feel it an hour afterward. She'd walked with just thirty-three dollars in tips, an all-time low. The stress of her day had been exacerbated by the stress of the day before, when Willa had succumbed to a full-blown panic attack. Susan had left midshift to pick her up, and Willa had been so shaken she couldn't even walk straight. And now, standing there on the parsonage doorstep, having knocked, she smelled the old-grease odor drifting up from her hideous teal polo and caught a reflection of herself in the glass—hair frizzing up from her ponytail and comically dark circles under her eyes. When Robert came to the door all gently surprised and smiling, an uncharacteristic anger reared up in her like a snake. She thrust out the money. Her face felt hard and mad.

"You left this," was all she said.

When he'd processed her words and taken the money, he continued to stand there, staring at her with a quizzical expression. She said, "I guess I'll be going then," and stomped back down the steps.

She'd already opened her van door when he finally found his voice and called out, "Wait," and then more urgently, "Wait! Can you—" He paused. "Do you have a minute?"

"I'm sorry but I've got to get home," she said.

"Do you have just one minute?" he asked.

Susan glanced down at the food stains splattered over the front of her shirt and the lumpy apron still tied around her waist.

"Please?" Robert said. He'd walked out onto the porch. He was wearing a droopy sweatshirt and a soft pair of khaki pants. His hair was sticking up on one side. He looked comfortable and solid and worn. "You don't owe it to me," he said. "But I would take it as a great kindness."

Susan sighed. She bent down to peer at the clock on the dashboard, then straightened up and studied him standing there, so transparently hopeful.

"All right," she finally said. "But I've only got fifteen minutes."

Inside, Susan stepped out of her shoes and folded her coat over the banister. They passed a moment in awkward silence before Robert clapped his hands and laughed a little. "Well," he said. "Hey. I guess I'll make us some coffee."

Susan seated herself at the dining room table while he scooped grounds into a filter, measured the water, and poured it in.

"I don't see your mother," she finally said.

"She's upstairs," he said. "Sleeping." He pressed the button on the coffee maker and walked over to sit down beside her.

"So you did it. You brought her home."

"Yes, well, the hospital didn't actually release her. She ran away. I had to find her. And then, yes, I brought her home. But she's dying, and the church has denied my request for funds to hire help. Now she needs twenty-four-seven care. So it's just going to be me with her, I guess, until the end."

Susan thought it over. "That's hard," she said.

"Yes," Robert said. "Yes, I think it will be."

They sat together in silence until the coffee maker finished its gurgling. Robert stood and walked to the cupboard, pulled down two mugs, poured them full, and carried them back to the table.

"I owe you an apology," he said as he sat. He pulled his mug close and wrapped his hands around it.

"For what, exactly?" Susan asked, trying to sound less interested than she felt. She turned her attention to her coffee, made a business of placing her palms over the top to collect the steam.

"For many things," he said, and he considered them for a bit. "For my mother's inviting you to Thanksgiving. For saying what I said then, about my feelings for you. And for saying what else I said at Karla's, implying that maybe you should separate from your husband. I am a pastor. I am supposed to help. Instead I've brought so much sadness upon your family."

"You couldn't help Thanksgiving. You knew nothing about it."

"No. But my mother only did it because she surmised my interest. And because she has really bad ideas and even worse judgment."

"And you can't help your feelings, either." This came out not kindly but dismissively. Susan tried to rein in her reactions. But Robert was safe, she realized. He would take whatever she threw at him and hold it without throwing it back. Which was all the more reason why she should take care not to abuse him.

"I suppose not. But that doesn't mean I had to go blabbing them to you."

"It was the situation that brought them out. And you had no control over that."

"No," Robert said. He blew on his coffee and sipped it, blew and sipped. "I think," he finally continued, "that I may be apologizing to myself even more than I'm apologizing to you."

"For what?"

"For choosing this vocation in the first place."

"I thought pastoring was a calling. Rather than a vocation."

"I think it can be," he said. "At the time, I told myself it was a calling, but now I think I really just heard what I wanted to hear. I didn't come to this job for the purest reasons, I'm realizing. I wanted to live this kind of life. And now I don't."

"What kind of life?"

Robert shrugged. "A life with clear guidelines, I guess. A life that was good. Or maybe not good so much as certain and safe."

"But what would you do if you left?"

Here his face brightened, and he straightened his back and patted his thighs. "Now that is an enjoyable question," he said. "I could do something else with my degree. Teach, perhaps. But I've also been wanting to learn a trade—you know, work with my hands. Between you and me, I've been considering a carpentry apprenticeship. I'm cautiously optimistic about the possibility. A good sign, I think."

He looked over at her and shook his head a little, noting, apparently, her changed expression. She was irritated. Specifically, she was jealous. Was it really so easy for other people to cast off what wasn't working and move on to something that suited them better? And shouldn't this make her happy for Robert, rather than sad for herself? This anger, this irritation, this jealousy—all these surprising emotions that kept rising up out of nowhere—they were so unlike her. Susan had always tended toward agreeableness in the presence of others; it came so naturally she never even had to try. She simply suppressed any negative reactions, or she at least saved them for later, when she could ponder them alone. Who was she becoming?

"But how did we get so far off topic?" he asked. "We were talking about you."

"No," she said. "We've been talking about you."

"I was trying to apologize for the pain I've caused you. However inadvertently."

Susan stood. "I've got to be home when the kids get off the bus," she said, and started walking toward the door.

"Wait!" he called. He rose and followed her to the entryway, where she bent over to pull on her shoes. "I'm sorry," he said. "I didn't mean to go on about myself."

When she rose to put on her coat, he was standing before her with such a pained expression that she felt herself soften. She sighed. "No, I'm sorry," she said. "It's just that I would give so much for a new beginning." She knew, as she spoke, that she sounded bitter. What did it matter? She was. She'd been bitter for some time. She just didn't have the energy to hide it anymore.

"Please," he said. "Don't be sorry." He took a deep breath in and let it out in a sigh. "You probably feel like life is going to be impossible forever. Right now, I mean."

Susan stared at him.

"It's not, though," he continued, watching her. He took a step closer and reached out, settled his hand on her shoulder. "Life is always changing. God surprises us in good ways, too."

Susan took a step backward, and Robert let his hand fall. She gulped down the tears rising in her throat and reached for the doorknob.

"I hope you'll come back. To church," he clarified.

"Maybe I will," she said. "Though I don't know how happy that would make the deacons."

"Ah," he said. "Don't worry about them. I think deep down they like a little excitement."

"Maybe," she said, and laughed a little. "Maybe not."

"But maybe," he said. He followed her out into the cold. "And please let me know if the church can help you out in any way," he said. "Please," he added.

He stood on the porch and gave a wave as she drove away.

49

It was Saturday at New Horizons, and Saturday was visiting day. Sunday could have been visiting day, too, and Susan could have driven the kids up after school a couple of nights a week if she'd wanted, but Sundays she said she had too much to do, and weekday evenings she said they didn't have enough time, even though they did, if you did the math. Randy was in no place to complain, he knew. And so he was trying to see his family's once-a-week visits as opportunities to demonstrate improvement.

Actually, that was Doc Nelson's idea. Randy had to retrain his brain, Doc said. He had to start thinking of challenges as chances to let go of all the shit that he couldn't control and focus on what he could control instead.

Randy wouldn't have admitted it to anyone, but it surprised him how much sense all the psychiatric stuff made. Sure, there were questions he didn't want to answer and more questions about things so far back they couldn't have mattered anymore—his mom dying, his dad kicking his ass, all the other stuff he'd tried his damnedest to forget. But therapy was also a lot more practical than he'd expected. There was a way, he'd learned, not to act on the anger—to wait the anger out. To stand within the wave of it until it peaked and fell. To breathe in a way that calmed you down. To release the pressure from the valve a little at a time instead of ignoring it until the whole thing blew to pieces.

There were strategies. Dr. Will called them "tools" that the patients could keep in their "toolboxes." All the language around them made Randy feel stupid, like a child, but damnitall if the tools didn't help. Randy hoped that when he got home, they would help even more.

At the hospital, his major challenges were dealing with all the memories that kept coming up in therapy. Memories of his mother, of how much she'd loved him. Memories of his father, of how jealous he'd been—jealous of his son, of all people, though it wasn't until therapy that Randy realized that. The funeral. The aftermath. Hiding in the basement, the mud room, the garage. Sobbing in the dark. He felt these physically now, like wounds. He tried to breathe through them, he tried to "release," even if he still couldn't figure out what the fuck that meant.

His other challenges were mostly small annoyances. Wibble Webster and the way he burst into the Weebles song at the top of his voice when you were trying to take a nap or eat your dinner or watch TV in the big room. Curly Strothers and how he would just walk in front of the screen and stand there rubbing his nose with the back of his hand until someone started shouting and an orderly had to usher him out of the way. Glenn Deeter and how he talked about Susan every chance he could (he'd seen her once) and called her "a fine piece of ass," which Randy knew he was supposed to take as a compliment. He breathed and he counted and he waited and he visualized and he identified solutions. He was trying as hard as he could with what life gave him.

Doc Nelson agreed that Randy was making good progress, but he still wasn't sure whether he'd be able to release Randy before Christmas. Randy tried to see this timeline as an opportunity, too—a chance to master his new skills, to sidestep the extra stress of the season and to kick off a new start in the new year.

Susan was giving them one more chance. She'd promised, and Susan's promises meant something. When they were all back together again in their old space, she would see how much he'd changed. If he kept on trying long enough, she'd have to see and believe. Trying was an opportunity, he told himself. Trying was something he could control.

Still, despite his optimism, Randy knew that in many ways it was easier to be locked away than it was to be free. Even though people complained about it, the food wasn't so bad, and there was more than enough of it. The temperature never got too hot or too cold. The hot water never ran out, and if you got up early enough, you didn't have to wait in line for a shower. You didn't have to shovel the driveway. You didn't have to punch in for work and get a talking-to when the weather made you late.

In the hospital, he moved along for hours feeling clear and good, better than he'd felt in years, and then he'd remember his life before the hospital, all his rages and suspicions. He'd remember Willa staring down at her thrown-up food and his stew bowl flying through the air and his fist punching through the pastor's wall, and the memory of his own actions would confound him. He'd been so violent then, so blind. What if only his surroundings had changed? What if he'd return home and switch back into the same maniac he'd been before?

No, he assured himself, he would not. He was different. Better. People changed like that. It was possible. People converted. People got wake-up calls and woke the fuck up. But then his thoughts would stray to Susan and the pastor and the life she might be making without him, and he'd have to remind himself that she visited him and asked how he was and had told him, at the end of their last visit, that she loved him. He'd said it first, but she'd said it, too. And Randy would breathe in for a count of four and hold it for a count of seven and exhale for a count of eight and ride the wave of panic until it passed.

Now it was Saturday, December 21, the last Saturday before Christmas. Randy had saved two Santa-shaped chocolates for Willa and Lukas. Anywhere else, they'd be wrapped in colorful foil, but in the psych ward, foil had been outlawed along with damn near everything else, probably because some crazy asshole had stockpiled a shit ton of it and tried to work it into a knife, and so Randy had wrapped them in a napkin. Without the foil, they didn't look much like Santas, but you could still tell what they were if you looked close enough, and the kids wouldn't mind anyway because chocolate was chocolate. Also, it would show Susan that he'd been thinking of them. Win-win.

The visiting room was full up, so they had to share a table with "the Duke"—Earl Cheatle—and his lady friend. Everyone called him the Duke because he really thought he was one, and his lady friend thought so, too, judging by the way she stared up at him all big-eyed and moony, like he'd just been awarded the kingship. He was dead skinny and almost seven feet tall, with long yellow teeth and long, straight silver hair that he always flipped over his shoulders with the back of his hands, like a woman. He looked batshit crazy, was the point.

Of course, the Duke's table was the only one with extra chairs, so Susan and the kids had already seated themselves there when Randy came in. Lukas didn't even look up at Randy because he couldn't stop staring at the Duke. Willa stood to hug him, but Susan stayed where she was. He bent and hugged her anyway, awkwardly, and then he wrapped his arm around Lukas's shoulders and shook him a little so that he finally said, "Hi, Dad."

There was one chair left. There should have been three chairs on his side of the table, but someone (probably one of his kids) had moved one of the chairs to the opposite side, so it was Randy and the Duke, the crazies, on one side, and the visitors on the other. Lukas, seated beside the Duchess, was still staring at the Duke, who was still talking nonstop, only louder now that his audience had grown and flipping his hair back more often with more and more ferocity. Willa was studying Randy too closely, with a worried face. Susan looked bored, or maybe distracted, like she was just there to get it over with.

"So what's new?" Randy asked a little loudly, so as to be heard over the Duke.

"Nothing," Susan said. "How are you?"

"Better every day," he called over the table. He had thought about it beforehand and decided to answer that question in just that way. He'd hoped the phrase would sound positive, but now, the way it came out, it sounded like he was picking a fight. He remembered the chocolates and took them out of his pocket. "Saved you kids something," he said. He placed the napkin on the table between them. Lukas finally broke his tractor beam on the Duke and leaned over to look inside.

"It looks like poop," he said.

"It's not poop," Randy said. He pushed down his annoyance. "It's chocolate. I saved it for you guys."

Willa leaned over and took one. "Thanks, Dad," she said, but then she set it on the table in front of her and left it there.

Lukas pulled the napkin close and leaned over it again. "Why does it look like that?" he asked.

"It's Santa," Randy said.

"Santa poop?" Lukas asked. He looked up at Randy with a sly smile.

"Never mind," Randy said. He reached out, wadded the napkin around the chocolate, and stuffed it back into his pocket.

"Randy," Susan said, already exasperated. "He's just playing with you."

"No he's not. He's trying to piss me off." It was like his anger had been sleeping and all of it woke up at the same time.

"I was going to eat it," Lukas said in a trembly voice.

"You can have mine," Willa said, and she slid hers down the table toward her brother.

"No," said Randy, picking up Willa's Santa and placing it firmly back down in front of her. "That's yours."

"It's okay," Susan said. "She doesn't like chocolate."

"What?" Randy asked. How could he not know that? "What kid doesn't like chocolate?"

Susan shrugged wearily. "She never has." She said it like she was blaming him for not knowing that already.

Lukas reached across Susan and snatched Willa's Santa. He bit into its head, which broke into pieces. Some of them fell out of Lukas's mouth and landed on the table. "It's empty," he whined. He was drooling a little.

Randy breathed deeply in and out. Doc Nelson: *Everything is practice.* He breathed in for four counts, held it for seven, and breathed out for eight. Then he realized that, to Susan, it might look like he was trying not to lose it. "How are things at home?" he asked. He tried to sound cheerful. "How's school?" he asked Willa.

"Okay," Willa said, and she gave Susan a look that meant something, only he didn't know what.

"Is it okay?" he asked Susan.

"Yeah," said Susan. "Everything's okay." And she reached her arm around Willa and gave her a sideways hug.

"Really?" Randy asked. "What aren't you telling me?" He was proud of himself for noticing, for caring. Susan should be proud of him, too.

At the other end of the table, the Duke and the Duchess stood up and sucked face for a while, rubbed their arms all over each other like they wanted to make sure everyone saw. Then they went their separate ways, out their opposite doors.

The visiting room had been emptying without Randy's notice, and the sudden quiet made him feel off-balance somehow. Susan hadn't answered him. She was still hugging Willa and running her hand up and down Willa's arm. Lukas was sitting in her lap now, licking the chocolate off his fingers. In one terrifying moment, Randy saw them physically moving away from him, sliding backward, like the table was getting wider or they were all getting smaller or he himself was being pulled back against his will, away from the rest of the world. He rubbed at his eyes and blinked a few times and pulled his chair closer to the table and reached across and ruffled Lukas's hair. Everything settled around him again, and the terror subsided. Doc Nelson: *No feeling is forever.*

"You okay?" Susan asked. She was staring at him the way you'd stare at a crazy person.

"Of course I'm okay," he said. "I just like to know what's going on, that's all. Just like anybody else."

Susan watched him a bit longer. "Willa had a little episode at school this week. A panic attack. But she got through it. I came to get her and took her home and now she's feeling lots better. Right, Willa?"

Willa nodded. She was looking down into her lap.

"You okay now, Willa?" Randy asked. She nodded again. "Good," he said. He looked at Susan. She looked so tired. She had a deep line between her eyebrows that he'd never noticed before and little pouches under the outside corners of her eyes. Lukas was trying to pull her sleeve down over her hand and smearing chocolate all over the fabric in the process.

"Good," Randy said again to Willa. "'Cause your mother doesn't need any more trouble."

"Randy," Susan said, and she shook her head.

"What?" he asked. "I'm trying to defend you here."

"It wasn't her fault," Susan said. "She couldn't help it."

"Well how am I supposed to know that?"

"It was a panic attack. Who tries to have a panic attack?"

"Hey, I know some things, too," he said. "I been learning a lot in here. It's all in your state of mind."

"Really?" she said, only she said it in her angry voice. She was glaring at him, tight-lipped and pale. He'd never seen her look this way before. She looked foreign. Ugly, even. "Would you like to share these revelations with the rest of us?"

"What the fuck, Suzy-Q?"

"Stop calling me that," she said through clenched teeth.

He stared back at her, felt an echoing anger swelling in his gut. But it rose and broke from his mouth as a weak, bitter laugh. "You must think I've got it so good in here."

She set Lukas firmly back in his chair, leaned forward over the table, and lowered her voice to a hissing whisper. "Do you know what I'd give for some help? For someone to cook my meals and someone else to listen to my problems? And someone else to make sure my kids had everything *they* needed?"

"You're right, Suzy. You obviously need a lot more help than I do."

They stared at each other across an icy silence. Then Susan shook her head. "It's not a competition, Randy. You're just not the only one who finds life impossible sometimes. The rest of us have to carry on anyway."

"Why don't you ask that pastor for help? Maybe he could meet some of your needs."

Randy had decided early on at the hospital not to bring up the pastor. It would sound jealous, paranoid. But it was like Susan had pulled out a plug and all the bad in him was spilling out. Of course she wouldn't call the pastor. She was the family caretaker—the better half, if he was being honest.

But now that he'd finally brought up the pastor, Susan wouldn't respond. She wouldn't even look at him. She just bent over and took a package of wet wipes out of her purse, pulled one free, and rubbed around Lukas's mouth with it, then started on his fingers. She looked guilty, was how she looked. Willa pulled a book out from somewhere and sank farther into her chair, hid her face behind the open cover. When Susan had finished cleaning Lukas off, she let him slide down from her lap and wander away. Finally she spoke.

"You just go ahead and think whatever you want to think," she said.

"Suzy," he said. He sounded desperate—scared. He was scared. He felt suddenly sick with fear. "You could at least tell me I'm being ridiculous."

Susan crossed her arms and shook her head. "No," she said. "I'm not going to play that game anymore. You're going to think whatever you want to think, and I'm not going to participate. It wouldn't be good for you if I did."

They locked glares across the table. He could see them from above, squared off across an impossible distance. It seemed that no matter how hard he tried, some invisible force kept working on them, pulling them back into battle positions. It occurred to him that the two of them would never be able to make things work. The thought came so naturally, like a given. Fear gushed up and drowned his anger.

"I'm sorry!" he almost shouted. He resituated himself. "We don't need to fight. I'm trying to be better." He sounded so desperate. He could feel his eyes dampening, and his face burned in embarrassment. "It's just so hard to be better."

Susan was watching him like this might all be a trick. Then her eyes softened, just a little, and she gave him a small nod. She turned her head to track Lukas, and Randy's gaze followed. The room had almost cleared out with only five minutes left until lunch.

"I don't know why we have to fight," he said. They had just enough time to talk about this, to try and smooth it over.

Lukas was standing in front of Wibble and his mom, staring. Wibble was rocking back and forth, like he always did, and his mom was kind of hugging him from the side. From across the room, Randy heard Lukas ask, "Why is he doing that?"

"Lukas!" Randy called. The boy glanced back at him but stayed where he was. Wibble's mom was explaining something in a quiet voice. "Lukas!" he called again, louder this time.

"He's fine," Susan said.

"He's rude," Randy said.

"He's curious," she corrected him. He hated it when she corrected him. Like she knew so much more about everything than he did. Susan stood and walked over to Lukas, said something to Wibble's mom. Together, they laughed softly. Willa was still absorbed in her book. She paid him no mind.

"Visiting time's almost over," he said. He said it to no one, really, but he said it loud enough for Willa to look up from her book and Susan to turn and lift one finger, a gesture that meant *wait*. Then she turned forward and kept listening to whatever Wibble's mom was saying. She stood there for a long time, her back to him. Wibble's mom finished talking, and Susan launched into an animated response. It was like she was showing off how little she cared to speak to her own husband. Wibble was looking up at her with excited eyes and a wet, open mouth, ogling Susan, relishing her attention.

Randy's chair screeched as he shoved it back, and the table shuddered as he stood, knocking his legs against the edge. "It's time for lunch," he called. Susan turned and nodded at him to show that she'd heard, then turned back. Wibble was going on and on about something, and Susan was just standing there, listening to him. She reserved her politeness for everyone else.

"All right," he said. "Bye, Willa."

Willa turned around. "Mom!" she called.

"Bye, Lukas," he said. Lukas didn't even turn, but Susan did.

"Just a second," she said over her shoulder, like he was a child.

He waited one beat.

"Your second's up," he said. "Merry fucking Christmas." And against his better judgment, he stomped out.

50

Robert next saw Susan on Sunday, when she came to church. She and Willa and Lukas slipped into the back pew during the opening hymn, with everyone standing and singing. Robert had been preoccupied with Leotie, who sat glumly in the aisle in a borrowed wheelchair. (She hadn't been eager to come, but Robert couldn't leave her so long alone in her current state.) He didn't notice Susan and the kids until he stepped up to the pulpit to lead the congregation in prayer, and when he did notice them, an expression of happy surprise crossed his face—so obvious that several in the congregation turned to locate the person at whom he was looking.

Robert quickly straightened his face and bowed his head, stumbled through the opening prayer only half conscious of the words he was speaking. He took the second hymn to compose himself, though when he again stepped up to the pulpit—this time to deliver the sermon—he was aware of a new ease and enthusiasm in his movements and a fresh confidence in the words he spoke. He wondered how noticeable it was.

Robert had recycled a sermon from his early years at Esau Baptist. He almost hoped his congregation would notice. He'd felt reckless over the past week, angry. Trying to manage the complexities of his mother's care had overwhelmed him, and he'd put off starting that week's sermon until right before Susan's visit on Friday. Then he began to think of the deacons' meeting a week before and his small, stagnant salary and the family fund he'd been padding. He'd been so humble, so stupidly trusting. A visceral anger possessed him. He had never recycled a sermon before, which he realized all at once was ridiculous. As it was less than a week until Christmas, he dug in his file drawer of sermons and found an Advent teaching he'd written about nine years back, before Cliff Grable informed him that an Advent series struck the congregation as "a little too, well, Catholic." So Robert crossed out all the specific references to Advent and then, when he sat down for his final Saturday run-through, he erased all his cross-out marks and circled the words instead.

Now, standing behind the pulpit, Robert read his sermon, aware that he was speaking smoothly and well and largely unaware of the meaning of what he was saying.

His mother rested her head against her chair and slept through the first half of Robert's teaching, her breath a gentle saw. Then the phlegm caught in her throat, her head snapped forward, and she began to cough in loud, garbled barks. At first Robert tried to carry on, hoping the fit might pass, but the coughing grew louder and harder. He thought maybe someone near Leotie might go to her aid, but no one did, and when he finally paused his sermon and stepped back from the pulpit to attend to her, Susan slipped out of her seat on the opposite side of the sanctuary, stole around the back and up the side aisle, and rolled Leotie out into the lobby. Robert resumed his sermon over Leotie's coughs and Susan's muttered comforts, over the *glug glug glug* of the water cooler. The coughing paused, then started up again, then tapered off. Susan rolled Leotie back in and parked Leotie's chair beside her own pew.

Afterward, Robert thanked Susan on her way out. He made his gratitude cursory enough not to draw too much attention from Clark Fisher, who had come before her trailing his sharp-angled wife and their perfectly pressed children, or from Cliff Grable, who stood next in line, no doubt waiting impatiently to revoice his concerns about the slippery slope of Advent. Robert simply said, "Thank you for helping my mother," to which Susan responded, "You're welcome," and that was that.

In the afternoon that followed, while his mother snored gently on the couch and Ethel Grable's cheesy potato casserole blistered in the oven, he reflected further on the moment. He wished he'd let himself linger more, let the deacons conjecture all that stood unspoken between Susan and himself. But for now, he supposed, for his mother's sake, it was best if he didn't rock the boat too much.

LEOTIE, ROBERT REALIZED, hadn't come with the intent of guilting him into caring for her. She had come because she loved him, because, as she let slip once when he'd helped her through yet another coughing fit in the middle of the night, holding her breathing mask over her nose and mouth and resting his hand on her shoulder until her breathing calmed, "You're still the best thing that's ever happened to me."

Leotie's perspective had begun to work on Robert. She saw him as bright and wise and worthy of better treatment, and she said so. And her observations, combined with his treatment at the hands of the deacons, had flipped a switch in his head, and now he couldn't unsee it everywhere. All the suspicions he'd raised without having done anything to justify them. His mother's coughing attack that morning, how everyone besides Susan had let her just sit there, choking. How he'd had to plead for the use of the money that he had set by. How his mother, after everyone's initial nosiness had faded, had been ignored—practically shunned. No one, besides Ethel Grable and the Wellers, had even asked how she was.

When Mildred Rider's mother, Ida, was dying years back in Clarence and Mildred's home, someone had circulated a list for congregants to provide meals. Robert himself had come often—every evening when Ida neared the end. He'd been there when she passed, he'd sat with them in silence, he'd led the family in prayer, and he'd preached the funeral. But now that his own mother was dying, he found himself alone.

It's because you're the pastor, so you don't have a pastor. It's because you knew what to do, but they don't. He told himself this, but he didn't believe it.

Ethel Grable kept bringing him his Sunday casseroles. A few parishioners would squeeze his hand in a meaningful way as they exited. Sandy Weller and Betty Clemens had both separately told him, "You let us know if you need anything." But what could he say?

Help, I don't know what I'm doing. Please don't let me be alone in this.
No.

As a pastor, he'd visited families with new babies, and he'd witnessed firsthand the frightened helplessness of new parents as they tried to figure out what they were supposed to do. He suspected that those new parents felt much the way he felt now. Leotie's hospital stay and consequent escape had emptied her. She'd come home much weaker than she'd been when she first arrived, and she'd only gone downhill from there.

Now Leotie kept exclusively to the bed or the couch. Robert had already mastered her medicines and breathing treatments, but now there were more medicines, each to be taken a different number of hours apart, and some of them made her nauseous, and others made her constipated, and Robert had to address these complaints by spending long stretches on the phone waiting for a nurse or a physician to advise him.

On top of the side effects, each day brought new challenges. Trips to the bathroom became difficult. Then, after an embarrassing accident (embarrassing for his mother and consequently for himself), he purchased several packages of adult diapers. So far he'd been storing them on the bathroom counter with a package of wipes so that his mother could change them herself, though that current level of independence, judging by her decrease in movement, was rapidly drawing to a close. She began developing bedsores, so he'd moved her to his own bed—a move she had long refused—so that he could help her rotate positions more easily. She developed rashes that itched, chapped patches on her cheeks and lips and arms, a cramp there that eventually passed, a sharp pain here that kept returning.

Then the day before, Saturday, on her way back from the bathroom, his mother had tripped and caught her arm on the edge of a chair and torn open the skin. Robert wrapped the wound tightly in a towel, but it bled and bled and would not stop, so he drove her again to the emergency room, where they stitched the skin shut and sent Leotie home with yet another bottle of pills.

Now it was Sunday. That evening was the Christmas pageant, which thankfully, due to his circumstances, he had only to attend rather than lead. He'd had to request this, too. He'd called up the sharp-elbowed Cecelia

Fisher, who'd requested he also enlist the help of two other mothers. So he'd dialed up Nelly Plonski, who was too busy with her eight children, and Rhonda Paisley, who was too busy with her three, and finally Sandy Weller, who had told him (he'd almost cried in gratitude) not to worry about a thing, just to show up at seven on Sunday night and she'd make sure everything else was taken care of.

So that evening was the pageant, and Wednesday was Christmas. His mother's last, if she made it that long.

Early Sunday evening he heated up another two helpings of potato casserole for an early supper, mashing his mother's, and then undertook the lengthy process of prompting his mother through everything she would want to do before they left the house—bathroom break, clothing change, swishing with mouthwash, attending to her hair—before helping her into her coat and boots and down the front steps into the borrowed wheelchair, which he had to shove hard to push through the inches of snow that had accumulated in the drive since he'd last had a chance to shovel.

Struggling in from the cutting wind, the church building was so warm and hushed and dark that Robert's breath caught in his throat. Someone— Sandy Weller, apparently—had decided to darken the building save for the stage bulbs, dimmed, and several strands of tiny golden lights draped in symmetrical lines over a shed with an empty manger centered beneath. Along the front pews, children bustled, and Robert caught the glints of halos and the silhouettes of angel wings and shepherd crooks. Ethel Grable was already at the organ, pressing "Silent Night" out through the hushed reeds. The scene so captivated him that he failed to look around until he rolled his mother to the side of the pew farthest back and seated himself beside her. When he finally turned to try and make out the audience seated in the dark, he found that he had inadvertently sat beside Susan.

"Ah!" he said, too loudly, then lowered his voice. "Didn't see you there."

Susan smiled in reply and sent him a small wave, leaning forward to include his mother. She was seated close enough for Robert to feel, he thought, the warmth of her body spreading toward him, through his clothes and into his skin. He allowed himself to close his eyes for a moment and surrender to the sensation of it.

Ethel finished the final chorus of the song, and the organ fell silent. On the stage, Caleb Plonski stepped up to the microphone and began to read. "And it came to pass in those days, that there went out a decree from Caesar Augustus that all the world should be taxed." His voice trailed on as Shawn Paisley shuffled onto the stage in slippers and a bathrobe, followed by Adrianna Fisher, Clark's daughter (who somehow always secured the part of Mary), carrying a stuffed horse head, presumably to signify the donkey.

The pageant continued on in the usual way. Willa was the one angel with a speaking role ("Behold, I bring you good tidings of great joy!"), and Lukas played one of the silent shepherds. Robert stole sideways glances at Susan throughout the performance, tried to fix in his mind the shape of her face, the soft sheen of the lights across it.

The story of Jesus's birth, despite Robert's many years of studying the Bible, had always remained his favorite. Its circumstances and its details made him feel at home in the world in a way he did not usually feel. The characters were so unlikely, for one thing—a pregnant teenage girl and her flummoxed new husband, helpless and homeless in a place that was not their own, along with a cadre of shepherds, which Robert had once likened in a sermon to the worst sort of used car salesmen. Hired shepherds, as those in the story likely were, carried a nasty reputation of taking advantage of those whose flocks they were charged with keeping, so much so that they were generally shunned by society and even banned from testifying at court. The first to receive news of Jesus's birth, therefore, with the announcement of angels, no less, represented not only the most humble but also the most despised and mistrusted. Robert had always marveled at what a radical move that had been, to underscore the worth of every single person by upending the social order from the very beginning.

Robert turned to check whether his mother was awake. He could just make out the glints of reflections in her half-open eyes. Her crooked profile, her small cloud of hair, looked even smaller in the dim light, and her tiny figure was swallowed up entirely in the darkness. He wanted to lean over and whisper, *This story is for you.* And then he thought, *No, it's for us.*

By the performance's end, his mother, he could tell, was exhausted, and to cover the interest he was afraid he'd betrayed in Susan throughout the evening, he stood as soon as Ethel kicked off "Joy to the World" and nodded perfunctorily in Susan's direction. "Merry Christmas then," he said, irked again at his loud volume.

"Merry Christmas," Susan replied, just loud enough to be heard. "Merry Christmas, Leotie."

On his way out, he thanked Sandy Weller for the beautiful evening and forgot also to thank Cecelia Fisher, who was standing next to Sandy until Sandy, nervously glancing between them both, said, "It was Cece's idea to turn out the lights—wasn't that neat?"

Robert finally remembered that Cecelia had stepped up to organize the pageant as well. "Thank you, Cecelia," he said, "I just couldn't have managed it—"

"You're welcome," she interrupted.

After that, there was nothing to be done but to push his mother back through the snow and help her up the steps and off with her things and back into bed. But after he'd settled her there and freshened her water and administered her breathing treatment and her several nighttime pills, he stepped back out onto the porch and stood there for a time, relishing the shock of the cold and the sharp points of the stars and the echoes of peace the pageant had brought him—a peace he knew he would carry with him, even if he left the church behind.

51

"Fear not," Willa had said at pageant practice.

"Louder!" Mrs. Fisher had yelled from the back of the room. "I can't hear you, Willow! Louder! Shout it out now!"

Mrs. Fisher yelled at her so many times that finally Willa was shouting, almost in anger, and she felt so good and strong and angry that she shouted it out at the pageant, too, as loudly as she'd dared.

"Fear not! For behold! I bring you good tidings! Of great joy! Which shall be to all people! For unto you is born this day a Savior! Which is Christ the Lord! And this shall be a sign unto you! You shall find the babe wrapped in swaddling clothes! And lying in a manger!"

Willa had shouted so loudly at the pageant, in a standoff against her own nerves, that by the time the performance finished and she exited the church and took from Mrs. Weller her own paper sack of peanuts and candies and an orange and climbed into the front seat of the van, she felt a comfortable combination of awakeness and tiredness that she eventually realized was relief, a feeling she had not felt in so long that she'd forgotten what it was. The night, as they drove away, felt magical somehow. The sky seemed taller and clearer than usual, with a painful number of stars. Just two days until Christmas, and no more school for two whole weeks.

The next morning, her mother would drop them off at their grandparents' house, where Willa could do whatever she wanted all day long, which meant diving into the stack of books she'd brought home from the library.

And Willa's relief and the promise of her warm bed and the whole break stretching out ahead of her gave Willa enough courage to ask, as the van slipped over the snow into the driveway, whether they might put up the Christmas tree that night.

"It's late, Willa. I'm sorry. I'm just not up for it tonight."

But Lukas joined in on the begging, too, and by the time they made it in the door and pulled off their coats and boots, their mother had relented. She pulled the giant tree box down from the attic and the three of them assembled the tree together, matching the colors at the ends of the branches to the colors of the holes on the pole. Then their mother heated milk on the stove for hot chocolate while Willa and Lukas wrapped the lights around as well as they could and hooked the ornaments onto the ends of the wire branches. Then they sat around the tree on the floor with their warm cups and only the strings of Christmas lights shining and the heat from the woodstove baking their backs.

"This is nice," said Lukas. "This is fun."

"This is peaceful," said their mother.

"It is," said Willa.

"Do you feel peaceful, too?" her mother asked her.

Willa said, "Yes."

"That's good to know," her mother said. "That we can all feel peaceful. "Even now, just the three of us." She smoothed Willa's hair back from her forehead. It took Willa a moment to realize what her mother was saying. Something within Willa clamped down, and the worry asleep inside of her snorted awake like a dragon.

"No," Willa said. "Not without Dad. Not without Dad," she repeated, louder. She had almost betrayed him. The dragon was squeezing her lungs. The lights of the tree flickered and began to blur. Her mother said something, but suddenly Willa couldn't understand what she was saying. Lukas chimed in, but Willa couldn't make out his words, either. That strange whistling sound was coming again from a place high above her, and she understood that she herself was making the sound, but she didn't understand how. Inside the dragon was roaring like a windstorm in her ears, and she could feel the fire of his breath burning her. She was dying this time, she was dying for sure, and the fear was a river of fire that filled her all the way up until it burned out all the light and left her in darkness.

WHEN WILLA WOKE, she felt almost too weak to open her eyes, and when she finally did open them to peek at the room around her, she quickly squeezed them shut again. The lights were too bright, and she couldn't tell where she was. Strange shapes surrounded her. Maybe she had died and ended up somewhere else. She was almost too tired to care.

"Willa? Willa, honey?"

Her mother's voice.

She pried her eyes open again, allowed them to focus. Now a dark shadow loomed above her, and her mother's face shifted into shape.

"You're okay, honey. Everything's okay." Her mother's hand on her forehead felt smooth and cool.

"Where are we?" Willa's voice was rough and croaky, like a frog's.

"We're in the hospital. You fainted. There's nothing wrong, though. You're going to be all right."

An unfamiliar voice said, "Is she up?" and the curtain around Willa's bed screeched open. A tall, white-coated man stepped forward, slipped his cold fingers around her wrist and held them there for a moment, then reached up without speaking and pulled back her eyelids and glared into them with a sharp look, as if he were angry. The doctor released Willa's eyelashes and nodded.

"Well, that's that," he said. "You're free to go."

"Just like that?" her mother asked. "Isn't there anything we can do? This is the second attack she's had in four days."

"Well, you can talk with a licensed professional to help identify any sources of stress in her life."

"I would, but like I said, our insurance won't cover—"

"Beyond that, there's really nothing you can do. There are medicines, but only psychiatrists can prescribe them."

"There's got to be something," she said, but another man in another white coat stepped inside the curtain and leaned close and whispered something into the first man's ear. The first man nodded to Susan and said, "Best of luck," and then he was gone.

Willa was pushing herself upright. Beside her bed lay Lukas, curled up asleep under his coat on two chairs pushed together. He looked the same way he used to look when he was a baby and Willa's mom had to hold Willa back from kissing him and waking him up—long lashes, round cheeks, puckery lips. Was he sick? Maybe he was sick. Why else would he be sleeping right then?

"Mom, what's wrong with Lukas?" Willa asked.

"Nothing. He's sleeping."

"Why is he sleeping?"

"Willa, it's the middle of the night. It's time for him to be sleeping."

"Why is it the middle of the night?"

"Because they gave you medicine, and it took some time for it to wear off. And now it's worn off, and it's time to head home." She sank down onto Willa's bed holding Willa's coat out by the collar, as if she was waiting for Willa to climb down and walk backward and stick her arms in the sleeves. Willa wasn't sure she could ever remember her mother looking so tired. She looked almost as if she was about to cry, but then, as Willa peered at her, she could see that it was just her mother's skin pulling down—down at her eyes and her cheeks, down at the corners of her mouth. Willa could make out her grandma then—her mother's mother—in her mother's face. And fear swelled up, like water swelling over a rock.

"Are you sick, Mom? Tell me you're not sick. Tell me you're not going to die." Usually when Willa had such thoughts, she tucked them away inside, but she wasn't strong enough to hold them in right then. As the words came out, so did the tears, and soon she was sobbing, and her mother's arms were around her and her mother's voice was speaking into her neck.

"Willa, you need to stop this. You need to get ahold of this. You can't go on like this anymore. Neither can I." And then her mother was crying, too, and they sat there crying together and holding on to each other until Willa felt better enough to say, "I'm sorry, Mom. I'll be better. I promise I'll be better," and for her mother to say, "No, honey. It's not your fault. I'm sorry. None of this is your fault at all."

Willa fell asleep on the drive home and woke only briefly when her mother pulled her out the van door and carried her (how long had it been since her mother had carried her?) up the steps and into the house.

WHEN WILLA WOKE the next morning, the sun had already risen, and Lukas's bed was a tangle of sheets and blankets with no Lukas in it. Willa could hear *Sesame Street* coming from the living room, and she thought she could smell something cooking—pancakes? She sat on the side of her bed and triple-checked her angel before heading down the hall. Lukas, as she'd expected, was parked in front of the TV and Willa's mother was in the kitchen, buzzing the electric mixer around a bowl. She clicked it off when Willa stepped into view.

"Well hello there, sleepyhead," she said, a little too cheerfully, but Willa tried to overlook that detail.

"Good morning," Willa said.

"Feeling any better today?"

Willa nodded.

"I thought maybe we'd decorate Christmas cookies."

Willa noted again the forced cheerfulness in her voice. Her mother was trying so hard, and so Willa tried, too. She made herself nod and smile. "You don't have to work today?" she said.

"Nope. Not today. Today I'm taking the day off to play with my kiddos."

"That sounds good," said Willa. "Cookies sound good."

"Yeah?"

"Yeah."

"Great. And then tomorrow is Christmas Eve, and I'll have to work until just after lunch, and so you and Lukas will spend the morning at the parsonage, and I'll pick you up just as soon as I'm done."

So that explained the cheerfulness.

Her mother turned the mixer back on and continued buzzing it around the bowl.

"No," said Willa.

"I'm sorry?" said her mother, clicking off the mixer, pretending like she hadn't heard.

"I'm not going to the parsonage."

"Willa," her mother said. "I'm not sure we have a choice." Her voice was still sweet, like she knew she had to plead, but Willa could just make out the warning underneath.

"Why can't we just go to Grandma's house?"

Her mother finally set the mixer down and turned to her. She put both of her hands on Willa's shoulders. "Because, Willa. I need you nearby. In case there's another . . . episode." Her mother paused before pronouncing the word *episode*, like she was considering whether to use the word *episode* or *accident*.

Willa considered her mother's reasoning and thought she could understand it. She would not want to have an attack at her grandparents' house, and if she did, she would not want her mother to be so far away. But the pastor's house? The pastor who her mother was half in love with? Wasn't there any other choice?

"Please, Willa," her mom said. "I know it's not ideal. But it's just for the morning. I promise. And then we'll figure out something else."

Willa stood there for a few moments in silence, her mind darting around for some other option, but nothing came to mind, and anyway, she felt guilty for being another one that had to be worried about, had to be watched so much more closely even than her baby brother. Her mother looked hopeful, but more than that, she looked tired.

She would go, then, to the pastor's house. But she would *not* pretend to enjoy it.

52

Susan had only asked Robert to watch her children as
a last resort, but she felt terrible about it nevertheless. When she called on
Monday, the morning after Willa's second panic attack, the pastor's voice,
though it had brightened when he realized who was calling, had sounded
so rough, so exhausted. And then she'd asked him, with as much reluctance
as she could make plain, if he might watch the kids the following morning.
She explained Willa's recent panic episodes and how Susan had to be very
close by and how there was no one else in Esau she could ask. It would just
be for the morning, she stressed, and she understood how much he had on
his plate and just what a gigantic favor she was requesting and she wouldn't
have asked him if there had been any other option at all besides possibly
losing her job.

When she finally finished her pleading outburst, Robert agreed, but
sounded distant somehow, and she could only speculate as to whether that
distance came from resentment, perhaps, for the request, or annoyance at
the big deal she made of asking for it, or even disappointment that she was
using him for a mundane task instead of reaching out in a way intended to
secure some deeper intimacy between them.

But no matter, she tried to tell herself. The only thing now was to keep
her family afloat through Christmas. She would drop the kids off at the
parsonage and work the abbreviated Christmas Eve shift, which was ru-
mored to be a profitable one, and then she would drive the kids down to her

mother's and drop them off before departing on her last-minute Christmas shopping at the Wal-Mart just down the road, where her mother could call and have her paged over the intercom system if it came to that. Susan would keep her job and keep her kids safe and give them a Christmas. Then, after their Christmas morning at home, they would pass the evening with Randy at New Horizons, where he'd been granted an outing of two hours in the place of dinner.

Beyond that, Susan could not bring herself to consider because beyond that posed the same impossibilities that Susan had already failed to resolve. Willa would still be at risk of panicking herself unconscious at any given moment, and Susan would still need to work, which meant she would still need to secure childcare closer to work, at least for the remainder of the children's winter break, and Randy would still be each moment closer to moving back home.

After Randy's blowup at Susan's last visit, he had called and apologized in all earnestness. He had taken full responsibility for his actions and asked her what he could do to make things right. Those had been, strangely enough, the exact words he'd used. It was as though he were reading from some script. "I want you to know I take full responsibility for my actions. Now what can I do to make things right?"

You can stop being an asshole, she wanted to say, but instead she said, "You can apologize to the children, too."

"Yes, of course," he replied, and she put them each on the phone in turn, and they each said, "That's okay, Dad," and "I love you, too," and that was that. She took the phone back from Lukas, and she and Randy talked a little more. She could hear the small triumph in his voice—how proud of himself he'd been—and she'd thought, *Leave it to a man to be prouder of his apology than he is ashamed of throwing the tantrum that preceded it.*

Still, she let it go, and she promised to be there on Christmas Day no matter the weather, as a warm front was supposed to be moving through and with it a storm.

She hadn't bought Randy anything for Christmas that year, since she assumed he hadn't the money or the means to get her anything, either. For all of his faults, Randy had always been dependable on that score. It had been one area in which his father had abysmally failed and in which Randy had determined to do better and had continuously done so. Every birthday, every Christmas, he had gifted her something. Usually they were stereotypically feminine gifts—a necklace, chocolates, a bottle of perfume. Once he bought her lingerie, black and poky and concealing nothing, only embellishing it with the shapes of the lace and a complicated system of bands and straps. She'd worn it once out of obligation and afterward had thrown it away and claimed to have lost it. It had felt like she was playing some ridiculous part—so fake, so impersonal.

But on a few occasions, Randy had proved so thoughtful in his giving that it had surprised her. One year he'd overheard her complaining about her sewing bag and how it didn't hold shut and kept spilling out her threads and pins. That year she'd found beneath the tree a beautiful sewing basket with a container inside of various-sized compartments and a woven lid that latched with a big wooden bead. Another year, the Christmas after Susan's grandma Claire had passed, Randy had hunted down photographs of Susan and her grandmother together and had them reprinted and resized, then assembled them into a collage frame. Susan had cried when she'd opened it, the gesture had moved her that much.

It was moments like those that Susan kept returning to when she came close to counting her losses and walking away from it all. There were two Randys, and she couldn't leave the one without abandoning the other. There was the Randy that the world would hold up as an argument to go—the Randy who lost his temper, who terrorized his children, who, with his volatile combination of machismo and insecurity, eventually chased all of her friends and aspirations away so that he might keep her hedged and lidded and all to himself. But then there was the Randy who hated himself for all of this, who would have been the Randy she loved much more often were it not for all the pain he'd endured. And that pain had been inflicted upon him when he was so young and so vulnerable. How could she, of all people—the only one who truly understood his story—be the one who injured him most of all?

And then there was Willa, who was so determined to prove her love for her father that the only wish she articulated these days was the wish that he'd come home. Susan suspected this to be far more act than truth. Still, her daughter's state was so delicate that it was impossible to tell. What would happen if Susan ripped off that Band-Aid? What if she whisked Willa away, against her will, from what Susan knew to be the biggest source of her suffering? Would the wound heal, exposed to air? Or would the pain prove too much? And what of Susan's own promise to give Randy one more chance? She would have to deliver on that promise, after all.

But what it really came down to was that Susan had just enough strength to keep going as things were, and barely enough for that.

On Tuesday morning, Christmas Eve, Susan woke the kids early and saw that they were fed well and dressed in clean pants long enough for their ever-lengthening legs and clean shirts with no holes or stains. She spent rather more time than usual on her face and hair, though she couldn't do anything about the garish teal polo Jeff insisted she wear. She could sense Willa looking at her extra efforts with suspicion.

"Why does it matter what we look like?" she asked. "You wouldn't care so much if we were only going to Grandma's house."

"You have to make more of an effort when people don't know you as well," Susan tried to explain with conviction. "Otherwise, they'll get the wrong impression."

"Why do you care what you look like, then? You're not sticking around. Why are you wearing makeup today? Why are you spending so much time on your hair?"

Susan was smoothing out her locks with a large curling iron. "I have to work today, Willa. You know that."

"Why don't you try so hard on all the other days, then?"

This final question Susan ignored. Willa was going to think what she wanted to think regardless, and Susan was reluctant to admit the truth even to herself.

Pastor Robert's admission of his feelings for Susan had come at the worst possible time, and after the horror that followed, Susan had tried to forget that moment, or at least to mitigate her impressions of it. Still, Robert's affections had been so apparent to his mother that she'd invited Susan to Thanksgiving without Robert's knowledge. This fact gave Susan a little thrill whenever she considered it. But the thrill was the thrill of being adored rather than the thrill of adoring, and Susan knew better than to confuse the two.

The pastor was a good man. He was the kind of man Susan should have fallen for all those years ago, when she'd had the chance to choose differently. But to trifle now with his feelings would be to play him along for her own distraction and amusement. It would be self-indulgent at best and cruel at worst. She regretted even having to lean on him for this relatively small favor. And yet, here she was, curling her hair. A sentence she'd heard once came back to her. *The heart wants what it wants.*

Yes, she agreed. *But it doesn't have to take it.*

They arrived a little later than she'd intended—Willa had been stalling—and Robert greeted them at the door, hair still damp from the shower and a smell of soap with some kind of spice in it. Susan had the ridiculous urge to lean close and breathe it in. His mother was sitting up in front of the television. She waved and called out a hoarse hello.

"I brought jungle Legos!" Lukas shouted, holding up his backpack.

"Jungle Legos?" said Pastor Robert. He sounded genuinely excited. "And hello, Willa," he said warmly, but Willa pulled her feet out of her boots and stalked over to the chair in the corner, where, still in her coat, she plunked herself down, opened her book, and stuck her nose in it.

"Willa," Susan said in a warning voice.

"It's okay," Pastor Robert said, and Susan could tell that he meant it and that he understood. She thanked him and resisted the urge to hug him and left.

Susan's shift that day did not go as well as she'd hoped, though she did earn more money than she typically earned on a Tuesday. Besides the usual patrons, that morning saw the addition of three bigger parties—a six-top, a seven-top, and an eleven-top. The six-top, however, was the staff of Larry's Garage, two of whom only ordered coffee to go with their cigarettes, and

Larry's tip was as shrewd as his reputation at exactly 10 percent (three dollars and eighteen cents) and all of it in change save for one balled-up dollar bill.

The seven-top, to Susan's embarrassment, turned out to be the ladies' quilting circle from Esau Baptist, most of whom behaved politely enough at the beginning but eventually ran her ragged, with the exception of sweet Lucy. Florence ordered an omelet, which she claimed, after eating all of it, not to have ordered in the first place. Marjorie's food was "practically frozen," though Susan spied the steam rising off it when Lenny slid it onto the counter. And Cecelia handed back her biscuits and gravy after devouring half of it, declaring that, no offense, she wouldn't have the heart to feed that to her dog and could she please just have one pancake with absolutely nothing on top of it. Still, four out of the seven ladies each left her a dollar, and Lucy Beamer, when she thought Susan wasn't watching, shuffled the money into the center of the table and slipped a five-dollar bill underneath.

The final party, the eleven-top, was Darlene Dickey and "her cronies" (Lenny's words), who, apart from the chain-smoking, would have been easy to serve were it not for the looks they kept giving her—looks of intense scrutiny that transformed themselves into false smiles every time Susan caught them watching. After Robert had visited Susan at the restaurant and informed her that the whole town had been openly discussing her private struggles, Susan had identified this look on the faces of her customers and had developed her own understanding of what it meant.

At first, she had tried to tell herself that the people of Esau were regarding her so closely out of sympathy and concern, but now, as a sort of public servant, Susan had experienced too much stinginess and chauvinism and even outright hostility to believe anymore that this was the case. Instead she had come to understand that they viewed her as something of a sideshow to capture their attention when the main acts of their lives ceased to be entertaining. It was probably a pleasure to consider that, for all their difficulties, at least their significant other wasn't locked up in a loony bin and at least they didn't have to wait tables in a tiny town where everyone and their brother could sneak a front-row peek at a life falling fantastically apart whenever they wanted. So Darlene Dickey's twenty-dollar bill, which she tossed into the middle of the table with a slightly exaggerated flourish, felt like a tip not only for Susan's service but also for her performance, for her generosity in giving them all someone to ogle and gossip about, and for the opportunity she gave Darlene to showcase her dazzling largesse.

Susan was still sliding the small heaps of change from Darlene's table into her apron when the phone rang. For once, Susan, in her annoyance at the general public, forgot to worry until she answered the telephone and Robert's voice responded.

"Willa's fine, and so is Lukas," he said first, an act that astonished Susan later, when she had time to consider how much he must have been grappling with at that exact moment and yet how he'd thought to allay her fears first of all. His voice lowered then almost to a whisper. "But I'm calling to tell you that my mother just died, and I thought you'd better come."

53

In her last days, when she wasn't stretched out on her son's bed, where he could roll her back and forth and, with a delicateness so kind it was almost painful, dab ointment on her sores, Leotie mostly just sat slumped in front of the television and let her mind wander. Then, when it wandered too far, she would try and bring it back to the program at hand.

It felt to Leotie that she'd already lived most of her life regretting. But as she neared the end, her regret kept finding new places to puddle—other holes in her history, other memories. She relived each of these over and over until the endless river of regret flushed her out of one and on into the next. It carried her forward and backward and over and down, close and clear and cruel. Little Bobby sobbing in the shower that long-ago December evening, so ashamed of her. Bobby tangled up in that old rottweiler's chain and how she'd slapped him for it, even though he was already covered in tears and filthy and terrified. Bobby at six years old, on the morning after his first tooth had fallen out and the tooth fairy had left him a penny instead of the dimes and quarters she left for the kids at school. It had pissed Leotie off then. She'd screamed at Bobby until he stopped crying. Now it made her whole chest hurt, remembering.

Back and back and back. All the times Bobby had asked her for some small thing—a game of hide-and-seek, a bus ride to the park, a library card—all the times she'd said no. The look he'd given her when she'd lost her new job at the Italian restaurant, the one that had let her take home leftovers at the end of each night. How the fear on her little boy's face had horrified her, that a child so small should already understand hunger. That look, and so many other looks of his throughout those early years, scared and tired and disappointed and sad, each face rising up out of the past, features fixed in place.

Down again and back. Bobby when he'd first learned to crawl at just five months old. She'd had a friend then, Callie, who'd gushed about how early he was. "Advanced," Callie called him. She'd looked at Bobby's hands and said he'd play the piano someday. Leotie had taken it as gospel truth. She'd figure out how to get him lessons. Of course she would. Bobby in the hospital, just born, mewling like a newborn cat. How he would startle and flail, and she knew somehow that he needed her to wrap him up tight and hold him. She wrapped him up, and she held him, and he stopped mewling, and she felt she could hold him like that forever. One of the nurses had said, "Would you look at that. You're a natural." And Leotie had thought, of course she was a natural. She was his mother, and he was her son. Of course she would always be able to give him exactly what he needed.

Back and back and back, all the way back to Leotie's mother. Her mother's dark curls, her plump, damp face and puffy eyes. Her mother leaning on the doorjamb of their trailer, with her arms crossed over her gut, the hand with the cigarette lifting up and down like a lever. Her mother leaning there, watching Leotie play in the street or skip to the bus stop, watching Leotie leave.

Leotie hadn't thought much about her mother since she ran away from home at sixteen. It seemed like she'd gone whole years without thinking of her mother at all. But when her Bobby memories ran out, and her lungs were still pulling in air slow and hard and loud like a backed-up drain, her mother washed up on the shore of her mind again and again. Her mother's arms, soft and always warm. Large enough to use as pillows. Long enough to swat or shove when Leotie wasn't expecting it. Her mother's nails, short and jagged and always black underneath, even though she never planted anything or picked up their tiny, scraggly strip of yard or even cleaned.

Nails were one thing Leotie had sworn she'd do differently. Nails and clothing and mothering, and by god, she'd kept her fingernails clean. On all other fronts, she had failed.

Before, when Leotie remembered her mother, all she remembered were the reasons why she left. The beatings, the screaming fits. Her mother's boyfriend, who "babysat"—pulled Leotie up onto his lap and rubbed her back and forth against his penis, sometimes made her jerk it up and down until it oozed. Leotie never told her mother. Her mother should have known.

The spectacle her mother made of herself wherever she went. There was an honors assembly once, in eighth grade, when Leotie made the honor roll. Her mom got wind of it and at the charity store bought a blouse as big as a house and bright red with sequins. She wore it with red clown lipstick that didn't quite match and ratty tennis shoes and black pants with a rip down the back of one leg that she pinned closed with a safety pin.

"Not bad, huh?" she'd asked Leotie, holding out her arms and stomping around in a circle. "Your old mom cleans up pretty good, huh?"

Leotie said, "Your pants are ripped." She could have said so much more, but she didn't.

"Oh." Her mom dismissed her with a flap of her hand. "No one'll be looking at me anyhow."

But wherever her mother went, she stuck out as far as she could. That evening, when the teacher called Leotie's name, her mom howled. The polite applause fell silent, and everyone turned toward her, planted smack-dab in the center of the bleachers, all red and shiny, like a big wound bleeding out. Then, in the dead quiet, her mother hollered, just as loud, "Go, Leotie! That's my girl!"

Leotie remembered the exact words because, for months afterward, kids would sneak up behind her and howl, "Go, Leotie! That's my girl!" They'd say "girl" just like her mother said it, landing hard on the *r* and drawing it out. Leotie swore she'd never make the honor roll again. She'd succeeded at that, too.

But her mother. Her mother in that big, red shirt with that slice of red lipstick she'd dug out from god knew where. It had taken Leotie over forty years to realize that maybe her mother hadn't been trying to embarrass her.

Maybe she did what she did because she was proud of Leotie and showing it the only way she could figure out how.

Her mother had at least kept custody. Her mother had at least given her kid an inhabitable home. She'd fought when they'd shut off the heat or the water, and she'd always gotten them turned back on.

Her mother had done a bang-up job compared to Leotie.

If Leotie's mother was still alive, she'd be pushing seventy. And she was still alive, for all Leotie knew, planted in a lawn chair in northern Oklahoma, taking smoke through the mouth and oxygen through the nose, jabbing her butts out with those same nasty fingernails. Maybe someone cleaned them now, scraped the dirt out from underneath. Leotie thought that someone should be her daughter.

As days passed, Leotie drank less and less water to lessen the times she'd have to get up and pee, and Bobby started bringing her meals instead of calling her to the table. Her mother arrived in her mind more and more often. She'd be sitting in the same lawn chair in the same backyard, bitching to another smoking white-hair about men and the weather. Really, it was probably a wheelchair in a drafty room in a state-run ward. Really, the woman was probably alone.

And here sat Leotie, with the space heater her son kept beside her feet and the sandwiches he made her for lunch on soft bread with the crusts cut off and applesauce and boiled carrots after she'd told him how hard it was to chew, and the honey buns he'd bought by the dozen after he'd learned how much she liked them.

And the coffee in the morning, first thing, with sweetener and powdered cream—she'd told him once how she liked it and he'd remembered. And the boxes of Kleenex and the fresh glasses of water four times a day, which had turned into Styrofoam cups once she'd started shaking more and asked did he have anything lighter maybe.

In the evenings, they'd watch the news together, then *Wheel of Fortune* and *Jeopardy*. Leotie had her boy and his silent forgiveness. She had some peace finally, and some company. She had some comfort, much more than she deserved.

Leotie's lungs shrank and pulled. She imagined the inside of her chest toughening into an animal's hide. She slept more, she lost track of the days. She woke to find herself in a chair when she thought she'd fallen asleep in a bed, and vice versa. She found her mother more and more often, and more and more often, she found her alone. Her mother's friend vanished. Her mother's fingernails grew black and long, her hair grew lank and patchy—sparse gray strands combed flat over a speckled scalp. The lawn chair turned to a wheelchair, the Oklahoma scrub grass to cold linoleum. The walls of her mother's room stood tall and bare and far away, with one high, small window of gray sky. Out in the hallway, children and grandchildren pushed other patients past, on their way to walks and picnics and family parties, while her mother lived out her final days at the mercy of underpaid strangers, with nothing to distract her from the end.

Leotie tried to tell herself that she'd made it all up, but she couldn't shake the vision. Her mother's life came to her unprompted and so clearly she couldn't help but believe it was real. Maybe, she thought, there was a God, and he let you see things at the end, when you really needed it.

She'd had a choice, though it hadn't struck her at the time, between finding her son, who didn't need her, and finding her mother, who did. Her final choice, and she'd chosen selfishly. Her final chance, and she'd chosen wrong.

Maybe she could still make it there.

No.

But maybe God would give her just one more good day, when she'd wake up to a body that was ready to move. She'd wait until Bobby was distracted, she wouldn't make him say goodbye. She'd leave a note with everything she needed to say, and she'd leave it at that.

When the day came, Leotie found she'd already written the note. She couldn't remember writing it, but there it was on the table beside her in a long white envelope with *Bobby* written across the top in her handwriting, so that's what it had to be. The woman's children were there—the boy with his warbly voice like a small bird and the girl with her big, sad eyes. Leotie reached into her pocket and found her mother's address on a scrap of paper all balled up. She knew it was her mother's address because the state read *OK*.

Leaving was easy, really. She just stood up and walked out, left Bobby's letter right there on the table where she'd found it.

Out in front of the church, a taxi pulled up with a boy driver, gangly, with belly-white skin and a shaved head. He turned toward her and smiled. His long teeth were spotted black with rot. Who was she to judge? She climbed into the back seat, and he said, "Train station?"

"Of course."

The station was mammoth and brick, with pillars out front that were beginning to crumble. She entered and found it empty. Outside, the building rumbled. The pillars, she knew, were giving way.

"We've got to get out of here," a voice behind her said. She turned to find a man in a pressed navy blue jumpsuit with red trim and gold snaps and zippers. He wore oversized sunglasses and an engineer's cap. "The building is falling today. You should have known. Everyone knew except for you."

"My mother," Leotie said. "I have to find her." And she reached into her pocket and pulled out the address.

He led her to a train. "This is my train," he said. "I will take you there. If you fall asleep, it will not take long."

Leotie was the only one on the train. The seats were long and soft and flat, like beds, with no buckles. She lay down across one and closed her eyes. The train pulled forward, and behind them she heard the station giving way. In her mind, she could see the brick walls buckle and fall. The building fell slowly enough for her to hear all the noises it made. The *thwump* of the bottom bricks and the roll of the rows higher up. The patter of smaller rock, the rain of dust, the crack of pipes and the burst and spray of water that slowed to a trickle. The groaning of the inside walls, which knew that their time had come to fall.

The engineer shook her awake. "We're there," he said. "We made it." He had stopped the train near her mother's nursing home. He led her down the train steps and pointed toward it. "There," he said.

The grass was thick and rich somehow, even in December. There were no roads, just gentle, treeless hills with a few houses scattered here and there and the nursing home, a one-story hall of windows honey colored in the twilight. She walked steadily toward it. Her lungs softened and opened and welcomed the air, cool in her throat and over her skin.

Inside everyone was standing in a semicircle, waiting for her. They had known she would come. They'd been waiting all day. Her mother stood in the center. Leotie knew it was her, even though she was standing, not sitting, and she looked as skinny as a movie star in a mint-green polyester pantsuit with tinted glasses and her silver hair combed back and curled and sprayed in place. She walked up and wrapped her arms around Leotie in slow motion, really savoring it, like the end of a movie. She smelled clean and fresh, like lemons and bar soap.

"I'm sorry," Leotie said into her mother's collar.

Her mother said, "Why be sorry?"

"Because," Leotie said. "I never knew that you loved me. And I didn't know that I loved you, either."

"But you did," her mother said.

"I did."

Leotie felt her chest give way. She was crying a current of tears, and they were flowing out of her mouth. Her eyes were too small for so much sadness. It had to pour. Her mother lowered her onto a couch.

"Let it all out," her mother said. "Now's the time to let it all go."

The current covered Leotie and warmed her. She felt herself sinking into the warmth, into the couch and past it, past the floor and past the surface of the earth and into the dark water beneath, where she floated weightless and painless until a current caught her, and she let it pull her down.

54

Willa preferred to read books about girls her age, ones where the main character had something that made her different from everyone else and lonely, too. Maybe the girl was really poor or painfully shy, or maybe she lived in a strange house in a normal town. Maybe she had no parents or a magical power, or she was really good at something unusual, like taming wild animals or solving really hard math problems—some characteristic interesting enough to fill up a whole book.

While Willa was reading these stories, she could forget her life. And they always ended so cleanly, with everything tying neatly together in the end. The problems, every single one of them, worked themselves out, and the girl wound up in a much better place than she'd been at the beginning, and the way the endings made it sound, things just kept getting better and better forever.

Were there any books, she wondered, where the problems didn't get fixed? Where the girl's life was hard, and things happened, but they didn't happen the way they needed to happen to make things better and so things just stayed the same? And eventually, when it got really boring and hopeless, the story just stopped?

Someday maybe she'd write a book like that, when she was a grown-up. And people would read it and say, "Yep, that's life all right, not like all them other stories," and they'd pay her lots of money to write more, and she'd buy a farm by a lake and ride horses and go swimming a lot.

Of course, that future story was a not-like-life story, too. Who was she kidding? Of course she'd write a not-like-life story, if she had the choice. Of course anyone would. That's why the world was full of them. Who would mope around in all the sad, hard things that never got better when you could write about a different world where they did? And who would want to read about the sad, hard world anyway? When she read a book where things got better, sometimes it gave her that feeling, when it ended, like things really had gotten better. And the feeling made the real world brighter and softer and neater, and it lasted sometimes for a whole day before it faded and Willa found another book to read and worked up the feeling all over again.

Willa had brought two books to the pastor's house—one to read the entire time she was there and another to start reading if she read too fast and finished the first one. She would not talk, she had decided. She would not eat. She would not play with Lukas. She would read until her mother came back to pick them up, and when Willa heard her mother pull in the drive, she would pull on her coat and her boots and be ready as soon as her mother came to the door so that the pastor couldn't talk them into staying a moment longer.

Willa didn't say hello to the pastor when they arrived. She kicked off her boots and marched into the living room. She climbed up into the armchair by the couch, where the pastor's mother was sitting, and plunged her nose, quick as she could, into her book.

Lukas said, "I brought my jungle Legos," and the pastor said, "Jungle Legos?!" like it was the best news he'd ever heard, and after their mother left, he led Lukas back to the dining room, where Willa heard them dump the bag out onto the table. They played with them all morning. The pastor's mother woke up and fell asleep and woke up and fell asleep again. Willa could tell because the woman snored when she slept, and then she jerked forward and snorted when she woke up.

Eventually, Willa lost interest in her book. It happened sometimes, especially when she'd made up her mind to read. It was weird. When she decided really hard to do something—even something she liked—she usually lost interest in doing it. But if she didn't decide hard to do something, she could lose herself in it for hours. Now the pastor called out that he was making lunch, and his mother snorted and Willa flat-out ignored him when he asked if she wanted a sandwich. Instead she bit down hard and long on both cheeks. It felt so wrong to ignore him that it was scary to do it, even though the pastor was too nice to punish her, and he'd probably go ahead and make her a sandwich anyway.

Her book was about a girl whose family had moved from the city to a big old crumbling house in the country that used to belong to a witch. No one had lived in it since, so there were bits of magic everywhere—wands and charmed pots and half-empty bottles of potions and so on. The girl, a lonely animal lover, had set a talking potion out for the animals, and they'd all begun to speak. There was a band of chatty little mice and an attic squirrel who bossed everyone around, and the family sheepdog, who had gobbled up a whole cupboard's worth of potion ingredients and transformed into a sleepy, dopey wizard.

Things got more complicated when the wild barn cat licked up some leftover growth potion and got really big and scary and hungry for the mice, who had become the girl's best friends. Then came lots of pages of the little mice scampering and squealing. Willa kept her eyes moving over and over the page and then she would turn one, for the sound, and then, after a little while, she would turn it back.

"Willa," the pastor called from the kitchen. "You've got a lunch out here if you want it."

"It's peanut butter and grape jelly, Willa!" Lukas called. "Your favorite! And your own box of raisins!"

No, Willa reminded herself.

Funny thing was, she liked the pastor. Or she would have liked him, if she'd met him some other way. He didn't push her around, and he didn't get mad, and whenever she said anything, he listened. In a way, liking him made her dislike him more because if she wasn't checking herself, she liked him more than she liked her own dad, which was wrong. Which would have hurt her dad a lot, if he knew. But no one knew, of course, except herself. And it was going to stay that way.

A noise. A strange noise. Not a Lego noise or an eating noise. The sound of dripping, almost, or bubbling. The sound of bubbling right next to her.

She turned toward the sound and found red bubbling down Leotie as she slept. Willa jumped up, and her book hit the floor with a thud and the cover slapped shut, but Leotie didn't move. She just sat there, slumped, with her eyes shut and her mouth hanging open and the blood falling out over her chin and onto her shirt. Her shirt was red from the blood and wet, and the wetness was moving down her front and it was the only thing moving.

In the kitchen, Lukas was talking about Power Rangers, and when he paused, the pastor said, "Mom? Mom? Are you ready for your lunch?"

The word *Mom* made Willa all twisted and choky inside. She led herself into the kitchen and told the pastor, "I think you need to go out there."

He smiled when he saw her, and then his smile fell. As he pushed back his chair and passed by Willa, the twisting inside of her worked its way up into her throat.

"Oh, God," she heard him say. "Oh, my God. Mom? Mom?"

Lukas was staring at Willa, his sandwich clutched tight in his two small hands. "Willa," he said. "Willa, what's wrong?" He dropped his sandwich and started to climb down from his chair.

"No!" Willa said, and Lukas paused. "You stay there." She swallowed hard. She would not vomit. She would think of Lukas and only of Lukas. She climbed up next to him. "I came in here to eat with you. Is it jelly? Is it grape jelly?" She smiled.

Lukas watched her smile, and then he smiled, too. He turned his bottom back into his chair and picked up his sandwich again. "It's grape jelly, Willa. Grape jelly! Just like you like it!"

In the living room, the pastor pushed the phone buttons. He mumbled something short and low and gave them an address. Then he walked back into the kitchen, pale and surprised. Willa stared at him, and he stared at her, and she could feel the silence tying them together in a big, complicated knot she might never be able to untangle.

"You okay?" he asked. He walked behind her and rested a heavy hand on her shoulder. He leaned into her and started to shake.

"I'm okay," she said. "I'm sorry." He was shaking hard now, not crying but shaking, like he was standing on his own little earthquake. She slid out of her seat and did what she'd seen others do. She reached her arms around his waist and patted his back. "It's okay," she said. "It's going to be okay." He felt so big, but then, shaking, he seemed so small.

Lukas asked, "What's going to be okay?"

Willa flooded with a dizzy, giddy goodness. She could see clearly, for the first time, how alive she was, could see her future stretching out along an endless road. She saw herself growing up and leaving her house and her school and her town and building for herself the life that she wanted. She could do that. She had a bright mind—all her teachers said so—and a body that kept getting stronger and no need for anyone else. She saw herself sitting alone on a bus seat beside a window, looking out at new places.

"Everything," she told Lukas. Everything would be okay. Better than okay. At that moment, she was absolutely certain.

Was she telling herself another not-like-life story? Well, so what if she was? Some not-like-life stories were true. People tamed wolves and built bridges and said things like *You can't make this stuff up.* So why couldn't she be who she wanted someday. Why couldn't she break off and take what she wanted from life.

55

The easiest part of Robert's mother dying was the hour or two just after she died. During that time, Robert impressed himself with his composure and presence of mind. He laid a sheet over top of her in case Lukas wandered into the room, and he called Susan at work and then the funeral home in town. Two men—gentle, sober, kind—arrived immediately and told Robert to let them know when he was ready. Robert replied that he was already ready. They told him to let them know when he'd said his goodbyes. He told them he already had.

Was he sure? Yes, he was sure.

Susan returned from her shift and after an anxious, fretful apology, she left right away with the children. (*Why did she seem so harried,* he wondered briefly, and then he remembered that his mother had died.)

The men laid a fresh, dark sheet over the white sheet, which was blooming with blood. They lifted his mother's body, still concealed, onto a stretcher. They carried her out and loaded her into their van and drove away.

He watched their vehicle navigate the potholes slowly, carefully, as though their cargo were still alive. At the time, he found this unnecessary, maybe even a little affected.

Was he sure? Yes, he was sure.

He bagged up his mother's clothes and carried them over to the church and stacked them neatly inside the missionary closet. Back at the parsonage, he took the caps off her medicines and shook the pills into the garbage and dropped the prescription containers in, too, and then the caps. He dismantled the homemade antennae and folded it into the trash, muscled the television set down the basement steps and slid it back onto its shelf. He reached her stack of Styrofoam cups back into a cupboard, then pulled them out and pushed them down into the trash can, along with the box of honey buns he'd bought the last time he went to the store and her breathing machine, which stood rinsed and air-dried and ready for its post-lunch session. He lifted out the bag of garbage and tied it and carried it into the garage. He pulled a fresh set of sheets back over his mattress and smoothed his comforter over the top, so that it looked exactly as it had looked every day before his mother had come.

Then he walked around his rooms, inspecting each surface and corner for any other items now irrelevant, trying to muster within himself a satisfaction at the his-ness of the house, though beneath his mustering lay a fresh realization that the house was not his, nor was anything inside of it, and now it was somehow his even less so.

He returned to the kitchen and ate, finally, the sandwich he had left sitting out for himself, and he ate a small pile of raisins, too, congratulating himself inwardly on his sensible appetite. After he had washed his own plate and Willa's and Lukas's, too, and settled them in the dishpan to drip-dry, he turned and on the far corner of the counter caught sight of his mother's lunch (how on earth had he missed that?), with the four crustless sandwich squares and the dim orange heap of boiled carrots. He stared at it for a long moment, frozen, as though the lunch itself had caught him in the midst of committing a crime and was about to pronounce some sort of judgment.

He shook his head, tried to bring himself back to his senses. *I took good care of her,* he told himself, *and now I don't have to anymore. It's as simple as that.*

Below his mind, his body revolted, and he made it to the toilet just in time for his stomach's contents to surge up his throat and splash down into the waiting water. The walls of the bathroom seemed to pulse toward him. He could not catch his breath. He buckled over and vomited again.

She had tried to tell him things. She had tried to pull him back and back to the past, and he'd dug his heels into the present. He had only half listened. What could he have learned, if he'd allowed himself?

He placed his palms on either side of the toilet seat, bracing himself as he hurled again. Mentally he dashed through the past month with his mother, snatching up each conversation he could remember and skimming its contents. Sweat beaded from his forehead and neck. Something. He had to have learned something.

"Your father was a bus driver. I met him riding the bus. I ever tell you that?"

"No," he had said. Just no. He could have asked why she had liked him, how long they'd known each other. He could have asked whether he and his father (a generous name for one so absent) had ever met. His mother had told him his father's name—Barr Sable—and said something about the man already having a family and not wanting another. He'd said, "Huh," or something similar, and she had dropped the subject.

Robert was beginning to wonder whether he had been poisoned. He felt so hot and so weak. He needed to lie down, but he could not stop retching.

There was the conversation about the doctor. He'd tried his hardest not to listen to that. It had sounded, straight off, like she was inventing excuses. She'd said, out of the blue over lunch one day, back when she'd been well enough to walk to the dining room without too much trouble, "Sometimes I think I could've done better by you if they hadn't done what they done to me when you were born."

Robert had sensed her need to tell, to explain her behavior in such a way that it became understandable. Mentally he'd planted himself in opposition. Still, basic politeness dictated that he ask, in as disinterested a tone as he could muster, "What was that?"

"I'll tell you what was that," she said. "They tied my tubes without asking me first." She waited a moment for him to react, and when he failed to do so, she continued. "They saw a knocked-up brown-skinned girl with no husband, and so when you were born, they just tied me up so I couldn't make more babies. Found out later it was something they did back then. Hell, they probably still do."

Robert had waited to see if she was done. She went on.

"Didn't even find out until just after they took you away. Went to the doctor for a physical so I could get you back. Then they told me I couldn't get pregnant no more. No brother for you, no sister."

Again, Robert had waited. He'd let the silence settle, hoped she was done.

"I know I failed you," she said. "But that kinda treatment does something to a person. It sends you a message you just keep hearing over and over."

He'd waited again. "What's the message?" he'd asked. At least he'd asked that.

"We don't want your kind," she'd said. "All what we got, you don't deserve it." She thought for a while longer before adding, in a quieter voice, like she was only talking to herself, "And the best thing in your life shouldn't've ever been yours."

She'd let the topic drop then as easily as he did, and he hadn't allowed himself to consider it any longer.

Robert continued to brace himself over the toilet until his stomach finally stilled. He sank onto the floor and scooted backward to lean against the wall. He had learned something. He had learned how little the world had wanted him. And he had learned that maybe that knowledge, more than anything, had been his mother's undoing.

He sensed his current life falling around him like a series of props, a backdrop of draped sheets. Everything he'd tried to convince himself he was, all his scrupulously built beliefs—all of it struck him suddenly as a story, like he'd spent all his years painting a fiction the size of life. He could see, suddenly, its flatness and falseness and how, as a painting, it had given off the appearance of dimension. His faith, both in the church and in his own importance, seemed like nothing more than a curtain he had carefully hung between himself and the horrors of life.

The remainder of the day passed in the same bewildering daze. At one point, he called Susan and let the phone ring until the machine picked up, then placed the receiver gently back down.

He could call someone else, but he couldn't think of who that might be. Certainly not the deacons. Certainly not Joe Cummings, with his endless political laments. Not Jim Hibbert, the irascible forty-year-old bachelor who had never asked Robert one single question about himself.

Not Clarence Rider, with his litany of medical ailments. Not Henry Gillis, kind but distant and beyond elderly. Not Arnold Oliver, elderly beyond even Henry's elderly. Not Lester Butts, whose response to every hardship, to the point of rudeness (here Robert was remembering the drowning of Rhonda Paisley's eight-year-old nephew), was *Well, the Lord giveth and the Lord taketh away and blessed be the name of the Lord.*

Not Alvin Clemens, an over-the-road trucker who rarely came, or Sherman Plonski, with his small country of children, or even Chet Weller, whom Robert actually liked a lot, far more than anyone else, with the exception of Ethel Grable. The truth was, Robert had leaned on no one before, not once in all his years in Esau, and so he had set no precedent for doing so now. The fault was perhaps his as much as anyone else's. Regardless, he was alone. And now, with his mother gone, he was even more alone, somehow, than he had been before she arrived.

That evening, Susan called to check on him.

"How are you doing? Are you holding up okay?" she asked, and the genuine concern in her question felt like a balm.

56

All Christmas Day, until his family arrived, Randy paced. He'd set his alarm for six thirty so that he wouldn't have to wait in line for a shower—his last shower in the nuthouse. Since the hospital barbershop would be closed on Christmas, he'd scheduled an appointment for a haircut and a shave just before close on Tuesday afternoon. He'd have a day-old shadow when Susan and the kids arrived, but at least he wouldn't have a full-on beard. He'd packed his duffel bag shortly after his Tuesday-morning session with Doc Nelson, after the doctor had told him that the next day, when his family arrived, he'd be free to go home. So the only thing he had to do on Christmas was to wait.

The day before, he'd marched straight from Doc Nelson's office to the nurses' station, where he'd written his name and number on the phone log and dialed Susan. But as soon as the line began to ring, he slammed the receiver back down. Maybe he shouldn't tell her ahead of time. Maybe he should wait and tell her face-to-face.

On her first visit, nearly a month ago now, he'd asked her to bring a few of the family photographs from the living room mantel, and as he shuffled them into a pile to slide inside his duffel, he came across their wedding photograph. Instead of packing it, he carried it to the activity room, where he wrapped it in red paper. He would hand it over at dinner. When Susan looked up, perplexed, from the picture in her lap, he'd say something like,

We get to start over again, right now. And if she still didn't understand, he'd say, *Susan, I'm coming home.*

Doc Nelson delivered the good news at the beginning of Randy's final session so that the doctor could spend the rest of the time prepping Randy for life "on the outside," as he called it, like Randy had been locked up in the big house for twenty-plus years.

Randy swallowed a laugh. "It's only been a month," he said.

"It's harder than you think," Doc Nelson warned. "People leave here with all sorts of high expectations. For themselves and for everyone else. And their loved ones have been out there building expectations, too. And then, when patients go home, all of those expectations meet with reality."

"Well I'm not planning to disappoint anyone's expectations," Randy said. He thought this was the kind of thing Doc Nelson would want to hear, but the doctor frowned.

"It doesn't matter if you're planning to or not," he said. "You will anyway. Just don't be too disappointed when it happens. That's when the real work begins."

The disappointment arrived much sooner than Randy had expected. First off, he'd forgotten that most restaurants would be closed on Christmas Day, so they ended up driving around for an hour until they spotted a blinking OPEN in the window of a strip mall China King—or CHI-A KIN-. Two letters had burned out, and the light in the big K kept blinking, threatening to join them.

Inside, Randy tried to rally. The food smelled good enough, and the buffet was all-you-can-eat. Susan helped the kids through the line, explaining their options and spooning food onto Lukas's plate when he struggled. Randy loaded up his own plate and then realized, when he arrived back at the table long before anyone else, that maybe he should help. So he left his cooling food on the tabletop and walked back to the buffet, where Susan was trying to coax Lukas into letting her add some green beans to his plate.

"You have to eat some vegetables," she told him. "Even on Christmas."

Randy scanned the line. Green beans were the only choice.

"Well that settles it," Randy said, and he scooped up a spoonful of green beans and dropped them onto Lukas's plate.

"No!" Lukas cried. He was staring down at the beans in horror. "They're all over my food!"

Susan shot Randy an aggravated glance.

"What?" he said. "I was just trying to help you."

She picked some of the beans off Lukas's plate and added them to her own. Then she corralled Lukas's remaining beans off to the edge, away from his other food. "Can we try not to make a fight out of it?" she asked Randy.

Why was she acting so bitchy?

"He's the one who made a fight out of it," Randy said. "He's just trying to get his way."

"He's a person, Randy. Of course he's trying to get his way. And can we please stop talking about him like he's not right here listening to everything we're saying?"

Lukas took this as his cue to carry his plate back to the table.

Randy said, "Give me a break, will you, Suzy? It's Christmas." He wanted to say more, about how hard he was trying, about how he didn't want to disappoint her expectations.

"Randy, I need a break, too. I've been keeping our family afloat this whole time. You've gotten a break from that. I haven't."

So that's what she thought the psych ward was like, like one extended vacation. He said, "Well maybe you could stop correcting me so goddamn much. That would give your mouth a break anyway." Immediately he regretted his words, and he regretted the reflex that made him pretend he didn't.

Susan leveled that gaze at him again, the one she'd started giving him just recently, after everything had started going so wrong—the one that said it was all his fault.

They stood there for a full minute, glaring at each other. Out of the corner of his eye, Randy could see that the kids had given up on waiting for them and started to eat. He thought of his and Susan's wedding photograph wrapped in Christmas paper and tucked in his coat pocket. Doc Nelson had said this would happen, and here it was.

"What do you want me to do?" he asked. "I'm trying my best."

"This is your best?"

"So I make mistakes. Your shit stinks, too."

"You said yourself you need to work on accepting responsibility, Randy. If you can't figure that out, then it's going to be that much harder when you come back home."

"News flash. I've already accepted it," he said. "That's why they let me go."

"What do you mean, they let you go?"

"I'm coming home," Randy said. "Tonight."

Susan swiveled her head toward their children seated at the table and then back to him. "Tonight?" she repeated.

Her face was unbelieving, maybe even frightened. Wow, had he blown it. "Yes. Tonight."

"Why didn't you tell me?" she asked.

"I wanted it to be a surprise," he said, and suddenly, horrifyingly, he felt an irresistible urge to cry. He was such a grade-A motherfucking moron.

"Well I'm surprised," she said.

And then Randy really was crying, his face twisting up against his will. His eyes and nose began to leak, and he couldn't breathe right. He blocked his face with one hand, hoping that the fit would pass, but it only grew stronger.

He could hear Susan saying, "It's okay to cry, Randy." Her voice sounded sorry. "Just let it out." After a minute she took his arm and led him away from the buffet line, where the worker was switching out a pan, past the single old guy in the nearby booth who was watching Randy (he could feel it, even with his face covered) like a TV show. She pulled him over to a booth in a corner, away from everything else, and told him to sit. She handed him a wad of napkins from the dispenser on the table, and he picked them up and pressed them to his face.

"I just thought it would be good news," he said, and then the crying came back when he realized how pathetic he sounded, what a stupid hope he'd been holding. He pressed the napkins back to his face. *You're such a disaster,* he told himself. *Pull yourself together, for fuck's sake.*

Susan reached across the table and halfheartedly patted his elbow. "It took me by surprise is all," she said. But he could read her much better than she thought he could. She didn't want him home—of course she didn't—and she was too tired to convince him otherwise. He couldn't make her want him there, he reminded himself, but once he returned, he could make it clear he'd changed for the better.

So Randy patted her hand and went to the bathroom and sobbed it all out in a stall before he rinsed his face and dried it and returned to the table.

After dinner they dropped back by the hospital so that Randy could pick up his duffel bag and sign himself out for good. The nurse at the desk was new—he'd seen her maybe twice before—and all the other residents were off somewhere else, so there was no one there to tell him goodbye. The new nurse buzzed him out. He rode the elevator down to the lobby and walked out into the night. The snow, which had been hit or miss throughout the day, was falling in earnest now. The van idled by the curb with his family warm inside.

Randy felt a stab of something like hope, but painful. He lifted the back hatch and tossed in his bag, slammed it shut to knock off the snow that had already landed there, and climbed into the passenger seat. They drove off in silence. As he looked back at the hospital windows bright and high and warm in the cold night, he realized he would miss it.

57

The morning after Christmas rose so glumly and reluctantly that it seemed like the world had stopped spinning as fast as it usually did. Karla's Kitchen was still closed for the Christmas holiday, which meant that Susan didn't yet need to worry about leaving the kids alone with their father. At least she'd have one day to feel him out, judge his soundness.

In part, the morning felt so late because Susan woke so early, if she even slept at all. Over the past month, she'd gotten used to sleeping alone and had found that she much preferred it. She'd almost forgotten how much Randy tossed and turned and how he jiggled the mattress, how he snored whenever he ended up on his back—like he was over there cranking a ratchet—until she used the strength of her arms and legs to roll him over onto his side.

The night Randy came home, Susan didn't even bother. She knew she wouldn't be falling asleep anyway.

When the merciless red segments of her clock switched from 3:59 to 4:00, Susan gave up entirely and slipped out of bed. She showered until the hot water ran out, then rubbed herself dry and shivered back into her pajamas and put on her bathrobe, too. She pulled on a pair of socks and stretched a pair of slippers over top of the socks, both to warm her damp, cold feet and to cover the gaping holes in her heels.

She always turned the thermostat down to fifty at night, after the kids had drifted off and she'd secured their blankets around them. Then she'd wait until six to turn it back up to sixty-two. The furnace always took too long to catch up, though, and so when the kids woke, they would still drag their blankets and their clothes into the living room and dress in front of the woodstove, whether Susan had kept the fire alive or not.

Instead of turning the furnace up early and wasting extra fuel, she pulled the armchair up to the woodstove and opened the door to poke at the embers. She halfheartedly tossed a log on top, without considering the likelihood of its catching fire. She pulled an afghan from the couch and wrapped it around her shoulders. This was good, she told herself. She could squeeze in some quiet time, maybe some prayer. She could try and wrap her mind around her day, around her new reality.

But why, she asked herself, did this reality suddenly seem so new? Wasn't it the same old reality she'd been dealing with for years, all the way until Randy's suicide attempt? His doctor had given him the go-ahead to return to work on January 3. That meant she could quit her job and get back to doing the same things she had always done, without the interruption of additional work. She began mentally to catalog the list. Feeding her family breakfast, lunch, dinner, and snacks; washing and mending their clothes; shopping for affordable new ones and affordable food and affordable whatever else they needed; growing as much food as she could and preserving it; cutting everyone's hair; scheduling everyone's appointments and chauffeuring them back and forth; cleaning up after them in the bathroom, the dining room, the kitchen, the bedrooms; answering all their mail; paying all their bills; using every ounce of her ingenuity to stretch the rest of Randy's paychecks as far as they would go. And in addition to all this, she must remain a loving mother who took the time to ask questions and listen to the answers, to help with homework and to help out in her children's classrooms, to protect her children from the world and from their father, to manufacture happy memories out of thin air.

And to handle the new problem of Willa's panic.

And to remain a wife.

It was still too much. It was all too much.

Susan blew again on the darkening embers. They flared a little. She stretched her palms forward to seek out the heat.

So what had changed? Willa had gotten worse. Randy, maybe, had gotten a little better. There was a chance he would be calmer, safer. There was a chance that the change would last, and probably a bigger chance that it wouldn't.

But Susan sensed that somehow, through all of this recent upset, what seemed to have changed most of all was herself. Maybe it was working a job outside her home—her first in almost a decade. Maybe it was just a funk brought on by all the chaos and change. Or maybe it had something to do with Pastor Robert and his goodness, which, she had learned, was somehow completely genuine. Damaged men, it turned out, did not always use their damaged pasts to justify bad behavior. Sometimes they grew kinder and stronger as a result.

Dread dawned in Susan's stomach when Randy's feet shuffled across the floor, his weight creaking and groaning over the floorboards. The children were too light to make such noises, and so Susan, having not heard the sound for four long weeks, now had the distance to recognize the effect it produced in her. The effect was one of, yes, dread, but also a sort of clenching, or a buttoning up. It was the same sense she'd had as a child when her father arrived home at the end of the day—guilty, sure that she'd done something wrong. She had only, in her laxness, forgotten what.

But that morning, Randy did not require as much as he usually did. He didn't ask what was for breakfast or inquire as to whether she'd made coffee. He simply sat on the end of the couch nearest her chair and yawned a long yawn as he pulled a blanket over his legs.

"It's freezing in here," he said.

Susan reached down and started to crumple some sheets of old newspaper. "I've been trying to do something about that," she said, even though she'd been largely ignoring the fire.

"Here," Randy said. He lifted Susan's log with the poker and propped two slender logs against it. He tucked Susan's newspapers underneath and blew, and the coals kindled a flame on the paper that swiftly grew. Soon the flames were licking and darkening the undersides of the logs.

Randy leaned back, and from one slight, arrogant twist of his neck, Susan could tell he was proud of himself. "Guess it's nice to have a man around again, huh?"

Susan watched the fire as it grew and grew. She would pretend she understood his comment to require no response.

"So," he continued, after waiting long enough to understand that his question had been dropped. "Today's a new beginning."

Susan nodded. "I guess it is."

"I'm gonna do better, Suzy," he said. "From here on out."

We'll see, she wanted to say, but instead she smiled, an old reflex. It was the close-lipped smile she always smiled when she could find no polite-yet-honest words with which to respond.

"I'm gonna prove it today, I'm telling you," he said. "I've got a surprise. Just for you. I just have to spend some time today putting it together."

The day moved along in much the same way days usually did. When the kids woke, Susan took the extra time to make pancakes, since pancakes were cheaper and filled the kids up more than cereal and anyway there was nowhere they needed to go. After breakfast, Randy disappeared down into the basement, where, judging by the occasional whistling and the absence of slamming and swearing, he'd found some project with which to distract himself. Willa finished two of the four books Susan had bought her for Christmas, and after *Sesame Street* ended, Lukas turned his attention toward his new set of Legos. Meanwhile, Susan cleaned up the pancake mess and threw in a load of laundry and cleaned the bathroom.

At noon, as always, Susan fixed peanut butter sandwiches for herself and the kids and two meat sandwiches for Randy and sliced up carrots and cheese and a few old apples whose bruises she carved carefully out. Randy devoured his sandwiches in record time and disappeared back downstairs. The children took longer and left behind more of a mess.

The kids grew restless shortly after lunch, so she sent them outside after helping locate all their snow pants and mittens and hats and scarves and boots. While they played, she cleaned up the mess from lunch and folded the laundry she'd found in the dryer. When they came back in, she heated cider on the stove and served it to them with some cookies she took from the secret stash she kept high up in the pantry.

After she'd cleaned up their snack, she turned her attention to what she could make for dinner, having depleted, over the course of the past month, the frozen meals she'd set aside in the freezer. She discovered she had just enough ham left over for a pizza topping, and so she mixed and kneaded a batch of pizza dough and placed it in a greased bowl under a wet towel and set it beside the woodstove to rise. While she riffled through the cellar for a jar of her pizza sauce and a garlic bulb, Randy called her over from his side of the basement.

"Suzy! Hey! Suzy-Q! Get over here! You gotta see this!"

She swallowed her annoyance and shouted back, "Just a minute!" But either he didn't hear her or she took longer than he'd expected, riffling through all her tomato-colored jars, because he kept on calling anyway.

"Suzy! Don't go upstairs yet! There's something you've got to see!"

By the time she finally made it over to his side of the basement with her jar, her annoyance had escalated into anger, though he looked so happy and hopeful—such a rare expression on such a familiar face—that she tried her best not to show it.

"Yes?" she said, her voice a little tight despite her trying.

"Check this out. Check out what I made."

His excitement reminded her of Lukas's when he'd built something he was particularly proud of, and Susan softened a little. He was holding out a plastic white rectangle with rows of tiny squares running across it. Susan vaguely identified it as a circuit board. Red wires looped in and out, and little beads and nodules stood up from its surface on skinny wire legs.

"Oh," she said.

"Wave your hand over it," he said, and she obeyed. "No," he said. "Stand over here."

Susan stepped closer and waved her hand at the circuit board again. A red light blinked feebly on and off.

"There!" he said triumphantly. "Did you see that?"

"The light?"

"Yeah!"

"I did."

"Isn't that great?"

"Yes." She waited a moment for him to explain. "What is it, exactly?" she asked.

"C'mon, Suzy. It's a motion detector. Obviously."

"Ah!" Susan said. She could tell that she was expected to act impressed. "Did you do that all by yourself?"

Randy picked up a book that Susan remembered him buying years back, before they'd married, when they'd both been in school. The cover read *Electrical Projects for Beginners*.

"Oh," Susan said. "So you followed the instructions in the book?"

Randy sighed in exasperation. "It's not that simple," he said. "You still have to figure out big parts of it for yourself."

Susan waved her hand back and forth again over the circuit board, trying to muster some interest. "That's impressive," she said.

"It is," Randy agreed. "Suzy, I have to talk to you." He set the circuit board on his workbench and palmed his hair back and jerked his neck around like he was really working up to something. "I had a lot of time in the hospital to think through things. And I had to talk through them and think a lot about my life."

Randy did seem different somehow. Was it age? Was that it? The hospital seemed to have dulled him, drained all the anger that had kept him barreling through life, and as soon as he slowed down, all those years he'd been running crashed into him. She could read it in the deeper lines of his forehead, in the slight droop of his back and shoulders. She had a hard time believing that this was the same Randy who had stormed into the parsonage, who had then tried to kill himself.

"That's good," she said. "And?"

Randy took a deep breath. "Suzy. I want to go back to school."

In the pause that followed, Susan tried to cobble together an appropriate response, but in her shock, all she could muster was, "Wow."

"I want to make a better life for us. For myself." He paused again, and when Susan still couldn't bring herself to speak, he went on. "Doc Nelson's the one who helped me figure it out. He even made some calls. JCC has a night program to become a certified electrician. If I worked really hard, I could keep my job at Mack and still finish in two years. I could even start in January. Suzy, you're looking at me like I'm dying. This is good news. This is the best news."

"I'm sorry," she said. "It's just such a surprise."

"Yeah," Randy replied. "A good surprise."

"It's just—" She fumbled for the words. "I had thought about doing a similar thing myself."

The open happiness on Randy's face steeled over. There. There was the Randy she could recognize.

"You," he said, disbelieving. "Why would you do that? You don't have to support the family."

"Because—because I, well, because I need it," she finished lamely.

"What the hell would you even study? Have you even thought about it?"

Susan's mind scrambled for an answer, but she came up empty. "I haven't had the chance," she said. "Yet."

"Well I have," he said. "I could take out loans to pay for the classes and then pay them back a little at a time. I could make over double what I'm making now. And I already know I'm good at it." He gestured to his motion detector. The little red light blinked on and off with the movement like a supporting witness. "Suzy, this is the second chance you promised me. I'm trying to make good on it. Not just for myself. For all of us."

Something inside Susan was shutting down. She could almost feel it physically as she stood there, an empty box collapsing in her chest. No, she didn't have a plan. No, she didn't have a demonstrated interest. How could she? But she really did think of it. She thought of it all the time. Just that morning, between the never-ending tasks of cooking and laundry, she'd picked up one of the magazines her mother ordered for her every Christmas, an inspirational magazine she'd never had the heart to tell her mother she didn't like. But she'd read the cover story because it was about a pregnant teen who had dropped out of college and later gone on to become an award-winning teacher. Susan was a sucker for stories like that. A widowed refugee taught herself English and built a successful business. A battered mother of five escaped her abuser with her children in tow and ended up earning her PhD.

Now, as Susan considered the reality of her life, she thought that such stories must be inventions. Dull minds that wanted to sell inspirational magazines. Why not? You take a picture of a woman hugging her children and smiling. You write a story, choose a name, a city. Who would bother verifying a piece like that? The truth was that people had to eat, and eating made messes, and then, a short while later, they had to eat again. And when they weren't eating, they were making other messes, and someone had to clean them up, and that someone was her. The truth was that back when she was young and stupid, she'd missed her chance and now there were other things that would always need doing.

"I'm sorry," Susan said. "This is good news. I guess I just need some time to process it, that's all." And before Randy could respond, she turned away with her jar of sauce and climbed the stairs and fetched the pizza dough from beside the woodstove. She beat it down on the kitchen counter over and over, as hard as she could, until her knuckles smarted against the bottom of the bowl.

58

Two days after Christmas, Willa's mom had to work, so she left Willa and Lukas home with their dad. When she'd said goodbye to Willa, the only one awake, she'd looked scared, and this had scared Willa, too. She'd set a bunch of food out on the counter so that, Willa knew, even if their father forgot to feed them, they'd still have something to eat—the HappyO's, the bananas with their brown polka dots, the peanut butter and the bread, the dented canister of raisins, and two cans of beef stew with a can opener balanced on the top.

The evening before, her parents had discussed it at the dinner table.

"I've got to work tomorrow," Willa's mom had said. "But I'm not sure what to do about the kids."

"Why wouldn't I just watch them?" Willa's dad asked.

"I mean," Willa's mom said, "you don't usually watch the kids. By yourself, you know. And after everything that's happened, and with Willa's panic attacks, I didn't know if you'd be up to it. Yet."

"You don't trust me to watch my own kids?" Willa's dad asked, in a voice that snapped Willa to attention.

Willa's mom paused, and in her head, Willa shouted, *Answer him.*

"Of course I do," her mother said, too late. "I just didn't want to throw too much on you at once."

Willa's dad laughed a little, but his laugh was more like a cough because it had no happiness in it. "How hard can it be?"

"Well," her mother said, considering, "you've got to feed them."

"Which I can do."

"And if you need me, I guess I am just a phone call away."

"I won't need you. I can handle this."

"But Willa could have a panic attack."

"Willa's not going to have a panic attack. Are you, Willa?" Willa said no right away, but then the big invisible hand dumped ice into her stomach and clamped it shut. She could feel the cold leaking out and spreading up through her chest and down into her arms.

"There," her dad said.

"Randy, she can't control it."

"Mom, it's okay." Willa managed to keep her voice bored, like her dad's.

Her mother studied her. "All right," she said, but she said it like she didn't really believe Willa, and that made Willa feel even worse. "Just call me if it happens," she said to Willa's dad.

"I won't be calling you, Suzy. No matter what happens, I can take care of it." The way he said it, Willa knew the conversation was over, and she also knew that she couldn't panic because her father wouldn't be able to handle it and he wouldn't be calling her mother for anything. Willa would be on her own.

That morning, when Lukas woke up, Willa poured them both cereal and carved the brown parts out of an old banana and split it between their two bowls. When they'd finished eating, she carried the bowls to the sink and carefully lowered them down before turning the TV on low so that Lukas could watch his morning shows without disturbing their dad, who was still sleeping. Willa looked at the clock on the microwave: 8:35. Seven more hours. She had to keep it all together for seven more hours.

The beginning of the day went well enough. Willa knew that Lukas's whining could set her dad off, so she did her best to keep that to a minimum. When Lukas's shows were over, after their dad had woken up and disappeared down into the basement, Willa played Legos with her brother for a while, even though she didn't really want to. Then she helped him into his outside clothes, and together they went out to play in the snow until Lukas began to get cold.

Willa found herself almost glad for all of Lukas's needs because when her mind tried to move toward the things she didn't want to think about, she could ask herself what Lukas might need and turn her attention toward that instead. All she needed was to go and check on her angel, which she did every thirty minutes, and that kept her calm enough to do everything else. She tried pretending her dad wasn't even there. She was watching Lukas all alone, and she had to watch him so often it was almost boring. A couple of times she tried to act annoyed, like a teenager, but that didn't work very well because it upset Lukas, and if he started crying, then it was all over for sure. So Willa spent most of her time and energy keeping Lukas happy.

For lunch, Willa made herself and her brother peanut butter and honey sandwiches, and she shook out a clump of raisins onto each of their plates and took the cheese from its little home in the refrigerator and cut Lukas a chunk of it. But then, when she tried to cut her own chunk, her pinkie finger slipped under the knife just as the blade pushed down, and suddenly the orange cheese was swimming in a pool of red and the top of the cheese was sprinkled with red, and the tip of her finger was tipping to the side in a weird, sickening way, and Lukas was screaming, and she was screaming, and their father was stomping up from the basement shouting, "What the fuck is going on?" When he found Willa standing in the middle of the kitchen holding up her bloody hand and oddly bent finger, he started yelling for real.

"What the fuck? What the fuck? What the fuck?" he kept shouting as he marched around the kitchen, pulling at his hair. He picked up the telephone and put it back down without dialing a number. "You're supposed to be the easy one, Willa. You're supposed to be the one I don't have to worry about." He marched up to her and glared at her finger. His face sickened suddenly, like he might throw up or faint. "It's gonna fall off. You're gonna have half a finger for the rest of your life. Your mom leaves me alone with you for one day," he said weakly, "and this is what happens."

Willa willed herself to listen to her father, even to feel badly for what she had done. She stared at her bloody finger, and she tried to keep herself there because that place was still a better place than where her mind kept trying to go, which was the pastor's mother dead on the couch with the blood moving down her chin, her mouth hanging open like one of those gargoyle fountains attached to old castles.

Willa brought her attention back to her finger, to the drip-drip-drip of blood down the side of her hand that slid past her wrist and streaked down her forearm and landed in the sleeve gathered around her elbow, where the white fabric pulsed a solid red. She had read about a similar situation in a book once, when a boy had fallen in the woods and sliced his leg on an old railroad spike. He'd kept alive by wrapping his sweater tightly around the wound.

"I'm bleeding a lot," Willa said, but her voice was small, and she couldn't seem to make her father hear her. He was off in the living room looking for something, maybe the phone book. She could hear him swearing, and she caught sight of a couch cushion flying through the air.

She had liked the pastor's mother. Lukas had thought she was scary, and she did look a little scary, but Willa had liked her anyway because she'd told them stories on Thanksgiving, and she'd looked at Willa and listened to her in a way that grown-ups almost never did—like Willa was a real person and not just some kid. Her eyes had held a special kind of look and then one day, they just screwed shut forever. It was the eyes that bothered Willa the most. The screwed-shut eyes, and the blood, and how the blood kept moving when everything else had stopped.

"Willa," Lukas said, "is your finger really going to fall off?" He had stopped crying and started eating his sandwich instead.

"Where's the fucking phone book?" Willa's dad shouted to no one.

Willa was starting to feel dizzy, weak. Maybe she was only imagining it. "I'm losing blood," Willa said. "I'm losing too much blood."

Her father was back in the kitchen. He was pulling out all the drawers and emptying them onto the floor. Lukas was still eating his sandwich. His snot was sticking to the top of the bread and stretching into strings whenever he pulled the sandwich away. Willa's body wobbled slightly, and she had to hold on to the counter. Now the blood was dripping from her elbow and landing on the kitchen floor in bright, splashy circles. Her mind moved to the bus ride she'd imagined just after the pastor's mother had died—that faraway day when she'd leave home all on her own and choose a place in the world where she wanted to be. She just had to get to that day.

"We need to wrap it up tight," she said, but again her father seemed not to hear her. Willa gulped the panic rising in her chest. She stepped over to her father and pulled on his shirt with her good hand until he stopped to look at her.

"Give me a washcloth," she said, and some quality of her voice kept him paused and listening. He handed her a washcloth from the drawer of kitchen linens he'd dumped on the floor. He watched as she folded it in half on the counter, placed her finger carefully inside, and rolled the washcloth around it.

"Now I'll hold this tight while you drive me to the hospital," she said.

"Hospital?" he said, like he wasn't even sure what a hospital was.

"Yes, Dad. I need stitches. They will give me stitches at the hospital."

For a moment, her father still looked terrified, and then his eyes cleared, and he nodded a little. "Yeah?" he said, and then nodded harder. "Yeah. That's what we'll do."

Willa and Lukas and their dad piled into the front seat of the truck, and besides the twinges that shot through her hand every time the pickup hit a bump, Willa actually enjoyed the ride. At the emergency room, the doctor poked her hand with shots until it all went numb, and she could barely even feel the tugging of the needle and thread as he sewed it all up.

Her dad acted different from how he usually did. After Willa had explained to the doctor what happened, the doctor sent her father an understanding look. "You bend over backwards to keep them safe," he said, shaking his head.

Willa's dad threw up his hands. "I know, I know."

"Then you turn your head for one minute."

Willa's dad said, "Exactly. That's how it goes," and he shook his head, as though he spent his whole life springing up between Willa and whatever new disaster she'd set her mind to.

For a moment, it embarrassed Willa that the doctor would think of her as that kind of kid when she was actually the exact opposite of that kind of kid. The only reason she'd cut herself in the first place was because she was trying very hard to make everything easier for everyone besides herself, especially for her father. But as she watched him sitting there with his arm slung around Lukas's shoulders enjoying the friendliness of the doctor, she spotted an unusual happiness in him, and she kept her thoughts to herself. He needed whatever he could get, and somehow, by some strange sort of luck, she didn't anymore.

Before they left, the doctor said, "No more playing with knives, young lady."

"You hear that, Willa?" said her dad.

Willa obediently nodded.

When they pulled in the driveway, Willa's mom sprinted out, coatless, and jerked open the side door of the truck.

"Who was bleeding?" she asked in a panicked voice. She spotted Willa's bandaged hand. "Willa!" she cried. "What happened?"

"Willa here damn near cut her finger off," her father explained. "I took her to the ER, and they sewed it up. They said everything's going to be fine. The stitches come out in two weeks. She'll just have a small scar, that's it." He said all of this like he'd been the one to keep his head, like he'd been the one who knew what to do. Willa didn't contradict him, and she didn't feel the need to, either.

"I was trying to cut a piece of cheese," Willa said. "For lunch. It was an accident."

"Well," said her mother. She looked at Willa and then back at Willa's dad. "I guess you took care of it," she said.

"I guess I did," he said, and Willa could see how proud he was, how much he had needed that.

She went down the hall to check her angel. She picked it up, put it back down, but it didn't feel scary anymore, like she had to make sure it hadn't moved. The angel was not going to move unless someone moved it, and that knowledge was all she needed. She could go look at it sometimes, and be reminded, but she didn't need to. She lay down and listened to the sounds of her family being calm together, her mother moving pans around in the kitchen, her father talking louder than he needed to, but in his happy voice. She didn't need things to stay the same anymore, and she didn't need them to change. All she needed was herself, just herself in all the world. The bird in her chest flitted and dipped and rose.

59

The following Sunday, Robert announced his mother's death at the beginning of his farewell sermon, which was received as benignly as all his other sermons. If he'd told anyone that this particular sermon would be his last, perhaps his congregation would have tried harder to look as though they were listening. Perhaps ancient Arnold Oliver wouldn't have blatantly snored through half of it as he always did, and Jack Allen wouldn't have spent the first ten minutes rethreading his string tie, and Clark Fisher would have looked up occasionally from his Bible, which he bent over in either study or slumber—most likely slumber, judging by the number of times the pointy Cecelia dug her elbow into his side. Robert had considered writing something borderline heretical, just to play with them a little, but ultimately he'd ended up salvaging yet another of his long-ago Advent sermons, even though Christmas, at this point, had already come and gone. No one had noticed his recycled sermons, or if they had, not even Cliff Grable had cared enough to mention it. The previous week had seen him too thrown by grief to write anything new when an infinitely easier option had availed itself. And so he stood there behind the pulpit and read aloud the words he'd barely even bothered to review and looked up occasionally to gauge whether anyone was paying attention. It appeared, as usual, as though no one was, and so Robert set his mind free to wander.

The previous Thursday, at the crematorium's front counter, he had filled out an index card, and a middle-aged blond had handed his mother over in a slim black box. The woman wore red-framed glasses that perfectly matched her red fingernails. On the way home, he couldn't stop wondering if the woman's fingernails always matched her glasses. What if she had purple-framed glasses and pink-framed glasses, too? What if she had taken the frames with her to the department store, where she held them up against the rows of polish, tracking down the perfect shade? It seemed like such a ridiculous thing to do—the ultimate vanity, the ultimate waste of time. Why bother, he'd thought. Why go through all that effort?

Out among the pews, Cecelia ritualistically dug in her elbow. Arnold Oliver's head dipped down and up, down and up, like an oil drill. Arnold always sat halfway up the sanctuary, which meant that he sat closer to the pulpit than anyone else. Why sit so close, Robert always wondered, if you knew you were going to take a colossal nap? Robert read through an entire excerpt from Micah before he realized that he'd located the right-numbered verses in the wrong-numbered chapter. The passage he'd read didn't relate to his sermon at all. No matter, he told himself. He smiled a little and kept on going.

He had brought his mother's remains home and moved her around the parsonage. For a while, he'd left her on the dining room table, but she looked wrong there—abandoned—so he moved her to her old cushion on the couch and stood back. It looked like a mistake. Now no one could sit there. So he tried the bookshelf, where she resembled an oversized VHS tape with no box. This was why people bought beautiful urns, he'd thought. Otherwise, it looked like you had just lugged your poor old mother home and shoved her in wherever she'd fit. The thought had made him snort, and then he laughed, and he kept on laughing until he cried.

"This is the promise of Christmas," he read from the pulpit. "That God will transform and descend. That God will come so close, we will be able to hold him in our arms." His voice broke on the word *arms*. His own sermon had surprised him. He paused to gather himself. Clark Fisher raised his head. Arnold Oliver snorted awake and swiveled from side to side, trying to figure out if the service was over. Even Hannah and Angelee, the two girls who spent his sermons drawing pictures on the backs of the bulletins, paused in their scribbling to watch. Robert had never choked up behind the pulpit before. He'd never even come close. He took a deep breath and tried to continue. "What a promise," he read, and his voice broke again. No matter, he told himself, and this time the thought was charged with determination. Everyone was listening now, frozen faces upturned. He read on, his voice warbly and uncertain.

"What a promise," he repeated. "That God will never again be far from us, that he will draw near enough to know, firsthand, exactly what it means to be helpless and hungry, thirsty and exhausted. To love and to lose, to mourn and to struggle. To be betrayed by those closest to him, those in whom he trusted, those in whose hands he had placed his life. Christmas," Robert read and gasped for air, "Christmas is a renewal of God's promise that, through Emmanuel, God will always be with us."

He looked up from his notes, which he'd finished reading, and scanned the congregation. "Regardless of everything," he added. The possessing emotion had passed now, and he stood there in the stunned silence, waiting for more words. When none came, he returned to his seat on the front pew. Ethel stepped up to the organ and started to play "It Came Upon a Midnight Clear."

Every other Sunday, when he'd finished his sermon, he closed with a prayer and then walked straight down the sanctuary's middle aisle to stand beside the foyer's big glass doors. But that day he didn't pray, and after returning to his seat, he continued to sit there, bent forward, consciously breathing, hands braced against his knees. He would let them all think he was having a moment. He would let them let themselves out.

And they did. Only Chet Weller came over to rest his hand on Robert's shoulder and say, in his gruff voice, "Hang in there, brother." Chet's was the only voice from the congregation, besides Ethel Grable's, that Robert would miss.

The church finally fell silent. Once everyone had gone, Robert conducted his standard walk-through, returning all errant items to their rightful places. After he finished, he retrieved the zippered deposit envelope from its file drawer in his office and approached the altar table, where he tipped out the tithes from the offering plates, tapped the checks and bills into one neat stack, and shuffled through them. Six hundred and thirty-two dollars and sixty-four cents. A tidy sum for a December Sunday.

He zipped everything into the envelope and carried it back to his office, unlocked the financial cabinet and flipped back through the files. Deductions, expenses, tax documents, family fund. Robert made all the deposits, though Clark Fisher, the treasurer, in a vestige of checks and balances, received the statements and filed them away. Over the course of ten trustworthy years, more and more had been heaped upon Robert's plate until he had eventually become responsible for pretty much everything save the decisions. Any decisions, in fact. Robert pulled out the file folder and opened it across his desk. The most recent statement lay on top. He skimmed down until he found *Current Balance* in bold. Twenty-three thousand, one hundred and thirty-three dollars. He'd been hoping for about that much. It had been a little under four thousand, he remembered, when he began.

So nineteen thousand. A significant amount. Not a lottery-winning sum. But enough. Surely, along with the seven-some-thousand he'd tucked away over the past ten years, enough.

60

From what Susan could tell, Randy actually had changed for the better since his hospital stay, though admittedly her chances to observe him had been limited. He'd be returning to work on January 3, two days before his classes began, so he'd mostly spent his time driving back and forth to Jefferson Community College, requesting papers and filling out forms, registering for classes and hunting teachers down in their offices to prove himself deserving of late registration. But when Randy was home, he moved through the house with a purpose, and his presence felt restless (albeit sometimes frantic) rather than angry.

Randy had arrived home from the hospital with two bottles of pills, each of which he took first thing every morning. Susan had checked the labels, but she didn't recognize the names, and despite his relative cheerfulness, she couldn't bring herself to ask him what exactly they did. She did wonder, however, just how much of his transformation they had effected. Were they revealing the person he really was? Or were they disguising it?

Regardless, Randy wasn't *so* very different from how he had been. It wasn't as though he had started paying more attention to the kids or helping Susan out around the house. But he was consistently civil and reasonable and calm, more calm than she could ever remember him being before. It was as though someone had charted the whole range of Randy's vacillations, chopped off the lows, and left the highs just as small and rare as they'd always been.

He still didn't want Susan to work. "You've had to take on way too much as it is," he'd told her, in an affected display of concern. "Let me take that off your plate." Susan didn't want to quit, but she didn't say so out loud. Somehow Randy's return had transformed her into a spectator rather than a participant. She felt oddly powerless, as if her only choice was to watch him and see what he would do.

The day Willa almost lost her finger, Randy had asked Susan if she'd put in her notice, and for the first time maybe ever, she had flat-out lied to him. Yes, she said, she'd talked to Jeff (which she hadn't), and he'd begged her to stay on through the holidays.

"So after the New Year," he said, "you're done." Maybe he'd intended it as a question, but his intonation was one of a command.

"I believe that's what he meant," Susan said.

"Well," said Randy. "I'd make sure if I were you."

Susan had even waited on Jeff the following day, when he came in to check the inventory, and she'd almost said something. Then he'd stiffed her, which she supposed was his right, as owner, but it had left a bad taste in Susan's mouth, and she'd thought that maybe he didn't deserve advance notice. Maybe she'd just keep quiet until the one day she didn't show up.

It wasn't that Susan loved her job. At times, like when a customer eyed her greasily or a table ran her ragged or a big party left her nothing but spare change, she downright hated it. But her job also carried with it a sense of order. Each task, each table, was marked with a clear beginning and a clear end. What's more, she was getting better at managing the rushes, pacing and prioritizing her duties so that details stopped slipping through the cracks, as they had when she'd started. It felt good to get good at something and to go on being good at it. By the end of each shift, she'd gleaned another small kernel of satisfaction and pride, ridiculous though it seemed, that the bundle of bills in her apron, however small, had been hard-fought and well-earned. The money she made was her own, at least until she deposited it into the bank account that she and Randy shared.

So it wasn't that she liked her job. It was more that she couldn't bring herself to give up the only thing that felt like it belonged entirely to her.

Besides, Susan had gotten the kids through Christmas. Willa hadn't

panicked in over a week, and she hadn't been sleepwalking, either. Her appetite had returned, and she seemed happier somehow, steadier. Susan had
reason to hope that her daughter's attacks had been two blips, two outliers.
Susan had earned the right, she thought, to coast for a while. And anyway,
most of the time it felt like coasting was all she could do. And so she coasted
along until Tuesday afternoon, New Year's Eve, when Robert dropped by
the restaurant.

He was sitting facing the window to the street, but Susan recognized
him anyway—his straight back and black hair and that particular set to his
shoulders, broad and oddly curvaceous, as though they led to wings rather
than arms. He turned as he heard her coming up behind.

"Susan." He smiled, though the smile, Susan noted, smarted somehow.
"I'd hoped to find you here." He was seated on the very edge of the chair,
as though unsure of whether to rise. His hair had outgrown its cut and one
damp lock curved down to his eyebrow. He looked harried, unlike his usual
self. "I need to tell you something, but it will take some explaining." He
turned partway around, surveying the dining room. "You may want to attend to your other tables first. In the meantime, I'd love some coffee, if you
could." He settled back into his chair, but his body kept its tension.

The lunch rush had finished up, so Susan's work at that time was nearly
done. She toured the dining room, topping off mugs and dropping off
checks. Once she delivered her final table's food, she returned to Robert
with two cups of coffee and seated herself in the opposite chair.

"I received your note," he said. "Thank you."

"Ah," Susan said. "Good." It had been an awkward note to write. She
had penned it hurriedly the day after Christmas, when Randy came home.
She'd managed to keep it hidden by tucking it into a cookbook, opening the
book to jot down each new line as it came to her. She'd had to convey her
genuine sympathy for his loss while also dropping the news that Randy had
returned home, which of course meant (this was implied rather than stated
outright) that he must not call her or expect her to call him. But just now,
sitting across from the pastor, his long, fine-boned fingers draped loosely
around his mug, his eyes keen, his forehead rumpled earnestly in thought,
she failed to grasp the necessity of that reality. Why should she deny herself

the tiny, innocent pleasure of sitting across the table from someone as remarkable as this?

"I truly am so sorry," she said. "And I'm sorry I couldn't be there for you, too."

Robert waved his hand as if to wave away the need for apology.

"No, Robert," she said. "I am sorry. You don't know how much."

He took a sip of coffee and swallowed before nodding once, eyes closed. "Thank you." Then he leaned forward and dropped his voice down. "But what I wanted to tell you is that I'm leaving."

"You're leaving what, your job?"

Robert nodded. He kept his voice low. "My job, my house." He paused and nodded some more, and if he was just beginning to understand it himself. "My life," he said. "Esau. I am getting out of Esau."

"But where will you go?"

"That I don't know yet," he said. "Maybe to Oklahoma, back to where I grew up, back to where my mother lived. Please don't tell anyone." He shook his head. "I know you won't. But I wanted to tell you so that you'd know. And I also wanted to tell you in case—" He halted and let out an impatient sigh.

"In case what?" she asked.

"In case you wanted to come with me."

Susan froze. She had wanted him to say that until he said it. She finally repeated, "You want me to come with you."

"You, and the kids."

She continued to stare at him, unmoving.

"I know. This seems so sudden. I mean, it is sudden. But maybe it's actually been coming on for a very long time."

"Okay," Susan said, turning the word up like a question.

"I have some money put away. Enough. It's mine, but it's not totally mine. I mean, it is totally mine, but I have to take it out of the family fund. But I'm the one who put it in there. So I'm going to take it back."

"It sounds like you're stealing it."

"No!" said Robert, and he laughed like she'd just told a joke. "I mean, maybe they'll say I'm stealing it. But I talked it over with a lawyer this afternoon. According to my contract, I am entitled to it. So it's legal, but I'm going to burn some bridges. Which is why I have to go. Which is where you come in. You and Willa and Lukas."

"Robert. You've been through way too much in the past few days. You just lost your mother. This is not the time to go throwing your life away."

"Now that is where you and I disagree," Robert said, his voice brightening. "I think that now is the perfect time. I'm beginning to think now is the only time."

"You sound half crazy," Susan said. "Where will you go? What will you do for work?"

"I don't know!" Robert said. He laughed, and in the periphery of Susan's vision, several heads turned in their direction. She gestured toward her mouth with a finger. "I don't know!" he said again, this time in a whisper. "It feels so good not to know!"

Susan shook her head. "Good for you," she said. "You don't know. Wonderful. For you. But that's not okay for me, and it's not okay for children. They need structure. Consistency."

"Right," he said. "Right. We will have to figure that out."

"Will? We *will*? *We* will?"

"Yes. *We will* figure it out," he said.

"You don't know that," she said. "You can't promise that. I—I can't believe I'm even discussing this."

"I'm not—I'm not asking you to marry me. I'm not asking you to run away and be my lover. Who knows what could happen someday, but that's not what I'm thinking of now. I'm thinking that you and your kids need a new beginning just as much as I do. Maybe even more. I could help you do whatever you wanted to do. We could help each other."

Susan studied him for a long time. For a moment, she allowed herself to imagine the possibilities, not because she thought they were possible but because she wanted to pretend, for a moment, that she lived in a world where they were. Finally, after too long a silence, she said, "No!" like something had surprised her. "Of course I can't do that. How am I even considering this? No," she said again. "The answer is no."

"Just think about it."

"I don't have to think about it. The kids and I are going to make do with what we have. I'm not going to throw their lives up in the air just because I want to run away."

"You do?"

"Stop."

A long silence.

"Well," Robert finally said. His voice came out lower and rough. He didn't sound angry, though, like Randy would have. He just sounded tired. Tired and sad. "Well," he said again. "I guess you've made up your mind. It was a crazy idea." He laughed a little. "But what did I have to lose?"

Through the afternoon and evening that followed, Susan tried to put the conversation with Robert out of her mind. She finished her shift and drove home, called downstairs to Randy, checked on the kids in their bedroom, brought Willa her pain medicine, set some frozen fish fillets out on the counter in a bowl of cool water. Then she sat at the dining room table and pulled the bills from her apron, flattened them and ordered them and carried them to the bedroom, where she added them to the stack on the dresser. She would treat herself to something, she decided. She had no idea what that something would be, but the thought of it warmed her nevertheless. Because she lived in this world, and she would go on living in it. Because she was faithful and hardworking and true.

At dinner, Lukas complained that Susan had given him too much fish, and Randy countered Lukas's complaint by complaining that Susan never gave him enough fish, which she suspected Randy intended as a compliment. He went on to talk loudly about his new schedule and how Susan might have to start packing him a dinner with his lunch or could she have dinner ready at four thirty rather than five thirty, and wow life was about to get crazy for all of them but it was all going to be worth it.

NEW YEAR'S EVE passed in the same way it had passed since the kids were born—so quietly that if Susan hadn't known the actual date, nothing in her life, besides the talking heads on the TV, would have reminded her of it. Randy had disappeared down into the basement after supper, and she'd tucked the kids into bed and then sat on a pillow between their beds, gazing off at the dim glow of the night-light.

Susan used to love New Year's Eve, not for the drinking and partying (she had spent a few New Year's Eves in her early twenties trying to enjoy the custom with no success) but for the new beginning it always signified. As a child, she used to spend the day cleaning her room, and the next day she would rise with a sense of possibility and resolve to keep it neat all year long. The deterioration of this goal a week or two later did not prevent her, the following New Year's, from fastening onto another, fresher resolution, revolving, as a child, around cleanliness or homework and later, as an adult, around a new exercise regimen or eating plan.

In the years since Willa was born, though, Susan had stopped trying to change anything on her own. Kids were the reason, she told herself. They kept you changing all by themselves. They broke you apart, and then you had to rebuild yourself from the ground up. Maybe some people could shovel extra resolutions atop those ever-present challenges, but Susan wasn't one of them. Besides, she thought, sitting on the pillow, slumped against the wall with the heating vent breathing into her back, she'd never been able to make the changes permanent anyway.

As Susan pondered the coming year, she tried to rouse in herself some motivation. At this time next year, Randy would be halfway done with his program. Willa would be in fifth grade, Lukas in second. And Susan? She would be one year older, nearly forty. She would be stretching the same paychecks to the same outlandish lengths. She would be bending over backward to feed everyone and juggle meals around Randy's new schedule and help her children with homework and clean up everyone's messes. She would quit her job. She would be alone again. And Robert? Robert would be one year gone, one year into building a better life for himself. She ached, to think of that. Susan breathed deep to try and dislodge the pressure in her chest, but it stayed there, heavy, like a hand pressing down.

In 1997, everyone's lives would be changing except hers. It gave her the sense of twin fires, one on each side of her, as the agony of powerlessness blazed against the agony of needing to make some desperate change. Susan sat there in the dim light and imagined the flames burning her down.

NEW YEAR'S DAY rose with an unseasonably clear sky and naked sun that softened the snow and melted spongy gray puddles along the ditches. Randy was happier than Susan had seen him in years. He took the kids out sledding in the afternoon, something he'd never done before, and Susan stood at the dining room window and smiled at the laughter ringing out from the hill behind their house.

That evening passed uneventfully with the same routine of dinner, dishes, bedtime, but Susan felt a freshness to it, and she assured herself, *This kind of work runs in circles, and just when you think you can't take it anymore, it shifts enough to keep you going. And if Randy and Willa and Lukas can be happy like this, then maybe I can be happy, too.*

The next day, ducking the crestfallen expression on Jeff's face, she told him she had to quit, and Susan's apathy helped her perform her job better. She walked away with nearly seventy dollars folded neatly in her apron.

Over the course of her shift, she'd finally decided what she'd spend her money on—a few luxuries to make the house a more enjoyable place to be, since she spent nearly all of her time in that one open room. She would buy fabric to sew new curtains, she decided, enough to sew a matching cover, too, for the hideous floral chair. She'd find another complementary print to make a tablecloth. With all she had saved up, she could even buy some paint to brighten up the walls, maybe some new contact paper for the insides of the cupboards. She would reclaim her home, recommit to it, she decided, make it more her own. But when she entered the bedroom to add her day's earnings to her tip pile and count up her total, she found that her money had disappeared.

Maybe Randy had moved it so that it wouldn't be sitting out, she thought. That was something he'd do. She peeked behind her jewelry box, lifted a pair of Randy's pants draped there and looked underneath. Nothing.

She shuffled through the dresser drawers slowly at first, then with increasing desperation.

The children wouldn't have taken it. She had left with them that morning, dropped them off to stay with her mother while she worked, and they'd only just gotten home. And then she remembered that Randy had been planning to buy his books for the coming semester, and when she remembered this, she froze, hands still plunged in the bottom drawer of the dresser, where she kept Randy's pants, pants that he never, ever put away.

He must have taken her money, then, and spent it on his books. She understood this, but still she stayed there on her knees, her left hand braced against the cool, smooth board at the drawer's bottom, her right hand lifting the folded edge of Randy's only pair of dress pants, her neck dropping forward to peer underneath.

He had taken her money and spent it on his books.

Her money was gone.

There was just enough in the bank account to meet the month's bills.

There would be no new curtains, no chair cover, no tablecloth, no paint. No job anymore where she could save up again for the things that would make her life a little easier to live.

She finally pulled her hands out of the dresser and sat back on her haunches, but she didn't rise to her feet. Something kept her seated there, puzzling it out.

It was almost as though she couldn't understand what he'd done. He'd taken the money, she told herself again, and that was that. The money was gone.

She tried to reason with herself. The money hadn't been necessary, it had been extra. Didn't it make sense for him to take it, since he could argue it was not hers but theirs, and that he needed it more than she did? It must have made sense for him, and he would no doubt communicate his reasoning to her.

But the road of her thoughts was still stopped at that critical juncture. A tree had fallen there, or an avalanche of stones, and she kept bumping up against the blockage over and over, and she couldn't get past it.

It wasn't the money she had needed. It wasn't the curtains or the tablecloth. It wasn't the explanation he'd give. It was the hope she'd held out that Randy, in his healthier state, could come to see her as someone who might need something just as much as he did.

"Mama?"

It was Lukas, standing at the door.

"Mama, I'm hungry."

Randy wouldn't see her. He would never, ever see her.

"Mama, what are you doing on the floor?"

"Just a minute, Lukey. Then I'll get you and Willa a snack, how about it?" But after he drifted off at her assurance, Susan stayed where she was until her feet fell asleep and her knees began to throb with the ache of being bent for so long, until Lukas came back twice to ask her for food and Willa came by once and asked if everything was okay, and Susan said, "Just a minute, just a minute, of course."

It wasn't until she heard Randy's truck pull in the drive that she stood and stretched out her knees, straightened her clothes, shook the blood back into her feet. The front door opened, and Randy called out in a loud, happy voice. She took one small step, and then she began to run.

61

"Good news!" Randy called. It was Thursday, the day after New Year's, and Randy had just returned from his final trip to campus. "I'm all set to go." He was carrying his plastic bag of new textbooks, which he'd had to buy with Susan's tip money. She kept it in a stack on their dresser until she had a chance to drive into town and deposit it.

There was something endearing about it to Randy, her stacking up her small savings just there, beside her jewelry box. Maybe it was the trust it displayed, placing it right out in the open, where anyone might take it. And Randy had taken it, because Susan had taken the kids to her mother's that day while she worked, and she'd taken the checkbook with her, and if Randy hadn't taken her tips, he would've had to drive into town for cash from the bank and then back out to JCC and then home, which would have cost him an extra forty-five minutes at least, not counting the cost of gas. So taking Susan's tip money just made sense.

But once he'd walked in the door and made his announcement, Susan came running out of the hallway, and her face stopped him short.

"Did you take my money?" she said.

"Well, hello to you, too."

"Did you take my money," she repeated. "From the dresser."

"Do you take *my* money every time I bring home *my* paycheck? Yes, I took *your* money. You took the checks, and I had to buy my textbooks."

Susan nodded. "Your books," she said. "You took my money to buy your books."

Randy tossed his bag into an armchair and threw up his empty palms. "What the hell did you want me to do, Suzy? Steal them?"

"That was my money," she said. "I was setting it aside."

"What the hell for?"

Susan shook her head. Her face had gone white with fury, her lips almost disappearing into two pale lines. "It doesn't matter," she said. "It was mine."

How fucking illogical. But Randy had been in too good a mood to get worked up over something so stupid. She'd get over it. He waved his hand. "You bring me back all my paychecks," he said, "and then we'll talk." He kicked his boots off, dropped down onto the couch, and reached for the remote. But Susan just kept standing there, staring at him and blinking like she couldn't see straight. He ignored her until she finally stalked out of the room and slammed the bedroom door behind her.

By dinner she seemed to have gotten over it, though she talked less than she usually did. Then the next day, when he called over lunch on his first day back, she didn't pick up, and when he finally made it home, he was relieved to find the van still in the driveway. Not that he thought it wouldn't be. But he'd felt a little bad about taking her money. He'd bought her a dozen roses at the Wal-Mart.

The house looked too dark in the fading evening light.

No. They were there. Of course they were there. The van said they were there.

Randy shifted the truck into park and quit the engine, cut the lights. The house was too dark. Something was wrong.

Lunch box in one hand, crinkly sheath of flowers in the other. Outside, his boots across the gravel—the only sound. Up the steps, try the door.

Locked.

No.

Drop the lunch box, fumble for the keys. Stop shaking. Kick back the door, call their names.

A trick, maybe. Or a surprise. Their names again, louder.

Check the rooms. Under the beds. Inside the closets. They're hiding. They must be hiding. Of course they're hiding.

The back room, under the heap of coats. The pantry. Behind the couch. Oh, God.

The bathroom, behind the door.

Behind all the doors.

The attic. Impossible. But still. A screwdriver to pry out the panel. Climb up. Black, freezing. The light. Nothing.

Outside! Of course! Running. The perimeter of the yard. No.

The field beyond. No.

The stream along the field. No.

No. No, no, no.

Everything dead and flat and cold. The dead stalks cracking. His breath loud and fast.

Gone. Oh, God. They were gone. Oh, God. Gone, gone, gone—the cadence of his running. The same word over and over, not from his mouth but his chest, his lungs heaving up the sound as each boot struck.

Up the back slope, around the side of the house, down the road. Gone, gone, gone, gone. He kept on running until the muscles in his legs began to burn, and still he ran, away from the house, away, away, and then back.

They were there now! He could sense it! When he came into view of their house, warm light shone from all the windows. A surge of mania, of joy, until he remembered, as he swung back the front door, that he had been the one to leave them on.

Down onto the floor of the entryway, gasping. He twisted sideways and slugged the drywall until it crushed inward and began to crumble. No, no, no. He would change. He would be good. He would keep being better. She would come back. She would bring the kids. She was too kind to keep them away forever, and too soft.

The flowers lay on the ground where he had dropped them. He kicked at their stems, and they spun to face him, the tips of their rich, red heads already touched with brown. Roses. Did she even like roses?

He would ask her when he saw her again. He would change in so many ways. It would make a different life, entirely, for all of them. She would see, she would believe. But what if she didn't—she would. She would, she would, she would. He moved to the couch and clenched his eyes shut, gripping the promise.

But when he woke much later, Carhartt chafing his cricked neck, work boots gouging his ankles, he found the house still empty and the dark sky growing gray with morning. Somewhere out beyond the clouds, the sun was rising.

Epilogue

For some time afterward, no one at Esau Baptist knew what had happened. The Wednesday-evening prayer service had been canceled, since it landed, that year, on New Year's Day. So it wasn't until the following weekend that the parishioners arrived, on the first, freezing January Sunday, to an equally freezing church. Cliff Grable had to drive back home to retrieve his set of keys. The small crowd entered together and then dispersed through the church building as though looking for something.

The children climbed up onto the pews in their coats and boots, slipping along and marking the thin cushions with mud. The handful of teenagers descended to the basement, where they opened all the doors to the Sunday school rooms, releasing the damp concrete odors and the pale, chalky air.

The adults began a silent inventory. The floor had been vacuumed, the curtains neatly drawn. Even the shelves in the pastoral office, from the looks of it, had been recently straightened and dusted. The missionary closet was tidy and fully stocked. The upstairs kitchen was so clean that every piece of metal reflected the dull winter light from the small window above the sink. The cupboards were just as full as they'd ever been, with everything in exactly the same place.

But still, each person thought to himself or herself that something seemed to be missing. Some decided it was the cold that made the church feel so empty. Some suspected Robert had stolen something, though they couldn't for the lives of them figure out what it was.

Only a handful of parishioners attributed the absence to Robert, who was wheeling, at that same moment, over the northeast corner of Oklahoma, the box of his mother's remains rattling atop the console beside him. His mother, heading back home. He would find her family, if he could. Maybe he would even find his own father, in time.

The morning he'd left, on his way out of Esau to pick up Susan and her children, his sense of exultation had only barely outweighed his sense of guilt. He passed the littered field for the last time, the empty park, the shadows of men he'd met but never come to know, scraping their snow shovels up and down their driveways, the smoke from their chimneys stretched and hovering over their low roofs like lazy ghosts, duller than the dull gray sky. Robert had come to save them, but in some backward, upside-down state of affairs, he was kicking off against them, toward a better future.

In the rearview mirror, Lukas swayed slightly in sleep. Beside Robert, Susan gazed out the passenger-side window at the distant, rocky Oklahoma dunes stippled with occasional shrubs. She had called Randy from a pay phone just outside Louisville to let him know they were all okay and that she'd call him again once they arrived.

"You have to come back," he growled, and she said, "No, I don't." His voice cracked into sobs then, and for a moment his naked sorrow terrified her. But Susan was too far gone to return. She had come to know what she needed to know, which was that God rarely gave you a second chance, if ever, and you either took it or you didn't. It would be hard for Randy to keep going, but not as hard as it would have been for Susan to stay.

Behind her, Willa watched the same dunes rise and fall. She, too, was thinking of her father, of how her mother had promised they would see him again, though she couldn't say when. Willa had placed her angel on the coffee table, where her dad would be sure to find it. She'd left a note folded underneath that told him she'd miss him, and she'd signed it *Love, Willie Bear*.

Before, she'd always thought of love as a good thing. But now she felt for the first time just how much it could hurt, how it could swell up so big that your whole body ached with it.

Acknowledgments

This book was the work of many dear souls, so please bear with me because this list is long. Endless gratitude to my gentle, discerning, and persevering agent Caroline Eisenmann, who locked arms with me and never gave up (I knew she wouldn't), along with everyone at Frances Goldin—your inspiration feeds my own.

To my editor Jenny Alton, whose striking insights and meandering conversations led me out of the trees and up to an overlook, and for all the folks at Counterpoint with all their staggering gifts: Yukiko Tominaga, Dan Smetanka, Wah-Ming Chang, Dana Li, Nicole Caputo, Laura Berry, Alisha Gorder, Rachel Fershleiser, Megan Fishmann, and Chandra Wohleber. To Helen Richard at Putnam, who, before it sold, cut this book in half and encouraged me to make it twice what it was. And to Sarah Clark for her close reading and meticulous feedback.

To the Ann Arbor Hens with Pens: Lonnie, Cathy, Hillary, Joy, Janet, Carrie, Gertrude, Katie, and Anna—cluck yes to all of you. And to all other early readers who have had a hand in this book—Sophfronia Scott, Joe Villella, Emily Langbehn, Connie Webster, Rory Webster, Margie Hein, David Hein, Ali Ziegler (a hoe among rakes), and Sarah Camp (please relay the happy news to Mike that Randy Shearer is actually an intergalactic robot overlord).

To my other friends and family who have supported my work from the beginning, including (but not limited to!) Tavia Gilbert, Gio Marcus, Julia

Kimball, Amanda Silva, David Heska Wanbli Weiden, Rich Farrell, Kali VanBaale, Jen Bowen, Robin MacArthur, Suzan Song, DeShauna Hollie, Ruth Cobban, Merri Rose, Katia Brinkman, Anne Heaton, Grace Helms-Kotre, Nicholas Hayes, Ken Hayes, Carmen Wyatt-Hayes, Donald Turner, Debra Belt, Becca Stam, Lynae Churgovich, Megan Matteson, and Melanie Sen. And to every single soul at Shalom Community Church, whose unflagging encouragement lasted the whole marathon long. You are the home of my heart.

To my advisers at Vermont College of Fine Arts—Larry Sutin, Robert Vivian, Ellen Lesser, Laurie Alberts, Sue William Silverman, Patrick Madden, Connie May Fowler, Douglas Glover, Trinie Dalton, Kurt Caswell, and Clint McCown—and to all of my VCFA classmates who lovingly pulled my work apart so that I could rebuild it better; I am a stronger writer for each of your efforts. To my high school English teachers, especially Margo Fenstermaker, who made us memorize poetry, and Cheri Oulette, who told me that I had some talent and that I should use it. And to Rocky Lee, a classmate who once said that a story of mine was the best thing he'd ever heard. He was most likely joking, but encouragement was scarce then, and I've carried his words with me ever since.

Because I wrote this novel wherever I could find space and time, I must also thank all the baristas, bussers, and dishwashers at Roaming Goat, Mighty Good Coffee, Zou Zou's, and Beezy's, along with whatever brilliant soul invented the McDonald's PlayPlace. I would be remiss if I did not thank my programmable coffee maker, too, which in the early days lured me out of bed long before my children woke. I never could have done this without you.

To my father Michael Webster, who through his music taught me how to hustle for what I loved. To my mother Connie Webster, who read to me endlessly and never wanted me to be anyone else. To Rory, my brother, who has always had my back, even in the fresh hell of high school, and to my sister Emily, who has cheered me on at the hardest times with the loudest voice and the most hilarious jokes.

To Alyosha and Silas, my true masterpieces. And to Scott, my closest reader, my most discerning critic, and my life's great love—this book belongs to both of us.

MICHELLE WEBSTER HEIN and her family work a small homestead in the southern Michigan countryside where she was born and raised. *Out of Esau* is her first novel. Find out more at michellewebsterhein.com.